THE JACOBEAN AND
CAROLINE STAGE

THE JACOBEAN
AND
CAROLINE STAGE

BY

GERALD EADES BENTLEY

VOLUME VI

THEATRES

OXFORD
AT THE CLARENDON PRESS
1968

Oxford University Press, Ely House, London W. 1

GLASGOW NEW YORK TORONTO MELBOURNE WELLINGTON
CAPE TOWN SALISBURY IBADAN NAIROBI LUSAKA ADDIS ABABA
BOMBAY CALCUTTA MADRAS KARACHI LAHORE DACCA
KUALA LUMPUR HONG KONG TOKYO

PRINTED IN GREAT BRITAIN

PREFACE

THESE two volumes conclude my survey of the writing, presentation, and publication of plays in London from the death of Shakespeare to the closing by law of all theatres in England. In volume vi I have considered the theatre buildings, private, public, court, and projected, which were in use during this period. In volume vii I have gathered into appendixes scattered material concerning Lenten performances and Sunday performances, and I have ordered chronologically a large number of dramatic and semi-dramatic events which may provide helpful contexts for students of the drama and theatre. This volume also contains an analytical index for all seven volumes.

The discussions of London theatres in use after the death of Shakespeare vary greatly in length ranging from that of Blackfriars, the house of greatest prestige throughout the period, to that of Le Fevre's Riding Academy, little known and little used. Since these volumes are intended for reference, I have tried to reduce to a minimum the amount of conjecture about theatres and their facilities for the staging of plays. In an area where there are so few seventeenth-century descriptions and so many twentieth-century hypotheses—too often asserted as demonstrable fact—I have found far more theatre material to reject than to include, particularly in the descriptions of individual stages and customary features of production. It is fervently to be hoped that some day we will be able to say with assurance that the Globe stage had so many entrances of such a size and position. That great day has not yet dawned, and until it does responsible reference books should severely restrict the space given to the weighing of conflicting hypotheses. Books on individual theatres must state the principal hypotheses and choose among them; reference surveys should not. The theatre volume was pretty well completed by the end of 1962, and books and articles appearing after that date have generally had to be ignored. They do not, I think, alter significantly the facts I have recorded, though several

offer support or contradiction to current theories about
staging.

In volume vii most of the space is devoted to an analytical
index for the seven volumes, an index to which I have perhaps devoted a disproportionate amount of time. The need
for a complete finding list for plays and playwrights has been
obvious and frequently expressed ever since volumes iii, iv,
and v began to be used, and it was apparent to me that such
an index, separated from the one to players and dramatic
companies in volume ii, would cause endless annoyance. The
index in volume vii, therefore, is planned to lead the reader
to all the material in any of the volumes, even that already
listed in volume ii. To these persons, places, and plays I have
added as many general subjects as I can think of. My hope
is that these subject heads may help students with interests
unlike mine to assemble scattered material I have used in
other contexts. Under these heads are collected references
concerning many subjects about which I have not written
and do not intend to write, but which may well provide a
start for someone else—Characters, Clergyman-dramatists,
Ghost titles, Misattributed plays, Plays in competition, Per-
sonal allusions in plays, Revised plays and Revived plays,
Roles in plays, Titles altered, and the like. No doubt there
are subjects of interest which did not occur to me, but after
two or three years of repeated rereadings of the various
volumes while flogging my brain for undiscussed relevancies
of incidental facts, I had to call a halt.

The index also includes the bibliography. Editions of
plays are simply listed, since full entries in every case are
given in the discussions of the plays; for the many non-
dramatic works—ballads, pamphlets, sermons, collections of
poems, treatises, histories, articles—the entries are fuller.

After it had been established that the remodelled Cockpit-
in-Court was opened in 1630 and that the features of the new
building recorded in the Treasury accounts correspond precisely to those of the Inigo Jones undated sketches, it became
important that those sketches should be reproduced in
volume vi. I am grateful to Dr. R. A. Sayce and to the Fellows of Worcester College for their permission to reproduce

the page of drawings from Jones's sketch-book now housed in their magnificent library.

The Annals of Jacobean and Caroline Theatrical Affairs in volume vii and the discussions of the Court theatres in volume vi repeatedly make use of the Declared Accounts of the Treasurer of the Chamber. In 1957 Professor F. P. Wilson very kindly loaned me his transcripts of dramatic entries in these accounts, and all the extracts I use were taken originally from his copy. When the Malone Society published these transcripts four or five years later in volume vi of the *Collections*, I simply checked the quotations I had used in the Public Record Office and changed the citations to the *Malone Society Collections*. But the characteristic thoughtfulness of Professor Wilson had not only brought them to my attention but had made it possible for me to use them when I was writing my first version of those sections. How many grateful scholars still miss David Wilson!

G. E. B.

Princeton
April 1967

CONTENTS

VOLUME VI

THEATRES AT COURT

PROJECTED THEATRES

VOLUME VII

APPENDIXES TO VOLUME VI

LIST OF ABBREVIATIONS FOR
VOLUMES VI AND VII

THE following References are those most used in this part of the present work. For other Abbreviations see Volume I, pages xi to xx.

Adams—Joseph Quincy Adams, *Shakespearean Playhouses* (Boston, 1917).

C.S.P., Dom.—*Calendar of State Papers, Domestic Series, of the Reigns of Edward VI, Mary, Elizabeth, and James I (1547–1625)*, 12 vols., edited by Robert Lemon and M. A. E. Green (London, 1856–72).

C.S.P., Dom.—*Calendar of State Papers, Domestic Series, of the Reign of Charles I (1625–49)*, 23 vols., edited by John Bruce, W. D. Hamilton, and Mrs. S. C. Lomas (London, 1858–97).

C.S.P., Ven.—*Calendar of State Papers and Manuscripts, Relating to English Affairs, Existing in the Archives and Collections of Venice, and in Other Libraries of Northern Italy (1202–1675)*, 38 vols., edited by Rawdon Brown, G. C. Bentinck, H. F. Brown, and A. B. Hinds (London, 1864–1947).

Chamberlain—*The Letters of John Chamberlain*, 2 vols., edited by Norman Egbert McClure (Philadelphia, 1939).

Chambers, *E.S.*—E. K. Chambers, *The Elizabethan Stage*, 4 vols. (Oxford, 1923).

Herbert—*The Dramatic Records of Sir Henry Herbert*, edited by Joseph Quincy Adams (New Haven, 1917).

Hotson—Leslie Hotson, *The Commonwealth and Restoration Stage* (Cambridge, Mass., 1928).

M.S.C.—*Malone Society Collections* (London: Printed for the Malone Society, 1907–62).

P.R.O.—Public Record Office.

R.E.S.—*The Review of English Studies* [in progress] (London, 1925–).

Variorum—*The Plays and Poems of William Shakespeare, with the Corrections and Illustrations of Various Commentators: Comprehending a Life of the Poet, and an Enlarged History of the Stage*, by the late Edmond Malone, 21 vols., edited by James Boswell (London, 1821.)

PRIVATE THEATRES

THE FIRST BLACKFRIARS

Adams, pp. 91–110.
Chambers, *E.S.* ii. 475–98.

The private theatre constructed by remodelling a part of one of the old Blackfriars monastic buildings in 1576 was not used for performances after 1584, and was later converted into private apartments.

THE SECOND BLACKFRIARS

Anonymous, 'Early London Theatres', *The Architect*, cvii, No. 2777 (10 March 1922), 184.
—— *The History from 1276 to 1956 of the Site in Blackfriars Consisting of Printing House Square . . . Being the Freehold Property of the Times Publishing Company Limited* (1956).
Adams, pp. 182–233. See also his 'The Conventual Buildings of Blackfriars, London, and the Playhouses Constructed Therein', *Studies in Philology*, xiv (1917), 64–87.
Armstrong, William A., *The Elizabethan Private Theatres: Facts and Problems*, Society for Theatre Research, Pamphlet Series, no. 6 (1958).
Bentley, G. E., 'Shakespeare and the Blackfriars Theatre', *Shakespeare Survey*, i (1948), 38–50.
Chambers, *E.S.* ii. 498–515.
Eccles, Mark, 'Martin Peerson and the Blackfriars', *Shakespeare Survey*, xi (1958), 100–6.
Feuillerat, Albert, 'Blackfriars Records', *Malone Society Collections*, ii, Pt. i (1913).
Fleay, F. G., *A Chronicle History of the London Stage, 1559–1642* (1890).
Harbage, Alfred, *Shakespeare and the Rival Traditions* (1952).
Isaacs, J., *Production and Stage-Management at the Blackfriars Theatre*, Shakespeare Association Pamphlet (1933).
McCabe, John, 'A Study of the Blackfriars Theatre, 1608–42', Unpublished Thesis, Shakespeare Institute, Stratford-upon-Avon (1954).
Mander, Raymond, and Mitchenson, Joe, *A Picture History of the British Theatre* (1957).
Wallace, C. W., *The Children of the Chapel at Blackfriars, 1597–1603* (1908).

In the Jacobean and Caroline period from 1616 to 1642 the Blackfriars was the premier theatre of England. Though the King's company—the sole tenants throughout the period—played also at the Globe, the Blackfriars is the house constantly associated with them in these years. It is also the theatre chiefly associated with court circles and the *élite* London audience, as many letters and allusions testify. On 8 January 1624/5 John Chamberlain wrote to Sir Dudley Carleton at the Hague: 'The Duke of Brunswicke went hence on Newyearesday after he had taried just a weeke and performed many visits to almost all our great Lords and Ladies as the Lord of Caunterburie, the Lord Keper, and the rest, not omitting Mistris Brus nor the stage at Blacke Friers.' (*Chamberlain*, ii. 594.) Viscount Conway wrote to the Lord Deputy in Ireland on 14 November 1635 with a similar assumption of the status of Blackfriars in courtly circles: 'The Affairs of this Summer make more Noise Abroad than at Home. The Gallants of the Court are more impatient to hear the News of a Battle, than they are to have a Play begin at *Black-Fryars*.' (*Strafforde's Letters*, i. 478.) And probably about the same time Sir John Suckling wrote an undated letter to two sisters in Anglesey using Blackfriars as the same status symbol: 'These things [boisterous winds in Wales] now we that live in *London* cannot help, and they are as great news to men that sit in Boxes at *Black-Fryars*, as the affairs of Love to Flannel-Weavers.' (*Fragmenta Aurea*, 1646, E$_8$.)

Of a different sort, though equally suggestive, is the address to the Reader of the Beaumont and Fletcher Folio of 1647, written by James Shirley, the last regular dramatist for Blackfriars. Such front matter for seventeenth-century literary works commonly contains exaggerated praise, but the more one sees of the casual allusions to Blackfriars and to Fletcher's plays, the clearer it becomes that many subjects of Charles I would have thought Shirley's statement not unduly exaggerated. Of the collection of plays he says: '*this being the Authentick witt that made Blackfriers an Academy, where the three howers spectacle while Beaumont and Fletcher were presented, were usually of more advantage to the hopefull young Heire, then a costly, dangerous, forraigne Travell, with the assistance of a governing Mounsieur, or Signior to boot*'. (1647 Folio, A$_3$.)

The Jacobean and Caroline Blackfriars was the second theatre of the name in London. The first had been built in 1576 in part of the Frater of the old Dominican monastery south-west of St. Paul's and within the walls of the city, and now part of the site

of *The Times* in Printing House Square.[1] The first Blackfriars had
ceased to be used as a theatre in 1584 (see Adams, pp. 91–110 and
Chambers, *E.S.* ii. 475–98). The second Blackfriars had been
made by James Burbage, the father of Richard and Cuthbert, from
a different set of rooms in the old conventual buildings. For the
sum of £600 he had purchased

All those Seaven greate vpper Romes as they are nowe devided
being all vpon one flower and sometyme beinge one greate and entire rome wth the roufe over the same coūed wth Leade . . . And also
all that greate paire of wyndinge staires wth the staire case therevnto
belonginge w[ch] leadeth vpp vnto the same seaven greate vpper
Romes oute of the greate yarde . . . (*M.S.C.* ii, Pt. i, 60–61.)

along with other rooms, stairs, walls, and yards. James Burbage
or his sons continued to buy property around their theatre in
Blackfriars, but the later purchases seem to have been for protection, convenience, or investment, not for enlargement of the hall.

In his major purchase James Burbage actually got two principal sets of rooms, one above the other, made from what has been
called the upper frater and the paved hall of the old Priory
(see Chambers, *E.S.* ii. 504–5). So far as present knowledge of
the two sets of rooms goes, either could have been converted into
his theatre, and there has been some disagreement as to which set
Burbage made over. Certain later allusions seem to me to demonstrate that it was the upper, reached by the 'greate paire of
wyndinge staires'. In *Love and Honour* (acted at the Blackfriars
in November 1634) by William Davenant, who had already
written at least four plays for the theatre, the speaker of the
epilogue says:

> Our Poet waits below to heare his destiny;
> Just in the Entry as you passe, the place
> Where first you mention your dislike or grace.
>
> (1649 ed., E₃.)

Thomas May in his *Life of a Satyricall Puppy called Nim*, 1657,
refers specifically to the stairs leading down from the theatre.

Which [plot] was, that I should go to see a Play in *Black-Fryars*:
and there (by all necessary consequences, or rather inspired assurance)
some rich Lady would cast her Eie on me . . . I enter'd the *Theater*,
and sat upon the Stage . . . Her uglinesse made me suppose that

---

[1] The location and history of the site are discussed in detail in Chambers,
E.S. ii. 475–96 and in *The History from 1276 to 1956 of the Site in Blackfriars* . . ., published by *The Times*.

nothing could be too base for her acceptance: therefore I (following her down the Staires) resolved to discover a good-will to her, either by a wanton gesture of my Body, or whispering in her Ear just as she came forth into the Street. (1657 edition, H_3^v–H_5^v.)

These references and others, probably but less certainly applying to Blackfriars, lead me to conclude that it was the upper and probably more lofty set of rooms which became the new theatre.

No records have been found to show precisely what James Burbage did to make a playhouse of his rooms, but presumably he removed the partitions, restored the original hall, and built a stage and galleries in it. The resulting area, including stage and tiring rooms, was 66 feet long by 46 feet wide (Wallace, op. cit., p. 39 n.), and references in the dramatic and satiric literature of the time show that there was more than one gallery, though they do not make clear whether there were two or three.

In spite of its fame, and the number of extant deeds and suits about it, Blackfriars has left surprisingly few details of its structure or appearance. The best-informed attempt to reconstruct it was made by J. H. Farrar and R. L. Martin, staff architects of the London County Council. Their sketch of the interior has been reproduced by Armstrong, op. cit., p. 1, and in Raymond Mander and Joe Mitchenson's *A Picture History of the British Theatre*, p. 14. Their model of the exterior of the theatre is displayed at the Shakespeare Memorial Theatre, Stratford-upon-Avon. They show a stage the full width of the hall, but some of this area must have been cut off by stage boxes. There are many references to the boxes at the Blackfriars, but only one, so far as I know, which makes clear the position of at least one of them. In a newsletter of 4 February 1631/2 John Pory reported to Viscount Scudamore several Star Chamber cases, one of them as follows:

Their lo:^{ps} made my lord Thurles of Ireland also to doe the like satisfaction to Captaine Essex. The occasion was this. This Captaine attending and accompanying my Lady of Essex in a boxe in the playhouse at the blackfryers, the said lord coming upon the stage, stood before them and hindred their sight. Captain Essex told his lo:^{p}, they had payd for their places as well as hee, and therfore intreated him not to depriue them of the benefitt of it. Wherevpon the lord stood vp yet higher and hindred more their sight. Then Capt. Essex with his hand putt him a little by. The lord then drewe his sword and ran full butt at him, though hee missed him, and might have slaine the Countesse as well as him.[1]

[1] P.R.O. C 115/M 35/8391. From a forthcoming article in *Studies in Philology* kindly sent me by Professor Herbert Berry.

If the noble lord, standing on the stage, could persistently obscure the view of Captain and Lady Essex in a box, their seats must have been in a box which was beside the stage, was nearly on a level with it, and which robbed the stage of at least part of the full width of the auditorium.

Lord Thurles's position in the theatre is a reminder of the fact that there are more references to sitting on the stage at Blackfriars than at any other theatre. Indeed, Professor Wallace was so struck by the number that he contended that the custom originated at Blackfriars, and was confined to that theatre until taken over by the other new private theatres, the Cockpit (1617) and the Salisbury Court (1629) (*Children of the Chapel at Blackfriars*, pp. 130–47). Though he is certainly wrong in thinking that the custom was initially or exclusively a Blackfriars one (see *Modern Philology*, viii [1911], 581–9) his examples do show its prevalence there before 1616. The early importance of the custom at the second Blackfriars was greater than Wallace knew, for a chancery suit of 1609 records the testimony of Henry Outlawe ' "That by the space of aboute fyftene wekes together in the first yere of the King*es* M^ties Raigne in Englande" [24 March 1603 to 23 March 1604] Evans, or others by his appointment, had received to the value of thirty shillings a week or thereabouts "for the vse of the stooles standinge vppon the Stage at Blackfryers"'. (Mark Eccles, *Shakespeare Survey*, xi [1958], 104.) At the usual rate of 6*d*. per stool this sum suggests that in 1603 there were usually at least ten spectators on the stage at each performance—more if the boys did not perform daily.

There is ample evidence that the custom continued into the later period. The entire prologue of Jonson's *The Devil is an Ass*, performed at Blackfriars in October or November 1616 (see above, iv. 616), is devoted to protests at the inconvenience caused by the custom. In 1619 Henry Hutton in his *Follies Anatomie. Or Satyres and Satyricall Epigrams* says:

> I durst not . . .
> Dine with Duke *Humfrey* in decayed *Paules*,
> Confound the streetes with *Chaos* of old braules,
> Dancing attendance on the Black-friers stage,
> Call for a stoole with a commanding rage.
>
> (A₆ᵛ.)

In 1623 Heminges and Condell recognized the custom as standard in their theatre when in the address *To the great Variety of Readers* for the First Folio they said: 'And though you be a

Magistrate of wit, and sit on the Stage at *Black-Friers*, or the *Cock-pit*, to arraigne Playes dailie . . .'.

Ben Jonson exploits the custom most fully in *The Staple of News*, acted at Blackfriars in February 1625/6, when his four gossips, as if members of the audience, sit on the stage throughout the play. Their introduction in the Induction shows their position, and their usurpation of a masculine privilege. Mirth interrupts the prologue speaker:

> MIRTH. . . . *Do you heare Gentleman? what are you? Gentleman-vsher to the Play? pray you helpe vs to some stooles here.*
> PROLOGVE. *Where?* o' *the* Stage, Ladies ?
> MIRTH. *Yes, o' the* Stage; *wee are persons of* quality, *I assure you, and women of* Fashion; *and come to see, and to be seene:*
>
> (1631 edition, Aa₂.)

In 1629 Francis Lenton referred to the same display of the aspiring wits in his *The Young Gallants Whirligig*:

> This golden Asse, in this hard Iron age.
> Aspireth now to sit vpon the stage,
> Lookes round about, then viewes his glorious selfe,
> Throws mony here and there, swearing hang pelfe;
>
> . . . . .
>
> Your Theaters hee daily doth frequent
>
> . . . . .
>
> The Cockpit heretofore would serue his wit,
> But now vpon the Fryers stage hee'll sit,
> It must be so, though this expensiue foole
> Should pay an angell for a paltry stoole.
>
> (1629 edition, B₃, B₄, C₃.)

Other allusions to the conspicuous spectators on the stage at Blackfriars might be cited, but these are characteristic and so spaced as to show the long continuation of the custom. It appears to have been finally abolished by royal order—at least one would assume that the King's command applied to all London theatres. The order is known only from a statement of instructions about allowances to the housekeepers at the Salisbury Court theatre, dated 14 September 1639: 'And one dayes p'ffitt wholly to themselves every yeare in consideration of their want of stooles on the stage, wᶜʰ were taken away by his Mᵗˢ comand.' (See above, ii. 687.) How long before the date of the Instructions the order of the King was issued is not known, but the context suggests that it was recent. If so, there were very few years in its long history when the second Blackfriars was free from the encumbrance of spectators on the stage.

Associated with the custom of sitting on the stage at Blackfriars is the custom of observing act intervals in the performances, a characteristic of productions at the private theatres, but apparently not in the public ones.[1] The customary act break at Blackfriars is several times recorded during the period of its occupancy by the boy actors. In the memoirs of Sir Richard Cholmley, who was born in 1580, his descendant writes:

> When he was of about the age of twenty-three years, coming to London, he went to see a play at Black Friars, and coming late, was forced to take a stool, and sit on the stage, as divers others did; and, as the custom was, between every scene [act] stood up to refresh himself. Whilst he was in that posture, a young gallant, very brave, clapped himself upon Sir Richard's stool. . . . (*The Memoirs of Sir Hugh Cholmley*, [1787], p. 18.)

Probably the most familiar example of the strongly marked act breaks at Blackfriars is the text of *The Knight of the Burning Pestle*, performed there by the boys in 1607 (see Chambers, *E.S.* iii. 220–1). Here not only is the end of each act marked, but the beginning of the next act is separately indicated. Three of the intervals are marked for music or dancing or both, and all act intervals are given extraneous dialogue by the Grocer and his wife, seated among the spectators on the stage.

Though the printed text is not marked so clearly, the same emphasis on the act breaks is indicated for Fletcher's *The Faithful Shepherdess*, acted at the same theatre a year or so later. Francis Beaumont, solacing Fletcher after the failure of his play in the theatre, says in his commendatory verses for the first edition,

> Nor wants there those, who as the Boy doth dance
> Betweene the actes, will censure the whole play.

[1] In his article 'Act-Divisions in Shakespeare' (*R.E.S.* iv [1928], 152–8), W. W. Greg examined for act divisions 172 plays printed between 1591 and 1610, and he classified them in various ways. He concluded: 'The data collected above point quite clearly to the fact that, as a general rule, the prompt-books of plays performed by children's companies at private theatres were divided into acts, and that the prompt-books of plays performed by men's companies at public theatres were not. I see no escape from this conclusion.' For all but the last year of the period here considered, all private theatres were occupied exclusively by boy companies, and public theatres exclusively by adults. When the men's companies acquired private theatres they took over the private-theatre customs, as will appear.

The article by Thornton Shirley Graves 'The "Act Time" in Elizabethan Theatres' (*Studies in Philology*, xii [1915], 103–34) tries to prove that act intervals were usual in most Elizabethan theatres; his confusion derives from the fact that he has not sufficiently discriminated between private-theatre plays and public-theatre plays.

These two plays had been performed by the boy actors before the King's men took over Blackfriars, but the same observation of act intervals evidently continued after the adult actors had moved in. Ben Jonson, who had much experience of Blackfriars, makes his character Fitzdottrell refer to the continuing custom in *The Devil is an Ass*, written for the King's men to be performed in that theatre in the autumn of 1616 (see above, iv. 614–17):

> Today, I goe to the *Black fryers Play-house*,
> Sit i the view, salute all my acquaintance,
> Rise vp betweene the *Acts*, let fall my cloake,
> Publish a handsome man, and a rich suite
> (As that's a speciall end, why we goe thither,
> All that pretend, to stand for 't o' the *Stage*)
> The Ladies aske who's that?
>
> (1. 6. 1631 edition, O₄–O₄ᵛ.)

In *The Fatal Dowry* by Massinger and Field (himself a member of the company at Blackfriars at the time), acted between 1616 and 1619 and published as a Blackfriars play in 1632 (see above, iv. 783–5), the act interval is utilized for the play. At the end of Act II occurs the stage direction

> *Hoboyes.*
> *Here a passage ouer the Stage, while*
> *the Act is playing for the Marriage of*
> *Charalois with Beaumelle, &.*
>
> (1632 edition, F₁.)

In the plays he wrote for the King's men Ben Jonson continued to make use of the act breaks in Blackfriars performances for dramatic purposes. In his *Staple of News*, given at Blackfriars in February 1625/6, he marks the act breaks strongly by preparing an 'intermean' for each intermission, during which the four Gossips who sit on the stage as an audience comment on the just finished act.

In the 'Dedication To The Reader' in the 1631 edition of *The New Inn* Jonson grumbles—as he does in the title-page statement for the play—about the failure of the piece at the King's men's performance (licensed 19 January 1628/9):

. . . there is more hope of thee, then of a hundred fastidious *impertinents*, who were there present the first day, yet neuer made piece of their prospect the right way. What did they come for, then? I will punctually answer: . . . To dislike all, but marke nothing. And by their confidence of rising between the Actes, in oblique lines, make *affidauit* to the whole house, of their not vnderstanding one Scene.

(1631 edition, sigs. (*)₂–(*)₂ᵛ.)

In this play Jonson also recognizes the act division by printing the argument of the play carefully set off, act by act.

In *The Magnetic Lady*, performed by the King's men in October 1632, the use of the act breaks is like that in *The Staple of News*. During each intermission the extraneous characters, Mr. Probee and Mr. Damplay, criticize the preceding act to the boy actor on the stage with them.

Finally, the customary Blackfriars performance with intermissions between the acts is assumed by Thomas May in his *The Life of a Satyricall Puppy Called Nim*: 'Which [plot] was, that I should go to see a Play in *Black-Fryars*: and there . . . I enter'd the *Theater*, and sat upon the Stage. . . . I stood up also at the end of every *Act*, to salute those, whom I never saw before. Two *Acts* were finished before I could discover anything . . . About the beginning of the fourth *Act*, my Face withstood a fresh encounter.' (1657 edition, H$_3$^{v}–H$_4$^{v}.)

It is evident from these examples that the custom of clearly marked act divisions which had been established by the boy actors at Blackfriars was continued in the productions of the King's men after they took over the theatre. Intermissions between the acts could always be expected by Blackfriars audiences.

Other facts about the theatre and its audiences are not made so clear by the allusions; the size of the audience is only vaguely noted. Nowhere is the capacity of the second Blackfriars precisely stated, though vague references describe each of the private theatres as small. Obviously an auditorium of 46 feet by 66 feet, including the stage, could not accommodate crowds the size of those at the Fortune, Globe, Red Bull, or Hope. Wallace estimated the capacity of the second Blackfriars as 558 to 608 (op. cit., pp. 50–52); Harbage estimated 696, 800, and 955, depending upon the number of galleries and the use of the upper or lower floor (op. cit., pp. 339–40). I see very little solid evidence for the claims of one set of figures over another, but in the light of repeated allusions to the small size of the theatre I should incline toward the lower ones.

Before turning to the history of Blackfriars in the hands of the King's company during our period, the distinctive character of its use as one of two different theatres operated by the same organization should be noticed. At the time of Shakespeare's death the company had for eight years been operating both the Globe on the Bankside and the Blackfriars. The complicated risk of the original planning and implementation of this unique enterprise in 1608 had involved not only the first attempt of any London troupe to own and operate two playhouses, but also the first attempt of any adult company to exploit the more exclusive and fastidious audience of the private theatres.[1]

This profitable and growing audience[2] was probably a greater incentive in the acquisition of Blackfriars than the more frequently mentioned avoidance of the cold, wet, and mud, which necessarily characterized attendance at most of the winter performances in the only partially roofed suburban Globe. The private-theatre audience became the important one in the Jacobean and Caroline period from 1616 to 1642. During these years all the principal competitors of the King's men were essentially or exclusively private-theatre companies—the Lady Elizabeth's company, Queen Henrietta's company, the King's Revels company, and Beeston's boys. It ought to surprise no one that during the late years of the reign of King James and throughout the reign of Charles I the King's men were generally known as the company of the Blackfriars and not as the old familiar company of the Globe. When Thomas Crosfield set down in July 1634 his notes on all the London acting companies, he designated the premier company as simply 'The Kings Company at yᵉ private house of Blackfriars', with no mention of the Globe. (See above, ii. 688–9.) The Lord Chamberlain in making out warrants for payments to the company normally called them 'the Kings Players' or 'His Maᵗᵉˢ Comædians' without mention of a theatre, but when he did

---

[1] See 'Shakespeare and the Blackfriars Theatre', *Shakespeare Survey*, i (1948), 38–50. It is conceivable, but not likely, that one or more of Beeston's companies, Queen Anne's, Prince Charles's (I), Lady Elizabeth's, or Queen Henrietta's, may now and then have made unrecorded use of the Red Bull and the Phoenix as summer and winter theatres (see above, i. 225 and n.). If such a device was ever tried by Beeston, it could not have been before 1616/17; it never received contemporary comment; and it would have been a manager's device, not a company policy, for none of the actors except Beeston is known to have been a housekeeper at the early Phoenix.

Rosseter's hazy amalgamation of companies (the Queen's Revels, Lady Elizabeth's, and Prince Charles's (I)) at one time had rights in the Hope, and in first the Whitefriars and then in Porter's Hall (q.v.). There is no evidence, however, that they ever used a public theatre and a private theatre alternatively (see Chambers, *E.S.* ii. 257–8).

[2] The private-theatre audience was the expanding one, as witnessed by the building of three new private theatres in the period: Rosseter's Blackfriars or Puddle Wharf in 1615–16; the Phoenix or Cockpit in Drury Lane in 1617; and the Salisbury Court in 1629. No additional public theatres were built after 1616, though the old Fortune was replaced (as the Globe had been) after a fire in 1621, and the Hope had replaced the Bear-garden in 1614.

mention a playhouse for them it was simply Blackfriars, with no indication that they were also associated with the Globe. (See *M.S.C.* ii. 378, 380, 388–9, 391, 397.) Sir Henry Herbert, like his superior, tended to ignore the Globe. In his extant records the Blackfriars is mentioned four times as often as the public theatre, and by 1662 he seems to have forgotten the existence of the Globe; for when, after the Restoration, he listed his fees in the old days, he set down 'The profittes of a summers day play at the Black-fryers . . . The profitts of a winters day, at Blackfryers' (*Variorum*, iii. 266), though the performances of the summer days were certainly at the Globe. Part of his own Caroline records, to which Sir Henry was referring so inaccurately in 1662, are still extant. They show that his receipts from these summer and winter revivals (admissions minus £2. 5s. 0d. for daily charges) in 1628–33 averaged £15. 15s. 0d. at the Blackfriars, but only £6. 13s. 8d. at the much larger Globe.[1] Evidently the Globe brought the company less profit as well as less prestige than Blackfriars.

The difference in prestige between the two playhouses run by the King's company is probably best reflected in the title-pages of the published plays. The fact that a play was printed at all was generally a reflection of some publisher's estimate of its prestige, that is, its appeal to literate people who had money to spare for book purchases; the title-page was itself a form of advertising which was expected to encourage sales. On the title-pages of the plays performed by the King's men between 1616 and 1642 the Blackfriars was mentioned 48 times, the Globe only 27. And if one considers the titles of all the company's plays published from 1616 to 1700, whether the company is known to have acted them in the period after 1616 or not, the prominence which the publishers gave to Blackfriars is even more marked. A rough count shows the Globe appearing on the title-pages of 31 editions, the Black-friars on 115.[2] Probably the Globe performances for a number of

---

[1] See above, i. 23–24. Several years earlier, late in 1612, Edward Kirkham had said in his replication to the answers of Edward Painton, Henry Evans, Richard Burbage, and John Heminges: '. . . ffor this replyant sayth, and the same will averr and proue to this honorable Courte, that duringe such time as the said defendants Hemings and Burbidge and theire Companye contynewed playes and Interludes in the said great Hall in the ffryers, that they gott & as yet dothe, more in one Winter in the said great Hall by a thousand powndes then they were vsed to gett in the Banckside'. (*Chronicle History of the London Stage*, p. 248.) Though this statement is not at variance with the later evidence, it should probably be discounted somewhat as lawsuit hearsay.

[2] Such a check of title-pages may be most conveniently made from

these plays were ignored for reasons of prestige. The second editions of *The Duchess of Malfi* and of *A King and No King*, for instance, mention Blackfriars only, though in each case the first edition had named both Blackfriars and the Globe. Similarly the Globe performance of *The Doubtful Heir*, mentioned by Shirley himself in a prologue, is ignored on the title-page of the edition of 1652. (See above, v. 1105–7.)

This evidence from receipts, allusions, and title-pages, showing that in Jacobean and Caroline times the Globe had been relegated to an inferior position, is confirmed by various direct statements in the plays themselves. William Davenant's plays were mostly prepared, as one would expect, for presentation at Blackfriars. (See above, iii. 193–225.) But one of them was intended for performance at the Globe. *News from Plymouth* was licensed for performance in the middle of the Globe season, 1 August 1635, and when Davenant published the epilogue for the play in 1638, in *Madagascar; With Other Poems*, he entitled it 'Epilogue, To a Vacation Play at the Globe'. The characters and the appeal of this play, which are much more plebeian than is usual with the aspiring Davenant, show that he was consciously writing for a different audience, and the lines of the prologue make explicit statement of his hopes and fears in this inferior Globe environment:

> *A Noble Company! for we can spy,*
> *Beside rich gawdy Sirs, some that rely*
> *More on their Judgments, then their Cloathes, and may*
> *With wit, as well as Pride, rescue our Play:*
> *And 'tis but just, though each Spectator knows*
> *This House, and season, does more promise shewes,*
> *Dancing, and Buckler Fights, then Art, or Witt;*
> *Yet so much taxt of both, as will befit*
> *Our humble Theame, you shall receive, and such*
> *As may please those, who not expect too much.*
> (*The Works of Sir William Davenant, Kt.*, 1673, Aaaa₁.)

The subordination of the Globe to the Blackfriars is also shown by their seasonal use, for the autumn, winter, and early spring

W. W. Greg's *A Bibliography of the English Printed Drama to the Restoration* (1939–59). Sir Walter's own list of theatre associations for plays (ibid., iii. 1470–1) is made on different principles, for he counts only one edition for each play, and he often counts plays whose provenance is not given on title-pages but is known from other sources. Even so, his list shows about the same proportions as mine for plays printed after 1615: Globe, 14; Blackfriars, 62.

were the seasons when the socially superior theatre patrons were in town; a summer theatre was almost necessarily an inferior theatre in the reign of Charles I. The summer and winter use of the two playhouses was first explicitly recorded by James Wright in his *Historia Histrionica*, 1699, in his enumeration of the Caroline theatres of London: 'The *Black-friers*, and *Globe* on the *Bankside*, a Winter and Summer House, belonging to the same Company called the King's Servants.' (See above, ii. 693.) Wright wrote from memory, but about a century later Edmond Malone made the same observation, first by conjecture and then from evidence in the now lost manuscripts of the Master of the Revels:

As the Globe was partly exposed to the weather, and they acted there usually by day-light, it appeared to me probable (when this essay was originally published) that this was the summer theatre; and I have lately found my conjecture confirmed by Sir Henry Herbert's Manuscript. The king's company usually began to play at the Globe in the month of May. (*Variorum*, iii. 70–71.)

When Nicholas Goodman wrote his facetious account of the Globe's neighbour, the brothel called Holland's Leaguer, he mentioned the 'three famous *Amphytheators*', i.e. the Globe, the Hope, and the Swan, which could be seen from the Leaguer. The Globe 'was the *Continent of the World*, because halfe the yeere a World of *Beauties*, and braue *Spirits* resorted vnto it'. (*Holland's Leaguer*, 1632, F$_2$v.)

The precise dates on which the King's company made its semi-annual moves across the Thames are not known, but I should guess that the timing was influenced as much by the movements of the gentry, the lawyers, and their clients as by the weather. During term-time one would expect to find the company at their private theatre, accessible to the haunts of the termers, the gentry, and the court: near the Inns of Court, and relatively near to the law courts at Westminster, and to the King's, Queen's, and Prince's courts at Whitehall, St. James's, and Denmark House. I should imagine them installed at Blackfriars for the opening of Michaelmas term on or about the sixth of October, and leaving Blackfriars for the Globe after the end of Easter term, i.e. between 3 May and 4 June, depending on the date of Easter. The precise records of Sir Henry Herbert, which led Malone to say 'The king's company usually began to play at the Globe in the month of May', he did not publish, and they have since been lost. But his 'usually' indicates that the date was not always the same, as I should expect from the fluctuating date of Easter. A few scattered records[1] locate the company sometimes at one theatre and sometimes at the other in May. In 1633 the King's men were at the Globe on 16 and 23 May, when Sir Humphrey Mildmay saw plays there;[2] in 1634 Queen Henrietta Maria saw *Cleander* at Blackfriars on 13 May, presumably in a private performance; Malone says that *Cleander* 'had been produced on the 7th of the same month' (*Variorum*, iii. 167), but I cannot be sure that he is not confusing acting and licensing date. In 1635 Mildmay saw *Othello* at Blackfriars on 6 May (see above, ii. 677), and in this same year on 19 May the Reverend George Garrard wrote to Wentworth in Ireland about a quarrel 'that lately broke out . . . in the *Black-Fryars* at a Play'. (See above, i. 47.) In 1640 Sir Humphry saw a new play at Blackfriars on 15 May, and in 1641 he saw an unnamed play at that theatre on 18 or 19 May. (See above, ii. 679.)

The only record I can find suggesting the September playing-

---

[1] Of course I am writing about the period 1616–42. I know of no careful attempt to determine how the King's men divided their time between the two houses from 1608 to 1616, but I should assume that the company had settled down to its Caroline programme within a year or two after taking over Blackfriars. This assumption is somewhat shaken by Simon Forman's *Booke of Plaies* (MS. Ashmole 208, Bodleian Library). Three of Forman's accounts begin:

> In Mackbeth at the Glob, 1610 [probably 1611], the 20 of Aprill . . .
> In Richard the 2 At the Glob 1611 the 30 of Aprill . . .
> In the Winters Talle at the glob 1611 the 15 of maye . . .
>   (Chambers, *William Shakespeare*, ii. 337–40.)

Since the attacks on the authenticity of Forman's *Bocke of Plaies* have been thoroughly refuted (*R.E.S.* xxiii [1947], 193–200) we have no reason to doubt that Forman saw the plays when and where he said he did, or that in 1611, or possibly 1610, the company had already begun to play at the Globe on 20 April. In 1611 Easter fell on 24 March, one of the earliest dates in the first half of the century, but even so the Easter term of the law courts would have been less than half over on 20 April, and I should have expected the King's men to remain at Blackfriars until at least 6 or 7 May. There would seem to be three possible conclusions from Forman's entries: (1) the Caroline limits of the winter and summer seasons had not yet been worked out in 1611; (2) for some unknown reason [repairs or alterations?] 1611 was an exceptional year; (3) my idea that the company continued at Blackfriars through the Easter term of the law courts is wrong. Of course I incline to (1) or (2), but a little more evidence would be welcome.

[2] See above, ii. 675. Unfortunately for our convenience, Sir Humphrey was generally out of town—like most of the rest of the gentry—in June, July, August, September, and early October, the normal months of playing at the Globe. His earliest recorded autumnal visit to the theatre was in 1638, when he saw Jonson's *Volpone* at Blackfriars on 27 October. (See above, ii. 678.)

place of the company is an uncertain one, but I think that probably an odd reference by John Pory should be taken as an indication that the King's men were still playing at the Globe on 15 September 1632. On that day Pory wrote to Viscount Scudamore: 'The Queens Majesty with some of her ladies, and maides of honour is daylie practizing upon a Pastorall penned by Mr Walter Montague. And Taylour the prime actor at the Globe goes every day to teache them action.'[1] Joseph Taylor was indeed the leading actor of the King's company in 1632 (see above, ii. 590–8), but in Caroline times he is commonly associated with Blackfriars or court performances rather than with the Globe. I take this unusual association of Pory's as an indication that in mid-September, when he wrote, Taylor and the rest of his company were still performing on the Bankside. This interpretation receives some support from another reference of Pory's in a letter to Viscount Scudamore two months later, when the same company had surely moved to Blackfriars. In his letter of 17 November 1632 he refers to them as 'The Players of the Black fryers'. (Ibid.)

In turning to the history of the theatre from 1616 to 1642, one observes that the King's company was solidly established as the dominant royal troupe and the Blackfriars as the most esteemed London theatre. One tends to think of their position as impregnable, but they were repeatedly threatened by their neighbours. The district of Blackfriars, though containing a number of noble establishments, was notably Puritan in its sentiments. Valerie Pearl, in her *London and the Outbreak of the Puritan Revolution*, 1961, says 'The suburbs and some of the liberties very quickly earned a reputation for Puritanism and, after 1640, for radicalism. . . . Two of the most radical and Puritan areas of all were the liberties of Blackfriars and Whitefriars. In Blackfriars, vast crowds assembled to hear a popular preacher.' (Pp. 40–41.)

The regular preacher in the parish of St. Anne's, Blackfriars, throughout the period of the occupancy of the Blackfriars theatre by the King's company was William Gouge, the Puritan writer and preacher who enlarged the church of St. Anne's and eventually became its Rector in 1621.

The power of the anti-theatre sentiment in the parish, probably marshalled by William Gouge, had been shown by the campaign from 1613 to 1617 to prevent the completion of Rosseter's Blackfriars theatre, and then to have it abolished. (See below, Porters'

---

[1] P.R.O., Scudamore Papers, C 115/M 35/8411. Quoted by J. P. Feil in *Shakespeare Survey*, xi (1958), p. 109.

Hall.) After this success the Godly of the parish still had Burbage's Blackfriars to offend them, and they proceeded to a new attack on it, using many of the same arguments and even some of the same phrases they had employed against Rosseter's playhouse. In undated petitions, probably of December 1618 or January 1618/19, they appealed to the Lord Mayor and the Corporation of London for the suppression of the Blackfriars theatre of the King's men. In the first petition, signed by the officers of the parish, headed by the name of William Gouge,[1] they recall a former petition against the theatre in 1596, and the ineffective order of 22 June 1600 limiting the London theatres to one on the Bankside and one in Golding Lane:

Neverthelesmay it please yor: Lo^p, and yor: brethren to bee aduertised, that contrary to the said Orders, The owner of the said playhouse, doth vnder the name of a private howse (respectinge indeed private Comoditie only) convert the said howse to a publique playhouse; vnto which there is daylie such resort of people, and such multitudes of Coaches (whereof many are Hackney Coaches, bringinge people of all sort*es*) That sometymes all our street*es* cannot containe them, But that they Clogg vpp Ludgate alsoe, in such sort, that both they endanger the one the other breake downe stall*es*, throwe downe mens good*es* from their shopps, And the inhabitant*es* there cannott come to their howses, nor bringe in their necessary provisions of beere, wood, coale or haye, nor the Tradesmen or shopkeep[er]s vtter their wares, nor the passenger goe to the comon water staires without danger of their lives and lymmes,[2] whereby alsoe many times, quarrell*es* and effusion of blood hath followed; and what further danger may bee occa$\check{c}$oned by broyles plott*es* or practises of such an vnrulie multitude of people yf they should gett head, yor wisedomes cann conceave; Theise inconvenienc*es* fallinge out almost everie daie in the winter tyme (not forbearinge the tyme of Lent) from one or twoe of the clock till sixe att night, which beinge the

---

[1] The prestige of William Gouge in the district is illustrated by the parish clerk's record of the death of his wife, entered in the burial registers. Other burials are given a single-line entry, but for 'Mrs Elizabeth Gouge wife to Mr William Gouge our Minister' there are four full lines, giving cause of death, number of children, place of death, and place of burial. All this in spite of the fact that she properly had no place in the record, since she died and was buried outside the parish. There is no other such detailed entry in two reigns. (Burial Registers for 1625, St. Anne's, Blackfriars. Guildhall MS. 4510/1.)

[2] This statement sounds like a Puritan anti-theatrical exaggeration, but it was not. The burial registers of the parish church of St. Anne's, Blackfriars, carry the entry under date of 19 January 1637/8: 'William Jordan a Beggar kild w^t a Coach com̄ing from the Play.' (Guildhall MS. 4510/1.)

tyme alsoe most vsuall for Christening*es* and burialls and afternoones
service, wee cannot haue passage to the Church for p[er]formance of
those necessary duties, the ordinary passage for a great part of the
precinct aforesaid beinge close by the play house dore. (*M.S.C.* i,
91–92.)

This well-set-out petition is signed first by Gouge, as 'Minister',
and then by two churchwardens, two sidesmen, two constables,
two collectors, and two scavengers, each pair testifying in a brief
sentence to the annoyance of the playhouse in the discharge of
their particular parish duties.

A separate supporting petition by 24 other residents of the
parish commends the officers,

hopeinge thereby to procure redresse of such disorders and inconvenienc*es* as arise there, by reason of the play house in that vnfitt
place . . . Wee desire yo.[r] L̃op and your Brethren to helpe vs to some
remedie therein, that wee may goe to our howses in safetie, and enioye
the benefitt of the street*es* w[th]out apparant danger, which nowe wee
assure yo[r] L̃õp, neither wee that are inhabitant*es*, nor anie other of his
Ma[tes]: subiect*es* hauinge occasion that waie, either by land or water
cann doe, ffor such is the vnruleines of some of the resorters to that
howse and of Coaches, horses, and people of all sort*es* gathered togeather by that occasion, in those narrow and crooked street*es*, that
many hurt*es* haue heretofore been thereby done, and feare it will att
some tyme or other hereafter, procure much more if it bee not by yo.[r]
wisedomes preuented. (Ibid. 93–94.)

These letters from the officers and inhabitants of the parish of
St. Anne's, Blackfriars, led to an order of the Corporation of the
City of London dated 21 January 1618/19. After summarizing
and quoting at length from the petition, the City document concludes:

whereupon, and after reading the said order and lettre of the Lordes
[i.e. of June 1600] shewed forth in this Court by the foresaid inhabi-
tauntes, and consideracion thereof taken, this Court doth thinke fitt
and soe order that the said playhowse be suppressed, and that the
players shall from henceforth forbeare and desist from playing in
that howse, in respect of the manifold abuses and disorders complayned
of as aforesaid. (Halliwell–Phillipps, *Outlines of the Life of Shakespeare*
[1887], i. 311.)

The order is very definite, but the Corporation evidently exceeded its authority. Not only did the King's men continue in
their private theatre, but two months after the order of the Lord
Mayor and Corporation the company's right to play in Blackfriars

was officially confirmed by royal patent. As Sir Edmund Chambers pointed out (*M.S.C.* i. 280) the company's patent of 1603 was still valid in 1619, and for most purposes they needed no new one. The patent of 1619 is practically a verbatim transcript of that of 1603, with two notable exceptions. The list of the Fellows of the company in the 1619 document drops the names of Fletcher, Shakespeare, Phillipps, Sly, Armyn, and Cowley, who had died, and adds the names of the eleven new members. More significant for our purposes the 1603 wording

> to shewe and exercise publiquely to theire best Cõmoditie . . . within theire nowe vsual howse called the Globe within our County of Surrey

is changed in 1619 to read

> to shew and exercise publiquely or otherwise to their best cõmoditie . . . wthin their two their now usuall houses called the Globe wthin o^r Coũ of Surrey and their private house scituate in the p^r-cinct*es* of the Blackfriers wthin o^r City of london. (Ibid., 264 and 281.)

It seems clear that the new patent, so unnecessary for most purposes in 1619, was issued at request as a guarantee of the right of the King's men to act in their private theatre in spite of the petition of the inhabitants of the parish and the order of the Corporation.

By the time the new patent was sealed (27 March 1619) Blackfriars, like all other London theatres, had been closed in official mourning for the death of Queen Anne. She had died on 2 March 1618/19 and presumably the theatres were closed immediately. John Chamberlain wrote to Sir Dudley Carleton at The Hague on 19 March 1618/19: '. . . the Quenes funerall is put of till the 29th of the next moneth, to the great hinderance of our players, which are forbidden to play so long as her body is above ground.' (*Chamberlain*, ii. 222.) The day of the state funeral was 13 May 1619, and Blackfriars was thus dark for more than two months. Since the funeral was so late in the spring, it is not unlikely that the company opened at the Globe after the restraint was removed and did not play again at Blackfriars during that season.

For the next few years there are no records of particular activities at Blackfriars, but in 1624 the King's men were in trouble because of the production of an unlicensed play there. On 20 December 1624 all but two of the patented members of the company signed a letter to the Master of the Revels apologizing for having 'not long since' acted without licence a play called *The*

Spanish Viceroy. (See above, v. 1412–13.) The date of the letter makes it fairly certain that the questionable play was acted at Blackfriars. One would guess that the company had been tempted into folly by the tremendous success of their production of Middleton's violently anti-Spanish play, *A Game at Chesse*, at the Globe during the previous summer. (See above, iv. 870–9.) Nothing at all is known of the play, *The Spanish Viceroy*; even the letter of apology is preserved only in a copy made by Sir Henry Herbert on the occasion of another company indiscretion nine years later.

For much of the year 1625 Blackfriars, like all other London theatres, was closed because of one of the worst outbreaks of the plague. Probably the playhouses were first closed in mourning for the death of King James on 27 March 1625, and, because of the mounting plague deaths, not allowed to reopen after the funeral on 7 May following. All theatres remained closed until late November or early December for the most deadly plague visitation in memory. (See above, ii. 654–7.)

Not long after the reopening of the theatres the parishioners of William Gouge were active again in trying to expel the actors from their parish. Perhaps they were encouraged by the long silence of the players during the plague time. At any rate, under the date of 28 February 1625 [/6] the Journals of the House of Commons record:

[Mr. Whitby] reporteth the Petition of the Inhabitants of the *Blackfryers*, against the Playhouse there:—Of the great Inconveniences the Inhabitants receive thereby:—Disturbance of Trade there; Hindrance of bringing in their Goods, and Victuals; Quarrels and Bloodsheds; Desertion of chief Dwellings by Noblemen and Gentlemen; Hinderance of carrying their Children to be christened, or dead Bodies to be buried; Danger of Infection.—The Committee thinketh fit, the Consideration and Redress hereof to be recommended to the Lord Chamberlain.

This ordered: And to be done by Sir *B. Rudyard*, and Sir *Wm. Herberte*, Sir *Tho. Hobby*, and Sir *Nath. Rich*. (*Journals of the House of Commons, 1547–1628* [1803], p. 826.)

Less than two weeks later the committee reported back:

Sir *B. Rudyard* reporteth that he hath delivered his Message to the Lord Chamberlain, about the Playhouse in the *Blackfryers*. That the Lord Chamberlain's Answer is (with Expression of great Respects to this House) that, though it belong not to his Place, yet he will recommend the Petition to his Majesty, with his best Endeavour to mediate the same, so as there may be Consideration had of the Players Damages by their Removal from thence. (Ibid., p. 834.)

Since the action was to be taken by the Lord Chamberlain and the King, both tried friends of the King's company, the matter was in good hands, but the doughty Puritans were by no means finished, as will appear later.

For several days in the late twenties and early thirties, receipts at particular performances at Blackfriars have been preserved. These unusual records derive from an agreement made by the Master of the Revels with the King's company in 1628. Herbert says:

> The kinges company with a generall consent and alacritye have given mee the benefitt of too dayes in the yeare, the one in summer, thother in winter, to bee taken out of the second daye of a revived playe, att my owne choyse. The housekeepers have likewyse given their shares, their dayly charge only deducted, which comes to some 2l. 5s. this 25 May, 1628. (*Variorum*, iii. 176.)

It should be noted that the category of play assigned to Sir Henry was one of the least attractive. Generally speaking, the largest audiences were attracted to new plays, the next largest to the first day of revivals. It is not clear from Herbert's statement whether the housekeepers' charge of £2. 5s. 0d. applies only to the Globe performance of 25 May 1628, to all Globe performances, or to all performances at either Globe or Blackfriars. In any case the housekeepers' charge would probably not have varied greatly—the Globe was larger and presumably required more cleaning and repairing, but the Blackfriars probably required candles and fires. (See above, ii. 687.) If we add £2. 5s. 0d. to the figures Sir Henry gives for the five winter performances we get the following receipts for particular days at Blackfriars:

1628	22 November	*The Custom of the Country*	£19. 15s. 0d.
1629	22 November	*The Moor of Venice*	12. 01s. 0d.
1630/31	18 February	*Every Man in his Humour*	14. 09s. 0d.
1631	1 December	*The Alchemist*	15. 05s. 0d.
1632	6 November	*The Wild Goose Chase*	17. 05s. 0d.

(*Variorum*, iii. 176–7.)

The selection of plays by Sir Henry Herbert—certainly one of the most theatrically knowledgeable of King Charles's subjects—is an interesting confirmation of the comparative reputations of dramatists. Literary allusions of the time show that the dramatists with greatest reputations were Jonson, Beaumont and Fletcher, and Shakespeare, and all the plays Herbert selected (Globe performances included) are from the works of these three playwrights, out of more than a score of writers represented in the company's repertory at this time. (See above, i. 109–34.) It is also noteworthy that each of Sir Henry's Blackfriars receipts is greater than any of his Globe receipts.

In 1629 a troupe of French players visited London, and a little over a fortnight before the performance of *Othello* at Black-friars recorded by Sir Henry Herbert they produced a French farce at the theatre. The Master of the Revels entered their payment to him 'For the allowinge of a French company to playe a farse at Blackfryers, this 4 of November, 1639 [error for 1629] —2*l*. 0*s*. 0*d*.' (*Variorum*, iii. 120.) The same performance was recorded with indignation by the Puritan William Prynne in his *Histriomastix*, 1633:

... as they have now their female-Players in Italy, and other forraigne parts, and as they had such *French-women Actors*, in a Play[t] [t In Michael. Terme, 1629] not long since personated in *Black-friers Play-house*, to which there was great resort.

.   .   .   .   .

In imitation of these some French-women, or Monsters rather on Michaelmas Terme 1629. attempted to act a French Play, at the Play-house in Blackfriers: an impudent, shamefull, unwomanish, gracelesse, if not more then whorish attempt. (*Histriomastix*, Ee₃ᵛ– Ee₄ and Ggg₃ᵛ.)

According to a letter printed by John Payne Collier the recep-tion of this French performance at Blackfriars was sensational. In the letter Thomas Brande says that there was a great disturbance at the performance. He says that the French actresses 'did attempt, thereby giving just offence to all vertuous and well-disposed persons in this town, to act a certain lascivious and unchaste comedye, in the French tonge at the Blackfryers. Glad I am to saye they were hissed, hooted, and pippin-pelted from the stage, so as I do not thinke they will soone be ready to trie the same againe.' (*History of English Dramatic Poetry and the Stage* [1879], i. 452–3.)

For reasons given elsewhere at length (see below, vi. 225–7) I doubt if this letter applies to the Blackfriars performance, but I cannot prove that it does not.

In 1630, for rather a long period, all London theatres were closed in another plague epidemic. The closing order went out from the Master of the Revels on 17 April, and the playhouses were not allowed to reopen until 12 November following. Thus the King's company lost the entire Globe season for the year, and the end of one Blackfriars season and the beginning of the next. (See above, ii. 657–8.)

It is probable that the Blackfriars season of 1630–1 was again interrupted by plague, but the evidence is not very decisive. There is some reason to think that for an uncertain period sometime between 18 February 1630/31 and 10 June 1631 there was a prohibition. (See above, ii. 658–9.)

In 1631 the attacks on Blackfriars by means of an 'humble petition of the Churchwardens and Constables of Blackfriars on the behalfe of the whole Parish' were renewed. This time they approached the Privy Council through Archbishop Laud—not the best intermediary for the Reverend William Gouge, one would have thought. Laud endorsed the petition of 1631: *The petition of the inhabitants of the Blackfriars about remove of the players. To the Council table. (C.S.P., Dom.,* 1631–3, p. 221.) The points of the petition are much the same as before, and the orders and petitions of 1596, 1600, and 1619 are annexed. The headings are itemized in the *Calendar of State Papers* but quoted in full in Collier's *History of English Dramatic Poetry.* Some of the points and the phraseology are suggestive of the popularity and the functioning of the theatre in 1631:

> Reasons and Inconveniences induceing the inhabitants of Black-friars London to become humble suitors to your Lordship for remov-ing the Playhouse in the said Blackfriers.
> 1. The Shopkeepers . . . suffer . . . by the great recourse to the Playes (especially of Coaches) . . .
> 2. The recourse of Coaches is many tymes so great, that the inhabi-tants cannot in an afternoone take in any provision . . .
> 3. The passage through Ludgate to the water is many tymes stopped up, people in their ordinary going much endangered, quarrells, and bloodshed many tymes occasioned; and many disorderly people towards night gathered thither, under pretence of attending and waiting for those at the playes.
> 4. Yf there should happen any misfortune of fier, there is not likely any present order could possibly be taken, for the disorder and number of the coaches . . .
> 5. Christenings and Burialls . . . are many tymes disturbed . . .
> 6. Persons of honour and quality, that dwell in the Parish, are restrained by the number of Coaches from going out, or coming home, in seasonable tyme . . . And some persons of honour have left, and others have refused houses . . .
> 7. [The order of 1600 limiting playhouses.]
> *(History of English Dramatic Poetry* [1879], i. 455–7.)

The points are well taken. It is noteworthy that the petitioners to the Archbishop avoid any mention of the subjects which were to get William Prynne into so much trouble with Laud two years later: the immorality of plays, playhouses, and players. They shrewdly confine themselves to the problems of traffic, fire prevention, church functioning, and neighbourhood deterioration, all of which the Archbishop and the Council must take seriously. There is no record of immediate action by the Council, but if the King's men knew of this new petition, as surely they did, Lowin and Taylor had good reason to be worried by this well-conceived attack.

Worry about their private theatre was not enough, however, to teach the company discretion, for in the autumn of 1632 they invited trouble at Blackfriars by their handling of Ben Jonson's *The Magnetic Lady*. The play was anticipated in September, for on the 15th John Pory had written to Viscount Scudamore: 'Ben Jonson hath written a playe against the Terme called the Magnetick Lady.' Five days later he repeated the information in a letter to Sir Thomas Puckering, adding the observation that he had thought Ben Jonson was dead.[1] The play was duly licensed for performance by the Master of the Revels on 12 October, and presumably opened at Blackfriars on or about that date. According to Alexander Gill, whose malice toward Jonson suggests that he should be discounted somewhat, there were only three performances of the play, and they were dismal.

> *To B Johnson on his Magnetick Lady.*
>
> Is this y^r Load-stone Ben that must attract
> Applause and laughter at each scene and act?
> Is this the child of your bed-ridden witt
> And none but ye black-friers to foster it?
>
> . . . . . .
>
> Foh how it stinkes! what generall offence
> Gives thy prophaneness such gross impudence?
> O how y^r freind Natt: Butter gan to melt
> When at the pooreness of your platt he smelt
> And Inigo with laughter then grew fatt
> That ther was nothing ther worth laughing att.
> And yet thou crazy wretch art confident
> Belching out full-mouth'd oathes wth foule intent
> Calling vs fooles and rogues vnletterd men
> Poore narrow soules y^t cannot judge of Ben.

---

[1] The first letter comes from the Scudamore Papers at the Public Record Office (C 115/M 35/8411) as transcribed by J. P. Feil, *Shakespeare Survey*, xi (1958), p. 109. The second version which Pory sent to Sir Thomas Puckering is in the British Museum (MS. Harleian 7000, art. 181) as transcribed by Henry Ellis in *Original Letters*, Second Series (1827), iii. 270.

Yet what is worse after three shameful foyles
The printer must be put to further toyles
                .   .   .   .

Fall to thy trade in thy old age agen,
Take vp thy trugge and trowell gentle Ben;
Let playes alone, or if thou needs will write
And thrust thy feeble muse forth into light,
Lett Lowin cease and Taylor fear to touch
The loathed stage, for now thou makst it such.[1]

The players cannot have been happy with this reception, but there was worse to come. In a letter of 17 November 1632 John Pory wrote again to Viscount Scudamore: 'The Players of the Black fryers were on Thursday [15 November] called before the high Commission at Lambeth, and were bound over to answere such articles as should be objected against them. And it is said to be for uttring some prophane speaches in abuse of Scripture and wholly thinges, which they found penned, for them to act and playe, in Ben Jonsons newe comedy called the Magnetique lady.' (Fiel, op. cit., p. 109.) Just how the King's men defended themselves against these charges is not clear, but a later note of the Master of the Revels suggests that they at first tried to put the blame on Sir Henry Herbert. That official noted in his Office Book under the date 24 October 1633:

Upon a second petition of the players to the High Commission court, wherein they did mee right in my care to purge their plays of all offense, my lords Grace of Canterbury bestowed many words upon mee, and discharged mee of any blame, and layd the whole fault of their play called The Magnetick Lady, upon the players. This happened the 24 of Octob. 1633, at Lambeth. In their first petition they would have excused themselves on mee and the poett. (*Variorum*, iii. 233.)

The two accounts seem to indicate that when the King's men were first called in after the failure at Blackfriars they claimed to have spoken only what Jonson had written and Herbert had allowed. If in the second petition they duly acknowledged Herbert's 'care to purge their plays of all offense' they must have admitted either that they themselves had added the 'prophane speaches in abuse of Scripture and wholly things' to Jonson's play, or at any rate that the text Herbert read did not contain the offensive matter.

[1] From a manuscript commonplace book in private hands. Transcribed in Bradley and Adams, *The Jonson Allusion Book*, pp. 177–9. Another manuscript of the poem is in Bodleian Ashmole MS. 38, p. 15.

In the autumn of 1633 the troubles of Blackfriars with the inhabitants of the parish came to the fore again, and this time the protests elicited more action. Apparently people of higher rank than churchwardens and constables had complained. At its sitting of 9 October 1633 the Privy Council ordered

Vpon Consideracon this day had at the Board of the greate incon venience and annoyance occasioned by the Resorte and Confluence of Coaches to the Play house in Black ffryers Whereby the Streetes being narrow thereabouts are at those tymes become impassable, to the greate p[r]iudice of his ma[ts]: Subiects passing that way vpon theire seuerall occacons and in pticular to divers Noblemen, and Councello[rs]: of State whose howses are that way, Wherby they are many tymes hindred from theire necessary attendance vpon his ma[ts]: pson and service. Theire Lopps calling to mynde that formerly vpon Complaint hereof made, the Board was of opinion, that the said Play house was fitt to be remoued from thence, and that an indifferrent Recompence & allowance should be giuen them for theire Interests in the said house, and buildings therevnto belonging. Did therfore thinke fitt and order, that S[r]: Henry Spiller and S[r]: William Becher K[ts]: the Alderman of the Ward Lawrence Whitaker Esq[r]: and [*blank*] Child Citizen of London, or any three of them be hereby required to call such of the pties interessed before them, as they shall thinke fitt and vpon heareing theire demaunds, and viewe of the place, to make an indifferent Estimate and valewe of the said house and buildings, and of theire Interests therin, and to agree vpon, and sett downe such Recompence to be giuen for the same, as shall be reasonable, and thervpon to make Report to the Board of theire doeings and pceedings therin by the 26: of this p[r]sent. (*M.S.C.* i. 386–7.)

Here was a greater threat to Blackfriars than any of the earlier ones. The committee did its work and reported back, as Secretary Windebank recorded in his notes of business transacted by the Privy Council on 20 November 1633: 'Blackfriars' play-house. The players demand 21,000*l.* The Commissioners (Sir Henry Spiller, Sir William Becher, and [Laurence] Whitaker,) valued it at near 3,000*l.* The parishioners offer towards the removing of them 100*l.* . . .' (*C.S.P.*, *Dom.*, 1633–4, p. 293.)

A more detailed statement of what the committee found is provided by a report endorsed 'Certificate from the Justices of the Peace of the County of Middlesex about the Blackfryers', which was printed by John Payne Collier. Though the authenticity of the document has been questioned, largely because Collier reported it and no one else has seen it, the certificate is probably genuine. (See *M.S.C.* i. 386.) The certificate reads:

MAY IT PLEASE YOUR LORDSHIPS,—According to the order of this
honorable Board of the 9th of October last, we have had divers meetings at the Black Fryers; and having first viewed the Playhouse
there, we have called unto us the chief of the Players, and such as
have interest in the said Playhouse and the buildings thereunto
belonging (which we also viewed): Who, pretending an exceeding
great loss, and almost undoing to many of them, and especially to
divers widows and orphans having interest therein, if they should be
removed from playing there, we required them to make a reasonable
demand of recompense for such interest as they or any of them had
therein. Whereupon their first demand being a gross sum, 16,000*l.*,
we required them to set down particularly in writing how and from
whence such a demand could rise, and gave them time for it. At our
next meeting they accordingly presented unto us a particular note
thereof, which amounted to 21,990*l.* But we, descending to an
examination of their interest in their houses and buildings they there
possess, and the indifferent valuation thereof, have with their own
consent valued the same as followeth.

   1. First for the Playhouse itself, whereof the Company hath
taken a lease for divers years yet to come, of Cutbert Burbidge and
William Burbidge (who have the inheritance thereof) at the rent of
50*l.* per Ann.: we value the same after the same rate, at 14 years'
purchase, as an indifferent recompense to the said Burbidges, which
cometh to 700*l.*

   2. For 4 tenements, near adjoining to the Playhouse, for the which
they receive 75*l.* per annum rent, and for a void piece of ground
there, to turn coaches in, which they value at 6*l.* per Ann., making
together 81*l.* per Ann.: the purchase thereof, at 14 years, likewise
cometh to 1134*l.* They demand further, in respect of the interest,
that some of them have by lease in the said Playhouse, and in respect
of the Shares which others have in the benefit thereof, and for the
damage they all pretend they shall sustain by their remove, not
knowing where to settle themselves again (they being 16 in number)
the sum of 2400*l.*, viz., to each of them 150*l.* But we conceive they
may be brought to accept of the sum of 1066*l.* 13*s.* 4*d.*, which is to
each of them 100 markes.

   All which we humbly leave to your Lordships' grave consideration.
Your Lordships' most humbly to be commanded.

<table>
<tr><td>'H. Spiller.</td><td>'Will. Baker,</td></tr>
<tr><td>'Humfrey Smith,</td><td>'Laur Whitaker,</td></tr>
<tr><td></td><td>'Willm. Childe.'</td></tr>
</table>

'20 Nov. 1633. (*History of English Dramatic Poetry*, i. 477–8.)

   The discrepancy between the valuation of the committee and
the offer of the parish gave the Council reason to proceed no
further with the project of buying out the Blackfriars theatre.

But they seem to have felt that something must be done, and they attacked the problem of the frequently denounced coaches at the theatre. At the same sitting of 20 November 1633 their Lordships declared that

Whereas yᵉ Board hath taken consideraçon of the great inconvenieñcs that growe by reason of the resort to the Play house of yᵉ Black-ffryars in Coaches, whereby the streets neare thereunto, are at the Playtime so stopped that his Maᵗˢ Subiects going about their neces-sarie affayres can hardly finde passage and are oftentymes endangered: Their lps remembring that there is an easie passage by water vnto that playhouse wᵗʰout troubling the streets, and that it is much more fit and reasonable that those wᶜʰ goe thither should goe thither by water or else on foote rather than the necessarie businesses of all others, and the publique Commerce should be disturbed by their pleasure, doe therefore Order, that if anie p[er]son man or woman of what Condiçon soever repaire to the aforesayd Playhouse in Coach so soone as they are gone out of their Coaches the Coach men shall de-parte thence and not retourne till the ende of the play, nor shall stay or retourne to fetch those whom they carryed anie nearer wᵗʰ their Coaches then the farther parte of Sᵗ Paules Church yarde on the one syde, and ffleet-Conduite on the other syde, and in yᵉ tyme betweene their departure and returne shall either returne home or else abide in some other streets lesse frequented with passengers and so range their Coaches in those places that the way be not stopped, wᶜʰ Order if anie Coachman disobey, the next Constable or Officer is hereby charged to com̃it him pʳsently to Ludgate or Newgate; And the Lo: Mayor of yᵉ Citie of London is required to see this carefully pformed by the Conestables and Officers to whom it apperteyneth and to punish every such Conestable or officer as shall be found negligent therein. And to the ende that none may pʳtende ignorance hereof, it is lastly ordered that Copies of this Order, shalbe set vp at Paules Chaine, by direction of the Lorde Mayor, as also at the west ende of Sᵗ Paules Church, at Ludgate and the Blackfryers Gate and Fleete Conduite. (*M.S.C.* i. 387–8.)

The letter was accordingly prepared for the Lord Mayor and is copied into the minutes of the sitting of 29 November 1633. (Ibid., 388.) And in a letter of George Garrard to Viscount Went-worth in Ireland, dated 9 January 1633/4, we have evidence that the Lord Mayor complied:

Here hath been an Order of the Lords of the Council hung up in a Table near *Paul's* and the *Black-Fryars*, to command all that Resort to the Play-House there to send away their Coaches, and to disperse Abroad in *Paul's Church-yard*, *Carter-Lane*, the Conduit in *Fleet-street*, and other Places, and not to return to fetch their Company, but they

must trot afoot to find their Coaches, 'twas kept very strictly for two
or three Weeks, but now I think it is disorder'd again. (*Strafforde's
Letters*, i. 175–6.)

Garrard was quite right in saying that the situation had become
disordered again by January. The reason is to be found in a supplementary order of the Privy Council issued at their sitting of
29 December 1633:

Vpon Informačon this day giuen to the Board of the discomoditie
that divers p[er]sons of greate quallity especially Ladies and Gentle-
women, did receiue in goeing to the Playhouse of Blackfriers, by
reason that noe Coaches may stand wthin the Blackfriers Gate or
retourne thither dureing the Play, and of the p'iudice the Players his
ma^{ts}: Servants doe receiue therby. But especially that the Streetes are
soe much the more incumberred wth the said Coaches. The Board
takeing into Consideračon the former order of the 20th: of Nouem-
ber last concerning this busines, did thinke fitt to explaine the said
order, in such manner that as many Coaches as may stand wthin the
Blackfriers Gate, may may [*sic*] enter and stay ther, or retourne
thither at the end of the Play. . . .' (*M.S.C.* i. 388–9.)

This series of documents about the attempts to suppress Blackfriars theatre in 1633 illuminates certain aspects of the enterprise of the King's men at Blackfriars. The settled hostility of the
parish and the determination of its officers become very clear,
but it is evident that whatever the moral indignation of Puritan
Blackfriars, it does not appear in their petitions. Their case is well
presented on sound grounds of civic need, and the Privy Council
was forced to conclude 'that the said Play house was fitt to be
remoued from thence'. The great discrepancy between the valuation of the players and the offer of the parish suggests a desire to
thwart the negotiations—probably by both parties. Finally, the
fate of the Council's coach order is eloquent testimony to the rank
and influence of the patrons of the theatre, who, by complaining
of their inconvenience, could persuade the Lords of the Council
to modify a published order. It may be significant that at the sitting at which the order was modified the King himself was present.
    While the serious threat to their theatre was hanging over them,
the players at Blackfriars were again involved in difficulties with
censorship. This time their performance was stopped after the
bills had already been posted. The players appear to have been
highly annoyed, and no doubt the audience, assembled at Blackfriars to see a play which was not given, were also annoyed. The
evidence suggests a misunderstanding, however, rather than an

attempt like the one of the previous year to circumvent the Master of the Revels. Sir Henry Herbert set out the facts more fully than usual in his Office Book.

On friday the nineteenth [18th] of October, 1633, I sent a warrant by a messenger of the chamber to suppress The Tamer Tamd [Fletcher's *Woman's Prize, c.* 1605], to the Kings players, for that afternoone, and it was obeyd; upon complaints of foule and offensive matters conteyned therein.

They acted The Scornful Lady [Beaumont and Fletcher, 1613–17] instead of it, I have enterd the warrant here.

'These are to will and require you to forbeare the actinge of your play called The Tamer Tamd, or The Taminge of the Tamer, this afternoone, or any more till you have leave from mee: and this at your perill. On friday morninge the 18 Octob. 1633.

To Mr. Taylor, Mr. Lowins, or any of the King's players at the Blackfryers.'

On saterday morninge followinge the booke was brought mee, and at my lord of Hollands request I returned it to the players yͤ monday morninge after, purgd of oaths, prophaness, and ribaldrye, being yͤ 21 of Octob. 1633.

Because the stoppinge of the acting of this play for that afternoone, it being an ould play, hath raysed some discourse in the players, thogh no disobedience, I have thought fitt to insert here ther submission upon a former disobedience, and to declare that it concernes the Master of the Revells to bee carefull of their ould revived playes, as of their new, since they may conteyne offensive matter, which ought not to be allowed in any time.

The Master ought to have copies of their new playes left with him, that he may be able to shew what he hath allowed or disallowed.

All ould plays ought to bee brought to the Master of the Revells, and have his allowance to them for which he should have his fee, since they may be full of offensive things against church and state; yͤ rather that in former time the poetts tooke greater liberty than is allowed them by mee.

The players ought not to study their parts till I have allowed of the booke.

[Here Sir Henry copied the King's men's letter of 1624 apologizing for acting the unlicensed play called *The Spanish Viceroy*]

Mr Knight,

In many things you have saved mee labour; yet wher your judgment or penn fayled you, I have made boulde to use mine. Purge ther parts, as I have the booke. And I hope every hearer and player will thinke that I have done God good servise, and the quality no wronge; who hath no greater enemies than oaths, prophaness, and publique ribaldry, wh^ch for the future I doe absolutely forbid to bee presented unto mee in any playbooke, as you will answer it at your perill. 21 Octob. 1633.

This was subscribed to their play of The Tamer Tamd, and directed to Knight, their book-keeper.

The 24 Octob. 1633, Lowins and Swanston were sorry for their ill manners, and craved my pardon, which I gave them in presence of Mr. Taylor and Mr. Benfeilde. (*Variorum*, iii. 208–10.)

The Master of the Revels twice notes that the objectionable material in the play was 'oaths, prophaness, and ribaldrye', the same offence as that of *The Magnetic Lady* at the theatre the previous year. Could oaths and ribaldry have had such a strong appeal to the Blackfriars audience as these accounts suggest? The offensiveness of *The Tamer Tamed* was easily eliminated, for a month later, on 28 November 1633, the company produced the play at St. James's Palace before the King and Queen, and Sir Henry himself reported that it was 'Very well likt'. (*Variorum*, iii. 234.)

From about this time comes an account which is interesting in its revelation of Blackfriars practice and Blackfriars audiences. In his memoirs for his children Bulstrode Whitelocke, at this time prominent at the Middle Temple and a rising young lawyer, wrote after his discussion of Shirley's *Masque of Peace*, which he had helped to arrange in early February 1633/4:

> I was so conversant with the musitians, and so willing to gaine their favour, especially at this time, that I composed an Aier myself, with the assistance of Mr. Ives, and called it *Whitelocke's Coranto*; which being cried up, was first played publiquely, by the Blacke-fryars Musicke, who were then esteemed the best of common musitians in London. Whenever I came to that house (as I did sometimes in those dayes), though not often, to see a play, the musitians would presently play *Whitelocke's Coranto*, and it was so often called for, that they would have it played twice or thrice in an afternoon. (Burney, *A General History of Music* [ed. 1935], ii. 299.)

Two notable aspects of the Caroline performances of the King's men at Blackfriars are emphasized by this passage. The first is the importance of the Blackfriars orchestra and its music, a tradition which had been carried over from the time of the boy company which had preceded the King's men at the theatre.[1]

---

[1] Probably the most explicit and best-known piece of evidence of the importance and distinction of the music at Blackfriars in the time of the boys is the account in the diary of Frederic Gerschow. He was in the train of the touring Duke of Stettin-Pomerania, and attended the performance at

Whitelocke's statement that the Blackfriars orchestra was then esteemed the best in London is corroborated for a later period by an observation made by Richard Ligon, who had left England in July 1647. He wrote in his history of Barbados:

As for Musick, and such sounds as please the ear, they wish some supplies may come from *England*, both for Instruments and voyces, to delight that sense, that sometimes when they are tir'd out with their labour, they may have some refreshment by their ears; and to that end, they had a purpose to send for the Musick, that were wont to play at the *Black Fryars*, and to allow them a competent salary, to make them live as happily there, as they had done in *England*: And had not extream weaknesse, by a miserable long sicknesse, made me uncapable of any undertaking, they had employed me in the businesse, as the likeliest to prevail with those men, whose persons and qualities were well known to me in *England*. (*A True and Exact History of the Island of Barbados . . .* [1657], Ee₂.)

The music in the performances of particular plays in the repertory of the King's company is most fully discussed by John P. Cutts in his unpublished University of Birmingham thesis, 'Music for Shakespeare's Company, The King's Men' (1956). Cutts limits his investigations to the period 1603–25.[1]

The second feature of Blackfriars performances illuminated by Bulstrode Whitelocke's memoir is the coterie character of the audience at that theatre. Only in such an audience would the orchestra be familiar enough with individual patrons to recognize Whitelocke on his entrance and play his composition on repeated occasions. Not only did the musicians have to recognize him, but they had to expect various members of the audience to recognize him too, in order for their gesture to be telling.

A series of events at Blackfriars in the seasons of 1634–5, and 1635–6 emphasize again the character of the audience and the functioning of the theatre as a meeting-place of the nobility and gentry. On 25 November 1634 Robert Leake wrote from Westminster to Sir Gervase Clifton: '. . . I make no doubt but you have heard that *actus secundus* plaid on Tusday last at Blackfriers

---

Blackfriars on 18 September 1602. Gerschow wrote of an hour's concert before the play and of the exquisite singing of one of the boys. (*Royal Historical Society Transactions*, New Series, vi [1892], 26–28.) The plays of boy companies at private theatres were distinguished by the amount of vocal and instrumental music they incorporated.

[1] Part of the material in this thesis is published in the author's *La Musique de Scène de la Troupe de Shakespeare: The King's Men sous le règne de Jacques Iᵉʳ* (1959), Eds. du Centre National de la Recherche Scientifique.

between Sir John Suckling and Mr. Digby; both of them with their companyes was committed to the King's Bench, but surely Sir John was bayld for I saw him this day in a coach.' ('MSS. of Sir Hervey Bruce', *MSS. in Various Collections*, vii [1914], *Historical MSS. Commission*, p. 408.)

At the end of the same season a similar affray in courtly circles is recounted by George Garrard in a letter to Viscount Wentworth in Ireland. On 19 May 1635 he wrote,

> The Quarrel that lately broke out betwixt my Lord *Digby* and *Will Crofts* in the *Black-Fryars* at a Play, stands as it did when your Brother went hence. *Crofts* stands confined to his Father's House, because by striking he broke his Bonds of 5000 *l.* but there was a great Difference in the Parties that stood bound; my Lord *Bedford* and Sir *John Strangwick* stipulated for my Lord *Digby*, Tom *Eliot* and *Jack Crofts*, Men of small Fortunes for the other, that they should keep the Peace, during the Suit depending in the *Star-Chamber*; the Lords have heard it, and reported their Opinions to the King, and there it rests. (*Strafforde's Letters*, i. 426.)

In the following season even more exalted members of the peerage were making a nuisance of themselves at Blackfriars. In another letter from Garrard in London to the Lord Deputy in Ireland, dated 25 January 1635/6, there is reported the following encounter:

> A little Pique happened betwixt the Duke of *Lenox* and the Lord Chamberlain about a Box at a new Play in the *Black Fryars*, of which the Duke had got the Key: Which if it had come to be debated betwixt them, as it was once intended, some Heat or perhaps other Inconvenience might have happen'd. His Majesty hearing of it, sent the Earl of *Holland* to command them both not to dispute it, but before him, so he heard it and made them Friends. (Ibid., p. 511.)

As the immediate superior of the Master of the Revels, the Lord Chamberlain ruled supreme in the London theatre. It is at first glance surprising to find anyone daring to dispute with him over a playhouse matter. But the Duke of Lennox outranked him in the peerage and was, moreover, the cousin of the King.

Even royalty itself is found at Blackfriars in these years. There are records of three visits to the theatre by Queen Henrietta Maria in 1634–6, and another in 1638. Sir Henry Herbert recorded in his Office Book: ' "The 13 May, 1634, the Queene was at Black-fryers, to see Messengers playe." [Malone adds the comment] The play which her majesty honoured with her presence was The Tragedy of Cleander, which had been produced on the 7th of the same month, and is now lost, with many other pieces of the same writer.' (*Variorum*, iii. 167.)

A year or so later the Queen was again at Blackfriars. Her nephew, Charles, Prince of the Palatinate, mentioned the visit to his mother, who had herself had a London company of players when she was the Princess Elizabeth. His letter is undated, but it must have been written some time between his arrival in England in November 1635 and the closing of the theatres on the following 12 May. He said: 'The King sate yesterday at Van Dyke's for the Prince of Orange, but y^r Mat^y hath forgate to send me the mesure of the picture; his howse is close by Blake Friers, where the Quene saw Lodwick Carlile's second part of Arviragus and Felicia acted, wch is hugely liked of every one. . . .' (*Duke of Northumberland's MSS*. Third Report [1872], *Historical MSS. Commission*, p. 118.) In the same season the Queen made another trip to Blackfriars with her nephew. The visit is known from the bill to the Lord Chamberlain for the twenty-two plays acted by the King's company for the court between Easter Monday 1636 and 21 February 1636/7. (Adams, *Herbert*, pp. 75–76.) The fourth item in the bill is 'The 5th of May at the Blackfryers for the Queene and the prince Elector - - - - Alfonso.' (See above, v. 1285–8.)

Finally a fourth visit by Queen Henrietta Maria to the Blackfriars is recorded in another bill presented to the Lord Chamberlain for the twenty-four plays acted by the King's company between 26 March 1638 and 7 January 1638/9: 'At the blackfryers the 23 of Aprill for the queene   the vnfortunate lou[ers].' (*Herbert*, pp. 76–77.)

Perhaps these royal visits are the most telling of all examples of the supremacy of Blackfriars in Caroline London. The performances attended by the Queen were almost certainly special night productions for the court, not the regular afternoon performances. The last two were clearly such, since we have payment records for them and know that they were paid for at the same rate as plays produced at the Cockpit in Whitehall. In the case of the last play we have evidence that though the company was paid a court fee, no afternoon performance had been cancelled. It was the custom in these years for the players to be paid £10 for each play given at court when the performance was near enough to Blackfriars for the company to perform as usual in their own theatre. But when a trip was involved—as for performances at Hampton Court or Richmond—and the company had to cancel their afternoon performance at Blackfriars, then the company was paid a double fee as compensation. In the bill for 1638-9 each performance involving the cancellation of the afternoon performance is marked with a tick for a double fee. The performance for the Queen on 23 April is not so marked, and therefore the company had taken their regular admission fees in the afternoon, and the Queen's performance was at night.

From a series of documents prepared in 1635 a few facts about the ownership, management, and profits of Blackfriars may be derived. The series of petitions, answers, and judgements are generally called the Sharers' Papers; they record the attempts of three of the principal actors of the King's company, Robert Benfield, Eyllardt Swanston, and Thomas Pollard, to force the housekeepers at the Globe and Blackfriars to sell them part of their housekeepers' shares in the theatres. (See above, i. 43-47.) We learn that at the time of the petition two housekeeping shares at Blackfriars were held by the actor John Shank, and one each by Cuthbert Burbage, Winifred Robinson, Joseph Taylor, John Lowin, Elizabeth Condell, and [?] Underwood, and that their part of the receipts at each performance consisted of half the takings from the galleries and half that from the boxes. The actor-sharers took the other half plus all the general admissions. The actors say that they pay all the 'wages to hired men & boyes musicke light[es] &c' amounting to 900 or 1000^{li} p[er] ann[um] [i.e. for both theatres] or thereabout[es] beeing 3^{li} a day one day wth another, besides the extraordinary charge which the sayd Actors are wholly at for apparell & Poet[es] &c.' (M.S.C. ii. 365-6.) The answer of John Shank gives his assertion of certain values at Blackfriars. He says that, two years before, he paid £156 for one share in the Blackfriars with six years to run, and one share in the Globe with two years to run. He does not assign the separate values. He says that on his Blackfriars share he paid a rent of £6. 5s., which would amount to £50 a year for the eight shares, but the other actors say that the rent for both theatres together is not more than £65 a year. Shank says that in the past year an actor-sharer's payment from the enterprise at both theatres was £180, but he says nothing of how much was from Blackfriars and how much from the Globe.

In response to the petition of Benfield, Swanston, and Taylor the Lord Chamberlain appointed a commission, including the Master of the Revels, to set a fair price on two of Shank's shares—presumably meaning one Globe share and one Blackfriars—for the petitioners. The commissioners were to report back. Nothing further is known, though at the time he made his will, five months after the appointment of the commission, Shank still had his shares. This alienation of the shares in their enterprise was one of the problems of the actors. As the original actor-house-keepers died, their shares tended to get out of the hands of the company; Shank's shares had come to him by purchase from the heir of John Heminges. Thus part of the strength of the company, which derived from almost complete control of their own affairs, began to dissipate.

One might imagine that these dissensions among the players had an ill effect on their performances, but the petitions and answers suggest that the quarrel was not a general company one, but a resentment of the younger players against John Shank, who says that in the course of the disagreement the others 'restrained him from the Stage'. This action must have taken place at the Globe, since it seems to have occurred between the Lord Cham-berlain's actions of 12 July 1635 and 1 August following. His appearances in the following Blackfriars season were probably few, for he made his will on 30 December 1635 and was buried on the 27th of the following January. (See above, ii. 646–8).

The company was probably still at Blackfriars on 12 May 1636, when all London theatres were ordered to close because of plague. The players were inhibited not only during the following summer season at the Globe, but for the Blackfriars season of 1636–7, which was entirely lost except for the week of 23 February 1636/7. (See above, ii. 661–5.) Not until 2 October 1637 were the play-houses allowed to reopen, after the longest prohibition on record. Probably the King's men opened at once at Blackfriars. It is likely that they began with a company strengthened by the addition of four or five of the principal actors of Queen Henrietta's men, whom Christopher Beeston had forced out of the Phoenix during the long plague closing. (See above, i. 237–9 and 56–57.)

In the season of 1637–8 the Blackfriars offerings were en-livened by at least two special productions. On 7 February 1637/8 George Garrard wrote to the Lord Deputy in Ireland: 'Two of the King's Servants, Privy-Chamber Men both, have writ each of them a Play, Sir *John Sutlin* and *Will. Barclay*, which have been acted in Court, and at the *Black Friars*, with much Applause. *Sutlin's* Play cost three or four hundred Pounds setting out, eight or ten Suits of new Cloaths he gave the Players; an unheard of Prodigality.' (*Strafforde's Letters*, ii. 150.) The two plays were Sir William Berkeley's *The Lost Lady* and Sir John Suckling's *Aglaura*. (See above, iii. 23–25 and v. 1201–7.) The extravagance of the *Aglaura* costumes was still remembered years

later, for during the Restoration John Aubrey wrote of them in
his notes on Sir John Suckling. 'When his *Aglaura* was ⟨acted⟩,
he bought all the cloathes himselfe, which were very rich; no
tinsill, all the lace pure gold and silver, which cost him . . . I have
now forgott. He had some sceanes to it, which in those dayes were
only used at masques.'[1]

Aglaura was evidently an admired spectacle, and it seems to
have profited the Blackfriars company through repeated performances as well as through the addition of spectacular costumes
to their wardrobe. The popularity is suggested by a poem in John
Phillips's collection, *Sportive Wit*, 1656, which recommends a series
of bequests to Fortune. For the actors he asks

> Lest the Players should grow poor
> Send them Aglauras more and more.

> (F₄ᵛ.)

(F$_4^{v}$.)

Aglaura and *The Lost Lady* are two of a fair number of courtier
plays produced in the thirties. They were written primarily for
the acclaim of Queen Henrietta Maria's circle, but they were
often given later to the commercial theatres (see Harbage,
Cavalier Drama, pp. 22–25), and most of them became part of the
repertory at Blackfriars. Great drama was not written by such
courtiers as Berkeley, Carlell, Killigrew, Habington, and Suckling,
but their plays roused jealousy on the part of professional playwrights like Richard Brome (see above, i. 59–60), and jealousy is
not normally elicited by failures.

During the last four years of the Caroline theatre there are very
few records pertaining to Blackfriars. That certain of the plays
opened there can be deduced from the dates of their licensing by
the Master of the Revels: Davenant's *The Unfortunate Lovers*
and *The Fair Favourite*; Massinger's *Alexius or the Chaste Lover*
and *The Fair Anchoress of Pausilippo*; and James Shirley's *The
Impostor*, *The Cardinal*, and *The Sisters*. But of specific records
of their performances there are none.

In 1640 the autumn opening of Blackfriars was delayed because
of another plague-closing. On 11 September the Privy Council
sent out its closing order, and the players were probably not
allowed to begin again until the end of October or the first week
in November—they were in operation on the 6th. (See above, ii.

---

[1] Clark, Andrew, ed., *Brief Lives . . . set down by John Aubrey . . .*,
2 vols. (1898), ii. 244. Aubrey's remark about scenes must refer to the court
performance. Even so it is not accurate, for previous plays at court, such
as Cartwright's *Royal Slave*, had been produced with sets.

665–6.) The King's men must have been forced to cut short their Globe season and to postpone their opening at Blackfriars.

Within four months another of the persistent enemies of the theatre was attacking: the petitions of the inhabitants of Black-friars against the theatre were renewed. Now other parishes joined with them. *The Journals of the House of Commons* for 26 February 1640/1 record 'The Petition of the Inhabitants of the *Black Friars, St. Martin's, Ludgate,* and St. Bride's, *London* was read; and is ordered to be referred to the Committee for Secretary Windebank's Business.' (p. 94.) What the petition was and some-thing of the temper of the House may be learned from the journal of one of the speakers for the petition. Sir Simonds D'Ewes entered in his journal for this day:

Then a petition preferred by the inhabitants of Blacke Friers and others against the play howse ther etc. hinderance of trade, by Alder-man Pennington. Hee spake to further it. I etc. A good petition. Gods howse not soe neare Divils. This a particular greivance this and the other a generall. All the objection men without them could not tell how to imploy them themselves etc. Others spake against this play-howse and others.

Then Sir Henry Fane being returned his reporting that the Lords would give us a present meeting brake offe our agitation. (*Journal of Sir Simonds D'Ewes,* p. 412.)

Apparently all three parishes had joined in petitioning against one theatre, as is indicated by Sir Simonds's use of the singular 'playhowse', though one would have expected the inhabitants of St. Bride's to complain of the Salisbury Court theatre in their own parish. The direction of the petition to the House of Commons rather than to the Privy Council or the Lord Mayor, as before, is symptomatic of the new political climate of 1641, a climate which was to prove fatal to all theatres in a few months.

In the late summer and autumn of this year the plague again became virulent, following much the same pattern as in the pre-vious autumn, though the death rate was not so high. The theatres were ordered to close on 5 August, and probably they were not allowed to reopen until the end of November. (See above, ii. 666–7.)

This final season at Blackfriars was not very successful. Though there was no further plague-closing, the plague deaths during the winter and spring were higher than usual; the political situa-tion was so feverish that one did not have to be a Puritan to find plays somewhat frivolous. The trying and theatrically disastrous times are complained against by James Shirley in his last play

to be performed at Blackfriars, licensed for acting on 26 April
1642. His 'Prologue at the Black-Fryers' for *The Sisters* begins:

> Does this look like a Term? I cannot tell,
> Our Poet thinks the whole Town is not well,
> Has took some Physick lately, and for fear
> Of catching cold dares not salute this Ayr.
>
> (See above, i. 67–68.)

When on 2 September 1642 Parliament ordered all theatres to
be closed, since they did 'not well agree with publike Calamities',
the company of Blackfriars and the Globe was by all odds the
best and most successful troupe in London. In the light of this
fact it is somewhat surprising that among the many records
of performances during the Commonwealth and Protectorate,
especially at the Red Bull, Fortune, Salisbury Court, and Phoenix
theatres there is no convincing evidence of surreptitious playing
at the Blackfriars. There is a newsbook statement asserting that
a reopening of the old private theatre of the King's men was
planned in 1647, when playing was indeed revived at the Fortune
and Salisbury Court. *The Perfect Weekly Account* for 6–13 October
1647 points out unsympathetically that 'Plays begin to be set up
apace neverthelesse not without disturbance yet they give out
that it shall go forward at three houses, and blacke Fryars is
repairing to the end that it may be one.'[1] (P$_2$^{v}.) The revival of
playing at Blackfriars in this year has been thought to be confirmed by a passage in another newsbook dated 27 November of
the same year. The passage seems to me, however, to be much too
facetious to be taken at its face value. Note particularly the solemn
citation of the hated Independent preacher and Army chaplain,
Hugh Peters, as a professional playwright.

The Comedy of Errors, had beene so often presented in publicke
to the rabble that it grew common and out of fashion, wherupon the
Houses commings in, began to impaire, and was not so full as it had
been wont to bee; which perceived by his Majesties servants of the
Blacke fryers, they petitioned for leave to set up their old trade againe;
no sooner was this motion of theirs whispered to the Army those
men of Action, but they conceived that it came to their turne by
succession to enter, and to play their parts now or never. . . . May it
please yee, this selected fraternity had beene often at rehearsall, and
intended their first show should be a King and no King, personated
to the life, but wholly Tragicall, altered into a new forme by their
Poet, H. Peters. (*Mercurius Vapulans*, 27 November 1647, A$_4$.)

---

[1] The passage was first noted by Leslie Hotson.

Since there are no other records about playing at Blackfriars, though there are several for the Red Bull, Fortune, Phoenix, and Salisbury Court, I should read the evidence as revealing perhaps an intention of reopening the Blackfriars theatre in 1647, but showing no actual performances there.

Probably a truer picture of Blackfriars after 1642 is that presented by Richard Flecknoe. It is part of a piece he entitled '*A whimzey written from beyond Seas, about the end of the year, 52. to a Friend lately returned into* England'. He speaks of the walk through Smithfield and past St. Pauls, and

From thence passing on to Black-fryers, and seeing never a *Playbil* on the Gate,[1] no *Coaches* on the place, nor *Doorkeeper* at the Play-house door, with his *Boxe* like a *Church-warden*, desiring you to remember the poor *Players*, I cannot but say for *Epilogue* to all the *Playes* were ever acted there:

> *Poor House, that in dayes of our Grand-sires,*
> *Belongst unto the* Mendiant Fryers:
> *And where so oft in our Fathers dayes*
> *We have seen so many of* Shakspears *Playes.*
> *So many of* Johnsons, Beaumonts & Fletchers,
> *Vntill I know not what* Puritan *Teachers*:
> (*Who for their* Tone *their* Language & Action,
> *Might 'gainst the Stage make* Bedlam *a faction*)
> *Have made with their Raylings the* Players *as poore*
> *As were the* Fryers *and* Poets *before*:
> *Since th'ast the tricke on't all* Beggars *to make,*
> *I wish for the* Scotch-Presbyterian's *sake*
> *To comfort the* Players *and* Fryers *not a little,*
> *Thou mayst be turn'd to a* Puritan *spittle.*
>   (*Miscellania*, 1653, I₆–I₆ᵛ.)

The last act in the history of the King's men's famous private theatre in the Blackfriars is revealed by some manuscript notes on the destruction of the theatre found in a copy of the 1631 edition of Stowe's *Annals*: 'The Blacke Friers plaiers play house

---

[1] The association of playbill advertising specifically with Blackfriars is not uncommon. Not long before, Robert Heath had written in the verse 'To my Book-seller' in his *Clarastella*, 1650, a request not to display his book

> nor poast it on each wall
> And corner poast underneath the Play
> That must be acted at Black-Friers that day.
>   (F₁₁.)

Jonson makes use of the Blackfriars playbill in the fourth scene of the first act of *The Devil is an Ass*.

in Blacke Friers, London, which had stood many yeares, was
pulled downe to the ground on Munday the 6 daye of August.
1655. and tennements built in the rome.' (*The Academy*, No. 547,
28 October 1882 [vol. 22], 315. Now at the Folger Library.)

Henry Fitz-Geoffrey's *Notes from Black-Fryers*

In 1617 Henry Fitz-Geoffrey published (S.R., 9 October 1617)
a collection of satirical pieces entitled *Satyres and Satyricall
Epigrams*. The third section of the little book is headed 'The
Third Booke of *Humours*: Intituled *Notes from* BLACK-FRYERS'.
These eighteen pages constitute the longest extant contemporary
passage on the theatre, as well as the least intelligible. Fitz-
Geoffrey has written a conventional set of satires, but he has
strung them together on the pretence that his victims were observed coming in to a play at the Blackfriars theatre. Most of the
individual satires have little of interest to say, but his connecting
material and a few of his satirical comments throw a little light on
the theatre, its audience, and the conduct of its performances.
The extracts printed here, constituting about one-third of the
third book, include all the comments which seem in any way to
reflect actual conditions at the playhouse.

Notes from Black-Fryers.

What (*friend Philelmo*) let me thy corpes Imbrace!
So jumpe met in this vnfrequented place?
Then, faith! 'lets Frolique 't: pre' thee what's y^e *Play* ?
(The first I visited this twelue monthes day.)
(They say) *A new Inuented Toy of* Purle
*That ieoparded his Necke, to steale a Girle
Of* 12: *And* (*lying fast impounded for't*)
*Hath hither sent his Beard, to Act his part.
Against all those in open Malice bent,
That would not freely to the Theft consent.
Faines all to's wish, and in the Epilogue,
Goes out applauded for a famous*—)

Now hang me if I did not looke at first,
For some such stuffe by the fond peoples thrust.
Then stay! Ile see't, and sit it out (what ere)
Had I at comming forth tooke a *Glister*:
Had *Fate* fore-read me in a *Croude* to dye:
To bee made *Adder*-deafe with *Pippin*-crye.
Come let's bethink our selues what may be found:
To deceiue *Time* with, till the second sound:

Out with these *matches* fore-runners of Smoake,
This *Indian pastime* I could neuer brooke.

See (*Captaine Martio*) he ith' *Renounce me* Band
That in the middle Region doth stand
Woth' reputation steele! Faith! lets remoue,
Into his *Ranke,* (if such discourse you Loue)
Hee'l tell of *Basilisks, Trenches, Retires*:

.   .   .   .

Look next to him to, *One* we both know well,
(Sir *Iland Hunt*) a Trauailer that will tell
Of stranger Things then *Tatterd Tom* ere li't of,
Then *Pliny*, or *Heroditus* e're writ of:

.   .   .   .

Bvt stay! see heere (but newly Entred,)
A *Cheapside* Dame, by th' *Tittle* on her head!
Plot (Villain!) plot! Let's lay our heads together!
We may deuise perchance to get her hither.
(If wee to-gether cunningly compact)
Shee'l holde vs dooing till the Latter *Act*,
And (on my life) Inuite vs Supper home,
Wee'l thrust hard for it, but wee'l finde her rome,
Heer *Mis* — (pox ont! she's past, she'l not come ore,
Sure shee's bespoken for a box before.

Knowest thou yon world of fashions now comes in
In *Turkie* colours carued to the skin,
Mounted *Pelonianly* vntill hee reeles,
That scornes (so much) *plaine dealing* at his heeles.
His Boote speakes *Spanish* to his *Scottish* Spurres,
His Sute cut *Frenchly*, round bestucke with Burres.

.   .   .   .

Now *Mars* defend vs! seest thou who comes yonder?
Monstrous! A *Woman* of the *masculine Gender*.
Looke! thou mayst well descry her by her groath,
Out, point not man! Least wee be beaten both.
Eye her a little, marke but where shee'l goe,
Now (by this hand) into the Gallants Roe.
Let her alone! What ere she giues to stand,
Shee'l make her selfe a gayner, *By the Hand*.

What think'st thou of yon plumed *Dandebrat*,
Your Ladyes *Shittle-cocke, Egyptian Rat*:
Yon *Musk-ball, Milke-sop*: yon *French Sincopace*:
That Vshers in, with a *Coranto* grace.
Yon *Gilded March-pane*: yon *All Verdingall*,
This is the *Puppet*, which the Ladyes all

Send for of purpose and solicite so
To *daunce* with them.

> .   .   .   .

A Stoole and Cushion! Enter *Tissue slop*!
Vengeance! I know him well, did he not drop
Out of the *Tyring-house* ? Then how (the duse)
Comes the mishapen *Prodigall* so spruse,
His year's *Reuenewes* (I dare stand vnto 't,)
Is not of *worth* to purchase such a *Sute*.

> .   .   .   .

A Pipe heere (Sirra) no *Sophisticate*.
(Villain) the *best*: what ere you *prize* it at.
Tell yonder Lady, with the *Yellow fan*,
I shall be proude to *Vsher* her anon:
My Coach stands ready.

> .   .   .   .

But h'st! with him Crabbed (*Websterio*)
The *Play-wright, Cart-wright*: whether ? either! *ho*—
No further. Looke as yee'd bee look't into:
Sit as ye woo'd be *Read*: Lord! who woo'd know him
Was euer man so mangl'd with a *Poem* ?
See how he drawes his mouth awry of late,
How he scrubs: wrings his wrests: scratches his Pate.
A *Midwife*! helpe ? By his *Braines coitus*,
Some *Centaure* strange: some huge *Bucephalus*,
Or *Pallas* (sure) ingendred in his *Braine*
Strike *Vulcan* with thy hammer once againe.

> .   .   .   .

Others may chance (that know me not a right,)
Report (iniuriously) all my delight,
And strength of studdy I doe wholly bend
To this *Losse-labour* and no other end.
To these I wish my scandald *Muse* reply
In as plaine tearmes as may bee *'Tis a lye*.
Heer's but a *Pate-pastime*: *Play-house Obseruation*,
Fruits of the vacants howers of a *Vacation*.
Then (say all what they can) I am sure of this,
That for *Play-time* it is not spent amisse.

To his worthy Friend, H. F.
vpon his *Notes from*
BLACK-FRYERS.

Had the *Black-Fryers* beene still vn-suppressd,
I cannot thinke their Cloysters had bin blessd
With better contemplations: Seeing now
Lesse may be gleand from *Puritanes* then you

Haue gathered from the *Play-house*. And I must
(Though't bee a *Players* vice to be vniust,
To Verse not yeelding coyne) let *Players* know
They cannot recompence your labour: Though
They grace you with a Chayre vpon the Stage,
And take no money of you nor your Page.
For now the *Humours* which oppresse *Playes* most,
Shall (if the owners can feele shame) be lost:
And when they so conuerted doe allow,
What they dislik'd once, *Players* must thanke you,
And *Poets* too: for both of them will saue
Much in true Verse, which hisses might depraue:
Since you haue so refin'd their Audience,
That now good *Playes* will neuer neede defence.

Io: STEPHENS.

LE FEVRE'S RIDING ACADEMY

In the year 1635 a French dramatic company, under the leader-
ship of Josias de Soulas, whose stage name was Floridor, visited
London and enjoyed the patronage of Charles's French queen,
Henrietta Maria, and of the circle around her. The presence of the
visiting company is first noted by the Master of the Revels in his
Office Book:

On tuesday night the 17 of February, 1634[/35] a Frenche company
of players, being approved by the queene at her house [presumably
Somerset House] too nights before, and commended by her majesty
to the kinge, were admitted to the Cockpitt in Whitehall, and there
presented the king and queene with a Frenche comedy called Melise,
with good approbation: for which play the king gives them ten
pounds.

This day being Friday, and the 20 of the same monthe, the kinge
tould mee his pleasure, and commanded mee to give order that this
Frenche company should playe the too sermon daies in the weeke,
during their time of playinge in Lent [i.e. the days on which the
regular playhouses were ordinarily closed], and in the house of
Drury-lane, where the queenes players usually playe. (*Variorum*, iii.
121 n.)

After a few other notices of the conditions of their playing at
the Cockpit in Drury Lane (see below, vi. 65–66) Herbert records
that the French played *Le Trompeur Puni* at court on 4 April and
Alcimedon on the 16th. The success of these productions and the
enthusiasm of the French faction at court are probably the grounds

for the much more notable favour of the King shown by a further entry in Sir Henry Herbert's Office Book:

> A warrant granted to Josias D'Aunay, Hurfries de Lau, and others, for to act playes at a new house in Drury–lane, during pleasure, y⁰ 5 may, 1635.
> The king was pleased to commande my Lord Chamberlain to direct his warrant to Monsieur Le Fevure, to give him a power to contract with the Frenchemen for to builde a playhouse in the manage-house which was done accordinglye by my advise and allowance. (*Variorum*, iii. 122 n.)

Actually, the warrant which Sir Henry Herbert records on 5 May had been issued more than a fortnight before. In the Lord Chamberlain's Warrant Books at the Public Record Office is the entry:

> His Majestye hath commaunded mee to signifie his royall pleasure that the ffrench Comædians (haueing Agreed *with* Mᵣ le Febure) may erect A Stage Scaffoldes & Seates, & all other accommodations which shall bee convenient, & act & present interludes & Stage playes at his house and Manage in Drury Lane during his Majesties pleasure without disturbance, hinderance or interruption, And this shall bee to them and Mᵣ Le Febure & to all others sufficient warrant & discharge in that behalfe, for such is his Majesties expresse commaund & pleasure. Apr. 18. 1635. (*M.S.C.* ii. 375.)

The precise location of M. Le Fevre's riding academy is not known, but since it was in Drury Lane it cannot have been far from the Phoenix theatre, which was about half-way down that short street which ran only a few hundred yards from High Holborn to the Strand. Probably there were recriminations among Queen Henrietta's men when they found their guests of February and March established as rivals in a near-by theatre. But the competition probably did not last long, for the French are last heard of when they were paid on 8 January 1635/6 for the performance of a tragedy at court in the preceding December. (Ibid., 378.)

It would be interesting to know more of the character of the theatre provided in the riding academy—assuming, of course, that it was really built and not simply allowed. 'A Stage Scafoldes & Seates' would suggest a platform at one end of the hall, rising tiers of seats in the back half of the hall, and seats in a spectators' gallery, but the words of the warrant are too few to give any clear indications of the plan.

If Le Fevre's riding academy really was converted to a theatre as planned, and if the French company did act there for six or

eight months, one would expect more comments on the pheno-
menon from playwrights and letter writers. The satiric episode
about French acting in Glapthorne's *The Lady's Privilege*, Act II,
Scene I (C₃), in which a character imitating a French player
'*Acts furiously*', is evidently intended for an audience which had
seen French actors. But they had not necessarily seen them at
Le Fevre's, and the date of the play cannot be fixed more closely
than 1632?–40. (See above, iv. 485–7.)

THE PHOENIX OR COCKPIT IN DRURY LANE

Adams, pp. 348–67.
Armstrong, William A., *The Elizabethan Private Theatres, Facts
and Problems*, Society for Theatre Research, Pamphlet Series,
no. 6 (1958).
Herbert, passim.
Hotson, pp. 88–99.
Keith, William Grant, 'John Webb and the Court Theatre of
Charles II', *The Architectural Review*, lvii (February 1925),
49–55.
Markward, William B., 'A Study of the Phoenix Theatre in
Drury Lane, 1617–1638', MS. Ph.D. Thesis, Shakespeare
Institute, Stratford-upon-Avon (1953).
Parton, John, *Some Account of the Hospital and Parish of St.
Giles in the Fields, Middlesex* (1822).
Wallace, C. W., *Three London Theatres of Shakespeare's Time*,
University of Nebraska Studies, ix (1909).

The Phoenix or Cockpit in Drury Lane was one of the two principal Caroline theatres. After Blackfriars it was the favourite
resort of the gentry, and for these two playhouses most of the
plays of the twenties and thirties which are still familiar to us
were written. These leading private theatres had much to do
with the shaping of later drama: the great majority of pre-
Civil War plays revived after the Restoration were Blackfriars
and Phoenix plays; William Davenant, the chief theatrical force
in the decade 1656–66, had written nearly all his early plays for
Blackfriars, and he had got his early managerial experience at the
Phoenix; many of the influential early Restoration actors had
been trained at the Blackfriars or the Phoenix or had been coached
by those who had. In the continuing English dramatic tradition
the Blackfriars and the Phoenix are more important that our
Shakespearocentric studies have generally allowed us to see.

The Phoenix was the property of Christopher Beeston, planned, built, owned, and managed by him until his death late in 1638. No other London theatre of the time is known to have been so dominated by one individual as the Phoenix was by this man.

Christopher Beeston, alias Hutchinson (see above, ii. 363–70), had been an actor at least as early as 1598, for he appears along with William Shakespeare and others in the Jonson First Folio cast for the original production of *Every Man in his Humour* in that year. His career was not, however, with the Lord Chamberlain's company, though he is probably the source of his son William's Restoration gossip about the early career of one of its principal members, William Shakespeare. From at least as early as 1602 until 1619 Beeston was a member of Worcester's–Queen Anne's company, a colleague and lifelong friend of Thomas Heywood, and from about 1612 to 1619 the most influential member—if not the manager—of that troupe. It was presumably in his position as the dominant member of Queen Anne's men that Beeston decided to prepare a private theatre for the company. No other London troupe of adult actors, except the King's men, had ever been established in a private theatre; but the King's company, by 1616, had demonstrated how profitable such a theatre could be made for an adult company. Apparently Beeston determined to set up a rival for the King's men at Blackfriars— at any rate that is what he succeeded eventually in doing.

The first step was the acquisition of property, and on 9 August 1616 Beeston leased from the trustees for John Best, Grocer,

All that edifices or building called the Cockpittes and the Cockhouses and shedds therevnto adioyning late before that tyme in the tenure or occupacon of John Atkins gent or his assignes Togeather alsoe with one tenement or house and a little Garden therevnto belonging next adioyning to the said Cockpittes then in the occupacon of Jonas Westwood or his assignes and one part or parcell of ground behinde the said Cockpittes Cockhouses three Tenements and garden devided as in the said Indenture is expressed To haue and to hold . . . from the feast daie of St Michaell the Archangell next coming after the date of the said recited Indenture vnto the ende and terme of one and thirty yeares from thence next ensuing and fully to be compleat and ended yealding and paying therefor yearely duringe the said terme . . . the yearely rent or some of fforty and five poundes of lawfull mony of England att ffower of the most vsuall feasts in the yeare by equal porcons[1]

----

[1] Disclaimer of Sir Lewis Kirke and Elizabeth his wife (widow of Christopher Beeston) to Complaint of Thomas Hussey, 8 November 1647. P.R.O. C 2, Ch 1,H 28/26. Discovered by Leslie Hotson.

A little more information about the property Beeston acquired can be gleaned from another suit in the same series, Thomas Hussey *v.* Robert Rolleston and Katherine Best, 9 July 1647. Hussey says that 'shortly after' the end of October 1609 John Best erected or caused to be erected on his property seven or eight dwelling houses with their appurtenances, 'as namely one messuage howse or tenement called a Cockpitt and afterwards vsed for a play house and now called the Phoenix with divers buildings thereto belonging and one other messuage howse or tenem^t with the appurtenances adioyneing to the said Messuage called the Phoenix wherein one William Sherlocke sometimes dwelt and now one John Rodes dweleth . . .'.[1]

Beeston's property lay between Drury Lane and Great Wild Street, north-west of Princes' Street in the parish of St. Giles in the Fields. In his history of the parish, John Parton lists 'COCKPIT COURT OR ALLEY . . . This latter was the site of the celebrated Cockpit Theatre, from which the present Drury-lane Theatre took its origin . . . . N.B. Cockpit Alley is now called "Pitt Place".'[2] For a private theatre, intended to appeal to a more well-to-do and sophisticated audience than that of the public theatres, the location was a good one, well outside the city, closer to Whitehall and St. James's than any other London playhouse, and within easy walking distance of all four inns of court. The neighbours whom Beeston probably hoped to allure into his new theatre are well indicated by Parton in a list which he gives in connexion with the rebuilding of the parish church in 1623:

> In Drury-lane, in 1623, there were the following inhabitants of ominence, all of whom were assessed towards rebuilding of St. Giles's church, viz. sir John Cotton, sir Thomas Finch, the right honourable the earl of March, sir Francis Kynaston, sir Lewes Lewknor, sir Edmond Lenthall, sir Edward Peto, sir Anthony Bugg, sir Anthony Henton, Philip Parker, esq., sir Gilbert Houghton, lady Henage, sir Lewes Tresham, sir John Sydnam, lady Lambert. (Op. cit., p. 173.)

Yet the neighbourhood must not be thought wholly exclusive; William Prynne happily reminds the readers of *Histriomastix* of other neighbours:

> . . . that our Theaters if they are not Bawdy-houses, (as they may easily be, since many Players, *if reports be true, are common Panders,*)

---

[1] P.R.O. C 2, Ch. I, H 44/66. Also discovered by Leslie Hotson.

[2] *Some Account of the Hospital and Parish of St. Giles in the Fields, Middlesex* (1822), p. 138. The site is shown in Rocque's *Map of London*, 1746, reproduced in Adams, facing p. 350.

yet they are Cosin-germanes, at *leastwise neighbours to them*: Witnesse the *Cock-pit*, and *Drury-lane*: *Black-friers Play-house*, and *Duke-humfries*; the *Red-bull*, and *Turnball-street*: the *Globe*, and *Bank-side Brothel-houses*, with others of this nature: . . . (Ddd₃ᵛ–Ddd₄.)

In his new project, therefore, Beeston not only had the advantage of an excellent neighbourhood for a private theatre, but he had also a garden, an adjoining house which could be used for a resident manager—probably Beeston himself at first, then William Sherlock, and finally John Rhodes (see above, ii. 572–3, 544–6)—and best of all a building already devoted to entertainment which could be converted to his purposes. His remodelling operations must have begun promptly after the beginning of his lease at Michaelmas 1616, for two weeks later the lawyers of near-by Lincoln's Inn were alarmed at his activities: at a Council held on the 15th of that month [October 1616] the Benchers of Lincoln's Inn decided to send a committee to 'the Queene's Councell, wᵗʰ others of the Innes of Courte, touchinge the convertinge of the Cocke Pytte in the Feildes into a playe house'.[1] The fact that the lawyers chose to send their committee to Queen Anne's Council rather than to another authority implies that they knew that Beeston intended to install the Queen's men in his new theatre. Subsequent records show that this is what he did; there is no indication that the visit of the committee had any significant result.

Of the physical characteristics of the new playhouse Beeston made from the old cockpit there is very little evidence. A circular or octagonal shape seems likely for a cockpit, and some such seems to be the implication of the prologue to James Shirley's *Coronation*, licensed for production on 6 February 1634/5, when Shirley was principal playwright for the Queen's men at the Phoenix. (See above, v. 1068.) Here the Prologue, toward the end of his address to the audience, turning to the ladies, says

> *You are the bright intelligences move,*
> *And make a harmony this sphere[2] of Love.*

> (1640 quarto.)

Dr. Markward's analysis of plays written for production at the Phoenix or Cockpit (op. cit.) shows fairly clearly that the stage

[1] W. P. Baildon, *The Records of the Honorable Society of Lincoln's Inn, Black Books*, ii. 186.

[2] There are similar references to the circular shape of the auditorium in John Ford and Thomas Dekker's *The Sun's Darling*, and in Thomas Heywood's *Love's Mistress*.

had three doors, as indicated in Heywood's *English Traveller*, written for the Phoenix:

Enter at one doore an Vsurer *and his Man,*
at the other, Old Lionell *with his seruant*: *In*
the midst Reignald.

and Reignald immediately speaks in consternation—

To which hand shall I turne me

(1633 quarto F_1^v.)

The same entrances, with the addition of a stage balcony, are specified in Thomas Nabbes's *Covent Garden*, produced by Queen Henrietta's company at the Phoenix in 1632/3. (See above, iv. 932–4.) The stage directions in this play repeatedly specify '*by the right* Scœne', '*by the middle* Scœne', '*by the left* Scœne', and '*in the* Balcone'.

Other stage details from the plays, such as trapdoors, upper windows, hangings, and so on are commonplaces. A number of plays require revelations, tableaux, and shops, and Dr. Markward thinks they are sufficient to indicate a permanent inner stage at the Phoenix.

It has been more than once suggested that the Caroline Phoenix may have been equipped for the use of scenery. The evidence is not sufficient to demonstrate such a radical innovation, but the inconclusive suggestions of something different in Drury Lane should be noticed. The most precise document put forward is a stage sketch among the Inigo Jones materials at Chatsworth. The drawing shows an arched proscenium with a stage set with sky borders, with tents on four pairs of wings, and with a back drop marked 'Citti of releue', obviously a set for an army encamped before a city. The sketch is marked 'for ye cokpitt for my lo Chāberalen 1639'.[1] The stage depicted here is clearly a proscenium-arch stage with scenery. The question is, What stage is it? Simpson and Bell said that the drawing belonged with three other extant sketches by Jones for the Lord Chamberlain's production of Habington's *Queen of Aragon* at the Cockpit-in-Court. When he reproduced the sketch in *British Drama* Professor Nicoll said in his note: 'This sketch was prepared by Inigo Jones for a production in 1639 of William Habington's *The Queen of Arragon* given at the Cockpit or Phœnix in Drury Lane.' (p. 9.) Both seem

---

[1] Percy Simpson and C. F. Bell (eds.), *Designs by Inigo Jones for Masques & Plays at Court* (Oxford, 1924), pp. 131–2. Here the sketch is described and discussed but not reproduced. It is reproduced by Allardyce Nicoll in *British Drama* (1955), p. 184 and by W. G. Keith, op. cit.

to be wrong, for the explicit records of production of *The Queen of Aragon* show that it was produced at the Hall in Whitehall and at the Blackfriars theatre, never in either the Cockpit in Drury Lane or the Cockpit-in-Court. (See above, iv. 522–5.)

Moreover, William Grant Keith pointed out (*Architectural Review*, February 1925, pp. 49–55) that the three other sketches for Habington's play have been made for a flat proscenium, whereas the questioned one shows an arched proscenium and therefore was not intended for the same play or the same theatre. Keith suggests that the sketch was prepared for Davenant's *The Siege* presumably at the Cockpit in Drury Lane. It is true that the setting would be more or less appropriate for the opening scene of *The Siege* (as for similar scenes of one or two other plays), but the sketch is dated 1639, and Davenant had nothing to do with the Cockpit until June 1640; up until May 1640 William Beeston was in charge at that theatre and in 1639 he appeared to be high in favour. Furthermore the Lord Chamberlain is not known to have had anything to do with the production of particular plays in Drury Lane. It seems unlikely to me, therefore, that the sketch 'for ye cokpitt for my lo Châberalen 1639' has any relation to the Cockpit in Drury Lane. What it does represent I cannot be sure, but I suggest that it may be the Cockpit-in-Court after all. The sketch is associated at Chatsworth with three others clearly intended for Habington's play. It is marked for the Lord Chamberlain, 1639, and it is notable that he did have a play produced in 1640, Habington's *Queen of Aragon*, which he presented to the King and Queen on 9 April 1640 and which, therefore, must have been in preparation in 1639/40. Could it be that the sketch really was intended for *The Queen of Aragon*, but that it was made when the artist assumed that the play would be produced at the Cockpit-in-Court and not, as was later arranged, in the Hall? Later it was superseded by the first of the three other sketches.

As an afterthought Miss Eleanore Boswell made another suggestion about the sketch: 'It occurs to me that this plan may have been made for Davenant's projected "opera house" in Fleet Street' (*Restoration Court Stage* [1932], p. 13 n.). This assignment does fit the date of 1639, but it flatly contradicts the part of the inscription 'for ye cokpitt'.

Other suggestive evidence about scenery at the Phoenix is more vague as to scenery but more specific as to the theatre. It is to be found in certain Cockpit plays. The prologue of *Hannibal and Scipio* by Thomas Nabbes, acted by Queen Henrietta's men at the Phoenix in 1635, has the lines

The places sometimes chang'd too for the Scene.
Which is translated as the musick playes
Betwixt the acts. . . .

(1637 edition, A₃^v.)

As promised, the play is carefully constructed with a different setting for each act, each place noted at the opening of the act, and no change within an act. Nabbes is similarly careful about his handling of place in his *Covent Garden* and *The Bride*, Phoenix plays of 1632/3 and 1638. In *The Bride* every scene except the first in each act begins 'To him', 'To them'; in *Covent Garden* each scene specifies the entrance used, '*by the right* Scœne', '*by the middle* Scœne'. The scenes are mostly interiors, the house of Sir Gervase, Dasher's tavern, Goodlove's house, Squirrel's tavern, though Covent Garden and a street also appear. Though settings are repeated, the changes in these two plays always occur, as in *Hannibal and Scipio*, between the acts. It may be that this careful manipulation of the action is simply pedantry on the part of the playwright, but it does provide for an easy manipulation of the background in production, and the self-conscious way in which Nabbes calls attention to what he has done may suggest some innovation. Possibly only the use of hangings and furniture is intended, but these plays do suggest something a little different at the Phoenix.[1]

Other evidence about the new theatre is less suggestive of the unusual. The comparative size of the Phoenix is noted by James Wright in his surprisingly well-informed *Historia Histrionica*, 1699. Truman, in response to Lovewit's question about the playhouses before the wars, replies:

The *Black-friers*, *Cockpit*, and *Salisbury-court*, were called Private Houses, and were very small to what we see now. The *Cockpit* was standing since the Restauration, and *Rhode's* Company Acted there for some time.

[1] These possibilities are more fully, though still inconclusively, discussed in William B. Markward's thesis on the Phoenix, pp. 644–53. He suggests elsewhere in his dissertation (p. 180) the possibility that in the opening scene of Nabbes's *Covent Garden* when Dungworth comes downstage with Ralph they actually describe the appearance of the house in the lines

What are all these things with rayles?
Ralph. I thinke mewes for hawkes, or ayrings for gentles. Other hawkes are not here in any request.
Dung. Mewes for hawkes, thou wouldst make me a Buzzard.
(Sig.B₁^v)

A description of the fronts in the new Covent Garden seems to me more likely.

Lovew. I have seen that.

Trum. Then you have seen the other two, in effect; for they were all three Built almost exactly alike, for Form and Bigness. Here they had Pits for the Gentry, and Acted by Candle-light. The *Globe*, *Fortune* and *Bull*, were large Houses, and lay partly open to the Weather, and there they alwaies Acted by Daylight.

(See above, ii. 694.)

The opening of Christopher Beeston's new playhouse (probably a special occasion) has left no record, but certain events enable us to date it rather closely. On 23 February 1616/17 the Queen's men were still at the Red Bull, where John Smith says he delivered costume materials to them (Wallace, *Three London Theatres*, pp. 32, 45–46). But less than a fortnight later, on 4 March 1616/17 (Shrove Tuesday), they were in the new Cockpit. The date is marked by one of the more sensational events in the history of the Jacobean theatre.

Shrove Tuesday was a traditional apprentices' holiday (see the closing scene of Dekker's *Shoemakers' Holiday*), and rioting and destruction on the occasion were common enough, but the holiday in 1616/17 was particularly distinguished. The most detailed account was transcribed by Halliwell-Phillipps from a letter among the State Papers in the Public Record Office. The letter was written by Edward Sherburne and is dated '8th Marche, 1616'.

> The Prentizes on Shrove Tewsday last, to the nomber of 3. or 4000 comitted extreame insolencies; part of this number, taking their course for Wapping, did there pull downe to the grownd 4 houses, spoiled all the goods therein, defaced many others, & a Justice of the Peace coming to appease them, while he was reading a Proclamacion, had his head broken with a brick batt. Th' other part, making for Drury Lane, where lately a newe playhouse is erected, they besett the house round, broke in, wounded divers of the players, broke open their trunckes, & whatt apparrell, bookes, or other things they found, they burnt & cutt in peeces; & not content herewith, gott on the top of the house, & untiled it, & had not the Justices of Peace & Shrerife levied an aide, & hindred their purpose, they would have laid that house likewise even with the grownd. In this skyrmishe one prentise was slaine, being shott throughe the head with a pistoll, & many other of their fellowes were sore hurt, & such of them as are taken his Majestie hath commaunded shal be executed for example sake.[1]

A letter from the Privy Council to the Lord Mayor, written the day after the riot, verifies Sherburne's account, identifies the

[1] Halliwell-Phillipps Scrap-Books, *Fortune*, p. 145. Folger Shakespeare Library.

players at the Phoenix, and notes that the rioting occurred 'especially in Lincolns Inne feildes and Drewry Lane, where in attempting to pull downe a Playhowse belonging to the Queenes Ma^{ts} Servants, there were diuerse p[er]sons slayne, and others hurte and wounded, the multitude there assembled being to the nomber of many thousands as wee are credibly informed.' (*M.S.C.* i. 374-5.) A few more details are given by John Chamberlain in his letter of 8 March 1616/17 to Sir Dudley Carleton. He says that the rioters

. . . beeing assembled in great numbers they fell to great disorders in pulling downe of houses and beating the guards that were set to kepe rule, specially at a new play house (somtime a cockpit) in Drurie Lane, where the Quenes players used to play. Though the fellowes defended themselves as well as they could and slew three of them with shot and hurt divers, yet they entered the house and defaced yt, cutting the players apparell all in pieces, and all other theyre furniture and burnt theyre play bookes and did what other mischiefe they could: in Finsburie they brake the prison and let out all the prisoners, spoyled the house by untiling and breaking downe the roofe and all the windowes and at Wapping they pulled downe seven or eight houses and defaced five times as many, besides many other outrages as beating the sheriffe from his horse with stones and dooing much other hurt too long to write. There be divers of them taken since and clapt up, and I make no question but we shall see some of them hangd this next weeke, as yt is more then time they were. (*Chamberlain*, ii. 59-60.)

Middleton and Dekker also refer to the riot and the attack on the Phoenix, as do the chroniclers Edmund Howes and William Camden.[1]

The reason for the violence of the attack on the Cockpit is unknown, though its proximity to the bawdy houses in Drury Lane, traditional targets for the Shrove Tuesday rioters, probably attracted the apprentices, who may have been enraged by the resistance of the players. Professor C. J. Sisson has contended that 'it [is] extremely likely that the riot at the Cockpit, which damaged it upon its opening, was a gesture of resentment by

[1] *Inner Temple Masque*, B$_3$^{v}; *Owles Almanacke*, C$_1$; John Stow, *Annales, or A Generall Chronicle of England* (1631), p. 1026; *A Complete History of England* (1706), ii. 647. One would expect a ballad to have been written on such an occasion, and John Payne Collier did print one in his *History of English Dramatic Poetry* (1879), i. 385-8, which he says 'we copy from a contemporary print, and which is written with a good deal of spirit and cleverness'. The comment is rather immodest, since no one else has ever seen the ballad, and it gives every appearance of a Collier forgery.

Clerkenwell for the desertion of the Red Bull and the injustice done to Susan [Baskervile] in a matter of local notoriety' (*Shakespeare Survey*, vii [1954], 68). Such a motive cannot be disproved, though it seems to me excessively precise and informed for thousands of rioters in several parts of London.

Punishment for the rioters does not seem to have been so severe as Sherburne and Chamberlain anticipated. Several were charged at a Middlesex Special Session of Oyer and Terminer on 20 March 1616/17, but the theatre is not mentioned, only 'the dwellinge house of Christopher Beeston'. (*Middlesex County Records*, ii. 219–23.) Presumably Beeston's dwelling-house was the 'tenement or house . . . next adioyning to the said Cockpittes' which was included in the property Beeston had leased from John Best. No doubt this house, so close to the theatre, would have been damaged in the rioting, but I do not understand why the playhouse itself is not mentioned in the charges.

While the theatre was undergoing repairs Queen Anne's company went back to the Red Bull, for an answer in a Chancery suit says that on 3 June 1617 Queen Anne's men were 'now comme, or shortlie to comme from the said Playhowse called the Redd Bull to the Playhowse in Drurie Lane called the Cockpitt'. (Fleay, *A Chronicle History of the London Stage*, p. 285.) If the Phoenix could be repaired in three months, the injury to the company in the loss of costumes and prompt-books must have been more serious than the theatre damage. Both Sherburne and Chamberlain refer to 'apparrell, bookes, or other things they found [being] burnt & cutt in peeces'. Playbooks and costumes were the principal investments of a company, and the statement two years later by Doctor Almanack in his charge to Shrove Tuesday, 'ruine the Cockpit, the/Poore Players ne're thriud in't' (Middleton, *Inner Temple Masque*, B₃ᵛ), indicates a struggling company at the new theatre. Prompt books could not be replaced so rapidly as tiles and benches.

On the first anniversary of the Shrove Tuesday riots another was proposed, aimed directly at Beeston's theatres. The Privy Council wrote to the Lieutenants of the County of Middlesex on 12 February 1617/18:

It is well knowne vnto yoʷ what disorder and tumulte was comitted the last Shroue Tuesday in diuers partes aboute the Cittie by Apprentices. . . . And though diuers of the offenders were comitted to Newgate, and proceeded wᵗʰall at the Sessions according to lawe: Yet they are soe farr from beinge warned by that example as they rather take occasion thereby, in regarde that some of their ffellowes were in dainger and punished the last yeare, to cast sedicious lybells into Playhouses in the name of some London ffellowe Apprentices, to Summon others in the Skirtes and Confynes, to meete at the ffortune, and after that to goe to the Playhouses the Redd Bull, and the Cock Pitt, wch they haue designed to rase, and pull downe. . . . (*M.S.C.* i. 377.)

Sherburne seems to say in his letter of the previous year that the players had killed one of the apprentices, and Chamberlain says three; the Privy Council letter indicates that it was in revenge that the apprentices planned raids on the two theatres where their opponents played. But there is no evidence that the proposed raids were ever carried out, and one must assume that the elaborate precautions recommended by the Privy Council proved effective.

Queen Anne's company had only about a year to play at the Phoenix after the authorities prevented the proposed second raid on their theatre. On 2 March 1618/19 their patron, the Queen, died, and all London theatres were presumably closed until her burial on 13 May 1619. (See above, i. 6–7.) Of course all London players suffered during this period of idleness, but the Queen's men were particularly unfortunate, for Beeston seems to have seized the occasion of the closing and the death of the sponsor to attach himself to a new company, evict Queen Anne's men, and bring Prince Charles's (I) troupe to his theatre. Probably he was high-handed; resentment of Beeston is clearly shown a few months later in the reply of three old Queen Anne's men, Ellis Worth, Richard Perkins, and John Cumber, in their answer, dated 18 November 1619, to the suit of John Smith concerning the company's alleged debt for costume materials. The three players say:

the said Beeston haueing from the begining a greater care for his owne privatt gaine & nott respecting the good of these Defend.^tes & the rest of his fellowes & companions hath in the place & trust aforesaid much enritched himself, & hath of late given over his coate & condic*i*on & sep*a*r*a*ted & Devided himself from these Defend.^tes cariing awaie nott onely all the furniture & app*a*rell . . . butt alsoe suffering the comp^lt to sue molest & trouble these Defend^tes. (Wallace, *Three London Theatres*, p. 38.)

Beeston himself verifies the break-up of the old Queen Anne's company at the Phoenix, and his transferred allegiance, in his own answer to Smith's suit, dated five days later than the answer of Worth, Perkins, and Cumber, '. . . the Company of Commedians that are supposed in the pl*ain*t*i*ffes bill to haue contracted with him the said Defendant for the said stuff*e*s (being since altered,

and the parties sep*a*rated and disp*e*rsed amongst other Companyes)'. Later in his answer Beeston is more specific about himself
and his fellows: 'true it is that about the time mentioned in the
said bill, the said Defendant was one of the said Company of
Comedians attendinge vpon the late Queenes Maiestie vntill after
her Ma^{tes} Decease, he entred into the service of the most noble
Prince Charles.' (Ibid., p. 40.)

Evidently, therefore, some time between March and November
1619 Beeston evicted his old company, Queen Anne's men, from
the Phoenix and brought in the company of Prince Charles, whose
service he took. Worth, Perkins, and Cumber allege that he
appropriated costumes and properties of their company, but their
obvious resentment of Beeston may have overcome their veracity.

In this change of companies at the Phoenix—as in all subsequent ones there—it is noteworthy that Beeston stayed with his
theatre and not with his company. For no other managerial figure
in the Jacobean and Caroline period do we have such clear evidence that the man went with the theatre and that he dominated
the company and controlled its fortunes. As more of his activities
come to light we may well find, I suspect, that various familiar
practices of the Restoration and eighteenth-century managers had
their origin in the methods and devices of Christopher Beeston.

The tenancy of the Phoenix by the Prince's men lasted not more
than three years, and little is known of the theatre in this time.
The Venetian ambassador said that in January 1619/20 the
company presented at court a play displeasing to the King, but
neither the title nor the punishment is known. (See above, i. 204.) It
was probably at the Phoenix that Prince Charles's men brought out
Dekker, Ford, and Rowley's *Witch of Edmonton*, and perhaps
Rowley's *All's Lost by Lust* and the anonymous *Man in the Moon
Drinks Claret*. (See above, iii. 269–72; v. 1018–21; v. 1370.) But
by May 1622 this company had left the Phoenix for the Curtain
and had been replaced by the Lady Elizabeth's company, a
troupe once resident in London, but more recently a provincial
organization. (See above, i. 176–83.)

Precisely when the new company arrived and why they came is
unknown. The first indication of a change at the Cockpit is in
the official allowance of the Master of the Revels for them to act
a new play. This licence was copied from the manuscript Office
Book by Malone, and never printed but transcribed on to the
fly-leaf of his copy of the first quarto of Middleton and Rowley's
Changeling: 'Licensed to be acted by the Lady Elizabeth's Servants at the Phoenix, May 7, 1622'. (*T.L.S.* 29 November 1923,

p. 820.) Of similar, though less exact, date is another record copied by Edmond Malone from the manuscript Office Book, an entry which, under the general heading of the year 1622, gives the chief members of the five companies then acting in London. For the Cockpit the entry reads: 'The chiefe of them at the Phœnix. Christopher Beeston, Joseph More, Eliard Swanson, Andrew Cane, Curtis Grevill, William Shurlock, Anthony Turner.' (*Variorum*, iii. 59–60.)

A company under the patronage of the eldest daughter of James I, Princess Elizabeth, who married the Elector Palatine (the Palsgrave) in February 1612/13 and became the Queen of Bohemia in 1619, had been formed in 1611. The troupe acted in the provinces and in London in various amalgamations from 1611 until 1616, when it seems to have been reduced to a provincial status. (See above, i. 176–82.) The organization at the Phoenix in 1622 appears to be a new one formed by Beeston for his theatre, for only Joseph Moore had appeared before as a Lady Elizabeth's man. Beeston had previously been in the service of Prince Charles, and the other five appear for the first time, as actors, in this record of the Master of the Revels. As in two later instances, Beeston seems to have been able to put together an essentially new acting company for his theatre.

To judge from the records which have come down to us, this new troupe achieved an enhanced reputation for the Cockpit in Drury Lane. In the three years of their tenancy, 1622–5, the Master of the Revels licensed for performance at the Phoenix: Middleton and Rowley's *The Changeling* and *The Spanish Gypsy*; Massinger's *The Bondman, The Parliament of Love*, and *The Renegudo*; Shirley's *The School of Compliment*; Dekker and Ford's *The Sun's Darling*; Dekker's *Match Me in London*; Davenport's *The City Night-cap*; Heywood's *The Captive*; Bonen's *The Cra . . . Merchant, or Come to my Country House*; and the anonymous lost plays, *The Black Lady* and *The Valiant Scholar*. Both the number and the quality of the plays imply the success of the Lady Elizabeth's men at the Phoenix.

Equally suggestive are records of gratuities paid by the politic Beeston to the Master of the Revels:

A Newyeres gift this 10 March 1623—Received as a newyeres gift from the Cockpitt company Sir Walter Rawleys booke worth 1[li]

Oct 30 1623 Gratuity—M[r] Shakerlye brought me with a note of Playes for Christmas as a gratuity from the Cockpitt companye 2[li]

From Mr. Blagrave, in the name of the Cockpit company, for this Lent, this 30th March, 1624. £2. 0. 0.

For a daye in Lent from the Cockpitt companye when their tyme was out 10ˢ. Mʳ. Biston sent mee for Lent by Mʳ. Blagrave in the name of the company this 5 April 2!¹¹

Such gratuities to the powerful Master of the Revels were of course good investments, but an insolvent company could not afford them, especially the Christmas and New Year's presents. Even more indicative of success are the surprisingly large contributions for the rebuilding of their parish church. John Parton says in his history of the parish:

... in 1623 ... the company acting there liberally gave £20 towards rebuilding the church, as we have shewn. This sum (which seems to have been the gift of the *performers*) not exempting the theatre itself from being assessed. We subsequently meet with an entry in the assessment book of the sum of £8. 14s. 5d. received from the house, but which is there termed the 'Phoenix' viz. 'the *Phoenix* playhouse viij¹¹ xiiij⁸ vᵈ receᵈ by Mr Speckart; and this contribution being probably thought too small, the house is immediately afterwards credited (in the handwriting of Dr Maynwaring [the rector]) for the further sum of £10. 7s. in terms which seem to leave no doubt as to the Cockpit and Phoenix being one and the same theatre, viz 'Rec' *more*, by Dr. Mayn from yᵉ *Cockpitt* x¹¹ vij⁸' the receipt of which sum is afterwards more regularly acknowledged as follows:—

Receaved from Mr. Biston, as from yᵉ Cockpitt,
for and towards yᵉ building of yᵉ church, yᵉ ⎫
sm̃ of tenn pounds & seaven shillings ⎭ £10. 7s.

So that the company and theatre contributed together on this occasion no less a sum than £39. 1s. 5d. (Parton, *St. Giles*, pp. 234–5.)

Only a successful theatre could have provided contributions of this size, and allusions of these years show that Beeston was drawing to his theatre the sort of audience he wanted. In their address '*To the great Variety of Readers*' for the Shakespeare folio of 1623 John Heminges and Henry Condell rank the Phoenix with their own Blackfriars as the haunt of the sophisticates: 'And though you be a Magistrate of wit, and sit on the Stage at *Black-Friers*, or the *Cock-pit*, to arraigne Playes dailie, know,

¹ The first, second, and fourth come from a transcript of Herbert's Office Book in a nineteenth-century hand, perhaps that of Craven Ord, which has been cut up and pasted into his Scrap-Books by Halliwell-Phillipps, and is now preserved in the Folger Shakespeare Library. The first and second are in the Scrap-Book labelled *Fortune*, pp. 150 and 149; the fourth is from *Appliances*, p. 127. The third was printed by Malone from the Office Book manuscript, *Variorum*, iii. 66. For the Lenten payments see below, vii. 3–6.

these Playes haue had their triall alreadie . . .'. The same coupling of Blackfriars and the Phoenix as the favourite theatres of the *élite* of the town occurs in a letter written by James Howell in London to R. Brown, Esq., and dated 20 January 1624/5:

> I have been already comforted with the sight of many of my choice friends, but I miss you extremely, therfore I pray make haste, for *London* streets which you and I have trod together so often, will prove tedious to me els. Amongst other things, *Black-Friers* will entertain you with a Play *Spick and span new*, and the *Cock-pit* with another; nor I beleeve after so long absence, will it be an unpleasing object for you to see. (*Epistolae Ho-Elianae* [1650], Section iv, Letter ii, sig. Gg₄.)

Very similar is the assumption—that the audience will accept the Cockpit and Blackfriars as the twin resorts of fashion in the town—made in the lines Sir Aston Cokayne gives to Lorece, 'A fantastick Gallant', in his courtship of a rich widow in the third act of *The Obstinate Lady*:

> *Lor.* I at any time will carry you to a Play, either to *Black-Friers* or *Cock-pit*: and you shall go to the *Exchange* when you will, and have as much money as you please to lay out. (1657 ed. F₁–F₁ᵛ.)

But dramatic enterprises are subject to many ills, and the Lady Elizabeth's men had scarcely completed three years at the Phoenix when all London playhouses were closed by the plague for over eight months. (See above, ii. 654–7.) From this terrible visitation, only the King's men, among the London players, survived intact. The Lady Elizabeth's company was reduced to a primarily provincial status (see above, i. 186 91), and again a new troupe was brought to the Phoenix.

During the eight or ten months when the plague of 1625 kept the theatres closed certain political events had presented Christopher Beeston with a new opportunity. In these months King James died, Charles succeeded, and very shortly thereafter he brought a new queen to the throne, when Henrietta-Maria of France reached London on June 16, after her marriage by proxy to Charles in Paris in the preceding May. A new company under the patronage of a new queen offered great possibilities, and this is what Beeston achieved. When the patent for the new company was granted, or by what means, is not known, but after the plague Queen Henrietta's company is found performing at the Phoenix with at least three of the old Lady Elizabeth's men—Beeston, Sherlock, and Turner—and with a number of plays from their repertory. (See above, i. 218–19 and 250–9.)

Another asset of the Lady Elizabeth's company retained by Beeston for his theatre and its new troupe was the services of James Shirley as dramatist. Shirley had written his first known play, *Love Tricks, or the School of Compliments*, for the Phoenix, to be performed by the Lady Elizabeth's men (see above, v. 1144–7); but his next twenty plays were prepared for Queen Henrietta's men at that theatre, and it seems likely that he ordinarily planned to provide for them a spring play and an autumn play each year. (See above, i. 226–7 and n. 3.) The regularity of his production for the company suggests that he may have had a contract with Beeston or with the theatre like that of Richard Brome with the Salisbury Court theatre. (See above, iii. 52–54.)

In this association of Shirley with the Phoenix the commendatory verses written by William Habington for the 1630 edition of Shirley's play *The Grateful Servant* have one passage more cogent than most such:

Confesse vs happy since th' ast giuen a name/ To the English Phenix, which by thy great flame/ Will liue, in spight of mallice to delight/ Our Nation, doing art and nature right. . . .

Shirley himself was satisfied—at one time anyhow—with his association with the company, for he wrote in his Address to the Reader for the same play: 'I must . . . do the Comedians iustice, among whom, some are held comparable With the best that are, and haue beene in the world, and the most of them deseruing a name in the file of those that are eminent for gracefull and vnaffected action.'

Just when Shirley's new company, Queen Henrietta's men, began to play after the plague of 1625 is not clear, but it was probably late in November, for on 6 December playing at the theatre was again ordered to be stopped. The Sessions of the Peace at Hickes Hall was troubled by the danger of the spread of infection in theatre audiences, and on that date they issued an order as follows: 'It is thought fitt, and this Courte doth prohibite the players of the howse at the Cockpitt, beinge next to his Majesties Courte at Whitehall, commaundinge them to surcease all such theire proceedinges untill his Majesties pleasure be further signified.' (*Middlesex County Records*, iii. 6.)

How long this restriction lasted is not known, but it cannot have been for long, and the association of Queen Henrietta's men with the Phoenix developed into one of the more notable ones in the Caroline theatre. Their plays were superior: in addition to the bulk of Shirley's work already noted, the best of

Ford and the late Heywood plays were written for this theatre and company; even the great Ben Jonson strayed from the dominant King's company to prepare *A Tale of a Tub* for them. The position of the theatre as the only—though inferior—rival to the Blackfriars was maintained. The Duke of Buckingham saw the company present Heywood's *Rape of Lucrece* (see above, i. 253) at the Cockpit in August 1628, and even the King and Queen seem to have gone to the theatre for a performance—probably a private one—of Heywood's *Love's Mistress*. (See above, i. 232–3.) Thomas Carew's commendatory verses for Davenant's *Just Italian*, which had failed at Blackfriars, in October 1629, clearly display jealousy of the Cockpit. (See above, i. 224–5.)

This period of success was interrupted by the plague of 1630 which kept all London theatres closed from 17 April until 12 November. (See above, ii. 657–8.) Such a long restraint must have been a severe strain on the Phoenix enterprise, but after the reopening it went on as before. A series of entries in the Office Book of the Master of the Revels is revealing about the conduct of affairs at the Phoenix.

18 Nov. 1632. In the play of The Ball, written by Sherley, and acted by the Queens players, ther were divers personated so naturally, both of lords and others of the court, that I took it ill, and would have forbidden the play, but that Biston [Christopher Beeston] promiste many things which I found faulte withall should be left out, and that he would not suffer it to be done by the poett any more, who deserves to be punisht; and the first that offends in this kind, of poets or players, shall be sure of publique punishment.

.   .   ,   .

Received of Biston, for an ould play called Hymens Holliday, newly revived at their house, being a play given unto him for my use, this 15 Aug. 1633, 3 *l*. o. o. Received of him for some alterations in it 1 *l*. o. o.

Meetinge with him at the ould exchange, he gave my wife a payre of gloves, that cost him at least twenty shillings. (*Variorum*, iii. 231–3.)

In this series one notices first that Shirley and the management at the Phoenix assumed that their theatre would attract an audience sufficiently conversant with court circles to recognize the impersonation 'both of lords and others of the court', not simply national figures. Clearly *The Ball* was not a play which would have been written for the Fortune or the Red Bull or the Globe. In the second place the influence of Beeston is apparent. Not many players could have talked an affronted censor into allowing an offensive play with the assurance that his function would be exercised in the theatre. Finally the glove entry and the *Hymen's Holiday* entry show the manager of the Phoenix cultivating the Master of the Revels in preparation for just such exigencies as that of *The Ball*.

There are two further examples, unfortunately not dated, of the efforts of the company and Beeston to keep the Master of the Revels sympathetic towards the Phoenix and its company. When Sir Henry Herbert, in December 1660, drew up the outline of his case against Killigrew's company, one item included was 'To proue that Mister Beeston payd me 60 li. per annum besids usuall Fees & allowances for Court plaies.' (Halliwell-Phillipps, *A Collection of Ancient Documents . . .*, p. 27.) Such a large annual fee is rather surprising and cannot now, of course, be proved, but most of the assertions in Herbert's outline of his case are verifiable. The profits at the Phoenix must have been considerable to provide perquisites of this size—and so must Herbert's, if there were many gratuities like the gloves and the £3 for *Hymen's Holiday* to be added to the annual £60 from the Phoenix.

The second example of policy at the Phoenix is found in an undated petition, probably of 1640, made by Dorothy Blagrave to the Lords:

> Peticion of Dorothy Blagrove Widdowe. That the Company of Players of the Cockpitt playhouse in Drury Lane graunted to Sir Henry Harbert under theire hands a play share dureing the time of theire enioying the Queenes Service, and Sir Henry Harbert for one hundred pounds consideracion to him paid graunted his said share to William Blagrove (since deceased) his deputy and assignes. . . . (*Hist. MSS. Com.*, MSS. of House of Lords, xi [New Series], 1962, p. 243.)

The advantage to the Phoenix of such a shareholder as the Master of the Revels is obvious. Mrs. Blagrave seems to say that the share was a gift and not a purchase by the Master, but her wording is not precise, and of course her information may have been faulty. Her husband, to whom Sir Henry had sold his share, was Deputy Master of the Revels, who sometimes licensed plays himself; a share of the Phoenix profits in his hands would have been only less beneficial to the players than a share in Herbert's.

Beeston at this time evidently thought well of the prospects of his theatre and company, for he persuaded the widow of John Best to extend his lease, and on 4 May 1633 they signed an agreement to lengthen the term for nine years so that it would not expire until 1656.[1] Long before the expiration of the extended lease regular playing in London had been prohibited by Parliament.

In February and March 1634/5 the Phoenix became for a time a centre for French drama in London. French influence at court had been rising as Queen Henrietta-Maria became more assured and more popular; the number of French men and women in her service was sometimes a matter of national concern. On 15 February 1634/5 she had a performance at her palace, Somerset House, of a French play presented by the visiting company of Floridor, and two nights later the troupe performed *La Melise* in Whitehall. (*Variorum*, iii. 121.) The subsequent events are listed by Malone from the lost manuscript of Sir Henry Herbert's Office Book:

> This day being Friday, and the 20 of the same monthe, the kinge tould mee his pleasure, and commanded mee to give order that this Frenche company should playe the too sermon daies in the weeke, during their time of playinge in Lent, and in the house of Drury-lane, where the queenes players usually playe.
>
> The kings pleasure I signifyed to Mr. Beeston, the same day, who obeyd readily.
>
> The house-keepers are to give them by promise the benefit of their interest for the two days of the first weeke.
>
> They had the benefitt of playinge on the sermon daies, and gott two hundred pounds at least; besides many rich clothes were given them.
>
> They had freely to themselves the whole weeke before the weeke before Easter, which I obtaynd of the king for them.
>
> .   .   .   .   .
>
> [In the margin] Thes Frenchmen were commended unto mee by the queene, and have passed through my handes, *gratis*. (*Variorum*, iii. 121, 122.)

Herbert's last note of the concern of the Queen with the French company probably provides the reason for the selection of the theatre of her company for the public performances. Though Sir Henry's account is none too precise, it appears that the French troupe acted at the Phoenix only on those days in Lent which were customarily forbidden to the English actors. (See below, vii. 4–5.) Presumably at the close of Lent the French company left the theatre to Queen Henrietta's men, after having played there about fourteen times.

[1] Disclaimer of Sir Lewis Kirke and Elizabeth his wife to the Complaint of Thomas Hussey, P.R.O., C 2, Ch. I, H 28/26. The suit was discovered by Leslie Hotson.

It is interesting that there is no record in the accounts of this visit of objections by the Phoenix audience to the actresses of the French troupe. The French visitors of 1629 had, according to one letter, been 'hissed, hooted, and pippin-pelted from the stage' at Blackfriars. (See above, vi. 23.) It is possible that there had been a great change in the English attitude toward actresses between 1629 and 1635, but I suspect an error in the accounts. In 1629 the French had played at the Red Bull and the Fortune as well as at the Blackfriars theatre; violence among the spectators was much more characteristic of Red Bull and Fortune audiences than of those at Blackfriars and the Phoenix. If the letter erroneously attributed conduct which took place at the Red Bull or the Fortune to the Blackfriars, then the various records would accord much better with Herbert's accounts of the 1629 visit, and with our knowledge of the differences between private-theatre audiences and public-theatre audiences in the reign of King Charles I. (See Bentley, *Shakespeare and his Theatre*, pp. 101–28.)

In 1636 and 1637 the Phoenix, like the other London theatres, underwent another long plague closing, and Christopher Beeston again seized the opportunity to get rid of one company at his theatre and to start another. The closing order went out on 12 May 1636, and except for one week at the end of February 1636/7 the playhouses remained closed until 2 October 1637. For reasons unknown the owner of the Phoenix took the occasion to break up the successful troupe of Queen Henrietta's men and to form a new boys' company, a type of acting organization which had not been known in London for twenty years.[1] Extant lists of actors in the company make it appear likely that though the new troupe is called 'Beeston's Boys', 'The King & Queen's young Company', and 'a company of boyes' it was not a true children's company like the Elizabethan Paul's Boys or the Children of the Revels, but a combination of an unusual number of boys and half a dozen or more adults. (See above, i. 324 n.)

The destruction of Queen Henrietta's company is recorded in

---

[1] Though one can only guess at Beeston's reasons for formation of the new company, Dr. William B. Markward has some interesting suggestions in his Birmingham thesis on the Phoenix, pp. 144–5. He notices the static and formal character of Thomas Nabbes's *Hannibal and Scipio*, acted at the Phoenix in the year 1635 (see above, iv. 934–6), as well as its use of spectacle and its hint at scenery. This play seems to demand an unusual number of boy actors, as do Rutter's *Shepherds' Holiday* and Ford's *Fancies Chaste and Noble* acted at the same theatre a year or so before. Possibly these plays testify to Beeston's observation of the effect of certain new appeals for his private-theatre audience.

three different documents. Mrs. Blagrave said in her petition to the Lords, already noted:

> ... And afterwards [i.e. after Herbert sold his share in the Queen's men to William Blagrove] one Mr. Beeston being Master of the said playhouse who alsoe subscribed with the rest takes occasion to quarrell with the Company to the end hee might have a Company that would take what hee would be willing to give them, And uppon this falling out some of them goe to Black Friers, and some to Salisbury Court Playhouses and those of Salisbury Court are made the Queenes Company. (Loc. cit.)

Essentially the same story of a broken company is told by Richard Heton in his papers about the affairs of the company a year or so later: 'When her M^{ts} servants were at the Cockpitt, beinge all at liberty, they disperst themselves to severall Companies, soe that had not my lo: of Dorsett taken care to make up a new Company for the Queene, she had not had any at all.' (See above, ii. 684.)

A similar account from a different point of view and with a few more details was set down by Sir Henry Herbert in his Office Book. Following his note on the reopening of the theatres after the plague on 2 October 1637 he says: 'Mr. Beeston was commanded to make a company of boyes, and began to play at the Cockpitt with them the same day. I disposed of Perkins, Sumner, Sherlock and Turner, to Salisbury Court, and joynd them with the best of that company.' (*Variorum*, iii. 240.)

The evidence that Queen Henrietta's men were expelled from the Phoenix is complete enough. The repertory of the boy company which succeeded them (see above, i. 337-42) shows that, as before, Beeston kept many of the plays of Queen Henrietta's and the Lady Elizabeth's men for the use of his new troupe. Surely this action must have been a source of hard feelings.

The new boy company was formed and rehearsed even earlier than Herbert's note implies, for the list of court performances in the winter of 1636–7 includes

> Cupides Revenge, at St. James, by Beeston's boyes, the 7 Febru.
>
> and
>
> Wit without Money, by the B. boyes at St. James, the 14 Feb.
>
> (*Variorum*, iii. 239.)

Both plays had been the property of former companies at the Phoenix.

Another step in Beeston's consolidating of his dominant position at his theatre is to be seen in the designation of his new official post. The Lord Chamberlain's Warrant Books at the Public Record Office carry the entry 'A Warrant to sweare Mr Christopher Bieston his M^{tes} servant in ye place of Gouuernor of the new Company of the King*es* & Queenes boyes. Feb. 21. 1636 [/37].' (*M.S.C.* ii. 382.)

Perhaps Beeston's success in evicting his old tenants at the Phoenix, and in forming a new company with double royal patronage, over which he would have more control, had gone to his head, for he was shortly in difficulties for presenting them to the public too soon. What he did was to prepare something like an opening 'by invitation only' to introduce his new troupe to the proper influential circles. The scheme itself tells us something about the Phoenix theatre and its audience. Apparently he assumed that the status of his guests made him immune to the plague-closing order. After the fact he presented his case most adroitly in an undated petition.

Petition of Christopher Beeston to the Council. Petitioner being commanded to erect and prepare a company of young actors for their Majesties' service, and being desirous to know how they profited by his instructions, invited some noblemen and gentlemen to see them act at his house, the Cockpit. For which, since he perceives it is imputed as a fault, he is very sorry, and craves pardon. (*C.S.P.*, *Dom.*, 1636–7, p. 254.)

What had caused Beeston to 'perceive it is imputed as a fault' is shown in a warrant issued by the Privy Council on 12 May 1637, after the plague-closing had been in effect for a full year.

A warrant to Iaspar Heyley Messenger to fetch before the Lords Christopher and Wm Biston Theophil Bird Ezech: Fenn & Michaell Moone wth a Clause to Command the Keepers of the Playhouse called the Cockpit in Drury Lane who either live in it or have relaĉon to it not to permit Playes to bee Acted there till further Order. . . . (*M.S.C.* i. 392.)

This staging of a private opening during plague-time was extremely presumptuous, but Beeston evidently had some reason to think that he and his theatre were privileged. The warrant of three months before to swear him *Governor* of the company was, so far as the extant records go, unprecedented since the time of the Elizabethan and early Jacobean boy companies. We have noted his privileged position with the Master of the Revels;

he seems to have been similarly influential with the Master's master, the Lord Chamberlain. Less than a month after his violation of the plague prohibition, when he might be expected to be in very bad odour, he was granted extraordinary privileges by the Lord Chamberlain. After being informed—presumably by Beeston himself—that some of the Phoenix plays were about to be printed, his Lordship ordered the Wardens of the Stationers' Company to see that no play should be printed without the written permission of John Lowin, Joseph Taylor, or Christopher Beeston to show that it did not belong to the repertories of either the King's company or Beeston's Boys. (See above, i. 54.) What better device could be conceived to insure Beeston's exclusive proprietorship of the large number of Phoenix plays which had been licensed for the Lady Elizabeth's and Queen Henrietta's companies, and to which Queen Henrietta's men, now at the Salisbury Court, might well have thought that they had some claim?[1]

The playhouses were permitted to open again on 2 October. Not long after, on 9 November, the Reverend George Garrard wrote to the Lord Deputy in Ireland of an event which again suggests the status of the Phoenix. Lady Newport was prominent in court circles; her husband, the Earl of Newport, was a conspicuous political figure. Garrard wrote: 'Here hath been an horrible Noise about the Lady *Newport's* being become a *Romish* Catholick; she went one Evening as she came from a Play in *Drury-Lane* to *Somerset-House*, where one of the Capuchins reconciled her to the *Popish* Church, of which she is now a weak Member.' (*Strafforde's Letters*, ii. 128.)

Audiences in which Lady Newport and her friends were notable are associated with the Phoenix, and many of the plays show evidence of having been designed for them. Yet these profitable audiences created a problem for Beeston's companies which they could not solve as the King's men had their similar difficulty at Blackfriars. The gentry, which formed a good part of the audiences at the two private theatres, were commonly out of town during the long vacation. At this time of year the King's men left the Blackfriars and played at the Globe, where a more plebeian audience was customary. Such a solution was not available for the Phoenix companies, but there is a suggestion that they tried for a more middle-class audience in the summer. The best identifiable example of such an effort is Thomas Nabbes's play *The Bride*,

---

[1] There is an interesting consideration of common, or at least popular, characteristics in the plays of the Cockpit repertory in William B. Markward's thesis, pp. 38–94.

produced in the summer of 1638. The prologue uses a tone and vocabulary quite different from the usual Phoenix address to the ladies and gentlemen, and the plot treats the middle class and its tastes far more sympathetically than was usual in Phoenix plays. (See above, iv. 929–32.) Unfortunately too few plays in the repertory can be dated with sufficient precision to show how characteristic this attempt to modify the bill during the summer was.

A few months after the performance of *The Bride* at his theatre Christopher Beeston died. In his will of 4 and 7 October 1638 he left his residuary estate, including the theatre, to his wife Elizabeth. The will says that there are six shares in the company of Beeston's Boys, of which he owns four, and he leaves two to the company and two to his wife. His son William is to be employed in the affairs of the company at a wage of £20 per annum. In a codicil he altered the bequest to William and directed his wife to make over to him one half share from her two shares 'for his care in the business, she finding and providing a stock of apparel for the said company as is within declared'. (See above, ii. 631–3.) Since he directed the exchange of £20 per year for half a share, Beeston seems to have estimated the annual value of a whole share at £40, or of the six shares at £240. His estimate of £40 for a share should be compared with Sir Henry Herbert's 1662 estimate of £100 (*Variorum*, iii. 266) ; Herbert had good reason to exaggerate, but it is not so obvious that Beeston would have minimized.

William Beeston took over his father's function as official manager of the troupe, for a warrant of 5 April 1639 orders that he be sworn 'vnder the Title of Gouuernor & Instructer of the Kings & Queens young Company of Actors'. (*M.S.C.* ii. 389.) In his new position as Governor and Instructor of his father's troupe, William Beeston secured the services of Richard Brome as playwright for the Phoenix. His first recorded play to be prepared for presentation in Drury Lane was—as Brome himself testifies—*The Antipodes*. To the 1640 edition of the play, which had been acted in 1638 by Queen Henrietta's men at the Salisbury Court, Brome appended a signed note in which he said:

Courteous Reader, *You shal find in this Booke more then was presented upon the* Stage, *and left out of the* Presentation, *for superfluous length* (*as some of the* Players *pretended*) *I thoght good al should be inserted according to the allowed* Original; *and as it was, at first, intended for the* Cock-pit Stage, *in the right of my most deserving Friend Mr.* William Beeston, *unto whom it properly appertained; and so I leave it to thy perusal, as it was generally applauded, and well acted at* Salisbury Court. *Farewell*, Ri. Brome. (1640 ed., L₄ᵛ.)

This transfer to Salisbury Court of a play planned for Beeston's Boys at the Phoenix was probably brought about by the insistence of Queen Henrietta's men that Brome should fulfil his contract with them. (See above, iii. 52–54.) At any rate Brome's last play for the Salisbury Court was delivered to that theatre before Easter 1639, and thereafter he wrote for the Phoenix and its young company under the direction of William Beeston. The relation between playwright and manager seems to have continued to be a friendly one, for Brome wrote for Beeston one of the very few early testimonials to the training of actors in the theatre. In the epilogue for his play, *The Court Beggar*, acted a year or so later by the boys at the Cockpit, Brome said:

> But this small Poet vents [no wit] but his own, and his by whose care and directions this Stage is govern'd, who has for many yeares both in his fathers dayes, and since directed Poets to write & Players to speak till he traind up these youths here to what they are now. I some of 'em from before they were able to say a grace of two lines long to have more parts in their pates then would fill so many Dry-fats. (1653 ed., S₈–S₈ᵛ.)

The skill of the new 'Gouuernor & Instructer' of the Phoenix is also memorialized by Francis Kirkman in the dedication of his translation, *The Loves and Adventures of Clerico and Lozia*, 1652, to William Beeston:

> *Divers times (in my hearing) to the admiration of the whol Company, you have most judiciously discoursed of Poësie: which is the cause J presume to chuse you for my Patron and Protector; who are the happiest interpretor and judg of our English Stage-Playes this Nation euer produced; which the Poets and Actors of these times, cannot (without ingratitude) deny; for I have heard the chief, and most ingenious of them acknowledg their Fames & Profits essentially sprung from your instructions, judgment and fancy . . . (1652 ed., A₂–A₂ᵛ.)*

And two years later in a postscript at the end of his tragi-comedy, *Love's Dominion*, Richard Flecknoe wrote similarly:

> *. . . if ever it be acted, I intitle to my right in it, (not departing in the mean time with my right of altering my mind) Mr. Will. Beeston, who by Reason of his long Practice and Experience in this way, as also for having brought up most of the Actors extant, I think the fittest Man for this Charge and Imployment. (1654 ed., F₈ᵛ.)*

Beeston as manager, producer, and coach at the Phoenix must have been a significant influence in the drama of late Caroline

London, and, through the young actors he trained, on the drama of the next generation.

About the time Brome came to the Phoenix there was trouble with the neighbours. One of Mrs. Beeston's houses adjoining the theatre had been converted to a tavern—one would assume with the consent of the owner, and partly for the use of the theatre. A petition of about June 1639 sets out the situation.

A minute.

It is humbly desired by the inhabitants of Drury Lane (of wch number are Mr Secr Windebanke, ye Lo: Mountagne, ye Ea: of Cleveland & divers other persons of qualitie) that, forasmuch as since George Lillgraves committment to a messenger, wine hath neverthelesse bene drawen, & sold in that house adjoyning to Mris Beestones playhouse, wch he attempteth to make a taverne in contempt of the severall orders of this board.

That Lillgrave may not be released untill he have put in sufficient securitie not to convert the house to a taverne.

And that power may be given to the next justice of the peace to committ any persons that shalbe found drawing & selling of wine there, or attempting to hang up a signe or a bush, or doeing any worke there towards the makeing of that house a taverne The disorder being there likely to be such in the taverne joyned to the playhouse as will not be possible to be suppressed.[1]

That a tavern adjoining a theatre might produce disturbances unwelcome to the neighbours is easy to understand, as is its possible profit to the theatre. In such a clash of interests one would expect residents of the standing of Secretary Windebank and the Earl of Cleveland to win, and they may have done so for the moment, but they were not eventually successful, for a Chancery bill of 9 July 1647 concerning the Cockpit property speaks of 'one other house or Tenement wth appurtenances wherein one Gilbert Jackson Lynner sometimes dwelt heretofore devised to one William Brittaine Esq. . . . and the same is since used for a Taverne called the George . . .'. An answer in the same suit dated 4 November 1647 refers a little more explicitly to the tavern, 'and the taverne in the tenure of one Lucas on the south and abutting on the Cockpit on the East . . .'.[2] The fact that the

---

[1] *State Papers, Domestic, Charles I*, vol. 424, no. 104, as transcribed in the Halliwell-Phillipps Scrap-Books, *Fortune*, p. 137. Printed in a somewhat modified form, *C.S.P., Dom.*, 1639, p. 358.

[2] *Thomas Hussey* v. *Katherine Best and administrators*, P.R.O. C 2, Ch. I, H 44/66, and the Answer of Robert Rolleston to the Complaint of Thomas Hussey, C 2, Ch. I, H 28/26. Both were discovered by Leslie Hotson.

tavern actually abutted on the playhouse makes it seem all the more likely that some relation between the operation of the two may have been intended. We cannot tell, however, how long the George of the 1647 suit had been in operation or how long George Lillgrave had been selling wine there before he was committed in 1639.

Later in the summer of 1639, when the residents of Drury Lane were trying to get rid of the tavern at the Phoenix, the Lord Chamberlain took steps to keep other London companies from performing any of the plays claimed by Beeston as part of his repertory. After listing the plays, the Lord Chamberlain says in his warrant: 'his Ma^{ty} hath signifyed his royall pleasure vnto me: therby requireing mee to declare soe much to all other Companyes of Actors heerby concernable: that they are not any wayes to intermedle wth or Act any of th'aboue mentioned Playes . . .'. (M.S.C. ii. 389–90.)

This list of 45 plays (see above, i. 330–1), almost all written for one or another of the predecessors of the boys at the Phoenix, formed the bulk of the repertory at the Cockpit at this time. The list does not, however, represent the complete repertory, for at least nine other plays are known to have been acted by the boys (see above, i. 337–42), but it shows well the type of dramatic fare to be expected at the Phoenix in the last years of the Caroline theatre. Fourteen of the plays are Shirley's, five Beaumont and Fletcher's, and five Massinger's: the rest are the compositions of a variety of dramatists. Almost none of those on the list can have been originally composed with Beeston's Boys in mind, and one wonders what modifications to exploit the talents of the young company were made before production.

It is noteworthy that this repertory protection warrant from the Lord Chamberlain explicitly vests the ownership of the plays in William Beeston and his theatre, not in the company:

Wheras William Bieston Gent' Gouuernor &c' of the kinges and Queenes young Company of Players at the Cockpitt in Drury Lane hath represented vnto his Ma^{tye} that ye seuerall Playes heerafter mentioned . . . doe all & euery of them properly & of right belong to the sayd House, and consequently that they are all in his propriety.

This conception of ownership had evidently been assumed by William Beeston's father, and it explains the retention at the Cockpit of plays of Queen Anne's company, Prince Charles's (I) company, Lady Elizabeth's company, and Queen Henrietta's company when those troupes left Christopher Beeston and his house.

Within a year of his fortunate attainment of the Lord Chamberlain's protection for his repertory William Beeston was in serious
trouble about the conduct of the theatre. There was always a
temptation for the managers to get a few easy audiences by putting
on a play with political allusions (see *Herbert*, pp. 18–23), and the
temptation seems to have been particularly strong for the boy
companies. In early May 1640 William Beeston produced at his
theatre a lost and nameless play which the Master of the Revels
says 'had relation to the passages of the K.s journey into the
Northe', that is, King Charles's unpopular expedition to Berwick
to suppress the Scottish revolt against the Prayer Book and the
bishops. It is significant that the Short Parliament was sitting at
this time and was dissolved by order of the King only a day or so
later. Sir Henry Herbert goes on to say that not only did the play
concern this controversial subject, but that it had never been
licensed and was produced after the Master had expressly forbidden
performance. (*Variorum*, iii. 241.)

In consequence of such folly Beeston, along with his players
George Estotville and Michael Moone, were arrested and confined
to the Marshalsea, and playing was prohibited at the Phoenix during
the pleasure of the Master of the Revels. The Master say that he
allowed them to act again after three days but that he confiscated
the manuscript of their offending play. (See above, i. 332–5.)

William Beeston, however, probably continued to languish
in the Marshalsea—at least he lost his company. Eight weeks
after his commitment the Lord Chamberlain issued a warrant
appointing William Davenant to serve in Beeston's place,

... to take into his Gou'nm^t & care, the sayd Company of Players,
to gouerne, order & dispose of them for Action and p^{r}sentmentes,
and all their Affyres in the sayd House, as in his discretion shall seeme
best to conduce to his Ma^{tes} seruice in that Quality. And I doe
heerby inioyne & cõmaund them all . . . that they obey the sayd
Mr Dauenant & follow his Orders & direccõns as they will answere
the contrary. (*M.S.C.* ii. 395.)

Here again is a Restoration type of situation set up, and for a man
who became a significant force in the Restoration theatre. Davenant had already written fifteen or sixteen plays and masques
(see above, iii. 197–225) and his desire for management is attested
by his endeavour just the previous year to set up a large theatre
in Fleet Street. (See below, vi. 304–9.) But so far as is known this
period as governor of the Phoenix was his only actual experience
in management before his momentous experiments at Rutland
House and Apothecaries Hall.

What Davenant's relations were with Mrs. Beeston, the owner of his playhouse and of most of the stock of his company, is not known. The situation must have been very difficult for her with a complete outsider forced by the Lord Chamberlain's warrant into a position of authority in what had for twenty-four years been a family enterprise. There is a suggestion, though only a vague one, that Davenant was intriguing against William Beeston. The hint is found in one sentence of Richard Brome's praise of Beeston in the epilogue for his play, *The Court Beggar*, acted in 1639 or 1640 (see above, iii. 61–65): 'And to be serious with you, if after all this, by the venemous practise of some, who study nothing more then his destruction, he should faile us, both Poets and Players would be at losse in Reputation.' (1653 ed., S₈ᵛ.) Since William Beeston was not known for his quiet life, 'the venemous practise of some' is not limited in its possible applications, but William Davenant seems a very likely candidate at this time. At all events there can be no doubt of Brome's attachment to Beeston, and his fear of someone's intrigue about the playhouse.

Shortly after Davenant took charge at her theatre Mrs. Beeston was in need of money. Whether her need was related to Davenant's actions as manager is unknown, but ten days after his appointment Mrs. Beeston borrowed £150 from William Wilbraham, once an actor at her theatre though of unknown affiliations at the time of the loan. For his money Mrs. Beeston mortgaged her theatre to him. Only the fact is known, from its mention in the papers of a law suit,[1] nothing of its causes or consequences. Presumably she still had to furnish costumes for the actors according to the stipulations of her husband's will, and it is not difficult to imagine Davenant demanding more elaborate displays, but this is the purest speculation.

Actually nothing at all is known of the Cockpit under William Davenant's management, though it may well be that this first handling of a dramatic troupe determined many of the policies he later adopted under his better-known managements. His term in Drury Lane was not long, for less than a year after his appointment he was involved in the Army Plot, and early in May 1641 fled London. It was presumably in 1641 that William Beeston was reinstated in his old post, for among the Lord Chamberlain's papers at the Public Record Office is an 'Establishment list of

---

[1] Joint and Several Disclaimers of Sir Lewis Kirke and Dame Elizabeth his Wife to the Complaint of Thomas Hussey, 8 November 1647, P.R.O. C 2, Ch. I, H 28/26; and *Rolleston* v. *Kirke*, 8 May 1655, C 5, H 21/89. Both discovered by Leslie Hotson.

Servants of the Chamber in 1641', which includes as 'Gouernor of ye Cockpitt Players' the name 'William Bieston'. (*M.S.C.* ii. 326.) This is the last record of the theatre before the closing order of 2 September 1642.

The Cockpit did not offer as much interregnum playing as the Fortune and the Red Bull did, but there are several notices of its use. The oddest is found in the records of the parish of St. Giles in the Fields: '1646. P^d and given to the teacher at the Cockpitt of the Children, 6d.' (Parton, *St. Giles*, p. 235.) This is the sum of the evidence, but it seems to imply that for a time the theatre was used as a school. One remembers that James Shirley, who had been principal dramatist at the Phoenix for eleven years, had been a schoolmaster before he became a playwright, and that he was a schoolmaster again after the theatres were closed. (See above, v. 1064–72.) But Wood says that Shirley taught 'mostly in the White-friars' and he gave that district as his residence in his will of 1666. Perhaps he tried the Phoenix before removing to Whitefriars.

Two or three pieces of evidence indicate that there was playing in Drury Lane in 1647. In one of the Chancery suits about the Cockpit properties found by Professor Hotson, Thomas Hussey says that the former Elizabeth Beeston and her second husband, Lewis Kirke, refuse to pay him rent, 'although they . . . do make a very great constant yearly profit of the said messuages, Tenements, & premises, & sometimes a very extraordinary profit, for in several nights since the said feast of Saint Michael 1647, they have gained by acting of plays there about xxx or xl^l a night'. (*Commonwealth and Restoration Stage*, pp. 94–95.) About the same time one of the newsbooks, *Mercurius Elencticus* for 29 October–5 November 1647, says that the members of Parliament 'cannot endure that their Elder brethren of the *Cock-pit* should live by them; because their Actions consist of Harmlesse mirth and Loyalty, whilst themselves Act nothing but tragicall and treasonable Scenes . . . .' (Ibid., p. 28.) And ten or eleven weeks later the same journalist, in his issue of 19–26 January 1647/8, twits Parliament: '. . . So that where a dozen Coaches *Tumble* after *Obadiah Sedgewick*; Threescore are observed to *wheele* to the *Cockpit*, which is very offensive to the Brethren.' (Ibid., p. 29.) They were still—or again—playing at the Phoenix at the time of the general raids on the Fortune, Red Bull, and Salisbury Court. *The Kingdoms Weekly Intelligencer* for 2–9 January 1648/9 says that 'The Souldiers seized on the Players on their Stages at Drury-lane and Salisbury Court . . . . They made some resistance at the Cockpit in Drury Lane, which was the occasion they were bereaved of their apperell, and were not so well used as those in Salisbury Court, who were more patient . . . .' (No. 293, pp. 1210–11.)

The later Cockpit history belongs with the beginnings of the Restoration theatre rather than with the last days of the Caroline. Christopher Beeston's widow and her son disputed the rights to the theatre with Robert Rolleston and with each other. William Beeston even made repairs to the theatre and trained a company in anticipation of a tenancy he did not attain. Davenant used the theatre for *The Siege of Rhodes*, and George Jolly and John Rhodes later had companies there. (*Commonwealth and Restoration Stage*, pp. 94–100, 155–60, and *passim*.)

PORTERS' HALL OR ROSSETER'S BLACKFRIARS OR PUDDLE WHARF

Adams, pp. 342–7.
Chambers, *E.S.*, ii. 472–4.
Hillebrand, Harold Newcomb, *The Child Actors* (1926), pp. 243–8.
Maxwell, Baldwin, 'A Note on the Date of Middleton's *The Family of Love* with a Query on the Porters Hall Theatre', *Elizabethan Studies and Other Essays in Honor of George F. Reynolds* (1945), pp. 195–200.
Wagner, Bernard, 'London's New Mermaid Theatre at Puddle Dock', *Shakespeare Quarterly*, x (1959), 603–6.
Wilson, F. P., 'More Records from the Remembrancia of the City of London', *Malone Society Collections*, iv (1956), 55–65.

Porters' Hall[1] or Rosseter's Blackfriars or Puddle Wharf theatre is a most obscure playhouse which left an unusual number of records of the attempts to build it, but almost none of its use by the actors. The confusion of our information about the project and its development has been somewhat clarified by the publication in 1956 of the dramatic items from a collection of letters of the mayoralty of Sir Thomas Hayes (1614–15), which were missing when the Analytical Index to the Remembrancia was published. These new letters, added to the old information, show that the enterprise was an attempt of Philip Rosseter and his associates

---

[1] The source of this name is not known. Professor Baldwin Maxwell suggests, loc. cit., that the building may have been the Hall of the Porters' Company for a short period in 1605 or shortly after. The suggestion is attractive but has not been confirmed.

to get a new house for the amalgamated Queen's Revels and Lady Elizabeth's companies, to which Prince Charles's company was later added. The first extant indication of this plan for a new house to replace the Whitefriars theatre, on which the lease had expired, is found in a letter from the Privy Council to the Lord Mayor of London, dated 29 July 1613:

> Wheareas Complaynt was this daie made to theire Lordshipps by my Recorder, and divers Aldermen of the Cittie of London, That one Sturgis havinge lately taken a lease from Sir Edward Gorge knight of a greate howse or Messuage in Whitefriers, hath lett the same to three or fower severall Tenauntes, as namelie one parte thereof beinge the Garden, to one Roseter Kynman, and others, whoe goe about to erect a Playehowse therevppon . . . It pleased theire Lordshipps, therevppon to order, that the Lord Maior and Alderman of that warde, shall take present order aswell for the staie of anie newe buildinge, to be there erected, as alsoe for devidinge of that howse into anye more Tenementes then hath bene heeretofore vsed there . . . . (M.S.C. iv. 58–59.)

This letter seems to have served its purpose to suppress the attempt of Rosseter and Kingman to build their new theatre in Whitefriars. But as an alternative they succeeded in securing higher authority to build in another place. This move is shown in a royal patent dated 3 June 1615:

> Iames by the grace of God &c . . . whereas wee . . . did appoint and authorise Phillipp Rosseter and certaine others from tyme to tyme to provide keepe, and bring vppe a convenient nomber of children and them to practise and exercise in the quallitie of playing by the name of the children of the Revelles to the Queene within the white ffryers in the Suburbs of our Cittie of london . . . And whereas the said Phillipp Rosseter and the rest of his said partners have ever since trayned vppe and practised a convenient number of children of the Revelles for the purpose aforesaid in a Messuage or mansion house being parcell of the late dissolved Monastery called the white ffryers neere ffleetestreete in london, which the said Phillipp Rosseter did lately hold for terme of certaine yeres expired, And whereas the said Phillipp Roseter, together with Phillipp kingman Robert Iones and Raphe Reeve . . . have latelie taken in lease and farme divers buildinges, Cellers, sollars, chambers, and yardes for the building of a Playhouse therevpon for the better practising and exercise of the said children of the Revells. All which premisses are scituate and being within the Precinct of the Blacke ffryers neere Puddlewharfe in the Suburbs of london called by the name of the lady Saunders house or otherwise Porters hall and now in the occupation of the said Robert Iones. Nowe knowe yee that wee of our

especiall grace certaine knowledge and meere mocion have given and graunted . . . lycense and authoritie vnto the said Phillipp Rosseter Phillipp kingman Robert Iones and Raphe Reeve, at their proper costes and charges to erect build and sett vppe in and vppon the said premisses before mencioned one convenient Playhouse for the said children of the Revelles, the same Playhouse to be vsed by the Children of the Revells for the tyme being of the Queenes Maiestie, and for the Princes Players and for the ladie Elizabeths Players soe tollerated or lawfully lycensed to play exercise and practise them therein . . . . (*M.S.C.* i. 277–9.)

This document must have seemed to Rosseter and his associates to assure their freedom in their new building enterprise; patents for companies are fairly common, but theatre patents which even name the companies to use them are unusual. The patentees began building operations at once.

These operations must have been fairly extensive. The various letters about the theatre show nothing of its size or cost, but Professor H. N. Hillebrand discovered a Chancery suit of 1623, brought by Edward Alleyn, son-in-law and executor of Philip Henslowe, in which the defendants assert that Philip Kingman and Robert Jones of the 1615 patent 'did transferr theire estate, or some parte thereof vnto one Hinslowe the Complainants father in lawe which said Iones, kingman, and Hinslowe, or some of them, by the advice, expences, and ayde of the said Hinslowe did cause some parte of the said Messuages, or Tenements [in Blackfriars] to be pulled downe, and indeavoured to build a playhouse there . . .'. (Hillebrand, op. cit., p. 246.) Alleyn said that he spent £1,500 on the property, and later made the entry in his diary for 28 September 1618: 'more disbursed for ye building in ye Blackfryars for this yeare and in ano 1617, when itt first begane wt ye 200l first disbursed by my father: [i.e. Henslowe] buyeing in off leases: chargis in lawe: and ye building itt selfe, wt making meanes to kepe them from being puld down, is 1105l 00s 02d.' (G. F. Warner, *Catalogue of the Manuscripts and Muniments of Alleyn's College of God's Gift at Dulwich* [1881], p. 174.)

The papers do not make clear how much of the money was spent on the theatre and how much on the other buildings in Blackfriars, but it is evident that the work on the playhouse was expensive. The revelation that first Philip Henslowe and then Edward Alleyn, both men of great theatrical experience, were associated with Rosseter in Porters' Hall and were spending money on it indicates how promising the project was thought to be and helps explain how it survived as long as it did against strong opposition.

To return to the activities about the theatre in 1615. Though the patent for their new theatre may have seemed to clear the way for Rosseter, Henslowe, and their associates, they had reckoned without the Puritan inhabitants of the precinct of Blackfriars, who frequently complained of the private theatre of the King's company already established in their neighbourhood and did not propose to have their troubles doubled. In August 1615 they petitioned the Lord Mayor and aldermen:

The humble petition of the Inhabitant*es*
of the precincte of the Blackfriers in London

Humbly shewe, That whereas there is nowe a Playehowse erectinge in the said Precincte which will tend to the greate annoyaunce daunger and inconvenience of the Inhabitant*es* there/. And wilbe a greevous Disturbaunce to the Devine service of God, the Church beinge soe neere) in respect of ffunerall Sermons, Christening*es* and eveninge praiers, which often happen in the weeke daies, and in the verie time of theire Playes, which throughe the div*ers* and variable noyses, they commonlie vse, wilbe greevouslie interrupted, which plaies are evill in themselues, for the matter they represent is corrupt and Dangerous for Imitation, and will likewise procure Tiplinge howses to Neighbour them, which doe occasion idle and dissolute people, to leave theire honest course of Lyfe, and assemble there/Where-vppon perticuler abuses and disorders, doe necessarelie ensue./ Besides divers Noblemen and gentlemen of qualitie, which inhabite in that place, are often indangered in theire passage to theire howses, and inforced to forsake theire Coaches. And by reason of the Diffi-culties and dissenc*i*ons, that many tymes happen in the narrowe passages, are often in daunger of Bloodshedd/. His maiesties Wardrobe greatelie indaungered, the doores of his Wardrobe and of the play-house openinge neere together/And the lord Evers his howse neere therevnto likewise adioyninge, is contynuallie indangered and annoyed, by contynuall suppressions of people in theire playe tymes/. Maye it therefore please yo*ur* honor and worshipps (the premisses considered) That you would be pleased to be a meanes to suppresse and put downe this theire newe erectinge Playehowse... [and] to make staie of the proceedinge of theire buildinge vntill his maiestie be informed of the Daielie annoyaunces which come by reason of theire plaies. (*M.S.C.* iv. 60–61.)

These 'Dailie annoyaunces' are the familiar objections to theatres as they are enunciated by puritanically inclined Lon-doners for years. The statement here is more reasonable and per-suasive than those of violent theatre-haters, like John Field or William Prynne, but it has not yet attained the suavity which anti-theatre petitioners of the parish later attained. (See above, vi. 18–19, 24–25.)

It was probably after seeing this petition of the inhabitants of Blackfriars that Sir Edward Coke, an official always unfriendly to players, wrote to the Lord Mayor on the problem of getting round the King's patent:

. . . The place for this Playehowse within your Cittie, is full of Inconvenience, both for the reasons alleadged in your letters, as alsoe for that it is neere his maiesties wardrobe, which in tyme of Infeccion and otherwise maye be dangerous/. They attempted the like neere Sergeantes Inne, [i.e. the attempt complained of in the Privy Council letter to the Lord Mayor of 29 July 1613] but his maiestie beinge informed of the Inconvenience thereof, caused it to be forbidden/. I knowe you and your Bretheren, will give that due reverence, to any thinge that his maiesties pleasure is to passe [i.e. the patent to build the theatre of the preceding 3 June] . . . But for that your Lordshipp was never called to it before it passed, in myne opynion you haue done well to staie it, vntill his Majesties returne, when after his maiestie be truelie informed of the cause, I knowe his pleasure therein shalbe to you all a lawe/ True it is, that there is an act of Councell grounded vppon such reasons, as I perswade my self his maiestie if hee had seene it, would not haue given way to the erectinge of a newe Playehowse in that place/. I praie you send mee a coppie of that which is graunted to them, [i.e. the patent of 3 June 1615] and then you shall heare further from me . . .
13 August./. (M.S.C. iv. 59–60.)

The receipt of Sir Edward's letter in August 1615 probably prompted the Lord Mayor and Aldermen to write their undated letter (presumably of September 1615) to the Privy Council. The position of the Lord Mayor and his brethren was a very delicate one: they were trying to persuade the King's Council to help them secure the cancellation of the King's patent. In their letter they set in order the two theatre proposals and make the old objections of the inhabitants of Blackfriars precinct plus a few new ones:

Our Duties to your Lordshipps most humblie remembred, Whereas in Iulie 1613, vpon our humble Complainte vnto your good Lordshipps, against the buildinge of a Playehowse, intended to be sett vpp in the Whitefriers, by one Rositer and others, It pleased your Lordshipp [sic] for the causes and reasons by vs alleadged, to give order for the staie thereof/. The said Rositer beinge prevented in that place, hath obtained another licence dated in Iune last past vnder the greate Seale of England, And by vertue thereof, haveinge pulled downe a greate messuage at Puddle wharfe, which was sometimes the howse of the Ladie Saunders within the precinct of the Blackfriers,

is nowe erectinge a newe Playehowse in that place/ The Inconveniences that will ensue thereby are soe manie, and of *that* consequence
as wee in our duties, as persons trusted with the governem*ent* of this
Cittie cannot but acquainte your Lordshipps therewith And wee
perswade our selves, yf his Ma*jesty* be informed, thereof it will
please him to revoke those letters Patent*es* of Lycence./. ffor we
finde that these playhowses in the Cittie, doe begett howses for
Tiplinge, and of worse Condition, to neighbo*r* by them, both which
together doe occasion greate numbers of persons to leave theire
honest and painefull course of life, Make Prentizes rob and run from
theire Maisters, and soe become Idle dissolute and dangerous people/
Besides the place wilbe verie inconvenient, for thoughe the common
waie be by Puddle Dock/. yet they haue a passage by ye Blackfriers,
where the kinges plaiers haue a howse already/Soe that by reason
of the contynuall multitude of Coaches, daielie standinge and attendinge at that playhowse divers noblemen and gentlemen of qualitie
which inhabite that place are often indangered in theire passage to
theire howses, and enforced to forsake theire Coaches/And by reason
of the Difficulties and impedimen*tes* in that narrowe passage, many
Broyles haue risen, not with out some perill of Bloodshedd. . . .
Which narrowe passage beinge nowe to be vsed for resorte of people
to both Playehowses, must needes increase that Inconvenience much
more then it was/Moreover this newe buildinge will not onely choake
vpp the Ayre, and the Lightes w*hich* was heeretofore an open place,
but will annoy the stree*tes* which beinge fowle cannot be clensed by
the Inhabitan*tes* from one weekes end to another for the standinge
of Coaches, which must needes be very dangerous and noysome for
infecc*i*on, and soe much the more to be feared and cared for (this
playhowse intended) beinge scituate neere his Maiesties greate ward-
robe/. And it alsoe incloseth the Church there, with Plaiehowses on
both sides/soe as Devine services, Sermons, Christeninges and
Eveninge praiers on the weeke daies (even in the tyme of theire
Plaies) must needes be verie much interrupted and disturbed by the
divers and variable noyses which commonlie proceede from Stage
plaies/.

Maie it therefore please y*our* good Lordshipps, my self and my
Bretheren restinge in some doubt what to doe in this matter, and the
parties (thoughe menn of meane qualitie) pressinge vs with his
maiesties Letters Patent*es* which wee acknowledge in thinges of the
smallest moment wee are bounde most dutifullie to obey; . . . Wee
haue humblie desired, that your L*ordshipps* will please to acquainte
his maiestie with the same, and that wee maie receave his maiesties
pleasure, and y*our* honors Direcc*i*ons for staie thereof, the patentees
proceedinge w*ith* speede in the erecc*i*on of that howse. . . . (*M.S.C.*
iv. 61–63.)

The Mayor and Aldermen are very clever in the presentation of
their case: they eschew entirely the Puritan cant about the

Devil's Chapels and wicked plays, and they confine themselves to the presentation of unquestionable civic problems. The emphasis on the annoyance to noblemen and gentlemen and on the danger to the King are well conceived for the Privy Council; so is the deference to the King and the humble plea for the Council's help. The hint that Rosseter and Kingman are waving the royal patent in the faces of the Aldermen and implying the disloyalty of their objections is probably not without foundation, for players are known to have employed similar tactics with town officials in the provinces, and the statement that the patentees are building 'with speede' suggests the desperation of both parties.

In response to this plea the Privy Council took action at its meeting of 26 September 1615:

> Whereas Complaint was made to this Boarde by the Lord Mayor and Aldermen of the Cittie of London That one Rosseter, and others havinge obtayned lycense vnder the great Seale of Englande for the buildinge of a Play house haue pulled downe a great Messuage in Puddle wharfe . . . are nowe erectinge a Newe Playhouse in that place . . . Their Lordshipps thought fitt to send for Rosseter to bringe in his Letters Patentes, which beinge seene, and pervsed by the Lo: Chiefe Iustice of England [Sir Edward Coke] . . . And that the Lo: Chiefe Iustice did deliver to their Lordshipps. That the Lycence graunted to the said Rosseter did extende to the buildinge of a Playhouse without the liberties of London, and not within the Cittie. It was this day ordreed by their Lordshipps. That there shalbe noe Play house erected in that place, And that the Lo Mayor of London shall straitly prohibit, and forbidd the said Rosseter and the rest of the Patentees, and their workemen to proceede in the makeinge, and convertinge the said Buildinge into a Play house; And if any of the Patentees or their workemen shall proceede in their intended buildinge contrary to this their Lordshipps Inhibicion, that then the Lord Mayor shall committ him or them soe offendinge, vnto Prison and certefie their Lordshipps of their contempt in that behalfe. . . . (M.S.C. i. 372–4.)

This action was, of course, just what the city fathers wanted, and they made no delay in their execution of the Council's welcome order. Two days after the sitting of the Privy Council the Court of Aldermen recorded payment for action: 'Item it is ordered by this Court that Mr Chamberlen shall pay vnto Mr Dyos the Citties Remembrancer the somme of iiili xvijs vjd by him disbursed about the restraint of building of the playhouse at puddle wharfe as by his bill of particulars allowed heere in Court may appeare.' (M.S.C. ii. 320.)

The victory of the City and Blackfriars precinct in their attempt to suppress the new theatre would seem to have been complete. Surely Rosseter and his backers would now abandon their project. But no; the next year the city fathers reported that he was active again. A letter of the Lord Mayor on 21 August 1616 is entered in the Tabula for the Remembrancia as: 'To my Lord Chamberlen to acquaint his maiestie with the order of the Lordes against the erectinge of the playehowse at puddlewharff, yf in case (as it is suspected) the parties should revive theire suite in the [Exchequer] [during the?] kinges progresse./' The letter itself reads:

May it please your good Lordshipp, whereas my self and my bretheren the Aldermen in September last, made complaynt . . . against the erectinge of a Playehowse, intended by one Roseter and others at puddle wharfe . . . wherevpon it pleased theire Lordshipps . . . to sett downe an order . . . to prohibite and forbidd the said Roseter and his workemenn to proceede in the buildinge thereof, Your Lordshipp maie please to be advertised, that as I am informed, the said Roseter and his partners, doe intend to revive theire suite to his maiestie that they maie proceede in the buildinge of the said playehowse, whereof I thought it my duetie to informe your Lordshipp, And humblie to praie that your Lordshipp will vouchsafe to acquaint his Majesty with the Order of the Lordes, and to be a meanes to his maiestie, that the said Roseter and his partners, maie not prevaile to haue theire purpose in a thinge held soe vnfitt by theire Lordshipps/ . . .   xxj°. August 1616. (M.S.C. iv. 64–65.)

Rosseter must have had influential backing if he intended to proceed in spite of the combined opposition of the Privy Council and the City corporation. One might suspect that the rumour reported by the Lord Mayor was false, but it was not, for it was confirmed in a letter from the Privy Council to the Lord Mayor five months later, at the sitting of 27 January 1616/17:

. . . Whereas his Majestie is informed that notwithstanding diverse Commaundementes and prohibicions to the contrary there bee certaine persons that goe about to sett vp a Play howse in the Blacke ffryars neere vnto his Majestys Wardrobe, and for that purpose have lately erected and made fitt a Building, which is allmost if not fully finished, You shall vnderstand that his Majesty hath this day expressly signifyed his pleasure, that the same shalbee pulled downe, so as it bee made vnfitt for any such vse, whereof wee Require your Lordshipps to take notice, and to cause it to bee performed accordingly with all speede, and therevpon to certify vs of your proceedinges. (M.S.C. i. 374.)

This letter of 27 January 1616/17 is the last in the correspondence of the Privy Council and the Lord Mayor about the Puddle

Wharf theatre; even a man like Rosseter must have ceased to struggle after this.

All the records cited speak of Porters' Hall or the Puddle Wharf theatre as a projected playhouse under construction; no one says that it had been used for performances. Yet two title-pages assert that plays had been acted in the new theatre. The clearest is the title-page of the first (1618) edition of Nathan Field's *Amends for Ladies*: 'As it was acted at the *Blacke-Fryers*, both by the Princes Seruants, and the Lady Elizabeths.' The Blackfriars mentioned cannot be the private theatre of the King's men, for neither company mentioned ever acted there. These companies were, however, two of the three for which Philip Rosseter planned his theatre, as the patent of 3 June 1615 shows. 'Blacke-Fryers' must, therefore, mean that *Amends for Ladies* had been acted at the third Blackfriars or Porters' Hall.

The other play whose publisher asserts that it was acted at Rosseter's new playhouse is Beaumont and Fletcher's *The Scornful Lady*. The title-page of the first (1616) edition says: 'As it was Acted (with great applause) by *the Children of Her Maiesties Reuels* in the *Blacke Fryers*.' This company was the third of the three mentioned in Rosseter's patent for the theatre. Performances of the play must have taken place during or after 1613, for there is a clear reference in the text to the negotiations for a Spanish match, and before 19 March 1615/16 when the play was entered in the Stationers' Register. Since the more familiar Blackfriars was in the exclusive possession of the King's men in these years, the theatre referred to on the title-page must have been the third Blackfriars.

Perhaps these performances and others—for it would be too much to assume that all plays acted at Porters' Hall got into print—took place in an unfinished building. All the correspondence refers to the theatre as under construction, though the letter of 27 January 1616/17 says that the building is 'allmost if not fully finished'. In any case production would have been possible while galleries were unfinished and decoration not even begun.

Such production surely cannot have continued for long in the face of the determined and powerful opposition. The later existence of the theatre is sometimes postulated from a remark in a letter of Edward Alleyn to his father-in-law, John Donne, concerning the unfriendly conduct of Donne and the marriage settlement of Alleyn's wife, Donne's daughter. Listing his property Alleyn says: 'I then towld you all my Land*es* wear stated on y*e* Coll: [i.e. Dulwich College] 3 Leases/I had one off them wase giuen to y*e*

Coll: ye other 2 being ye manor/& recktory off Lewsham worth 130^l a year & diuers tenement*es* in y^e/black fryars *as the plaiehowse theare* worth 120^l ye year boath wch cost me 2500^l . . ..' (*R.E.S.* vi [1955], 367.) The words in italics have been inserted between the lines in a disguised modern hand. Presumably this and other insertions about Blackfriars theatre in the manuscript of Alleyn's diary are forgeries by John Payne Collier, who wanted to make Alleyn Shakespeare's successor in his shares in the King's men's Blackfriars. (See Warner, *Catalogue of the Manuscripts . . . at Dulwich* [1881], p. 115.) Now and then the forgeries are still included in transcripts as if they were genuine.

Alleyn's accounts and letter do show that he held Blackfriars property for at least ten years before his death, but they show nothing about Porters' Hall theatre, though that building or its foundations or its successor must have been part of his estate.

It is pleasant to know that Bernard Miles's Mermaid Theatre has now revived the drama at Puddle Wharf. Probably his theatre has presented more performances than the original one ever did, and certainly his enterprise has had far greater approval from the City of London than Rosseter's ever had.

ST. PAUL'S

Adams, pp. 111–18.

The obscure private theatre in the precincts of St. Paul's Cathedral has never been precisely located. Acting there seems to have been sporadic, and there are no records of any performances after 1606.

THE SALISBURY COURT

Adams, pp. 368–83.

Bentley, G. E., 'Randolph's *Praeludium* and the Salisbury Court Theatre', *Joseph Quincy Adams Memorial Studies* (1948), pp. 775–83.

Bordinat, Philip, 'A Study of the Salisbury Court Theatre,' MS. Thesis, University of Birmingham (1952).

—— 'A New Site for the Salisbury Court Theatre', *Notes & Queries*, New Series iii, vol. 201 (1956), 51–52.

Cunningham, Peter, 'The Whitefriars Theatre, the Salisbury Court Theatre, and the Duke's Theatre in Dorset Gardens', *Shakespeare Society's Papers*, iv (1849), 89–109.

Hotson, *passim*.

Parry, John Jay, ed., *The Poems and Amyntas of Thomas Randolph* (1917), pp. 226–31 and 370–1.

Rollins, Hyder E., 'A Contribution to the History of the English Commonwealth Drama', *Studies in Philology*, xviii (1921), 267–333; also xx (1923), 52–69.

Rosenfeld, Sybil, 'Unpublished Stage Documents', *Theatre Notebook*, xi (1956–57), 92–96.

Smith, G. C. Moore, *William Hemminge's Elegy on Randolph's Finger Containing the Well-Known Lines 'On the Time-Poets'* (1923).

The Salisbury Court was the last theatre built in London before the wars: the lease of the ground and of the buildings to be re-modelled was not signed until 6 July 1629, and the first perform-ance in the new house probably took place in November 1630.

There was London gossip about the preliminary arrangements for the new theatre in the autumn of 1629. On 24 October 1629 Sir George Gresley wrote from Essex House to Sir Thomas Puckering:

> My Lord of Dorset is become a great husband; for he hath let his house in Salisbury Court unto the queen for the Ambassador Leiger of France, which is daily expected to come over, to lie in, and giveth for it £350 by the year, and for the rest of his stables and outhouses towards the water side, he hath let for £1000 fine and £100 by the year rent, unto the master of the revels, to make a playhouse for the children of the revels. (R. F. Williams, ed., *The Court and Times of Charles I*, ii. 35.)

Other documents concerning the preliminary arrangements for the theatre roughly confirm Gresley's gossip. The most explicit state-ment about the acquisition of property for the theatre was set out on 2 July 1667 by Edward Fisher and Thomas Silver in a petition which recapitulated the early history of the Salisbury Court enterprise.

> Whereas, the said Edward Fisher and Thomas Silver exhibited their petition into this Court, thereby setting forth that the Right Honble Edward, late Earl of Dorset, and his Trustees, by Indenture dated the sixth day of July, [1629] in the fifth year of the reign of the late King Charles the First, in consideration that Richard Gunnell and William Blagrave should at their costs and charges erect a playhouse and other buildings at the lower end of Salisbury Court, in the parish of St. Bridget, in the ward of Farringdon Without, did demise to the said Gunnell and Blagrave a piece of ground at the same lower end

of Salisbury Court, containing one hundred and forty foot in length, and forty-two in breadth, To hold to the said Gunnell and Blagrave, their executors and assigns, from thenceforth for forty-one years and a half, paying therefore to the said Trustees, or the survivors of them, twenty and five pounds for the first half year, and one hundred pounds per annum for the remainder of the term, by quarterly payments; That the said late Earl and his Trustees, by indenture dated the fifteenth day of the said July, [1629] in the said fifth year of the same late King, in consideration of nine hundred and fifty pounds paid to the said late Earl by John Herne, of Lincoln's Inn, Esquire, did demise to him the said piece of ground and building thereupon to be erected, and the rent reserved upon the said lease made to Gunnell and Blagrave, To hold to the said John Herne, or his assigns, from the eighth day of the said July, for sixty and one years, at the yearly rent of a peppercorn. . . . (*Shakespeare Society's Papers*, iv. 102–3, from B.M. Additional MS. 5064, fol. 225.)

The indenture to Herne, mentioned in the Fisher and Silver petition, was found by Peter Cunningham and printed by him. This document gives more precise limits for the property which Gunnell and Blagrave leased for their theatre:

. . . All that soyle and grounde whereupon the Barne, at the lower end of the great Backe Court or yard of Salisbury Court now stands, and soemuch of the soyle whereupon the whole south end of the great stable in the said court or yard stands, or conteynes from that end of that stable towards the north end thereof, Sixteene foote of Assize and the whole breadth of the said stable, and all the grounde and soyle on the east and west side of that stable lyeing directly against the said Sixteene foote of grounde at the south end thereof, betweene the wall of the great Garden belonginge to the Mansion called Dorsett house and the wall that severs the said Court from the lane called Water lane, And all the grounde and soyle beinge betweene the said walles on the east and west parte thereof, and the said Barne, stable, and grounde, on both sides the same on the south and north parts thereof, wch said seu'all p'cells of soyle and ground therein before menconed to bee demised conteyne, in the whole in length, from the Brickwall of the said Garden, att the east thereof, to the said wall dividinge the said Court or yard from the said Lane called Water lane at the West One hundred and fforty foote of Assize; and in breadth, from the outside of the said Barne towards the south into the said stables and grounde, on both sides thereof towards the north, fforty and two foote of Assize, and lyes together att the lower end of the said Court . . . Together w^th . . . free ingresse, egresse, and regresse, for the said John Herne . . . there comonly nowe used, or w^ch, att anie tyme hereafter, shalbee made or comonly used dureinge the terme thereby granted as were together, wth the demised and

bargained p'misses unto *Richard Gunnel and Will'm Blagrove* . . .
dated the *sixt daye of this instant July* . . . *To have and to hould* the
same for the terme of *Threescore and One yeares* from the *eight* daye
of July last past, under the rent of a peppercorne. . . . (Ibid., 91–95.)

Herne agreed that, if the Earl on 16 July 1634 paid him £950
with interest, he would surrender the property. Dorset's agreement made over the rents and reversion of the property, and in
effect made John Herne the landlord of the theatre so long as
Dorset's debt of £950 remained unpaid.

The information given in the suit and the indenture is clear
enough so far as it goes: on 6 July 1629 Blagrave and Gunnell
leased from the Earl of Dorset for forty-one and a half years a
piece of ground at the lower end of Salisbury Court containing
140 feet from east to west by 42 feet from north to south, which
contained a barn and part of a stable. The ground abutted on
Water Lane on the west and on the wall of the garden of Dorset
House on the east.[1] For this plot and the buildings Blagrave and
Gunnell agreed to pay £25 rent for the first year and £100 for
each subsequent year, and to erect a theatre and other buildings
on the site. Other documents show a little of what they did in
preparing their theatre.

A petition of the late 1650's by the heirs and assignees of Gunnell and Blagrave says that they converted the barn to a playhouse at a cost of £1,200:

To the Right Hon[ble]: the Earle of Dorsett. The humble peticon of
Elizabeth Heton William Wintersall and Mary Young now the wife of
William Jones, &c.

Sheweth

That yo[r]: peticone[rs] about 30 yeares last past did by S[r]. Henry
Herbert interest in yo[r]. hono[rs] late Father take a lease from him of an
ould barne standing in Salisbury Court which barne they were tyed
by Covenants to lay out uppon 800[li] for Converting the same into a
playhouse and to pay for the same play house y[e] rent of 100[li] p[r]
annu' for the full terme of 41 yeares w[ch] was duly paid to yo[r] late
Father untill the proffitts & priviledges of the said house were
absolutely taken from yo[r] pet[rs] and they made uncapable of Continuing the said payment.

---

[1] Bordinat's article 'A New Site for the Salisbury Court Theatre' shows
that the plaque now exhibited in Salisbury Square to mark the site of the
theatre is in the wrong place. He argues convincingly for a location a little
to the south-west and abutting on Water Lane. This is approximately the
site shown in the map in Adams, p. 371.

That your peticon[rs] expending neare the sum of 1200[li] in building & finishing the said play house and have paid neare three hundred pounds since theire house was taken from them.

May it therefore please yo[r] hono[r] to Consider both the losses and Sufferings of yo[r] pet[rs], and graciously to Continue unto them the terme of yeares yett unexpired in theire said lease they paying the said rent of 100[li] a yeare from the time of theire Entire [sic] into quiet possession and giveing good Security for payment thereof.

And yo[r] pet[rs] shall ever pray &c.

Elizabeth Heton
William Wintersall
William Jones.[1]

This petition shows that the Salisbury Court theatre was indeed the barn converted, that the petitioners' estimates of the costs were £1,200, and that £300 had been expended on the place since the closing of the theatres.

Also interesting is the petitioners' statement that Gunnell and Blagrave had secured their lease from the Earl 'by S[r] Henry Herbert interest in yo[r] hono[rs] late Father'. Gresley had heard that the lease was made to Herbert, and the connexion of the Master of the Revels with the theatre must also have been recorded in his Office Book, which was the basis of the statement of Edmond Malone that in December 1631 '. . . Sir Henry Herbert received on account of the six representations [of Marmion's *Holland's Leaguer*] but *one pound nineteen shillings*, in virtue of the *ninth* share which he possessed as one of the proprietors of that house'. (*Variorum*, iii. 178.)[2]

---

[1] Printed by Sybil Rosenfeld, loc. cit. The petition is now among the Sackville papers deposited in the Kent Archives Office at Maidstone— U269 E 136/1. Miss Rosenfeld points out that though the petition is undated, it must have been prepared after the death of Edward, Earl of Dorset, on 17 July 1652, and before acting was renewed at the theatre under Beeston in 1660.

[2] Professor J. Q. Adams thought that Malone had misinterpreted what he saw in the Office Book and that Herbert was not 'one of the proprietors of that house', but merely the recipient of some sort of annual gratuity. (*Herbert*, p. 45.) In support of his position Adams cited the document Herbert prepared in December 1660 for his case against Killigrew: 'To proue a share payd by the Fortune Plaiers and a share by the Bull Plaiers and a share by Salsbery Court Players' (Halliwell-Phillipps, *A Collection of Ancient Documents* . . ., p. 27); and the similar document concerning his former fees, prepared two years later: 'For a share from each company of four companyes of players (besides the late Kinges Company) valued at 100*l* a yeare, one yeare with another, besides the usuall fees, by the yeare . . . 400.00.00' (*Variorum*, iii. 266). Adams's implication was that the 'shares'

Another fact or two about the Salisbury Court enterprise can be gleaned from the early history of the theatre given in a Bill of William Beeston against the Earl of Dorset on 25 June 1658: '. . . the said Gunnell and Blagrave by the consent of the said Edward Earl of Dorset did erect and build vpon the said p^rmisses one dwelling house and playhouse wherein Plays & Interludes were vsually Acted. The building whereof cost the said Gunnell and Blagrave the sum of one Thousand pounds. . . .'[1] Though Beeston differs somewhat from the Gunnell and Blagrave heirs in his estimate of the sum spent, both were using round figures, and the heirs perhaps had the stronger motive for exaggeration. The new fact which Beeston records is that a new house as well as a new theatre was erected by Gunnell and Blagrave. Later documents show that this house was connected with the playhouse and may have been in part over the stage. The house was probably occupied by Gunnell as manager of the theatre.

One or two more facts about the physical features of the playhouse built by Gunnell and Blagrave were noted by Leslie Hotson, who discovered the papers of a suit concerning alterations of the building in 1660. (*Commonwealth and Restoration Stage*, pp. 107–13.) By this time William Beeston, who had managed the Phoenix before the closing of 1642, had precarious control of the Salisbury Court and employed the carpenters Edward Fisher and Thomas Silver to repair, alter, and enlarge the decayed and mutilated theatre. In 1666 there was a suit about the character of the repairs and alterations and the payment for them. In their answer to Beeston, Fisher and Silver say that they agreed on 5 April 1660 to repair and amend the 'messuage Tennemon^ts and playhouse of the said Comp^lt in or neare Salisbury Cort in ye p ish of St Brides als Brigitt aforesaid the walls thereof whereof [*sic*] were then already built or almost built wth brick . . .'. (P.R.O. C 10/80/15.)

This is a clear enough indication that the walls of the Caroline playhouse were brick, but other items in the agreement are less clear; they might refer to the new building to be done for the

mentioned were not proper proprietor's shares but some sort of extra fee or gratuity paid to an official.

Nevertheless I am inclined to accept Malone's conclusion that Sir Henry Herbert's share was like Blagrave's or Gunnell's and he was indeed 'one of the proprietors of that house'. Malone saw among the Herbert papers documents and accounts which he often used for generalizations, but did not quote. Besides, both Gresley's letter and the petition of Heton, Wintersall, and Jones attest Sir Henry's peculiar association with the Salisbury Court.

[1] P.R.O. C 10/53/7. The suit was found by Leslie Hotson.

reconstructed theatre or they might refer simply to alterations of the existing parts of the old theatre. Of this sort are the several references to 'the tymber belonging to the private house & over the stage' and 'the timber belonging to the dwelling house and over the stage'. Were the apartments of the manager built over the stage in the original building of 1629, or was this a new construction made by Fisher and Silver in 1660?

A little more revealing is Beeston's statement in his complaint of 8 May 1666. He says that Fisher and Silver agreed that they would

within the space of half a yeare or thereabouts therafter build and erect on the said theatre or stage a large Roome or Chamber for a danceing school of forty foote square which was to bee done with good sufficient & substantiall tymber and should allsoe well and substantially and firmly repaire and amend the said Theatre and the seates and boxes and vejwing roomes thereto belonging and should allsoe raise the roofe of the said howse thirty foote higher then it was . . . (P.R.O. C 10/80/15.)

We could have assumed seats, boxes, and viewing rooms in the theatre of 1629, but the agreement to erect a 40 feet by 40 feet chamber over the theatre or stage must give us one dimension of the original playhouse—a width of 40 feet, or 6 feet less than the width of the second Blackfriars. This square chamber above also implies that the theatre below was square or rectangular.[1]

This suit gives us no evidence of the other dimensions of the Caroline Salisbury Court playhouse, but literary references speak of it as small, implying that it had fewer accommodations than the Phoenix or Blackfriars. In the epilogue to Thomas Nabbes's

---

[1] It has been thought that the prologue to Shakerley Marmion's *A Fine Companion*, acted at the Salisbury Court in 1632 or early 1633 (see above, iv. 742–5), implies that the auditorium was round:

> In that you wrong th' approved judgments of
> This noble Auditory, who like a Spheare
> Mooved by a strong Intelligence, sit round
> To crowne our Infant Muse, whose cælestiall
> Applause, shee heard at her first entrance.

The diction of these lines, 'noble', 'Spheare mooved by a strong Intelligence', 'cælestiall', now seems to me inappropriate for a commercial theatre but suitable for the court. Since the title-page says that *A Fine Companion* was acted 'before the King and Queene at White-Hall' is it not likely that this is the court prologue and the references are to the King and court in the octagonal Cockpit-in-Court?

Tottenham Court, whose title-page records that it was 'Acted in the Yeare MDCXXXIII. At the private House in *Salisbury-Court'*, the Hostess refers to the small house and the struggling troupe:

> *If I winne*
> *Your kinde commends, 'twill bring more* custome *in.*
> *When others fill'd* Roomes *with neglect disdaine yee;*
> *My little* House *(with thanks) shall entertaine yee.*
> *And if such* Guests *would dayly make it shine,*
> *Our* POET *should no more drinke* Ale, *but* Wine.

The inferior size is again referred to in the first lines of the pro-logue of Lewis Sharpe's *The Noble Stranger*, acted at Salisbury Court, probably between 1638 and 1640 (see above, v. 1051-2):

> *Blest Fate protect me! what a lustre's here?*
> *How many Starres deck this our little spheare?*

It seems likely that inferior size is also implied in Edmond Malone's previously noted comment on Sir Henry Herbert's receipts from the theatre: 'Sir Henry Herbert received on account of the six representations [of *Holland's Leaguer*] but *one pound nineteen shillings*, in virtue of the *ninth* share which he possessed as one of the proprietors of that house.' These figures indicate that the total return to all housekeepers for six performances must have been £17. 11s. When one recalls that a *single* performance of a revived play at Blackfriars had brought the housekeepers £17. 10s. in 1628; £9. 16s. in 1629; £12. 4s. in 1630; £13 in 1631; and £15 in 1632 (*Variorum*, iii. 176-7), it is evident that the paid admissions at Salisbury Court can have been only a fraction of those at Blackfriars.

The inferior size of the Salisbury Court is denied by James Wright, who, in 1699, said of Blackfriars, the Phoenix, and the Salisbury Court, that 'they were all three Built almost exactly alike, for Form and Bigness'. (See above, ii. 694.) I can only say that such evidence as I can find seems to contradict him.

The builders of the Salisbury Court theatre, so frequently named in the documents about it, Richard Gunnell and William Blagrave, were men of a good deal of theatrical experience. Richard Gunnell was already a mature enough actor to be one of the patented members of the Palsgrave's company in January 1612/13. He was one of the housekeepers of both the old and the new Fortune; he wrote at least three plays for the company; and he appears to have been manager at the Fortune in the 1620's. (See above, iv. 516-18.) Gunnell had far more acting experience than

Blagrave, and he probably served as manager at the new theatre. Such a function is strongly suggested by Thomas Crosfield's record of what the wardrobe keeper at the Salisbury Court told him about the organization in 1634, 'The cheife whereof are 1. Mr. Gunnell a Papist'. (See below.) As manager he probably lived in the house connected with the theatre which William Beeston said had been part of the construction work in 1629. Gunnell certainly moved from the parish of the Fortune theatre, where at least eleven members of his household had been christened or buried from 1613 to 1631, to Whitefriars. In the parish registers of nearby St. Bride's, Fleet Street, is the record of the burial of 'Elizabeth daughter to Rychard Gunnell' on 23 January 1632/3. On 7 October 1634 in the same register is the entry for his own burial: 'Whitefriars. Mr Gunnell ye Player in Salsburie court'.[1]

Gunnell's partner William Blagrave, though inexperienced, so far as we know, in acting and management, had the very great advantage of an official position in the entertainment world. He was deputy to Sir Henry Herbert, Master of the Revels, and was continuously engaged with theatres and companies and court performances, even licensing plays now and then in Sir Henry's stead. (See above, ii. 380–1.) When he was paid in January 1634/5 for plays acted at court by the company from Salisbury Court, he was receiving money for performances which his own office had ordered. The combination of Gunnell's experience and Blagrave's influence promised well for the new theatre.

The company assembled by Blagrave and Gunnell for their new house was a troupe called the King's Revels, or the Children of the Revels.[2] The company opened at the new theatre and played there a year or so before moving on.

There is no direct evidence as to the opening of the new Salisbury Court theatre, and it has been surmised that the King's Revels company began playing there late in 1629 or early in 1630. The evidence suggests to me now, however, that the opening was not until November 1630. Eight or nine months is not an unduly long period for the transformation of a barn into a private theatre, even without complications, and if the builders

[1] From the burial registers of St. Bride's, Fleet Street, deposited in the Guildhall Library, MS. 6538.

[2] The company was not made up wholly of boys, like the old choir troupes, but of some combination with more boys than usual, probably like Beeston's Boys (the King and Queen's young company) of a decade later. It may have been formed for the new playhouse, but it seems more likely that it was already in existence when the leases were signed in July 1629. (See above, i. 283–91.)

took so long the opening would have been delayed until November 1630, for all London theatres were closed in that year from 17 April until 12 November. (See above, ii. 657–8.)

As to the date of the opening of the new theatre, two references by William Prynne offer an interesting suggestion. In the dedication to his *Histriomastix*, 1633, he mentioned '*two olde Play-houses* being also lately reedified, enlarged, and one *new Theatre* erected' [White Friers Playhouse]. (*Histriomastix*, *₃ᵛ.) White Friars was, of course, the district of the new Salisbury Court theatre, and the name is used for the new playhouse elsewhere. Later in his treatise Prynne refers again to the new house:

> The grand Objection of our present dissolute times for the justification of these Playes is this; (*y*) That none but a companie of Puritans and Precisians speake against them; all else applaud and eke frequent them; therefore certainly they are very good recreations, since none but Puritans disaffect them.
>
> (*y*) This Obiection as I have heard was much urged in a most scurrilous and prophane manner in the first Play that was acted in the New-erected Play-house: a fit consecration Sermon for that Divels Chappell. (*Histriomastix*, Iiiii₃.)

Though one can never be positive about such vague identifications, Prynne's comments are very apt for Thomas Randolph's *The Muses' Looking Glass, or The Entertainment*. (See above, v. 986–9.) That play explicitly demonstrates that objectors to plays are 'Puritans and Precisians' in a fashion which Prynne would have found 'scurrilous and prophane'. At the opening there enter 'Bird *a Featherman, and* Mʳˢ Flowrdew *wife to a Haberdasher of small wares; the one having brought feathers to the Play-house, the other Pins and Looking-glasses; two of the sanctified fraternity of* Black-friers.'[1] They mount the stage and comment on the audience, 'the lew'd Reprobate', and Bird remarks on the new playhouse:

> Sister, were there not before Innes,
> Yes I will say Inns, for my zeale bids me
> Say filthy Innes, enough to harbour such
> As travell'd to destruction the broad way;
> But they build more and more, more shops of Satan.

[1] The selection of characters and occupations is apt for the neighbourhood of the Salisbury Court theatre. The districts of Whitefriars and Blackfriars were known as Puritan centres, and the Puritans of these districts were more than once ridiculed for trading in the vanities of dress they deplored. The registers of St. Bride's, Fleet Street, the parish of the Salisbury Court, list burials for a 'featherdresser' and for a 'haberdasher of small wares'.

Mrs. Flowerdew replies:

> Had we seen a Church,
> A new built Church erected North and South,
> It had been something worth the wondring at.

After these comments on the new theatre Mr. Bird and Mrs. Flowerdew remain on stage throughout the action, often making observations in Puritan cant, but gradually being converted to a recognition of the salutary nature of what they see. At the end of the play the two members of *'the sanctified fraternity of* Blackfriers' admit their conversion in a fashion which must have been most enraging to Prynne and to their fellow Puritans:

> *Flow*[erdew]. . . . Most blessed Looking-glasse
> That didst instruct my blinded eyes today,
> I might have gone to hell the Narrow-way!
> *Bird.* Hereafter I will visit Comedies,
> And see them oft, they are good exercises!
>
> (1638 edition, M₃ᵛ.)

William Prynne was not alone in noting the offensiveness to the Puritans of Randolph's play for the new Salisbury Court; another contemporary pointed out their indignation toward Randolph. William Heminges, son of the long-time financial manager of the King's company, wrote a rambling mock elegy making comments on a number of Caroline dramatists. This piece, never printed until the twentieth century, is called 'Heminge's Elegy on Randolph's Finger'. It was written about 1630–2, and it contains, among other remarks on Randolph, these assertions of the Puritans' animus against him for what he had written at Cambridge and had composed more recently for boy players. They

> wisht the man weare slayne:
> such was thayr Charritye cause his sarsnett hood
> so vilye wrote a gaynst the Brotherhood,
> And wᶜʰ was worse that lately he did pen
> vyle thinges for pigmeyes [boy actors] gaynst the
>   Sonns of men,
> The Righteous man and the regenerate
> being laught to scorne thare by the reprobate.
> 'brother, sayd on, you spurr youʳ Zeale to slow
> to checke att thes thinges when the learned knowe
> Thes arre but scarrs: the woundes dothe deeper lye:
> Who knowes but hee wrightes to a Monastarye [Whitefriars?]
> and those whome wee call players may In tyme
> Luther abuse and fence for Bellermyne?

The Pope has Iuglinge trickes and can vse slightes
to Conuerte Players Into Iesuittes.

                    (G. C. Moore Smith, ed., lines 192–206.)

Now if Randolph's anti-Puritan play, *The Muses' Looking Glass*, was indeed the play presented at the opening of the new Salisbury Court theatre, we can date that opening in November 1630. Edmond Malone never printed a transcription of the licence for the play from Sir Henry Herbert's Office Book, but he did record it twice in his annotations in the books in his library, as W. J. Lawrence discovered (*T.L.S.* 29 November 1923, p. 820). In his Langbaine, Malone wrote:

> *The Muses' Looking Glass* was not printed till 1638 (at Oxford by Leonard Lichfield and Francis Bowman), and the titlepage has only 'by T. R.,' without any preface or mention of the theatre where it was acted. But it was acted by the Children of the Revels under the title of the Entertainment in the summer of 1630 and licensed by Sir Henry Herbert, November 25, 1630.

And the gist of this information he repeated in another note on the title-page of his copy of the play.

The question immediately arises, why should a play acted in the summer of 1630 have remained unlicensed until November? A likely answer would be that the play was never acted in London until November, but had been performed in the summer on the road, when all London theatres were closed; when it was brought to London it was duly licensed for performance and became 'the first Play that was acted in the New-erected Play-house'.

It may be that we can identify another feature of the opening at Salisbury Court after the plague of 1630. In B.M. Add. MS. 37425 is a poem called 'Praeludium' (misread 'Prologue' by J. J. Parry, ed. cit.) endorsed in the hand of Edward Hyde, later Earl of Clarendon, 'T. Randall after ye last Plague'. The piece is a dialogue between *Histrio* and *Gentleman* about the hard time the players have had during the recent plague, which covered a period longer than June to October. The allusions in the dialogue fit the year 1630 (see Bentley, 'Randolph's *Praeludium* and the Salisbury Court Theatre') and no other plague closing in Randolph's maturity. It may be that this rather unusual curtain-raiser was prepared by Randolph for the opening of the Salisbury Court after the plague. It contains, however, none of the expected allusions to the newness of the theatre or the company, and I have now some misgivings about its presentation as part of the opening bill.

Though the *Praeludium* mentions no theatre, one would expect Randolph to have prepared it for the King's Revels company. These associations of Randolph with the Salisbury Court theatre (his *Amyntas* was licensed for performance there the day after *The Muses' Looking Glass*) appear to have constituted regular employment by the house. (See Bentley, op. cit.) It is possible that he was working under contract for Gunnell and Blagrave. This conjecture is not so radical as it may seem, for a number of his theatrical allusions show a conversancy with theatre affairs, and Richard Brome is known to have had such a contract with the management of the Salisbury Court a few years after Randolph's death. (See above, iii. 52–54.) Such a formal arrangement would presumably have been part of the preparations of Gunnell and Blagrave in the autumn of 1629 for the opening of the King's Revels company at their new theatre.

In or just before December 1631, for reasons unknown, the King's Revels company was replaced at Salisbury Court by Prince Charles's (II) company, a new troupe, of which the popular clown, Andrew Cane, a former associate of Richard Gunnell, was the leader. (See above, ii. 398–401.) The company is not known before it appears in Whitefriars; indeed, Richard Heton, the successor of Gunnell and Blagrave at Salisbury Court, implies that they had been newly organized there. About 1639 he wrote: 'And wheras my lo: of Dorsett had gotten for a former Company at Salisberry Co't the Princes service . . .'. (See above, ii. 684.) His assertion has some probability, since the Earl had a good deal of influence at court and some interest in the prosperity of the theatre, and since his wife had recently been appointed 'governess' to the young prince.

In spite of its promising auspices, the new troupe was never a very successful one. One of the first plays—perhaps the very first—they acted at Salisbury Court was Shakerley Marmion's *Holland's Leaguer*, and we have already seen that the housekeepers of the theatre received only £17. 11s. as their share of the takings for six consecutive performances, no more than the housekeepers at Blackfriars sometimes shared from a single performance of an old revived play. And the prologue and epilogue of Shirley's *The Changes* emphasize the struggles of the troupe (see above, i. 305–6), the former even going so far as to say

> *Wee have no name, a torrent overflowes*
> *Our little Iland, miserable wee,*
> *Doe every day play our owne Tragedy.*

How long Prince Charles's men remained at the theatre is unknown, but before July 1634 they had been replaced by the return of the King's Revels company. (See below.) It is not clear which of the two companies occupied the theatre when the management got into trouble over a lost anonymous play, *The City Shuffler*. (See above, v. 1309–10.) The incident is known only from the extract Malone copied from Sir Henry Herbert's Office Book as an example of censorship on the application of an individual.

Octob. 1633. Exception was taken by Mr. Sewster to the second part of The Citty Shuffler, which gave me occasion to stay the play, till the company [of Salisbury Court; Malone's addition] had given him satisfaction; which was done the next day, and under his hande he did certifye mee that he was satisfyed. *MS. Herbert.* (*Variorum*, iii. 172.)

Since the play is lost, one can only guess what it was and what offended Mr. Sewster. Both the title and the complaint would fit a satirical London comedy; the certified satisfaction of Mr. Sewster suggests an expurgation like that of Ben Jonson's *Tale of a Tub* at the complaint of Inigo Jones five months before.

A playhouse event more sensational than the staying of *The City Shuffler* is hinted at a few months later. The Burial Registers of the nearby parish church of St. Bride's, Fleet Street, contain, under date of 27 March 1634, the laconic entry: 'George Wilson kild at ye play house in salesburie court'. (Guildhall MS. 6538.) Was it a stage accident like that at the Red Bull, in which the actor Richard Baxter stabbed an apprentice named Gill in the spring of 1622? Was it a riot like that at the Phoenix on Shrove Tuesday 1616/17, or the one at the Fortune in May 1626? Since no other allusion to the event is known, it may have been simply a street accident which the parish clerk was recording, but his most unusual particularity suggests more.

Later in 1634 the Salisbury Court company was on tour, and when they visited Oxford in July their wardrobe keeper, Richard Kendall, told a good deal about the company—and a little about other London companies—to Thomas Crosfield, Fellow of The Queen's College. Crosfield has in his diary a sentence or two about each of the four other London companies, and then notes:

5. The Company of Salisbury Court at ye further end of fleet street against ye Conduit: The chiefe whereof are 1. Mr. Gunnell a Papist. 2. Mr. John Yongue. 3. Edward Gibbs a fencer. 4. Timothy

Withdrawn

Reed. 5. Christof*er* Goad. 6. Sam. Thompson. 7. Mr. Staffeild.
8. John Robinson. 9. Courteous Grevill. These are ye cheife whereof
7 are called sharers i.e. such as pay wages to ye servants & equally
share in the overplus: other servants there are as 2 Close keepers
Rich*ard* Kendall Anth*ony* Dover &c. Of all these Companies ye first
[King's men] if they please may come to Ox*õ*n, but none without
speciall le*tt*res from the Chancellor obtained by meanes of ye Secretary to the ViceChancelo*ur*./Mr. Gunnell akin to ye Nappers. A Crosse
mischance happened to this company bec*ause* of a boy y^t quarrelled
with a Scholar in ye Taverne./They came furnished with 14 playes.
And lodged at ye Kings Armes, where Franklin hath about 3^li a day
while they stay, i.e. for every play 4 nobles besides ye benefit of seats.—
(See above, ii. 688–9.)

The prominence of Richard Gunnell in the list one would expect
from his position as manager. It is noticeable that Kendall omitted
to name Richard Blagrave, presumably an indication that his
association with the company was financial and he had little or
nothing to do with the management. The inclusion of a fencer
in the list is a little surprising for a private theatre; it might be
interesting to try to deduce his parts in the company plays.

Kendall named no boys, and the number of adults listed indicates
that any right the company still had to be called a children's
troupe rested on the larger-than-normal group of boys, not on
their preponderance. The fourteen plays he mentions as the touring repertory of the company probably comprised only a selection
from those they owned, but the selection is larger than the total
number of titles we can assign to them now. (See above, i. 300–1.)

One wonders how long this tour kept the Salisbury Court dark.
The players seem to have been back in London a month after
their Oxford visit, for Sir Henry Herbert licensed a revised play
for them on 16 August: 'An ould play, with some new scenes,
Doctor Lambe and the Witches, to Salisbury Courte, the 16th
August, 1634,—£1.0.0.'. (*Variorum*, i. 424.) It is likely that this
revision was an attempt to exploit the excitement about the
Lancashire witches of 1633; for Doctor Lambe had been dead
for six years, but the Lancashire witches had only recently been
brought to London. Indeed, the revised play at the Salisbury
Court is probably the one the King's men complained about in
a petition to the Lord Chamberlain on 20 July 1634:

A petic*õ*n of the Kings Players complayning of intermingleing
some passages of witches in old playes to ye p*r*iudice of their
designed Comedy of the Lancashire witches, & desiring a prohibition
of any other till theirs bee allowed & Acted. Answered *per* Refer-

ence to Blagraue in absence of Sr H. Herbert./ Iuly 20. 1634 (*M.S.C.* ii. 410.)

Since the Lord Chamberlain referred the petition to the deputy to the Master of the Revels, this occasion is perhaps one of those on which the Salisbury Court players profited from the official position of one of the owners of their house. The month which elapsed before the licence of the Salisbury Court play suggests, however, that the King's men had their way as usual.

Later in 1634 Richard Gunnell died, and was buried at St. Bride's on 7 October. This loss of their manager and most experienced member must have been very serious for the Salisbury Court players, but too little is known of their affairs to assess it. Eventually Gunnell was succeeded in his function, and presumably in his residence, by Richard Heton, but the date of Heton's first association with the theatre is not known. It can only be said that on 18 February 1636/7 he received payment for plays the troupe had performed at court in October 1635 and February 1635/6, but he may have been only collecting for performances arranged by a predecessor.

In February 1634/5 there was trouble at the Salisbury Court, though the only account of it makes no charges against the company. Sir Henry Herbert noted in his Office Book:

> I committed Cromes, a broker in Longe Lane, the 16 of Febru. 1634, to the Marshalsey, for lending a church-robe with the name of JESUS upon it, to the players in Salisbury Court, to present a Flamen, a priest of the heathens. Upon his petition of submission, and acknowledgment of his faulte, I releasd him, the 17 Fehr 1634. (*Variorum*, iii. 237.)

It seems likely that the church-robe had been actually used on the stage and not simply intended for use when Cromes was arrested. If so, the company would surely be thought to have offended as seriously as the broker in Long Lane, and there must have been at least a prohibition of the play presenting a Flamen, if not more serious penalties. However, no records of restrictions suffered at the theatre have come to light.[1]

---

[1] Sufficient status for the Salisbury Court in this year was assumed by William Lilly, the astrologer, to make it a suitable setting for one of the stories he tells in vindication of his art.

'In 1634, or 1635, a Lady living in *Greenwich*, who had tried all the known Artists in *London*, but to no purpose, came weeping and lamenting her Condition, which was this: She had permitted a young Lord to have the Use of her Body, till she was with Child by him; after which time he could not

In July 1635 the managers of the Salisbury Court succeeded in luring the dramatist Richard Brome away from the Red Bull theatre and attaching him to their own house by a contract with a term of three years. Such contracts between dramatists and theatres or companies were probably common, but Brome's is the only one known, and its terms are of much interest in showing what was probably a normal relationship between poet and theatre. Brome agreed to write exclusively for the Salisbury Court and to provide the players with three plays a year for three years. He also agreed to publish none of his plays without the consent of the company. In the event, Brome provided the players with only six of the promised nine plays, but he did prepare for them 'numerous songs, epilogues, and revisions of scenes in revived plays', a service which was probably normal for theatre poets. For his services the dramatist received a salary of fifteen shillings a week plus the first day's profits from each new play, which on one occasion was estimated at £5 or more. Brome is said to have given one or two of his plays, in violation of his contract, to a rival theatre, the Phoenix or Cockpit in Drury Lane. Nevertheless, the Salisbury Court must have been satisfied with him, for at the expiration of his contract in 1638 they offered him a seven-year extension, with an increased stipend of twenty shillings a week. It is not clear whether this new contract was signed, but Brome gave the company another play just after Christmas 1638, and a second before Easter 1639. Thereafter he left the Salisbury Court to write for the Phoenix. (See above, iii. 52–54.)

Of Brome's eight plays, said to have been written for the Salisbury Court, we can now identify only *The Sparagus Garden*, *The English Moor*, *The Antipodes*, and *The Queen and the Concubine*. The first, performed in 1635, was a resounding success, and the suit which reveals Brome's contract says that the company made a profit of £1,000 on the play. Probably this figure is a great lawsuit exaggeration, but such an estimate could be attached only to a production known to have been very successful.

A good part of Brome's contract with the Salisbury Court was fulfilled after the King's Revels company had ceased to act there. Less than a year after the document was signed the theatres were

---

or would not endure her Sight, . . . Her Desire unto me was to assist her to see him [which he did, thus preventing her suicide. On another occasion,] when the Lord was out of the Prison, then I ordered her such a Day to go and see a Play at *Salisbury-Court*, which she did, and within one quarter of an Hour the Lord came into the same Box wherein she was.' (William Lilly, *History of His Life and Times From the Year 1602 to 1681* [1715], p. 34.)

again closed as a measure of precaution against the raging plague. The closing order went out on 12 May 1636, and except for one week at the end of February 1636/7 they remained closed for a year and a half, until early October 1637. (See above, ii. 661–5.)

In the affairs of London players such protracted idleness produced many changes, one of which was the disappearance of the King's Revels company, and another the breaking up of Queen Henrietta's troupe at the Phoenix. The remnants of the two organizations were joined and, after the lifting of the ban, reopened at the Salisbury Court theatre as a new Queen Henrietta's company. The changes are inadequately recorded by Sir Henry Herbert in undated Office Book entries during the plague period.

> Mr. Beeston was commanded to make a company of boyes, and began to play at the Cockpitt [the theatre in which Queen Henrietta's men had been acting for years] with them the same day.

> I disposed of Perkins, Sumner, Sherlock and Turner, to Salisbury Court, and joynd them with the best of that company. (*Variorum*, iii. 240.)

Another feature of the transfer is mentioned by Richard Heton, the new manager of the Salisbury Court, in a document prepared in 1639 and called 'Instructions' for his patent: 'When her M^ts servants were at the Cockpitt, beinge all at liberty, they disperst themselves to severall Companies, soe that had not my lo: of Dorsett taken care to make up a new Company for the Queene, she had not had any at all.' (See above, ii. 684.) Again the interest of the Earl of Dorset in the Salisbury Court theatre appears. He would have been active in the arrangements for maintaining a company for Queen Henrietta, as he had been, since 1628, Lord Chamberlain to the Queen.

The man Richard Heton, who records Dorset's action, is a very obscure figure, though clearly important in the last four or five years of the Salisbury Court theatre before the wars. Just when he became manager of the playhouse is not known, but it must have been after the death of Gunnell in December 1635, and perhaps after the death of William Blagrave, who disappears during the period of plague closing.[1] His 'Instructions' for his patent, his

---

[1] A play licensed for publication by Blagrave appears in the Stationers' Register 6 August 1636, but five other plays entered in the Register in March and April 1637 are said to be licensed by 'Mr Thomas Herbert Deputy of Sr Henry Herbert'. (Greg, *Bibliography*, i. 45–46.) Heton's draft patent for Queen Henrietta's implies that he had been manager during at least part of the plague period, for he says that he 'hath lykewise disbursed good somes of money for the maintayning and supporting the said Actors in the

draft of the patent, and various of his proposals show a good deal about the condition of the enterprise at Salisbury Court, and about the changes Heton expected to carry out there. Though the documents belong to the year 1639,[1] various remarks refer to the period immediately following the plague-closing, and all illuminate Heton's term as manager of the theatre and of Queen Henrietta's men. Heton proposes that complete control of the troupe at the theatre be vested in him, and that if the company leaves the Salisbury Court it should then cease to be the Queen's company. Otherwise, he says, when the company could find another house they would 'leave us as in one yeare and halfe of their being here they haue many tymes threatned, when they might not exact any new imposicons upon the housekeepers at their pleasure. And some of them have treated upon Condicons for the Cockpit playhouse, some gone about to begge o^r house from the King . . .'. (See above, ii. 684.)

In his 'draught of his pattent' the manager proposes himself as patentee, with none of the players of the troupe named. He wanted the new patent to 'lycence and aucthorize o^r said servant Richard Heton, or his assignes, from tyme to tyme, and at all tymes hereafter to select, order, direct, sett upp, and governe a company of Comedians in the said private house in Dorset house yard, for ye seruice of o^r deare Consort the quene . . .'. (See above, ii. 685.)

Heton's intention to make himself not manager, but governor of the company—perhaps in imitation of William Beeston at the Phoenix—is shown in another of his notes, which is headed 'My Intencon for the rest'.

That such of the company as will not be ordered and governed by me as of their governor, or shall not by the M^r of his M^{ts} Revells and my selfe bee thought fitt Comedians for her M^{ts} service, I may have power to discharge from the Company, and, wth the advice of the M^r of the Revells, to putt new ones in their places; and those who shalbe soe descharged not to have the honor to be her M^{ts} servants, but only those who shall continew at the aforesaid play-house. And the said Company not to play at any tyme in any other place but the forsaid playhouse without my consent under my hand

sicknes tyme, and other wayes to keepe the said Company together, wthout wch a great part of them had not bene able to subsist . . .'.

[1] The 'Instructions' refer to conditions at the Salisbury Court during the tenancy of Queen Henrietta's men 'for a yeare and a halfe last past', i.e. since the summer or autumn of 1637. He also refers to Davenant's licence to build a new playhouse in Fleet Street, a document dated 26 March 1639. The final document, 'Instructions touching Salesbery Co^{r}t Playhouse', is dated 14 September 1639. (See above, ii. 684–7.)

in wryting, (lest his M^ts service might be neglected) except by speciall comand from one of the Lo. Chamberlaines, or the M^r of his M^ts. Revells, &c. (See above, ii. 686.)

How many of these intentions Heton succeeded in carrying out, we cannot now tell, but his purpose is clear enough. The old idea of an independent troupe making its own decisions, as the King's company still did, was not to be allowed at the Salisbury Court. All power was to be vested in the hands of the manager, and players were to be hired and fired at his dictation. Probably Heton did not get as far in carrying his plan into effect as the Restoration and eighteenth-century managers did, but he has it clearly stated.

Another of Heton's papers concerns the relation between the company and the housekeepers at the Salisbury Court, and seems to compare a superseded agreement with a new one. These notes, though they give a good deal of insight into the conduct of the theatre, are not entirely clear. I take it that the document is an outline of Heton's presentation to the players of a new agreement with the housekeepers; it is intended to demonstrate how much the players are gaining by the new agreement. The housekeepers are to gain no benefits not enjoyed before, but they are to pay more of the expenses. The statements about halves are confused, but I take it that, however he states it, Heton means that for the item in question the housekeepers pay half the cost and the players pay half. This paper is endorsed 'Instructions Touching Salesbery Co^rt Playhouse, 14 Septem., 1639':

The diffrence betwixt the first Articles
and the last.

The housekeep^s enioy not any one Benefit in the last wch they had not in the first.
And they paid only by the first.
1, All Repaires of the house.
2, Halfe the gathering plačs.
  Halfe to the Sweepers of the house, the stagekeep^s, to the Poor, and for carying away the soyle.

By the last Articles.

We first allow them a Roome or 2 more then they form'ly had.
All that was allowed by the former Articles, and
Halfe the Poets wages wch is 10^s a week.[1]

---

[1] The twenty-shilling weekly wage indicated here for the theatre poet is the same as Brome was to be paid on his new contract at this house in 1638. Evidently the rate was standard. It is not known who Brome's successor was.

Halfe the lycencing of every new play wch halfe is also xx^s. [Herbert's fee for licensing a new play at this time was £2.]

And one dayes p'fitt wholly to themselves every yeare in consideration of their want of stooles on the stage, wch were taken away by his M^ts comand.

We allow them also that was in
noe Articles.

Halfe for lights, both waxe and Tallow, wch halfe all winter is near 5^s a day.

Halfe for coles to all the Roomes.

Halfe for rushes, flowers, and strowings on the stage.

Halfe for all the boyes' new gloves at every new play, and every revived play not lately plaid. (See above, ii. 686–7.)

Several of Heton's articles allude to familiar customs of the private theatres, but others appear to indicate practices at Salisbury Court which are less well known. The contribution to the poor has been noted elsewhere; probably all playhouses made such a contribution to the poor of the parish; the practice is found at the end of the sixteenth century. (See Chambers, *E.S.* i. 283, 301, 317; iv. 325, 327–8.) The 'Roome or 2 more' allowed the housekeepers were probably boxes for any performance; it may be that the Lord Chamberlain had such a box at Blackfriars. (See above, vi. 34.) The benefit performance in lieu of 'stooles on the stage' is another allusion to the familiar practice of sitting on the stage (see above, vi. 7–8), but the reference to the recent prohibition is new. Presumably this excellent royal order applied to all London theatres and not to the Salisbury Court alone, but nothing more is known of it.

The reference to 'all winter' in the article about wax and tallow candles implies that during other seasons of the year candles were not needed at the Salisbury Court. Apparently this playhouse had more window area than is usually assumed for private theatres. Can Heton mean that there were not even stage lights during the months of longer daylight?

The article about 'coles to all the Roomes' would seem to indicate that there were fires in the private rooms or boxes, for 'all the Roomes' suggests more than just the tiring-house and perhaps the music room. What was done about smoke? Surely there could not have been a fireplace for each box.

The rushes on the stage in the next article are familiar enough from many other allusions, though I recall none so late as this one. The flowers are not familiar. Were they among the rushes strewn on the stage? Were they decorations?

New gloves for the boys are mentioned elsewhere, and go back at least as far as the Elizabethan boy companies, but this statement is unusually specific in its indication of the regularity of their use. Like one or two other items in Heton's analysis of the articles of agreement with the housekeepers, it suggests more elegance in an afternoon at the Salisbury Court theatre than might have been expected.

It was probably after the plague restraint was removed in the autumn of 1637 that Thomas Nabbes's *Microcosmus, A Moral Masque* was presented at Salisbury Court. (See above, iv. 936-8.) The sub-title is an accurate description of the piece, and the requirements for staging are so expensive that one would assume no commercial theatre could manage it. Yet the 1637 title-page makes the assertion that *Microcosmus* was 'Presented With generall liking, at the private house in Salisbury Court'. Moreover, Richard Brome, at that time under contract as the regular dramatist of the theatre, wrote commendatory verses for the play, referring to the plague closing as current, and anticipating profits for the theatre after the restraint was taken off, when *Microcosmus* could be presented. Apparently he did not consider the masque too much for the Salisbury Court. If the stage directions can be trusted, the piece was presented with a special proscenium and five scene changes. Though there are no detailed descriptions of the scenes, there is enough to show that they were similar to those for Inigo Jones's court masques; obviously they must have been greatly reduced in size, elaborateness, and splendour, compared with those Jones designed.

After describing the costumes of thirty-six or more characters, Nabbes goes on to the proscenium arch:

The Front.

Of a workmanship proper to the fancy of the rest, adorn'd with brasse figures of Angels and Divels, with severall inscriptions: The Title in an Escocheon supported by an Angell and a Divell. Within the arch a continuing perspective of ruines, which is drawne still before the other scenes whilst they are varied.

The Inscriptions.

Hinc gloria.	*Hinc poena.*
Appetitus boni.	*Appetitus mali.*
	(B₂.)

It would have been necessary to build this front, or proscenium, for the production, as was done at court. No doubt the construction could have been much cheaper and smaller than that at

Whitehall; the 'perspective of ruines' would have to be painted to order unless the players had found some way to borrow it. I take the 'drawne still' to mean that this flat was drawn aside to reveal the tableau in each act and was pushed across again at its close. Though the demands of this proscenium would have been severe for the Salisbury Court, the rest of the play demands more.

After five pages of dialogue and a dance there is a stage direction: *'Whilst the following song is singing, the first Scene appeares; being a spheare in which the 4. Elements are figur'd, and about it they sit imbracing one another.'* There follows a song, a little dialogue, and a dance. After which Love says,

> *Now to the other worke; our art*
> *Shall make all perfect e're we part.*

and the stage direction reads: 'They returne into the Scene, and it closeth.' (C_1v.) About the middle of the second act the next construction is introduced: *'The second Scene is here discover'd, being a perspective of clouds, the inmost glorious, where* Bellamina *sits betwixt* Love *and* Nature; *behind her the* Bonus *and* Malus Genius.' (C_3v.) After a long speech by Nature comes the stage direction for their descent: *'Whilst the following song is singing, they descend from the Scene and present* Bellamina *to* Physander.' Finally, after a speech and the song, 'Love *and* Nature *returne to the Scene, and it closeth.' (C_4v.)

In the middle of the third act comes the next presentation: *'During the following Song, the third Scene is discover'd, being a pleasant arbour, with perspectives behind it, of a magnifique building: in the midst thereof* Sensuality *sits.' (D_4.) The closing of this scene is not marked for Act III, but two-thirds of the way through the fourth act comes the next presentation: *'Here the fourth Scene is suddainly discover'd, being a Rock, with a spring of water issuing out of it. At the foot thereof a cave; where* Temperance *sits betwixt a* Philosopher, *an* Hermite, *a* Ploughman *and a* Shepheard. *Behind the Rocke a Lantskipt.' (F_1.) At the end of the act is the direction, *'Temperance with the rest of hers being return'd into the Scene, it closeth.' (F_2v.) The 'Scene' in the last act is very near the end, and it is more elaborate than the previous ones:

> *Here the last Scene is discover'd, being a glorious throne: at the top whereof Love sits betwixt* Iustice, Temperance, Prudence *and* Fortitude, *holding two crownes of starres: at the foote upon certaine degrees sit divers gloriously habited and alike as* Elysij incolae; *who whil'st Love and the Vertues lead* Physander *and* Bellamina *to the throne, place themselves in a figure for the dance.* (G_4.)

And after a song and speech (there must have been a dance also, though it is not marked) the play ends with the direction, '*The daunce ended, they returne to their first order, whils't Love speakes the Epilogue: which done, he is receiv'd into the Scene, and it closeth.*'

All this display seems much too elaborate and expensive for a theatre like Salisbury Court, and I cannot believe that the players were able to pay for such creations as the explicit stage directions demand. Yet the statement on the title-page is clear enough, and so are Brome's expectations for the masque. The further statement on the title-page, 'Set down according to the intention of the Authour', could mean that a good deal of the spectacle was omitted in performance, but I do not see how it could all have been cut. Could the masque as it is printed have been prepared for some private production which was cancelled, as appears to have been the case with another of Nabbes's masques? (See above, iv. 938–9.) Could the theatre have fallen heir to some of these structures paid for by others? So far as I can tell there is nothing in these scenes described by Nabbes which would have been physically impossible for a private theatre stage. A special proscenium could have been erected well forward on the stage, and with some crowding the spectacles might have been built behind it. The large cast of characters could have been doubled by an ordinary company, since most of them appear in only one act. It is the cost of carpentry and painting that seems to me impossible for a commercial theatre in Caroline London, but the work might have been available had they been provided at someone else's cost. In any case I see no clear evidence in *Microcosmus* that the Salisbury Court stage was radically different from those at Blackfriars or the Phoenix. Other plays produced there do not seem to require a distinctive stage, and there are no contemporary comments on anything sensationally different at Salisbury Court. I can imagine a somewhat distorted production of *Microcosmus* there, but I am puzzled about the financing.

Presumably *Microcosmus* was produced under the management of Richard Heton, and it is possible that the new manager arranged a very risky production, but he says nothing of it in Heton's Papers. In spite of the determination shown in his 'Instructions' for his patent and his 'Intencon for the rest', events at the playhouse under Heton have left very few records. The most interesting is the Praeludium written for a play acted in the Salisbury Court theatre, probably in 1638, *The Careless Shepherdess*. (See above, iv. 501–5.) The play proper is rather academic, and probably it was old in 1638, but the Praeludium is topical, colloquial, and evidently specially written for this theatre. Bits of the dialogue in this Praeludium indicate customs and prices at the theatre.

Præludium:

The Actors.

Spruce, *a Courtier.*
Sparke, *an Inns of Court-man.*
Landlord, *a Country Gentleman.*
Thrift, *a Citizen.*
Bolt, *a Door-keeper.*

Prologus.

The Scene

SALISBURY COURT.

Bolt. A Door-keeper, sitting with a Box on the side of the Stage. To him Thrift *a Citizen.*

Thrift. Now for a good bargain, What will you take to let me in to the play?

Bolt. A shilling Sir.

Thri. Come, here's a groat. I'le not make many words.

.   .   .   .   .

When will it begin?

Bolt. Presently Sir.

Thri. Thou once didst tell me so
When the first Act was almost done.

Bolt. Why then
They presently began to make an end.

Enter Spruce, *a Courtier.*

Spruce. How oft has't sounded?

Bolt. Thrice an't please you Sir.

.   .   .   .   .

Enter Landlord, *a Country Gentleman*

Landl. God save you Gentlemen, 'tis my ambition
To occupy a place neer you: there are
None that be worthy of my company
In any room beneath the twelve peny.

.   .   .   .   .

Landl. Why I would have the Fool in every Act,
Be't Comedy, or Tragedy, I 'ave laugh'd
Untill I cry'd again, to see what Faces
The Rogue will make: O it does me good
To see him hold out's Chin hang down his hands,
And twirle his Bawble. There is nere a part

About him but breaks jests. I heard a fellow
Once on this Stage cry *Doodle, Doodle, Dooe,*
Beyond compare; I'de give the other shilling
To see him act the Changling once again.
Thri. And so would I

　　　.　　　.　　　.　　　.　　　.

I never saw *Rheade* peeping through the Curtain,
But ravishing joy enter'd into my heart.

　　　.　　　.　　　.　　　.　　　.

Landl. Well, since there will be nere a foole i' th' *Play,*
I'le have my money again; the Comedy
Will be as tedious to me, as a Sermon,
And I do fear that I shall fall asleep,
And give my twelve pense to be melancholy.

　　　.　　　.　　　.　　　.

　　　　　　　　　　Loud Musique sounds.
But hist, the Prologue enters, *Landl.* Now it chimes
All in, to the Play, the Peals were rung before.

　　　.　　　.　　　.　　　.　　　.

[Two Prologues forget their lines and retire in confusion.]

Spru. Perhaps our presence daunteth them, let us
Retire into some private room, for fear
The third man should be out. *Spar.* A match.
　　　　　　　　　　　Exeunt Spru, Spar.
Landl. I'le follow them, though't be into a Box.
Though they did sit thus open on the Stage
To shew their Cloak and Sute, yet I did think
At last they would take sanctuary 'mongst
The Ladies, lest some Creditor should spy them.
'Tis better looking o're a Ladies head,
Or through a Lettice-window, then a grate.

　　　　　　　　　　　Exit Land.

Thri. And I will hasten to the money Box,
And take my shilling out again, for now
I have considered that it is too much;
I'le go th' Bull, or Fortune, and there see
A Play for two pense, with a Jig to boot.　　　*Exit.*
　　　(*The Careless Shepherdess* [1656], B$_1$–B$_4$^{v}.)

Most of the features of the house and the performance alluded
to here had been mentioned for one theatre or another in the
previous forty years—the gatherer's box, sitting on the stage,
the private-theatre admission price and comparative prices, act
division in private-theatre performances, the triple sounding,
and private boxes screened by lattice. But I can think of no other

account, with the possible exception of Jonson's allusions to the Hope in the Induction to *Bartholomew Fair*, which specifically assigns so many features to a particular theatre at a particular time.[1] One allusion, that to Timothy Reade peeping through the curtain, is unique, and suggests a particular following for Reade in at least a section of the Salisbury Court audience, a following which seems to have continued for some time, as later allusions to Reade show. (See above, ii. 540–1.)

In the last three years of the legitimate Caroline theatre there are few records of activities at the London playhouses, and the Salisbury Court is no exception. They were all closed in 1640, from 11 September to about the first week in November, because of plague. And again in 1641 there was an intermission. Though the records are not clear, the prohibition seems to have lasted from 5 August until the last week in November. (See above, ii. 665–7.)

I know of no records at all of the Salisbury Court in 1642, but presumably Queen Henrietta's men were still playing there in September, when Parliament issued the order to close all theatres while 'these sad Causes and set times of Humiliation doe continue'. (See above, ii. 690.) So far as is known, the house was dark until the recrudescence of playing at several theatres in 1647. The Salisbury Court is first mentioned in this revival in the sequel to *The Parliament of Ladies*, issued on 2 August 1647, and entitled *The Ladies, A Second Time, Assembled in Parliament*:

the first thing they fell upon, was, a Complaint that was made against Players, who contrary to an Ordinance, had set up shop againe, and acted divers Playes, at the two houses, the Fortune, and Salisbury Court. Whereupon it was demanded what Plaies they were, and answer being given, that one of them was the scornefull Lady, the house tooke it in high disdaine . . . . (B₃. Cited by Rollins, *Studies in Philology*, xviii. 279.)

A less facetious account of renewed activities at the theatre was published in the newsbook *Perfect Occurrences* under date of 6 October 1647:

A Stage-Play was to have been acted in Salisbury Court this day (& Bills stuck up about it) called *A King and No King*, formerly acted

---

[1] A good deal of the confusion about features of Elizabethan playhouses and performances derives from the indiscriminate collection of evidence from plays of different theatres and different companies at different times, and the consideration of these allusions with others derived from non-dramatic sources naming no theatre or company at all. Behind many of these essays lies the unstated assumption that all Elizabethan theatres and performances were more or less alike.

at the Black-Fryers, by his Majesties servants, about 8. yeares since, written by *Francis Beaumont*, and *Iohn Fletcher*.

The Sheriffes of the City of *London* with their Officers went thither, and found a great number of people; some young Lords, and other eminent persons; and the men and women with the Boxes, [that took moneys] fled. The Sheriffes brought away *Tim Reade* the Foole, and the people cryed out for their monies, but slunk away like a company of drowned Mice without it. (Qq₄. Cited ibid., pp. 283–4.)

The singling out of Reade in this account suggests that his reputation, attested by Landlord in *The Careless Shepherdess*, was not forgotten after five years of suppressed theatres. The same raid at the Salisbury Court is reported by *Mercurius Pragmaticus* in his issue for 5–12 October 1647

. . . for though the House hindred the Players this weeke from playing the old Play, *King*, and no *King*, at *Salisbury* Court, yet believe me,

> *He that does live, shall see another Age,*
> *Their Follies* stript *and* whipt *upon the* Stage.
>
> (D₄ᵛ. Cited ibid., p. 284.)

Finally, the same event is much more unsympathetically noticed in the issue of *Mercurius Melancholicus* for 2–9 October 1647. The covert allusion to the old story about the real Devil appearing in the devil's dance at a performance of *Doctor Faustus* is a nice example of the continuity of anti-theatre propaganda.

The Common Inns of sin, and Blasphemy, the *Playhouses* began to be custom'd again, and to act filthinesse and villanny to the life; but on Tuesday last, there appear'd more Actors then should be, (yet no Devills) at *Salisbury-Court*, the Lord Mayjor and Sheriffe was there, who put the puppy-Players so out of countenance, that they had not one word to say; Why should *Play houses* be cry'd up, and *Pamphlets* be cry'd down; are they bawdy-houses too. (F₂ᵛ.)

Such a well-known raid might have been thought enough to put an end to playing at the theatre, but it did not; a year later regular playing is reported at three theatres, including the Salisbury Court; it was reported to Parliament on 'Wednesday Septemb. 13' that 'Stage-playes were daily acted either at the *Bull* or *Fortune*, or the private House at *Salisbury-Court.*' (*The Kingdom's Weekly Intelligencer*, 12–19 September 1648. Cited by Rollins.) This report produced more effective action on the part of Parliament, though in the case of the Salisbury Court it was delayed for several months. *The Kingdom's Weekly Intelligencer* in its issue of 2–9 January 1648/9 tells of better planned suppressive action.

> The Souldiers seized on the Players on their Stages at Drury-lane, and Salisbury Court. They went also to the Fortune in Golden-lane, but they found none there, but John Pudding dancing on the Ropes, whom they took along with them. In the meane time the players at the Red Bull, who had notice of it, made haste away, and were all gone before they came, and tooke away all their acting cloathes with them. But at Salisbury Court they were taken on the Stage the Play being almost ended, and with many Linkes and lighted Torches they were carried to White-Hall with their Players cloathes upon their backs. In the way they oftentimes tooke the Crowne from his head who acted the King, and in sport would oftentimes put it on again. Abraham had a black Satten gown on, and before he came into the durt, he was very neat in his white laced pumps. The people not expecting such a pageant looked and laughed at all the rest, and not knowing who he was, they asked what had that Lady done ? They made some resistance at the Cockpit in Drury Lane, which was the occasion that they were bereaved of their apperell, and were not so well used as those in Salisbury Court, who were more patient, and therefore at their Releasement they had their cloaths returned to them without the least diminution: After two days confinement, They were Ordered to put in Bayle, and to appeare before the Lord Mayor to answer for what they have done according unto law. (Cited by Hotson, pp. 40–41.)

This performance and its conspicuous aftermath is the last one known for the Caroline Salisbury Court. If the players dared to try again in the next ten weeks, no evidence of their attempt has been found. After that their playhouse was unfit for use. The final event is recorded in a manuscript note in the 1631 edition of Stow's *Annales*: 'The playhouse in Salsbury Court, in fleetstreete, was pulled downe by a company of Souldiers set on by the Sectuaries of these sad times. On Saterday the 24 day day [*sic*] of March 1649. by the same Souldiers.' (Folger Shakespeare Library, Phillipps MS. 11613.) This is probably the demolition referred to by William Beeston in his bill of 25 June 1658 in a Chancery suit about the rebuilding of the theatre: '. . . divers Souldiers by force & Armes entered ye said Playhouse Cutt down ye Seates, broke downe ye Stage and vtterly defaced ye whole buildinges. In regard whereof your Orator did not pay ye residue of ye said money to ye said Mr Herne . . .'. (P.R.O. C 10 53/7.)

Although the Salisbury Court theatre was not completely and finally destroyed as the Globe was, the raid marks the end of the Caroline playhouse. The repairs and enlargement of the ruined

Caroline theatre carried out by William Beeston are really the beginnings of the Restoration theatre. They are well set out by Leslie Hotson, who discovered the documents. (Hotson, pp. 107–13.)

THE WHITEFRIARS

Adams, pp. 310–23.

Chambers, *E.S.* ii. 515–17.

Cunningham, Peter, 'The Whitefriars Theatre, the Salisbury Court Theatre, and the Duke's Theatre in Dorset Gardens', *Shakespeare Society's Papers*, iv (1849), 89–90.

Dickson, M. J., 'William Trevell and the Whitefriars Theatre', *Review of English Studies*, vi (1930), 309–12.

Dowling, Margaret, 'Further Notes on William Trevell', *Review of English Studies*, vi (1930), 443–6.

Hillebrand, Harold Newcomb, *The Child Actors* (1926), pp. 220–36.

The obscure private playhouse in Whitefriars had a rather shadowy existence before 1613, and it was not certainly used at all after that date. One or two assertions of its later use have been made, however, and it may be helpful to put them in context.

The theatre was in the precincts of the old Carmelite monastery, between Fleet Street and the Thames, just west of Water Lane, but its precise location in the old monastic buildings is not known. It was in use by the Children of the Revels in 1608. On 3 June 1615 a licence was issued to Philip Rosseter and his associates who had

trayned vppe and practised a convenient number of children of the Revell*es* for the purpose aforesaid in a Messuage or mansion house being parcell of the late dissolved Monastery called the white ffryers neere ffleetestreete in london which the said Phillipp Rosseter did lately hold for a terme of certaine yeres expired, And whereas the said Phillipp Roseter together with Phillipp kingman Robert Iones and Raphe Reeve to continue the said service for the keeping and bringing vppe of the children for the solace and pleasure of our said most deere wife . . . have latelie taken in lease and farme divers building*es* . . . for the building of a Playhouse . . . All which p*r*emisses are scituate and being within the Precinct of Blacke ffryers neere Puddlewharfe . . . . (*M.S.C.* i. 277–9.)

This royal licence to build the Puddle Wharf theatre was taken up and building was started. (See above, vi. 78–86.) There is no good evidence that any London company ever acted in the Whitefriars theatre after the expiration of the lease mentioned in this patent.

But there are two later allegations about the theatre which seem to suggest its later use. John Payne Collier wrote in his *New Facts Regarding the Life of Shakespeare in a Letter to Thomas Amyot, Esq., F.R.S.* (1835):

> ... I have in my possession an original survey of some part of the precinct [of Whitefriars] made in March 1616, which contains the following paragraph regarding the Theatre in Whitefriars.
>
> 'The Theatre is scituate near vnto the Bishopps House, and was in former times a hall or refectorie belonging to the dissolved Monastery. It hath beene vsed as a place for the presentation of playes and enterludes for more then 30 yeares, last by the Children of her Majestie. It hath little or no furniture for a playhouse, saving an old tottered curten, some decayed benches, and a few worne out properties and peeces of Arras for hangings to the stage and tire house. The raine hath made its way in and if it bee not repaired, it must soone be plucked downe, or it will fall.' (p. 44.)

Collier never gave any more precise description of his document, and no one else has ever seen it. The phraseology, especially that 'old tottered curten', strongly suggest Collier's own composition, and only occasionally has his 'original survey' been taken as genuine.

The other late reference to the theatre was made by Peter Cunningham in 1849 in his paper on the three seventeenth-century theatres in the general Whitefriars area—Whitefriars, the Salisbury Court, and Dorset Garden. After noting a payment of £20 to Sir George Buc on 13 July 1613 (*Variorum*, iii. 52) for 'a license to erect a new play-house in the White-friers' Cunningham continues:

> The theatre in the Whitefriars was not, I believe, rebuilt, though the case of Trevill *v.* Woodford, in the Court of Requests, informs us that plays were performed at the Whitefriars Theatre as late as 1621; Sir Anthony Ashley, the then landlord of the house, entering the Theatre in that year, and turning the players out of doors, on pretence that half a year's rent was yet unpaid to him. (p. 90.)

Since no records of dramatic activities at Whitefriars theatre after 1613 have been found, I can only conclude that there is some error, either in the statement of plaintiff or defendant, or in Cunningham's interpretation of the statement about

Sir Anthony Ashley's actions. Unfortunately the papers Cunningham saw are not now available.[1]

Occasionally confusion about this theatre has arisen from loose references to the Caroline Salisbury Court theatre as Whitefriars. In his complaint about the proliferation of the Devil's Chapels in London William Prynne refers to the two old theatres lately rebuilt and 'one *new Theatre* erected'. This new theatre he annotates 'White Friers Playhouse'. (*Histriomastix*, $*_3$v.) In his *Lady Mother* written for the Salisbury Court in 1635 (see above, iv. 483–5) Henry Glapthorne makes one of his characters say, after a song in the first scene of the second act, 'Now on my life this boy, does sing as like the boy at the *Whitefryers* as ever I heard'. And in the usual self-advertising vein of the actors in the Jacobean and Caroline theatres his companion replies, 'I, and the Musicks like theires'.

In the same way the 1641 pamphlet called *The Stage-Players' Complaint* refers in its sub-title to the chief comedians at the Fortune and the Salisbury Court as '*Cane of the Fortune and Reed of the Friers*'. (See above, ii. 540–1.)

All these references are fortunately in such contexts as to make it clear that the authors were referring loosely to the theatre erected in 1629 just outside the precinct of Whitefriars and usually called the Salisbury Court theatre.

[1] Cunningham cites 'Trevill *v.* Woodford, in Court of Requests, 18 Charles I—(Documents at the Chapter House, Westminster)'. These records were removed from the Chapter House to the Public Record Office in 1859. Though many of the earlier records of the Court of Requests have now been calendared, most of those of the reign of Charles I have not; presumably *Trevill* v. *Woodford* is among the 500 uncalendared bundles from that reign

PUBLIC THEATRES

THE BELL INN

Adams, pp. 7–17.
Chambers, *E.S.* ii. 381–2.

Playing is first heard of at the Bell Inn in Gracious (Grace-church) Street during the season immediately preceding February 1576/7. No reference to playing there after 1588 is known.

THE BEL SAVAGE INN

Adams, pp. 7–17.
Chambers, *E.S.* ii. 382–3.

Playing at the Bel Savage Inn on Ludgate Hill is first referred to in 1579. The last reference is Prynne's in 1633: '. . . the *visible apparition of the Devill on the Stage at the Belsavage Play-house, in Queene* Elizabeths *dayes* . . .'. (*Histriomastix*, Ggg*₄.) The absence of allusions to playing at this house in Jacobean and Caroline times implies that it was no longer used by the actors, a suggestion which seems to be confirmed by Prynne's *'in Queene* Elizabeths *dayes'*.

THE BOAR'S HEAD INN

Adams, pp. 7–17.
Chambers, *E.S.* ii. 443–5.
Hotson, Leslie, *Shakespeare's Wooden O* (1959), pp. 264–5, 268–70, 287–8.
Sisson, C. J., 'Mr. and Mrs. Browne of the Boar's Head', *Life and Letters Today*, xv (winter, 1936), 99–107.
—— 'The Red Bull Company and the Importunate Widow', *Shakespeare Survey*, vii (1954), 57–68.

There is no reliable evidence that the Boar's Head Inn was used by the actors as a playing-place after 1616, but so much significant information has come to light since the publication of *The Elizabethan Stage*, where it properly belongs, that I feel some obligation to discuss it here.

There were at least six London inns called the Boar's Head (Chambers, *E.S.* ii. 443), and there has been some confusion as to which was the theatrical one, but Professor Sisson notes that in the litigation about the property: 'We are told by those defining [the Boar's Head's] position during these debates that it stood on the North side of Whitechapel Street in the parish of St. Mary Matfellon or Whitechapel [outside Aldgate]. It is commemorated even today by the local name of Boar's Head Yard. . . .' ('Mr. and Mrs. Browne . . .', p. 107.)

The building has usually been thought of as just another of the several London carrier inns that were from time to time adapted for the temporary use of the players (see Adams, loc. cit.), but the research of Sisson and Hotson shows that it was far more, for it had permanent theatrical accommodations built at no little expense. Perhaps the Boar's Head's approximation to regular theatrical status should have been deduced earlier from the mention of it in several contexts unusual for carrier inns. When the Duke of Newcastle wrote his odd and inaccurate recommendations 'To K Charles', not long before the Restoration, he pontificated on the subject of popular entertainment:

Firste for London Paris Garden will holde good for the meaner People. Then for severall Playe Houses as ther weare five att least In my Time, [he was born in 1593]—Black-Friers, the Cock-Pitt, Salisburye Courte, the Fortune, & the Redd Bull,—Ther weare the Boyes thatt played att Black-Friers, & Paules, & then the kinges Players played att the Globe—which Is nowe Calde the Phenixe,—Some Played, att the Bores heade, & att the Curtin In the feildes & some att the Hope which Is the Beare Garden, and some att White Friers,—Butt five or Sixe Playe Houses Is Enough for all sortes off Peoples divertion & pleasure In thatt kinde . . . . (Sandford A. Strong, *A Catalogue of Letters . . . Welbeck* [1903], p. 226.)

The inclusion of the Boar's Head with ten fairly well-known public and private theatres suggests that in Cavendish's mind it did not fall into the same category as the Bell, the Bel Savage, the Bull, or even the Cross Keys. Cavendish's memory of theatrical affairs is obviously faulty—confusion of Globe and Phoenix, late dating of boys at Paul's—but the status he implies for the Boar's Head can now be confirmed by other evidence.

A similar and contemporary implication of permanent theatrical status for the Boar's Head is to be found in the draft licence for Queen Anne's men of about 1604, a document in which they are licensed to play 'Aswel w[th]in there now vsuall Howsen, called the Curtayne, and the Bores head, w[th]in our County of Midd, [or] *as in* any other play howse not vsed by others. . . .' (*M.S.C.* i. 266.)

The Boar's Head was not a new acquisition for the Queen's company at this time, for a year or so earlier, when they were still called the Earl of Worcester's company, they had already designated the Boar's Head as their regular playing place. The circumstances are suggestive of the desirable accommodations at the Boar's Head. The Privy Council, on 31 December 1601, had reiterated their order of a year and a half before, limiting London playing-places to the Globe for the Lord Chamberlain's men and to the Fortune for the Lord Admiral's. (*M.S.C.* i, 80–85.) Then in a supplementary order dated 31 March 1602, under the heading 'A leře to yᵉ l. Maior for the Bores head to be licensed for yᵉ plaiers', they require that the company resulting from the combination of the Earl of Oxford's men and the Earl of Worcester's men be confined to one place:

And as the other Companies that are alowed, namely of me the L. Admirall and the L. Chamberlaine, be appointed there certaine howses, and one and noe more to each Companie. Soe we doe straightly require that this third Companie be likewise to one place. And because we are informed the house called the Bores head is the place they haue especially vsed and doe best like of, we doe pray and require yow that that said howse namely the Bores head may be assigned onto them and that they be verey straightlie Charged to vse and exercise there plaies in noe other but that howse. . . . (Ibid., pp. 85–86.)

Since the two orders, made just three months apart, establish the new Globe (1599), the new Fortune (1600), and the Boar's Head as the only chosen and allowed London theatres, ignoring the available Swan, Rose, and Curtain, there is a strong implication of the superior accommodations available at the Boar's Head, in spite of the fact that the orders appear never to have been seriously enforced. The designation of the Boar's Head as the third legally sanctioned theatre because it was the company's accustomed location—'the place they haue especially vsed and doe best like of'—provides a clear demonstration of the inn's usefulness to the company.

Similarly indicative of the status of the Boar's Head in the theatrical world is a remark of Edward Alleyn's wife Joan in a letter to her actor-husband dated 21 October, during the terrible plague year of 1603. In a sentence about theatrical affairs she says: 'All the Companyes be Come hoame & well for ought we knowe, but that Browne of the Boares head is dead & dyed very pore, he went not into the Countrye at all. & all of yoʳ owne Company ar well at theyr owne houses.' (*Henslowe Papers*, pp. 59–60.) Uncertainty as to which Browne and which Boar's Head Joan

Alleyn referred to (see Greg's note, ibid.) is settled by the Sisson-Hotson suits, which show that 'Browne of the Boares head' was the leading actor, Robert Browne, who had a principal interest in the Boar's Head inn-theatre. If Mrs. Alleyn identified such a well-known theatrical figure to her actor-husband as 'Browne of the Boares head', the reputation of that playing-place as much more than a carrier inn is again indicated.

Finally, there is a suggestion, though not a clear statement, that in 1608 or 1609 the Duke of York's (Prince Charles's) players were customarily acting at the Boar's Head. In the Leicester accounts for 1608–9 one payment record reads: 'Itm̃ given to the Princes Players of the White Chapple, London, xxˢ.' (William Kelly, *Notices Illustrative of the Drama* . . . [Leicester, 1865], p. 248.) Since, except for the Boar's Head Inn, no Whitechapel playing-place is known, and since there is no other information as to where Prince Charles's company performed in London, it seems reasonable to assign them to the Boar's Head.

This is the information about the Boar's Head Theatre that was available, though not adequately assessed, before the law suits examined by Sisson and Hotson had revealed how much more elaborate than our ordinary conception of an inn-yard theatre the Boar's Head was. The theatrical historian trying to order and evaluate their information is seriously handicapped because neither scholar has yet published transcripts or full analyses of his documents. Still, the extracts or comments they have used in pursuing other arguments or in telling other stories are useful.

Hotson notes that the documents involved, but so seldom cited with any precision, are these:

(1) A Star Chamber proceeding, *Samuel* v. *Langley et al.* Sta. Cha. 5/S74/3 and 5/S13/8. The date is 1600 and an encounter of 16 December 1599 is recounted.
(2) Chancery Town Depositions *Samuel* v. *Woodliff*, C24/278/71. No date given.
(3) Chancery Town Depositions *Browne* v. *Woodliff et al.*, C24/290/3. No date given.
(4) Uncalendared Proceedings of the Court of Requests, *Woodliff* v. *Browne et Jurdaine* (1603) P.R.O. Req. 2/466, Pt. ii. (Op. cit. 269 n., 264 n.)

All the information quoted by either man seems to come from these records, but Sisson seldom gives sources for his quotations or summaries, and Hotson never gives context. Evidently one of the suits shows that 'The Boar's Head was owned in copyhold by

Jane Pooley, a widow. On 28 November 1594 she leased it to Oliver Woodliffe, yet another speculator in theatres, and to his wife Susan. Woodliffe employed Richard Samuel to prepare the inn afresh for use as a theatre, building a stage and "galleries" for spectators in the yard, early in 1595, during Woodliffe's absence abroad.' (Sisson, 'Mr. and Mrs. Browne . . .', p. 102. No reference.) This information is repeated with one further detail in a note to the Red Bull company article: 'The theatre, a converted inn, was built in 1595, and rebuilt on a larger scale in 1599, when Browne became lessee of both inn and theatre. It is specifically described as a "winter house".' (Sisson, 'The Red Bull Company . . .', p. 67, n. 16. No reference.)

One of the difficulties of ordering the scattered bits of information from these suits is that neither reporter makes it clear whether the details he uses apply to the original inn-theatre of 1595 or the enlarged one of 1599. I take it that most of them refer to the latter, which seems to have given rise to most of the litigation. One set of details given by Sisson applies to the inn itself, presumably both before and after the remodelling of the acting facilities: 'Altogether, the Elizabethan theatre must have been something like a club for its habitués and for its locality. The Boar's Head had, to be exact, a hall, a general "drinking room," four "parlours" for more select potations or for dinners and suppers, and eleven bed-chambers.' ('Mr. and Mrs. Browne . . .', p. 100. No reference.)

The accommodations of the Boar's Head theatre of 1595 were remodelled after July 1599. Hotson says, 'In the summer of 1599 Richard Samuel was at great expense remodelling the theatre built in the quadrangular yard of the Boar's Head . . .'. (*Shakespeare's Wooden O*, p. 264, apparently from P.R.O. Req. 2/466, Pt. ii.) And several details of the remodelling are given in Sisson's 'Mr. and Mrs. Browne of the Boar's Head':

Towards the end of his [Oliver Woodliffe's] stay abroad he disposed of his control of the inn itself to Samuel [i.e., Richard Samuel, the contracting carpenter who had prepared the inn for use as a theatre in 1595], giving him a lease for eighteen years at a rent of £40 a year, keeping the theatre for himself. In July 1599, on Woodliffe's return, he came to see his theatre, and was dissatisfied with its equipment. The stage was too small: so were the galleries, accommodating an unprofitable number of high-priced seats. He desired to rebuild all on a large scale. [The extensive renovations of course required that Woodliffe provide a large amount of capital.] But he was not prepared to lay down the necessary money. He therefore proposed that Samuel should undertake the work, and agreed that, in recompense, he should extend his lease to cover the yard and all its equipment for stage purposes and exploit the theatre for his own profit. Woodliffe kept an interest in the theatre, in the shape of a share of the takings, as well as his rent on the lease. (Op. cit., p. 102. No reference.)

There were further complications in the property transfers of the inn and theatre—now separately owned though physically entwined—while the reconstruction was taking place. Sisson continues in his summary of events from his suits:

> This further lease was a verbal agreement, made before witnesses, valid enough if sufficiently testified to. Samuel took it as sufficient, and agreed to rebuild the theatre on these conditions. But he soon found that his financial resources were inadequate, and looked round for a supporter. What more natural then that he should turn to the actors who were using the theatre, especially to their leader! Robert Browne had money, and was willing to come in. He lent Samuel £200. The work progressed. But more money was still needed. Samuel gave it up, the fat kine devoured the lean kine, Browne put up a further £160, £360 in all, and in return Samuel conveyed to him all his interest in his lease of the inn and theatre. So Browne became lessee of the whole inn on the terms of Samuel's lease from Woodliffe. (Ibid. No reference.)

This acquisition of the entire property, inn and theatre, by Robert Browne, is what made Joan Alleyn's reference to 'Browne of the Boares head' perfectly clear to her husband, though it has been heretofore obscure to so many readers of the *Henslowe Papers*.

A few of the features in Browne's enlarged theatre in the Boar's Head are indicated in other extracts or summaries from the suits. Hotson, in his attempt to prove the physical orientation of all London public theatres, quotes two sentence-fragments about the reconstruction:

> the stage tyreing howse & galleries on the west side of
> the greate yarde
> the said weste galleryes over the said Stage
> (*Shakespeare's Wooden O*, p. 264, from P.R.O. Req. 2/466, Pt. ii.)

And Sisson, with less quotation and more summary, offers these statements, based on information from the suits about the Boar's Head:

> Bagnall [a whitebaker hired to clear up rubbish after the alterations] let fall a revealing phrase: which leads us to consider the nature of this inn-yard theatre. The rubbish which he had to clear away was mostly 'cast under the stage'. The stage was, in fact, a permanent

structure, far removed from the conjectural waggon-top of early days or the moveable trestle-stage so frequently assumed. As for the 'galleries' so much referred to, they were defined as 'galleries or rooms for people to stand in to see the plays,' set up in the yard, independent structures of considerable size. They had nothing to do with the ordinary galleries of chambers running round the yard like a verandah on the first floor. More than this, there are definite statements which show that the buildings at the stage end of the yard comprised not only a stage, but also a covering or 'heaven' over it, two 'tiring houses' or greenrooms and a balcony over the 'tiring-houses'. ('Mr. and Mrs. Browne . . .', p. 106. No reference.)

No other details about the structure of the theatre in the Boar's Head Inn have been revealed, but these are sufficient to show that the place clearly provided a permanent theatre in regular competition for several years with the Globe, the Fortune, the Rose, and the others.

Other facts about the customs, ownership, financing, and profits of the Boar's Head are revealed in scattered quotations and summaries. Professor Sisson says:

There is much further information on details of administration and sharing of takings. I will only add that on playing days, Browne had the right and the power to close the gates of the inn at eleven in the morning to prepare for the play, which began at two o'clock in the afternoon, after dinner. After the gates were thus closed, none could enter without paying entrance money, first to the 'gatherers' at the gates, and then a further payment for a place on the galleries erected in the yard. Browne's own share, as lessee of the theatre as well as leader of the company of actors, was the 'housekeeper's half' of the whole takings, a very enviable perquisite. ('Mr. and Mrs. Browne. . .', p. 106. No reference.)

One cannot be sure whether this statement about payment at the gates and for gallery places derives from specific disclosures in the suit or from general knowledge of the conduct of public theatres, but the information about the handling of the regular inn business on playing-days is new and illuminating. Clearly on those days the Boar's Head's function as an inn was severely curtailed. One wonders if the situation could have been the same at the Cross Keys, the Bell, the Bel Savage, the Bull, and the Red Lion, where no player is known to have had any financial control of the inn. The stated hours are also interesting. Was the three-hour interval necessary for performance preparations? Did any spectators appear so far in advance? (In 1624 John Chamberlain said that it was necessary to be at the Globe before one o'clock to get a seat for the great hit, *A Game at Chess* [see above, iv. 875], but clearly he thought the situation phenomenal.) Did the company at the Boar's Head normally have a run-through of the play late on the morning of performance? Perhaps the long interval was only insurance against delay in shutting off the inn business in the yard.

Other scattered bits of information add to our knowledge of the financial affairs of the company.

Langley's rent [he had a conflicting lease; see below] and other demands upon the company's purse had made playing at the Boar's Head unprofitable. To Langley's £3 a week, we learn, had to be added 15s. a week to the Master of the Revels, 5s. a week to the poor of the parish, and 'much money' for constant suits at Court to defeat attempts by the City to close the theatre. For the Boar's Head was in a vulnerable locality. ('The Red Bull Company...', pp. 61 and 67 n. From Decrees in a Chancery suit, C33/1601A/ff. 573, 611, 643, 648, 735, 798.)

The payment for the poor of the parish can be duplicated from incidental records of other theatres. (See below, vi. 250.) The amount of the weekly payments to the Master of the Revels seems high. Is the weekly sum of fifteen shillings just an average of the usual payments for play licences and special charges, or does it represent a regular independent weekly payment? The expenses for contesting City suits provides further evidence of the reasons for the location of later theatres well outside the jurisdiction of the Lord Mayor and Corporation.

Finally, these extracts and statements in the two Sisson articles provide additional details of the financial affairs of the company and of the ownership of the Boar's Head theatre. The interest in the theatre which Woodliffe had leased to Richard Samuel by a verbal agreement, during or soon after July 1599, had soon been made over by Samuel to Robert Browne, the player. But

Woodliffe had a bad memory.

Only a few months later his memory failed him completely. In November of the same year [1599?] he made a fresh deal altogether, oblivious of any lease to Samuel. Francis Langley was then fresh from his adventure upon the Swan Theatre. . . . The Swan seems to have fallen into disuse. But Langley, it appears, was still an optimist concerning real estate and theatres as investments. . . . So he got into touch with Woodliffe and bought from him the lease he held from Mrs. Pooley. For this he paid £400, £100 down, and £300 in bonds. Having thus completed his bargain, he came down to take possession and make terms with the actors at the Boar's Head, and with their leader Browne. . . . Under the strain of Woodliffe's injurious secrecy, whatever natural sense of justice Langley may have had broke down, and he denied the validity of the verbal lease. . . . Langley proceeded against Woodliffe in Chancery, while Browne proceeded impartially against both of them. For both were equally concerned to deny the verbal lease. And both proceeded against Browne in several suits at Common Law to recover possession of the theatre, but were invariably non-suited. ('Mr. and Mrs. Browne . . .', p. 103. No reference given.)

This combination of fraud and surprising innocence or carelessness in property transactions seems to have characterized a great many Elizabethan business deals, at least those involving theatres. However lamentable they may be as reflections of character, such deals and the consequent litigation are the welcome sources of a large part of our knowledge of Elizabethan and Jacobean actors and theatres—the Theatre, the Red Bull, the Globe, the Hope, the Blackfriars. In the case of Woodliffe, Langley, and Browne, the frauds and the consequent bitterness not only made the financing of the playing enterprise chaotic, but they are alleged to have produced certain sensational actions no less hampering to the players:

It is fully evident that the actors' tenure of the stage during these events was uncertain and eventful. More than once, indeed, Langley, weary of the law's delays, took matters into his own hands. With a hired force of bullies he invaded the theatre, and sat upon the stage itself, bristling with arms, grinning like Bunyan's giant at the affrighted pilgrims, swearing at the poor Thespians and protesting that he would kill or slay any that sought to resist him. On one occasion, Langley and Woodliffe, with their gang of bullies forced their way into the yard and found a play actually in progress on the stage. Whereupon the two financiers, with the help of Mrs. Woodliffe, laid hands on the pay-box, turned out Browne's 'gatherers,' and sat during the rest of the performance at the receipt of custom. Their haul amounted to four pounds. ('Mr. and Mrs. Browne . . .', pp. 103–4. No reference given.)

Such interference with their professional activities must have grievously compounded the troubles of a company already faced with financial problems. Their response is indicated in another summary made from Chancery decrees:

In Michaelmas 1600 the sharers in the company, numbering six and led by John Duke and Thomas Heywood, exhibited a Bill in Chancery against Browne, who was suing them for the breach of their bonds to play only at the Boar's Head Theatre. Their suit was dismissed finally on 28 June 1601, as 'no meet matter for this Court,' and they were ordered to pay 26s. 8d. costs to Browne, whose Answer was found 'sufficient.' The company, in fact, had moved from Browne and the Boar's Head to Henslowe and the Rose, vacant upon the building of the new Fortune Theatre. Langley's rent and other demands upon the company's purse had made playing at the Boar's Head unprofitable. ('The Red Bull Company . . .', pp. 60–61. Mostly from Chancery Decrees C 33/1601A/ff. 573, 611, 643, 648, 735, 798.)

A somewhat confusing comment about the affairs of the troupe is to be found in 'The Red Bull Company and the Importunate Widow'. Though the statement appears to refer to events of 1600, I assume that, given the date of the Chancery suit of John Duke, Thomas Heywood, and the other actors, against Browne, and given the date of the building of the Red Bull, it must refer to events of 1604 or 1605.

In 1600 Langley enforced a payment of £3 a week for the use of the theatre. There can be little doubt that the company found their situation impossible, and sought a new permanent theatre. The building of the Red Bull by Aaron Holland was the consequence, designed for occupation by this company and under a bargain with them. A leading member of the company, Thomas Swinnerton, was indeed a founder-sharer in the house as to one-eighteenth part, almost certainly in return for a contribution to the building costs and for the assurance of the occupation of the theatre by the company. ('The Red Bull Company . . .', p. 60. From *Woodford* v. *Holland*, October–November 1623, C 3/390/47.)

Sisson's previous statement about the players' abandonment of the Boar's Head for Henslowe's Rose conflicts with what this later one appears to say. I can only conjecture that, after abandoning the Boar's Head for the Rose before Michaelmas 1600, the company returned at a later date to the Boar's Head. Such an hypothesis would fit the clear statement in the Privy Council letter of 31 March 1602 that 'the Bores head is the place they haue especially vsed and doe best like of', and it would also fit the statement found in the Queen's men's draft patent of about 1604 that the company is 'to shew and exercise publikly . . . wᵗʰin there now vsuall Howsen, called the Curtayne, and the Bores head'. (See above, vi. 122–3; *M.S.C.* i. 266.) Presumably then it is the departure of the Queen's men for the Red Bull after a second sojourn at the Boar's Head that Professor Sisson is referring to.

What happened to the Boar's Head after 1604 I do not know. The wording of the reference to the Prince's men at Leicester in

1608–9 suggests that it was used for a time by the Duke of York's (Prince Charles's) company. This troupe might have played there a good deal, for no regular theatre for them is known until they were attached to the Hope in 1615. The absence of any clear theatrical allusions to the Boar's Head after 1604 suggests, however, that if there was any use of the converted inn as a theatre in the middle years of the reign of James it must have been sporadic.

THE BULL INN

Adams, pp. 7–17.
Chambers, *E.S.* ii. 380–1.

The Bull Inn in Bishopsgate was used as a place of public entertainment in the 1570's, 1580's, and 1590's, first for fencers' prizes and later for both fencers and players. The last known reference to the acting of plays there is in 1594.

THE CROSS KEYS INN

Adams, pp. 7–17.
Chambers, *E.S.* ii. 383.

The first known reference to playing at the Cross Keys Inn in Gracious (Gracechurch) Street is found in the year 1579, and the last in 1594.

THE CURTAIN

Adams, pp. 75–90.
Chambers, *E.S.* ii. 400–4.
Hook, Lucyle, 'The Curtain', *Shakespeare Quarterly*, xiii (1962), 499–504.
Hotson, Leslie, *Shakespeare's Wooden O* (1959), pp. 304–9.

In the Jacobean and Caroline period the Curtain, the second public theatre to be built in London, was the oldest playhouse in town and seldom in regular use. It had been built very shortly after The Theatre, probably in 1577, near Finsbury Fields, and probably close to the south-west corner of Hollowell Lane and Shoreditch, in the parish of St. Leonard's, Shoreditch, and not far south of The Theatre.[1]

---

[1] Adams, pp. 75–79. This account is supplemented by Lucyle Hook from late Treasury records and a review of the maps. Her survey indicates that the theatre was closer to Shoreditch than Adams thought, and 'immediately across [Hollowell Lane] from the dismantled Priory'.

In 1585 it was owned by Henry Lanham, and he may have been the builder, though nothing is known of the origins of the building. In shape it was probably round, for the epilogue of *The Travels of The Three English Brothers*, acted in 1607, and one of the few extant plays which can be surely associated with the Curtain, speaks of 'Some that fill vp this round circumference'. (1607 edition, H$_4$v.) What appears to be the Curtain can be rather dimly seen in a unique copy of an anonymous undated engraving bearing the legend 'The View of the Cittye of London from the North towards the Sowth' now in the library of the University of Utrecht. The flag and the hut in a three-storey building are visible, as well as what appear to be two external staircases. The dates of the engraved view and of the drawing upon which it was based are unknown.[1] The name of the Curtain came from the plot of ground on which it was built, and not from a sign with a green curtain as has been sometimes said. (Adams, pp. 75–76.)

The early history and occupancy of the Curtain—as, indeed, the later—are very obscure. At no time does the house seem to have been of very high repute, though the Lord Chamberlain's company was probably playing there in 1597 and 1598, and inconclusive allusions suggest that *Romeo and Juliet*, *Every Man in his Humour*, and possibly *Henry V* may have been presented there. (Chambers, *E.S.* ii. 196–7, 402–3; Hotson, *Shakespeare's Wooden O*, p. 309.) The undistinguished reputation of the Curtain is eloquently attested by the fact that though it stood longer than any other playhouse of the time the London publishers used its name on the title-page of only one play in all those years, W.

---

[1] In *The Times* (London) for 26 March 1954, p. 14, about two-thirds of the view was reproduced from a photograph in the print room at the British Museum. The picture of the Curtain is discussed in an article by Leslie Hotson, 'This Wooden O', on page 7 of the same issue. Hotson's article is reprinted under the title 'Shakespeare's Curtain Theatre Identified', as Appendix B of his *Shakespeare's Wooden O*, 1959, pp. 304–9. In the Appendix an enlarged section of the view, showing the theatre, is printed as an illustration. Whereas Hotson dates the view only vaguely in the *Times* article, he has attempted a precise date in another appendix (Appendix C, 'Alleyn's Fortune in the Making'). Here he reproduced an enlargement of another building in the view, which is on or near the location of the Fortune. Hotson is sure the second building represents the Fortune theatre, but since the building shown in the view has only two stories, no hut, no flag, no external staircases, and no clear roof line, whereas the Fortune contract calls for three stories, tile roof, and two external staircases, Hotson jumps to the conclusion that the picture represents the unfinished Fortune, and therefore dates the view between the January and late summer of 1600. The evidence is inadequate. It is doubtful that the building represents the Fortune, and therefore the date of the view is still unknown.

Smith's *The Hector of Germany*, published in 1615, '*As it hath beene publickly Acted at the* Red-Bull, *and at the* Curtayne, *by a Company of Young-men of this Citie*'. At least one other printed play was known by its publisher to have been acted at the Curtain, for in June 1607 he entered Day, Rowley, and Wilkins's *The Travels of The Three English Brothers* in the Stationers' Register, 'as yt Was played at the Curten', but when the play was printed in the same year the company but not the theatre was named on the title-page.

In 1604 and for a year or two thereafter the Curtain, along with the Boar's Head, was one of the regular houses of Queen Anne's players, but it was superseded by the new Red Bull. (Chambers, *E.S.* ii. 229–32.) What company, if any, succeeded them is unknown, but references to the house as the home of jigs and vulgarity accord with the lines in Edward Guilpin's *Skialetheia* of 1598:

> And she [the Thalia of base poets] with many a salt *La volto* iest
> Edgeth some blunted teeth, and fires the brest
> Of many an old cold gray-beard Cittizen,
> *Medea* like making him young againe;
> Who comming from the Curtaine sneaketh in,
> To some odde garden noted house of sinne.
>
> > (*Skialetheia. Or, A shadowe of Truth, in certaine Epigrams and Satyres*, 1598. B₈ᵛ.)

The same assumption that the Curtain is the normal environment for the vulgar work of the lowest poets appears twice in George Wither's *Abuses Stript and Whipt* in 1613. In the first satire 'Of the Passion of Love' he writes of the verse of the foolish lover:

> His *Poetry* is such as he can cul,
> From plaies he heard at *Curtaine* or at *Bul*,
> And yet is fine coy Mistres *Marry Muffe*,
> The soonest taken with such broken stuffe.
>
> > (C₄ᵛ.)

Again in the third satire of the second book he makes a similar association of the Curtain and low entertainment:

> base fellowes, whom meere time,
> Hath made sufficient to bring forth a *Rime*,
> A *Curtaine* ligge [i.e. jig], a libell, or a ballet,
> For fidlers, or some rogues with staffe and wallet
> To sing at doores.
>
> > (P₈ᵛ.)

Apparently the Curtain was an appropriate place for the conduct of the Venetian ambassador, Foscarini, which was reported to

Venice by a colleague in a letter undated but sent during the ambassador's incumbency, 1611–15.[1]

Possibly Samuel Rowley, the actor-playwright, was performing at the Curtain at about this time, but the evidence is vague and suspicious. In 1647, when the violently hated militant Independent preacher, Hugh Peters, was being assailed with all sorts of charges by the royalist writers, *Mercurius Pragmaticus* made his contribution to the campaign against Peters by declaring in the issue of 21–28 September: 'he has a fine wit I can tell you, *Sam Rowley* and he were a *Pylades*, and *Orestes*, when he played a womans part at the Curtaine Play-house, which is the reason his garbe is so emphaticall in the Pulpit'. (Quoted by Hotson, p. 15.) As there is no other evidence at all that Peters was ever a player, this statement is almost surely pure slander. But the best designed slander—and *Mercurius Pragmaticus* was no amateur—uses the truth as much as possible, and the selection of a companion and a theatre for Peters should have been deliberate. *Mercurius* wasted good malice if Rowley had never been associated with the Curtain in the public mind; and since Peters was born in 1598, the best years for his alleged acting of 'a womans part at the Curtaine Play-house' would have been about 1608–18. Probably I am pushing the craftsmanship of a hard-working slanderer too far. At least we have some slight cause to associate Samuel Rowley, whose only known dramatic activity after 1616 is the composition of three plays for the struggling Palsgrave's company at the new Fortune in 1623 and 1624 (see above, i. 149–51 and v. 1009–14), with the Curtain theatre. Moreover, since Peters would look worse if his associations were kept low, *Mercurius Pragmaticus* would seem to be concurring in the estimate of the Curtain suggested in the other allusions.

In 1620, and perhaps a little earlier, the Curtain theatre was being used by the company of Prince Charles.[2] In February 1619/20 'Iohn Drew one of the Ordinary groomes of the Prince his Chamber' asked to be paid for travelling 'from the Courte at San Iames into London so far as Shoredich wᵗʰ a mesuage to Roulle one of his highnes players'; in the same month William Price, another groom of the Prince's Chamber, also asked to be paid for 'beinge sent by the Commaund of mr Peter Newton . . . of one message from the Courte at whithall to the Prince his players in

---

[1] Transcribed by Sir Edmund Chambers in *R.E.S.* i. (1925), p. 186.

[2] This date is earlier than the one I conjectured in the history of this company (see above, i. 204–5); the evidence quoted here did not become available until twenty years after that account was published.

shorediche to warne them to attend his highnes'. (*M.S.C.* vi [1961], 148.) Since the Curtain, after the demolition of The Theatre in 1599, was the only London theatre in Shoreditch, it must have been to the Curtain that Drew and Price were sent with their messages for Prince Charles's players.

A slanderous poem of the late summer or early autumn of 1621 indicates that there was playing at the Curtain at that time, but unfortunately it gives no hint of the company there, though it does impute a fairly low character to the playhouse. On 26 August 1621 the undergraduates of Christ Church, Oxford, presented a revival of Barton Holyday's tedious comedy, *Technogamia, or the Marriages of the Arts*, before King James at Woodstock. There are various allusions to the failure of the performance and to the overt boredom of the King. (See above, iv. 589–96.) One long, derisive poem, which is found in several extant commonplace books, was written by Peter Heylyn, at that time a Fellow of Magdalen College and a rising light in the University. In one passage, addressed in mock indignation to a critical soldier of the King's guard, Heylyn says:

> He [Holyday] hath a zelous sword if you he heares
> Be sure heele cut of your rebellious eares,
> fly to yᵉ Globe or Curtaine with your trul,
> Or gather musty phrases from yᵉ Bul,
> This was not for your dyet he doth bring
> what he prepar'd for our Platonique King.[1]

Two further bits of evidence suggest that the Prince's men were still at the Curtain at the end of 1621 and were therefore the company Barton Holyday advised the guard to visit with his trull. In one of the Lord Chamberlain's Warrant Books, now Inner Temple MS. 515, No. 7 (see J. T. Murray, *English Dramatic Companies*, ii. 193), there is a warrant for payment of twenty marks 'for two plaies to the Princes Servauts [for presenting plays at court] the one 27 Decembris *1621*, called the man in the moone drinks Clarrett . . .'. The play is now lost and is otherwise unknown. But there is a ballad in the Roxburghe collection entitled 'The Man in the Moon Drinks Claret. As it was lately sung at the Curtain, Holy-Well'. (*The Roxburghe Ballads*, ed. William Chappell [1874], ii. 256–8.) The ballad is undated and there appears to be no entry for it in the Stationers' Register. The Curtain was,

---

[1] Folger Library commonplace book (MS. 452. 5, fols. 140–2), as quoted by Sister M. Jean Carmel Cavanaugh in her edition of Barton Holyday's *Technogamia* (1942), p. xxxv.

however, the theatre of the Prince's men in early 1621 and in 1622, and the identity of the titles of play and ballad suggest that the ballad was sung by the Prince's men in the course of Curtain performances of the play they acted at court on 27 December 1621. Of course they may have sung it there *after* the court performance, but first performance at the Curtain is at least as likely. The ballad is a song about riotous drinkers and suggests a roistering, possibly a satiric, play.

Definite, official evidence that the Prince's Servants were the company in residence at the Curtain in 1622 comes from Sir Henry Herbert's Office Book. Edmond Malone, whose quotations from this now lost manuscript are the most precise and extensive, summarized a portion of his observations:

> It appears from the office-book of Sir Henry Herbert . . . in the year 1622, there were but five principal companies of comedians in London; the King's Servants, who performed at the Globe and in Blackfriars; the Prince's Servants, who performed then at the Curtain; the Palsgrave's Servants, who had possession of the Fortune; the players of the Revels, who acted at the Red Bull; and the Lady Elizabeth's Servants . . . who performed at the Cockpit in Drury Lane. (*Variorum*, iii. 57–59.)

In June of 1622 the audience at the Curtain presumably saw the Prince's men present another new play, now lost. Sir Henry Herbert's Office Book, under date of 10 June 1622, carries the licence: 'A new Play, called, *The Duche Painter, and the French Branke* [*Brawle? Branle?*] was allowed to be acted by the Princes Servants at the Curtayne.' (See above, v. 1324–5.) For this lost play there is no ballad to suggest its character, and even the meaning of the title is uncertain. It might be entertaining to make up a plot about the King's Dutch painter, Anthony Van Dyck, who had been painting in London a year or two before, but there is not the slightest evidence that the play concerned him.

Late in 1622 performances were still going on at the Curtain and were evidently expected to continue in 1623, for Jack Dawes's mock prognostication for the year 1623 includes the passage:

> About this time, new Playes will be in more request, then old: and if company come currant to the *Bull* and *Curtaine*, there will be more money gathered in one after-noone, then will be giuen to the *Kingsland* Spittle in a whole moneth. Also, if at this time, about the houres of foure and fiue, it waxe cloudy, and then raine downe-right, they shall sit dryer in the Galleries, then those who are the vnderstanding men in the yard. (*Vox Graculi, or Iacke Dawes Prognostication . . . for 1623* [1623], I₁ᵛ–I₂.)

Presumably the performances at the Curtain, during which, 'Jack Dawe' shrewdly predicted, rain would wet those standing in the open pit but not the gentlemen in the covered galleries, were given by Prince Charles's men, but that company did not remain much longer at the Curtain, for by 19 August 1623 they were at the Red Bull, where the Master of the Revels, on that date, re-licensed to them an old play called *The Peaceable King or the Lord Mendall*. (See above, v. 1393.)

At the Curtain the Prince's men were succeeded by an unknown troupe, not one of the regular London companies—Prince's, Lady Elizabeth's, King's, Palsgrave's, and possibly the dying Revels company. What this company was is unknown, but one would guess that it was some provincial troupe trying to gain a foot-hold in London. For them the Master of the Revels licensed another lost play with a title even more titillating—at least for Americans. In August 1623 Herbert made an entry which reads, in an unfamiliar transcript, probably made by Craven Ord: 'A Tragedy of the Plantation of Virginia, the [prophaness left out] contayninge 16 sheets & one May be acted [els not for the] com-panye at the Curtune Founde fault with the length of this playe & [commanded a] reformation in all their other playes.' (See above, v. 1395–6.) No other Jacobean or Caroline play devoted largely to the American colonies is known, and it may be thought suggestive that this one was licensed for the lowly Curtain, that it was too long, and that it contained too much 'prophaneness'.

This tenancy of Prince Charles's men in 1622 and 1623 con-stitutes the last known use of the Curtain as its customary theatre by a regular London company. However, John Underwood, one of the King's men, evidently did not think the playhouse aban-doned in October 1624, for in his will he left to his five children 'my part and share or due in or out of the playhovse called the Curtaine scituate in or neere Holloway in the parishe of St: Leonard in Shoreditch London or any other place ...'. (See above, ii. 651.) Irregular use of the theatre is indicated by a somewhat cryptic record Sir Henry Herbert made of a commission dated 9 March 1624/5 which allowed the provincial troupe of William Perry to act for limited periods at the Curtain:

It determines 9 March 1624—[5]—A license to Perrye & others in [confirmation of a] pattent from the Revels for a yeare after date hereof this [9th Apr. 1624. 3 *li*.] He hath given his bonde for 6*li* more to bee payd in sixe [months in respect of] the weakness of his commis-sion for the Revels their having [a latter grant of] more force; att the same tyme   dayes libertye to [acte with his companye] in this

towne of London att the Curtin—10ˢ —Of this [hath byn payd] for
the compisition by Mʳˢ Fleminge this 17 Apr. 1624—2¹ᐧ¹

The precise significance of this document in the tangled affairs of
the provincial company often called the Children of the Revels
to the late Queen Anne (see above, ii. 529–31) is now impossible
to determine, but it is clear enough that the licence provided by
someone in 1624/5 gave them the privilege of occasional short
seasons at the Curtain. No evidence that this provincial troupe or
any other Caroline acting company ever so used the Curtain is
known, but the licence shows that such use was contemplated
and therefore that the theatre was available.

Evidently Edmond Malone, who saw the original Herbert
manuscripts, could find in them no evidence of dramatic use of
the Curtain in the last fifteen years or so that acting was allowed.
He said that from shortly after the accession of King Charles the
Curtain 'seems to have been used only by prize-fighters'. (*Variorum*, iii. 54, n. 2.) The theatre was not, however, demolished.
In February 1627/8 'the common shoare neer the Curtaine Playhouse' is mentioned (Jeaffreson, *Middlesex County Records*, iii.
164); and Dr. Hotson noticed that in a 1660 list of disreputable
characters is found 'Mrs Mails by the Curtain Playhouse'.
(Hotson, p. 92, from John Garfield's *The Wandering Whore Continued* [1660].)

The meaning of the word 'Playhouse' in these documents cannot, unfortunately, be confidently given its ordinary meaning, for
a Treasury warrant of 21 April 1698 lists a number of properties
in Shoreditch, including 'garden and houses called the Curtain
Playhouse in Hallowell Lane in Shoreditch'. (Lucyle Hook, 'The
Curtain', loc. cit.). If 'Curtain Playhouse' meant a garden and
houses in 1698, how long had it had that meaning? Apparently
at some time the old theatre had been converted to tenements,
though retaining its old theatrical name. One wonders if
Christopher Beeston could have been responsible for the conversion. His will of 4 October 1638 left unspecified land and
tenements in Shoreditch (see above, ii. 632), and a suit of 1666,
discovered by Leslie Hotson, seems to indicate that part of this
property may have been the Curtain. (Hotson, p. 92.)

But this is mere speculation. We know that no records of regular
playing at the Curtain have been found after the reign of James I,

¹ Halliwell-Phillipps Scrap-Books, *Fortune*, p. 85 (Folger Shakespeare
Library). The bracketed sections are in a different hand; they indicated
the replacement of words cut off when the MS. was cut up for pasting in the
scrap-books.

and that Malone found only prize-fight records after 1625. Before the end of the century the old theatre appears to have been converted to tenements, but the date of the conversion is unknown.

THE FIRST FORTUNE

Adams, pp. 267–93.
Archer, William, 'The Fortune Theatre, 1600', *Shakespeare Jahrbuch*, xliv (1908), 159–66.
Chambers, *E.S.* ii. 435–43.
Greg, W. W. (ed.), *Henslowe's Diary* (1904–8), ii. 56–65.
—— *Henslowe Papers* (1907), pp. 4–7.
Hotson, Chapters I and II, *passim*.
—— *Shakespeare's Wooden O* (1959), pp. 87–91, 310–13.
Lawrence, W. J., 'New Light on the Elizabethan Theatre', *Fortnightly Review*, xcix, New Series (1916), 820–9.
Rollins, Hyder E., 'A Contribution to the History of the English Commonwealth Drama', *Studies in Philology*, xviii (1921), 267–333 and xx (1923), 52–69.
Warner, George F., *Catalogue of the Manuscripts and Muniments of Alleyn's College of God's Gift at Dulwich* (1881).
Young, William, *The History of Dulwich College*, 2 vols. (1889).

The first Fortune, like the first Globe, was destroyed by fire in Jacobean times; the second Fortune, like the second Globe, was rebuilt—though after a somewhat longer interval—on the same site; and the second Fortune, again like the second Globe, has been much less fully studied than its predecessor.

The first Fortune was in regular use until it burned to the ground on the night of 9 December 1621. It had been built as an important move in the competition of Philip Henslowe and the Lord Admiral's company with the Lord Chamberlain's company at the new Globe. Their Bankside theatre had been completed about the middle of 1599, and on 8 January following Philip Henslowe and Edward Alleyn signed a contract with Peter Streete, carpenter and builder, for the construction of the new Fortune. Not only does the close proximity of the dates imply an episode in the rivalry of the then principal dramatic companies of London, but the selection of Peter Streete as the builder and the wording of his contract show quite clearly that competition with the Globe was uppermost in the minds of Henslowe and Alleyn. Peter Streete was the 'heade Carpenter' or 'Cheefe carpenter' who had supervised the dismantling of The Theatre in preparation for the building of the Globe. In the Court of Requests suit, *Burbage* v. *Allen*, in April 1600, John Goborne deposed that he was present at the tearing down of The Theatre and that Peter Streete was there as 'the Cheefe carpenter'. Henry Johnson, present on the same occasion, deposed:

he this deponent did perceave that the same Theater was appoynted to be soe pulled downe by the Complainant by his Brother Richard Burbage and one Thomas Smythe: and one [Peter] Streete who was heade Carpenter that gaue assistance therein: And when he had soe Charged them not to pull the same Theatre Downe they the said Complainant and Thomas Smythe and [Peter] Streete the Carpenter tould him this deponent that they tooke yt downe but to sett yt vpp vppon the premisss in an other forme and that they had Couenanted wth the Carpenter to that effecte . . .[1]

Since Peter Streete seems to have been in charge of the workmen at the demolition of The Theatre, preparatory to the transportation of the timbers across the river for the erection of the Globe, it seems most likely that he was the building contractor for the new theatre. This likelihood is enhanced by certain specifications in the contract which Henslowe and Alleyn made with him: in three different instances Streete agrees to build major features of the new Fortune as they are 'made & Contryved in and to the late erected Plaiehowse . . . Called the Globe'. (*Henslowe Papers*, p. 5.) In a fourth and even more suggestive instance it is agreed that he will 'alsoe make all the saide fframe in every poynte for Scantling[es] lardger and bigger in assize Then the Scantlinges of the Timber of the saide newe erected howse Called the Globe . . .'. (*Op. cit.*, p. 6.) Surely Henslowe and Alleyn would not have relied on such comparative specifications, and Streete would not have bound himself to observe them, unless he had such intimate knowledge of the Globe as its builder would have acquired. In any case the paramount consideration of successful competition with the Globe is made obvious by the contract.

Henslowe and Alleyn selected for their new theatre a site north-west of the City which, as Sir Edmund Chambers notes, 'would be convenient for the well-to-do population, which was establishing itself in the western suburbs, along the main roads of Holborn and the Strand. The Fortune on the north, and the Blackfriars,

---

[1] *Court of Requests Proceedings, Uncalendared, Bdl. 242. Depositions ex parte Allen*, 26 April, 1600, as printed by C. W. Wallace, '*The First London Theatre: Materials for a History*', University Studies of the University of Nebraska, xiii (1913), 222.

opened about the same time on the south, delimited a region which has remained almost to our own day the head-quarters of the stage'. (*E.S.* ii. 435.) The land was in the parish of St. Giles without Cripplegate, between Whitecross Street and Golding Lane. Since the plot also contained six tenements, five on the east side of Golding Lane and one on the west side of Whitecross Street, the exact amount of ground devoted to the theatre cannot be determined from the contract. The size of the plot of ground on which stood the *second* Fortune, erected on the same site in 1622 and 1623, is given in a survey of the ruined theatre made for the Masters and Warden of Dulwich College in July, 1656: 'That ye sd late playhouse and Tapphouse: belonging to ye same: standeth vpon a peece of ground Conteyninge in length from East to West one hundred Twenty and seven ffoote: and a halfe: a little more or lesse: and in breadth from North to South: one hundred twenty and nine ffot a little more or les . . .'. (*Henslowe Papers,* p. 96).[1]

On this ground Henslowe and Alleyn contracted with Peter Streete to build the Fortune theatre. Their contract, still extant among the muniments of Dulwich College, is the most precise set of specifications we have for any theatre of the time; it is therefore worth quoting almost in full, for purposes of reference:

This Indenture made the Eighte daie of Januarye 1599 And in the Twoe and ffortyth yeare of the Reigne of our sovereigne Ladie Elizabeth by the grace of god Queene of Englande ffraunce and Jrelande defender of the ffaythe &c^e Betwene Phillipp Henslowe and Edwarde Allen of the pishe of Ste Savio^rs in Southwark in the Countie of Surrey gentlemen on thone pto And Peeter Streete Cittizen and Carpenter of London on thother parte witnesseth That whereas the saide Phillipp Henslowe & Edward Allen the daie of the date hereof Haue bargayned compounded & agreed wth the saide Peter Streete ffor the erectinge buildinge & settinge upp of a newe howse and Stadge for a Plaiehouse in and vppon a certeine plott or pcell of grounde appoynted oute for that purpose Scytuate and beinge nere Goldinge lane in the pishe of Ste Giles w^thoute Cripplegate of London To be by him the saide Peeter Streete or some other sufficyent woorkmen of his provideinge and appoyntem^te and att his propper Costes & Chardges for the consideracōn hereafter in theis pñt^e expressed / Made erected, builded and sett upp Jn manner & forme followinge (that is to saie) The frame of the saide howse to be sett square and to conteine ffowerscore foote of lawfull assize everye

---

[1] For the leases see *Henslowe Papers*, pp. 14–18 and 25–30. The ownership of the property from 1546 is traced from Dulwich deeds in *Henslowe's Diary*, ii. 56–57.

waie square w^thoutt and fiftie fiue foote of like assize square everye
waie w^thin wth a good suer and stronge foundacōn of pyles brick lyme
and sand bothe w^thout & w^thin to be wroughte one foote of assize att
the leiste aboue the grounde And the saide fframe to conteine Three
Stories in heighth The first or lower Storie to Conteine Twelue foote
of lawfull assize in heighth The second Storie Eleauen foote of lawfull
assize in heigth And the Third or vpper Storie to conteine Nyne foote
of lawfull assize in height / All which Stories shall conteine Twelue
foote and a halfe of lawfull assize in breadth througheoute besides a
Juttey forwarde in either of the saide Twoe vpper Stories of Tenne
ynches of lawfull assize with fflower convenient divisions for gentlemens roomes and other sufficient and convenient divisions for Twoe
pennie roomes wth necessarie Seates to be placed and sett Aswell in
those roomes as througheoute all the rest of the galleries of the saide
howse and wth suchelike steares Conveyances & divisions w^thoute
& w^thin as are made & Contryved in and to the late erected Plaiehowse
On the Banck in the saide pishe of Ste Savio^rs Called the Globe W^th
a Stadge and Tyreinge howse to be made erected & settupp w^thin
the saide fframe wth a shadowe or cover over the saide Stadge w^th
Stadge shalbe placed & sett As alsoe the stearecases of the saide
fframe in suche sorte as is p^rfigured in a Plott thereof drawen And
wch Stadge shall conteine in length ffortie and Three foote of lawfull
assize and in breadth to extende to the middle of the yarde of the
saide howse The same Stadge to be paled in belowe wth good stronge
and sufficyent newe oken bourdes And likewise the lower Storie of
the saide fframe w^thinside, and the same lower storie to be alsoe laide
over and fenced wth stronge yron pykes And the saide Stadge to be
in all other proporcōns Contryved and fashioned like vnto the Stadge
of the saide Plaie howse Called the Globe W^th convenient windowes
and lighte glazed to the saide Tyreinge howse And the saide fframe
Stadge and Stearecases to be covered wth Tyle and to haue a sufficient
gutter of lead to Carrie & convey the water frome the Coveringe of
the saide Stadge to fall backwardes And also all the saide fframe and
the Stairecases thereof to be sufficyently enclosed w^thoute wth lathe
lyme & haire and the gentlemens roomes and Twoe pennie roomes
to be seeled wth lathe lyme & haire and all the fflowers of the saide
Galleries Stories and Stadge to be bourded wth good & sufficyent
newe deale bourdes of the whole thicknes wheare need shalbe And
the saide howse and other thinges beforemencōed to be made &
doen To be in all other Contrivitions Conveyances fashions thinge
and thinges effected finished and doen accordinge to the manner and
fashion of the saide howse Called the Globe Saveinge only that all the
princypall and maine postes of the saide fframe and Stadge forwarde
shalbe square and wroughte palasterwise wth carved proporcōns
Called Satiers to be placed & sett on the Topp of every of the same
postes And saveinge alsoe that the said Peeter Streete shall not be
chardged wth anie manner of pay[ntin]ge in or aboute the saide

fframe howse or Stadge or anie pte thereof nor Rendringe the walls wthin Nor seeling anie more or other roomes then the gentlemens roomes Twoe pennie roomes and Stadge before remembred / **notwe theiruppon** the saide Peeter Streete dothe coveñnt promise and graunte . . . That he the saide Peeter Streete his executo^{rs} or assignes shall & will . . . make erect, sett upp and fully finishe . . . All the saide fframe and other woork*e* whatsoever Jn and vppon the saide plott or pcell of grounde (beinge not by anie aucthoretie Restrayned, and haveinge ingres egres & regres to doe the same) before the ffyue & twentith daie of Julie next Comeinge after the date hereof **And shall alsoe** at his or theire like costes and Chardges Provide and finde All manner of woorkmen Tymber Joyst*e* Rafters boord*e* dores bolt*e* hinges brick Tyle lathe lyme haire sande nailes lade Jron Glasse woorkmanshipp and other thinges whatsoever wch shalbe needefull Convenyent & necessarie for the saide fframe & woork*e* & eu^{r}ie pte thereof **And** shall alsoe make all the saide fframe in every poynte for Scantling*e* lardger and bigger in assize Then the Scantlinges of the Timber of the saide newe erected howse Called the Globe / . . . **Jn consideracõn** of all wch building*e* and of all stuff & woorkemanshipp thereto belonginge . . . the saide Phillipp Henslowe & Edward Allen or one of them Or the executo^{r}s admĩstrato^{r}s or assignes of them or one of them Shall & will well & truelie paie or Cawse to be paide vnto the saide Peeter Streete his executo^{rs} or assignes Att the place aforesaid appoynted for the erectinge of the saide fframe The full some of ffower hundred & ffortie Poundes of lawfull money of Eng-lande in manner & forme followeinge / **Jn witnes whereof** the pties abouesaid to theis pñte Jndentures Jnterchaungeably haue sett theire handes and seales / Yeoven the daie and yeare ffirste aboue-written.

P S

Sealed and deliu^{r}ed by the saide Peter Streete in the p^{r}sence of me william Harris Pub Sc¡ And me Frauncis Smyth appr to the said Scr /

[seal wanting; endorsed:]

Peater Streat ffor The Building of the ffortune[1]

From the specifications in this contract, Mr. Walter H. Godfrey, the English architect, constructed at the instigation and with the advice of William Archer a scale model of the first Fortune. (Archer, *Shakespeare Jahrbuch*, loc. cit.) One model is now in the Dramatic Museum at Columbia University, and another in the Museum of European Culture at the University of Illinois. The

---

[1] *Henslowe Papers*, pp. 4–7. A convenient sketch, scrupulously limited to those features of the theatre explicitly measured in the contract, and nothing more, is to be found in C. Walter Hodges, *The Globe Restored*, p. 188.

Jahrbuch article reproduces two of Godfrey's sketches and two of his plans. Models, plans, and sketches have often been reproduced, and they have had a great deal of influence on popular ideas of Elizabethan theatres.

Unfortunately, as both Godfrey and Archer were well aware, many important features of the theatre are barely mentioned in the contract or are referred to the Globe. Since there is no way to leave blanks in a model, Mr. Godfrey was forced to build into his miniature Fortune William Archer's conjectures about such items as stairs, the shadow, many features of the stage, the galleries behind the stage, the tiring-house, the stage doors, &c. Most of the enthusiastic writers and teachers who have used the models or the illustrations have made little distinction between those features which are based on conjectures and those based on the specifications of the contract.

The distinctive or memorable features of the Fortune emerge from this contract—its shape, in the first place. It was square, 80 feet each side, whereas all the other public theatres whose shapes are known were round or nearly so. For the Fortune only do we have exact over-all measurements—80 feet square outside, 55 feet square inside; stage 43 feet in width, and $27\frac{1}{2}$ feet, plus anything which may have been taken from the first gallery, in depth; three galleries (as for several other theatres)—the first 12 feet high (as at the Hope) and 12 feet 6 inches deep, the second 11 feet high and 13 feet 4 inches deep, the third 9 feet high (as implied, but not specified, in the Hope contract) and 13 feet 4 inches deep. The stage was to be paled-in below with new oak boards, as was the lower story of the frame, and the latter was to be fenced with iron pikes.

Unfortunately the contract relies on the lost 'Plott thereof drawen', on Peter Streete's experience, and on his specific knowledge of the Globe, for the building of those parts of the theatre we should most like to understand: the tiring-house, the upper and inner stages, if any, the height, position, and extent of the 'shadow', the location and size of the lords' room and the musicians' room, the position, size, character, and number of the staircases and entrances, the traps, hoists, and curtained stage areas, the height of the stage. It would also be interesting, though less important, to know what Alleyn did in his painting after Peter Streete and his carpenters finished; for the painting, probably the simulation of marble, must have been effective in making the Fortune 'the fayrest play-house in this towne', as John Chamberlain described it at the time of the fire in 1621. (*Chamberlain*, ii. 415.)

It has recently been asserted that an undated engraving, found in the manuscript journal of a Dutch East India Company agent who lived in London from 1629 to 1636, shows the Fortune theatre under construction between January and autumn 1600.[1] Since the map is undated, the only reason for identifying the building as the Fortune is its position—extremely hazardous to determine from such a view. The building shown has only two stories, no hut, no flag, no external staircases, and no clear roof line. Since the Fortune contract calls for three stories, two external staircases, and a tile roof, no characteristics of the Fortune are recognizable. Under the circumstances it is most ingenious but scarcely convincing to set a date arbitrarily narrowed to half a year, simply to account for the fact that the building shown in a very rough approximation of the right location shows none of the features specified in the contract for the Fortune.

When the new theatre was ready, apparently in the autumn of 1600,[2] the Lord Admiral's company moved in, and this troupe under its successive names—the Lord Admiral's company to 1603, Prince Henry's company 1603–12, and the Palsgrave's company 1612–25—played at the Fortune until the house burned in December 1621. The history of the theatre up to 1616 is set out by J. Q. Adams (pp. 267–83) and by Sir Edmund Chambers (*E.S.* ii. 435–42 and 173–92), but there are a few events and situations of significance for the later history of the theatre which need to be considered here.

At the time of the building of the Fortune by Henslowe and Alleyn in 1600 the company there was a serious rival, for pre-eminence in London, of Shakespeare's troupe, the Lord Chamberlain's men; for their large and well-known repertory included most of the Marlowe canon, some of the more distinguished plays

[1] *Shakespeare's Wooden O*, Appendix C, 'Alleyn's Fortune in the Making', pp. 310–13. The unique engraving of London from the north was first printed in *The Times* (London), 26 March 1954, but with no mention of the Fortune in the accompanying article. The Fortune identification, with the part of the engraving showing the building in question enlarged, appears in the Appendix.

[2] Though Streete's contract called for him to finish on 25 July, he had the escape clause 'beinge not by anie aucthoretie Restrayned'. Moreover, Alleyn's painting, which may well have been very elaborate, had to be done after Streete finished. The Admiral's men had left their old theatre, the Rose, before the end of October, for Henslowe records that Pembroke's company 'begane to playe at the Rosse the 28 of octob[er]' (*Henslowe's Diary*, i. 131), but Edward Alleyn's rent payment 'for the firste weckes playe' is recorded in an undated diary entry between 11 November and 14 December. (Ibid., p. 124.)

of Dekker, the early Jonson pieces, now lost, as well as the largest
body of lost plays that we can now assign to any company. But
in Caroline times the Fortune, along with the Red Bull, had become
notorious as one of the lowest theatrical resorts in town. The
deterioration which led to this Caroline state began in the first
decade of James's reign, as certain pieces of evidence indicate.

On 1 October 1612 the General Sessions of the Peace at Westminster issued 'An Order for suppressinge of Jigges att the ende
of Playes'. The Order began:

> Whereas Complaynte have [*sic*] beene made at this last Generall
> Sessions that by reason of certayne lewde Jigges songes and daunces
> vsed and accustomed at the play-house called the Fortune in Goulding-
> lane divers cutt-purses and other lewde and ill disposed persons in
> greate multitudes doe resorte thither at th' end of euerye playe many
> tymes causinge tumultes and outrages wherebye His Majesties peace
> is often broke and much mischiefe like to ensue thereby, Itt was here-
> uppon expresselye commaunded and ordered. . . . That all Actors
> of euerye playehouse within this cittye and liberties thereof and in
> the Countye of Middlesex that they and euerie of them utterlye
> abolishe all Jigges Rymes and Daunces after their playes And not
> to tollerate permitt or suffer anye of them to be used vpon payne
> of ymprisonment and puttinge downe and suppressinge of theire
> playes. . . . (Jeaffreson, *Middx. Co. Rec.* ii. 83.)

Clearly the Fortune was thought to be the chief offender in this
unsavoury situation, though all the theatres were to suffer the
consequences. The actors at the Fortune were well aware of at
least some of the offensive aspects of their reputation, for they
allowed their poets Thomas Dekker and Thomas Middleton to
write into their comedy *The Roaring Girl, or Moll Cut-Purse*
certain lines which contain a surprising allusion, quite compatible
with the statement in the order of the General Sessions. The play
exploits in its chief character, Marion Frith, a well-known London
female roisterer who frequently dressed in men's clothes, and who
is depicted in a rare woodcut on the title-page of the 1611 edition
so habited, carrying a sword, and smoking a pipe. In the first
scene of the fifth act Moll, who uses her underworld knowledge
to help her upper-class friends, sees a very well-dressed cutpurse
enter with several accomplices. Lord Noland and Sir Thomas
Long are taken in by his gallant appearance, but Moll warns them:

> Pox on him, a gallant? shaddow mee, I know him: 'tis one that
> cumbers the land indeed; if hee swimme neere to the shore of any of
> your pockets, looke to your purses. . . .

one of them is a nip, I tooke him once i' the twopenny gallery at the
Fortune. . . . (1611 quarto, L_1^v.)

Thomas Dekker, one of the authors of the play, as if to explicate
his own text, wrote about the same time: 'suffer me to carry
vp your thoughts vpon nimbler winges, where (as if you sat in the
moste perspicuous place of the two-penny gallerie in a play-house)
you shall cleerely, and with an open eye beholde all the partes . . .'.
(*The Ravens Almanacke* [1609], B_2^v.) Allusions to theatres and
players in Jacobean and Caroline plays are generally complimen-
tary if alluding to the theatre in which the play is to be acted,
unfavourable if referring to competitors; this allusion in a play
printed in 1611, 'As it hath lately beene Acted on the Fortune-
stage by *the Prince his Players*', suggests that the company at the
Fortune was willing to advertise its dubious audience.

Another record implies that the Fortune was intent on the
vulgar appeal. In the *Consistory of London Correction Book* under
the date 1605 appears the following entry:

Officium dñi contra Marion Frith.

This day and place the said Mary appeared personally and then and
there voluntarily confessed that she had long frequented all or most
of the disorderly and licentious places in this cittie as namely she
hath usually in the habit of a man resorted to alehouses taverns tobacco
shops and also to play houses there to see plaies and proses [prizes ?]
and namely being at a play about three quarters of a yeare since at
ye Fortune in man's apparel and in her boots and wth a sword at her
syde she told the company then present y^t she thought many of
them were of opinion that she was a man, but if any of them would
come to her lodging they should finde she is a woman, and some other
immodest and lascivious speaches she also used at y^t time and also
sat upon the stage in the public viewe of all the people there present
in man's apparel and played upon her lute and sange a song and she
further confessed y^t she . . . hathe also usually associated herself
wth ruffianly swaggering and lewd company as namely with cutpurses
blasphemers drunkards and others of bad note . . . and further con-
fesseth y^t she was punished for the misdemeanours aforementioned in
Bridewell. . . . (Francis W. X. Fincham in *Transactions of the Royal
Historical Society*, Fourth Series, iv [1921], 111–13.)

Evidently Middleton and Dekker had exploited for the Fortune
company a notorious character who had already exhibited herself from the Fortune stage to the scandal of some.[1] Of course the

---

[1] See R. C. Bald, *Modern Language Review*, xxxii (1937), 37–39 for a
good case that the play dates from 1607–8.

play sentimentalizes Moll, but the policy which directed the cultivation of the popular appeal of Miss Frith is consistent with that which made the Fortune, by 1612, the chief London centre for the jig, and caused 'divers cutt-purses and other lewde and ill disposed persons [to] resort thither at th' end of eurye playe many tymes causinge tumultes and outrages'. It could well be that one of the 'tumultes and outrages' referred to in the order of the General Sessions of the Peace was that for which, on 28 February 1610/11, 'John Shawe of Grubstreete butcher and Gilbert Borne of Whitcrosse Street . . . and . . . John Lynsey of St. Andrew's Undershafte butcher' posted a total of £80 bail for Lynsey's appearance at the next Middlesex Sessions of the Peace to answer 'for abusing certen gentlemen at the Play House called The Fortune'. (Jeaffreson, *Middx. Co. Rec.* ii. 71.) Certainly the jig order did not eliminate the 'tumultes and outrages' at the Fortune theatre, for nine months after it was sent out, a true bill was issued, 5 June 1613, declaring that 'on the said day at The Fortune . . . near Gouldinglane . . . Richard Bradley late of St. James's at Clarkenwell yoman assaulted Nicholas Bestney junior gentleman, and with knife gave him two grievous wounds, by stabbing him with the said weapon in the first place on the right breast, and then in the left part of his belly, of which two wounds the said Nicholas languished and still remains in danger of death'. (Ibid., pp. 88–89.) Bradley confessed the indictment. Such frays are reported now and then from almost every Elizabethan and Jacobean theatre, but no other playhouse is charged with anything like so many as the Fortune and the Red Bull.

By 1614 the reputation of the Fortune as a house of uncultivated audiences and vulgar fare was sufficiently widespread to be exploited at Trinity College, Cambridge. When King James and his court visited Cambridge during a royal progress, they had performed for them in the Hall at Trinity, on 9 March 1614/15, Thomas Tomkis's play, *Albumazar*. Trincalo, the stupid farmer who is enamoured of Armellina, soliloquizes over her charms and his desire to win her. As she approaches in the first scene of the second act, he says: 'O 'tis *Armellina*: now if she haue the wit to beginne, as I meane shee should, then will I confound her with complements drawne from the Plaies I see at the Fortune, and Red Bull, where I learne all the words I speake and vnderstand not.' (1615 edition, C_4^v–D_1.) A few lines later he emits a sample of the 'complements drawne from the Plaies I see' at the Red Bull and Fortune: 'O lippes, no lippes, but leaues besmear'd with mel-dew! ô dew no dew, but drops of Hony combs! ô combs no

combs, but fountaines full of teares! ô teares no teares, but . . .'.
(D₁-D₁ᵛ.) This parody of the most notorious lines of *The Spanish
Tragedy* (III. ii. 1-3) is again suggestive. The play belonged to the
company at the Fortune and it is not unlikely that at least some
members of the Trinity College audience could be expected to
identify both the play and the theatre in which it was commonly
presented. By 1614 *The Spanish Tragedy* was very old-fashioned
and thought of as a bombastic favourite of the naïve and the
vulgar,[1] an opinion which constitutes a further commentary on
the Fortune and its audience.

It would appear, then, that by 1616 the Fortune, in spite of
the fact that John Chamberlain had called it 'the fayrest playhouse in this towne', had developed a rather low reputation, and
the Palsgrave's company, its then occupants, were less esteemed
than they had been when, under the name of the Lord Admiral's
men, they had moved in during the autumn of 1600. When Philip
Henslowe died on 9 January 1615/16 his holdings in the Fortune
passed to his wife Anne or Agnes, but Sir Walter Greg said, after
his analysis of the Henslowe records: 'It is clear . . . that Alleyn
assumed the direction of Henslowe's theatrical affairs immediately
upon his death, and it would appear that upon the death of the
widow [April 1617] most of Henslowe's property passed into
Alleyn's hands, probably in right of his wife.' (*Henslowe's Diary*,
ii. 64.) One of Alleyn's first acts after the Fortune property came
entirely into his hands was to arrange that a group of actors from
the company should become housekeepers for the Fortune, as the
King's men were for the Globe.[2] In 1618, after a series of preliminary meetings, a lease was drawn up making over the Fortune
with its taphouse and garden for thirty-one years to ten of the
leading members of the Palsgrave's company. They were to pay

---

[1] Hugh Dick, in his excellent edition of *Albumazar* (University of
California Publications in English, xiii [1944]) says that 'virtually all the
topical allusions fall into two clearly defined groups, those relating to
1610-11 and those to 1613-14' (p. 50).

[2] Apparently Alleyn and Henslowe had had the idea for such a partici-
pation in the profits by the players several years before. Among the
Dulwich papers is a lease dated 1608, but with the month and day still
blank, to Thomas Downton (see above, ii. 426), one of the sharers of the
company, of one thirty-second part of the net profits of the Fortune for
thirteen years, for £27. 10s. 0d. and an annual rent of 10s. Downton agrees
to pay his part of the charges and repairs for the building and to play at
the Fortune and no place else in London without the written consent of
Alleyn and Henslowe, and he agrees not to sell his share. But the lease was
never executed, and apparently the plan fell through. (*Henslowe Papers*,
pp. 13-14 and *Henslowe's Diary*, ii. 64.)

to Alleyn an annual rent of £200, plus a rundlette of sack and another of claret at each Christmas. (See above, i. 137–9 and *Henslowe Papers*, pp. 27–28.) On 31 October 1618 the lease was signed by the ten members of the company who now became housekeepers for the Fortune: Edward Juby, William Birde alias Bourne, Frank Grace, Richard Gunnell, Charles Massey, William Stratford, William Cartwright, Richard Price, William Parr, and Richard Fowler. The players agree that 'they nor any of them their executo^rs admĩstrato^rs or assignes shall not at any tyme hereafter alter transpose or otherwise Convert the said playhowse to any other vse or vses then as the same is now vsed'. This lease made the Palsgrave's men masters of their own affairs to an extent which characterized no other London company, so far as is known, except the King's men at the Blackfriars and the Globe. Unfortunately for them, their independence did not last long, for their theatre and many of their other assets were destroyed by fire three years later. It may be that an undated letter to Alleyn among the Dulwich muniments testifies to their new independence. One item in their lease allowed them a rent of 24s. a year from John Russell, who had a 99-year lease on a tenement of two rooms adjoining the playhouse. The man may have been some sort of dependant of the Henslowes, for Agnes Henslowe had left him a legacy which Alleyn had paid. (Warner, op. cit., p. 181.) At any rate the players found him untrustworthy at the theatre, and in or about 1617 William Birde, one of the senior sharers, wrote to Alleyn an undated letter which indicates one of the problems at the Fortune and suggests the players' increasing voice in the management of their own affairs:

> Sir there is one Jhon Russell, that by yowr apoyntment was made a gatherer wth vs, but my fellowes finding often falce to vs, haue many tymes warnd him ffrõ taking the box. And he as often, with moste damnable othes, hath vowde neuer to touch, yet not wth standing his execrable othes, he hath taken the box, & many tymes moste vnconsionablye gatherd, for wch we haue resolued he shall neuer more come to the doore yet for yor sake, he shall haue his wages, to be a nessessary atendaunt on the stage, and if he will pleasure him-self and vs, to mend our garment[es], when he hath leysure, weele pay him for that to, J pray send vs word if this motion will satisfye yo^u; for him his dishonestye is such we knowe it will not. . . . (*Henslowe Papers*, 85.)

The problem of dishonest gatherers must have been constant when all theatres were forced to rely on cash admissions;[1] the complaint

---

[1] In J. D.'s Fortune play of about 1638, *The Knave in Graine, New*

which William Birde in the name of the Palsgrave's company passed on to Edward Alleyn is simply more explicit than others.

It has several times been said that there is a description of a Fortune audience in a letter written on 8 December 1617 by Orazio Busino, chaplain to the Venetian Embassy in London. But the audience and performance Busino tells about sound more like the Blackfriars than like the Fortune. He writes:

> To distract me, they took me, at the suggestion of Sig. Giovanni Battista Lionello, to one of the numerous theatres here in London where comedies are recited and we saw a tragedy performed there, which moved me very little, especially as I cannot understand a single word of English, though one may derive some little amusement from gazing on the sumptuous dresses of the actors and observing their gestures, and the various interludes of instrumental music, dancing, singing and the like. The best treat was to see and stare at so much nobility in such excellent array that they seemed so many princes, listening as silently and soberly as possible, and many very honourable and handsome ladies come there very freely and take their seats among the men without hesitation. That very evening the secretary was pleased to play off a jest upon me. I was surrounded by a number of young ladies, and after I had been seated awhile a very winning dame in a mask took her seat beside me and spoke to me as if I had been her husband. She asked me for a rendezvous in English and French, and as I turned a deaf ear to both, she showed me some fine diamonds which she wore removing no less than three gloves which she wore one over the other. She was richly dressed from head to foot. (*C.S.P.*, *Ven.*, 1617–19, xv. 67–68.)

In this passage Busino mentions the name of no theatre, and if the audience was really as aristocratic, well dressed, and well behaved as he thought, and if the ladies were indeed ladies, his description is quite at variance with other references to the Fortune audience.

Vampt (see above, iii. 187–90), the rogue says in the closing scene of the play:

> But Gentlemen; what need we more repeating?
> Knowing, that even in all Trades there is cheating?
>
> . . . .
>
> Tis frequent 'twixt the Pander and the Whore,
> We our selves finde it at the Play-house doore.
>
>   (1640 quarto, $M_2{}^v$.)

A gatherers' favourite technique of cheating is noted in *The Actors Remonstrance*, 1643: 'Nay, our very Doore-keepers, men and women, most grievously complaine, that by this cessation they are robbed of the priviledge of stealing from us with licence: they cannot now, as in King *Agamemnons* dayes, seeme to scratch their heads where they itch not, and drop shillings and half Crowne-pieces in at their collars.' ($A_3{}^v$.)

If the singing, music, and dancing was really in interludes, as he says, and not concentrated in a jig at the end of the play, this aspect of his entertainment also sounds more like the Blackfriars than like the Fortune. But the anonymous writer who first quoted Rawdon Brown's translation of the letter (*The Quarterly Review*, cii [1857], 416), a translation differing from the *Calendar of State Papers* text only in occasional phrases and in an extended description of the lady's dress, introduced it with the statement, 'the whole Venetian embassy repaired to the Fortune Theatre on the following melancholy occasion', and his identification of the Fortune was followed by Furnivall in his edition of Harrison's *Description of England* (New Shakspere Society, 1878, pp. 55*–56*) by J. Q. Adams (pp. 280–1), and by others, including me. (See above, i. 136–7.) It is possible that Rawdon Brown had additional information not appearing in the letter, and information not seen by Allen B. Hinds, the editor of the *Calendar* of 1909, though he says in his Preface that he has made full use of Brown's work. It seems more likely, however, that the author of the *Quarterly Review* article was mistaken, and that Busino mentioned no theatre.

Two years later we find an incidental description of a familiar and apparently regularly repeated performance at the Fortune of Marlowe's *Doctor Faustus*, a play which had been in the repertory of the Fortune company for more than a quarter of a century. John Melton, in his satiric attack on the prognosticators, entered in the Stationers' Register on 8 April 1620 (dedication dated 10 June 1620), cites a number of the trick prophecies which the 'Figure-Casters' can be expected to make for the year:

> Another will fore-tell of Lightning and Thunder that shall happen such a day, when there are no such Inflamations seene, except men goe to the *Fortune* in *Golding-Lane*, to see the Tragedie of Doctor *Faustus*. There indeede a man may behold shagge-hayr'd Deuills runne roaring ouer the Stage with Squibs in their mouthes, while Drummers make Thunder in the Tyring-house, and the twelue-penny Hirelings make artificiall Lightning in their Heauens. A third will foretell. . . . (*Astrologaster, or the Figure-caster* [1620], E₄.)

Melton evidently expected his illustration to be easily recognized as a frequent performance. It is just the sort of old-fashioned spectacular which other references would lead one to expect at the Fortune, but not the sort of performance that Busino and the other members of the Venetian embassy seem to have witnessed at their unnamed theatre.

But it would be easy to imagine Fortune audiences as too consistently crude and vulgar. An ambassador with his train *did* go there on occasion, as the letter writer John Chamberlain has recorded. In 1621 Gondomar, the Spanish Ambassador, was one of the most conspicuous figures in London, hated by the populace, notoriously influential with King James, and popular with the Spanish faction at court. His activities were common talk. On 21 July 1621 Chamberlain wrote his friend and regular correspondent, Sir Dudley Carleton, Ambassador at The Hague, about the movements of several of the great nobles:

> All the lords and great men about this towne go to visit and congratulate with the earle of Northumberland. The earle of Arundell supt with him the first night, and dined there the next day, whether came likewise unbidden the Spanish ambassador, who is growne so affable and familiar, that on Monday [16 July] with his whole traine he went to a common play at the Fortune in Golding-lane, and the players (not to be overcome with curtesie) made him a banket when the play was don in the garden adjoyning. (*Chamberlain*, ii. 391.)

So far as I know this entertainment of an ambassador by players at a banquet in their own garden (presumably the impaled strip 123 feet by 17 feet on the south side of the theatre, referred to in the lease of 1618) is unique. Was it part of Gondomar's public relations? Was it arranged by Alleyn, who noted in his diary nine months later 'I dind w^t ye Spanish Embasadore gondomarr'? (Young, *History . . . Dulwich*, ii. 235.) Whatever the circumstances, Chamberlain's record is a warning not to imagine the audience or the bill at any Jacobean theatre as too unvarying.

Five months after the entertainment of Gondomar the Fortune burned down. There are a number of contemporary references to the fire: the most precise is Edward Alleyn's entry in his diary: 9 Dec. 1621—'m̃d this night att 12 of ye clock ye fortune was burnt.' (Young, *History . . . Dulwich*, ii. 225.) The most detailed record is John Chamberlain's: 'On Sonday night here was a great fire at the Fortune in Golding-lane the fayrest play-house in this towne. Yt was quite burnt downe in two howres and all their apparell and play-bookes lost, wherby those poore companions are quite undon: there were two other houses on fire but with great labour and daunger were saved.' (*Chamberlain*, ii. 415.) 'Quite undon' is an accurate assessment of the state of the Palsgrave's men after the fire, for costumes and playbooks represented the principal investment of any Jacobean company; though the troupe struggled on for a few more years, they never recovered. (See above, i. 141–53.)

Edward Alleyn was soon busily engaged in the construction of a new Fortune theatre. No contract for the second theatre is extant, but some of the steps in the building operations can be reconstructed from Alleyn's diary and expense accounts, and from the leases for the enterprise. Within four months of the fire a contract must have been drawn up, for on 16 April 1622 Alleyn noted that he had paid 3s. for 'Dinner att ye Hart in Smithfeeld wt ye builders off ye fortune', and ten days later he entered 12d., which he paid for 'wine wt ye fortune workmen'. (Young, *History . . . Dulwich*, ii. 234, 235.) A number of subsequent entries show his activities in connexion with builders, investors, and players of the company until, on 6 September 1622, he noted: 'I seald att vnderwoods ye fortune Leases . . .'. (Ibid., p. 249.)

A few features of the new Fortune which was under construction at least from April to September 1622—unfortunately Alleyn's diary does not go beyond October 1622—can be assembled from scattered references here and there. One would expect Edward Alleyn to plan the second building to outdo the first. William Prynne said that the second Fortune was enlarged, but his reference is so vague and his bias so obvious that one hesitates to accept his statement:

*The Fortune and Red bull.	**two olde Play-houses* being also lately reedified, enlarged, and one
*White Friers Playhouse.	**new Theatre* erected, the multitude of our London Play-haunters being so augmented now, that all the ancient Divels Chappels . . . being five in number, are not sufficient to containe their troopes, whence wee see a sixth now added to them. . . . (*Histriomastix* [1633], Epistle Dedicatory, *₃v.)

In his continuation of Stow's *Annales* Edmund Howes asserts the improved appearance of the rebuilt theatre but says nothing about its size: '. . . a fayre strong new built Play-house, neere Gouldinglane, called the Fortune, by negligence of a candle, was cleane burnt to the ground, but shortly after, rebuilt farre fairer'. (John Stow, *Annales* . . . [1631], I$_{iii}$v.)

The anonymous author of the manuscript notes in a copy of Stow's *Annales*, 1631, who wrote comments on the destruction of the theatres in the 1640's and 1650's, said of the Fortune: 'The Fortune Playhouse betweene White Crosse streete and Golding

lane was burnd downe to the ground In the yeare 1618. And built
againe with bricke worke on the out-side in ye yeare 1622.'
(Now at the Folger Shakespeare Library, Phillipps MS. 11613.)
Brick construction is also noted by the two surveyors who reported to the Master of Dulwich College on the ruinous condition
of their property in 1656. They said that 'by reason ye lead hath
bin taken from ye sayd building: the Tyling not secured and y^e
foundation of ye sd play house not kept in good repair, great pt
of ye sayd play house: is ffallen to ye ground, the tymber thereof
much decayed and Rotten: and the Brick walls soe Rent: and torne:
y^t ye whole structure is in noe condition capable of Repaire . . .
and ye brick walls much shaken . . .'. (*Henslowe Papers*, p. 96.)
The tiles and the lead on the roofs might have been expected from
the various extant comments on the tile roof of the second Globe,
after the first had been burned because of the gun wadding which
caught in the thatch. Brick walls for theatres were less common;
they must have been expensive, and one would guess that they
were another fire precaution. Brick walls are also suggested by
the fact that the two builders named in the leases are 'Thomas
Wigpitt Cittizen and Bricklayer of London and Anthony Jarman
Cittizen and Carpinter of London'. (See above, i. 143.) If only the
foundations of the building had been brick it would surely not
have been necessary to make the bricklayer a joint contractor.
Very late testimony from James Wright's dialogue *Historia
Histrionica*, 1699, also mentions the brick. Truman responds to
Lovewit's question about Edward Alleyn: '. . . he was Dead before
my time.) He was Master of a Company of his own, for whom he
Built the *Fortune* Play-house from the Ground, a large, round
Brick Building'. (See above, ii. 694.) So far as I know, Truman's
'round' is the only reference to the shape of the second Fortune.
The first one had been square, but there is no record that any
other public theatre was, and it would not be surprising if the
second Fortune had conformed to the normal pattern; it would,
however, be comfortable to have evidence earlier than Wright's.

   That the new theatre had two entrances and two only is implied
by the record of a raid on the Fortune during the surreptitious
performance of a play in October 1643. *The Weekly Account* of
4 October 1643 reports: 'At the Fortune in Golding Lane . . . this
day [2 October 1643] there was set a strong guard of Pikes and
muskets on both gates of the Play-house.'[1]

   [1] Quoted from the British Museum copy (Burney, 17) by Leslie Hotson,
Shakespeare's Wooden O, p. 266. Hotson uses the passage, with another
noting that in 1648 many coaches stood in Golding Lane during a Fortune

It has been asserted that the second Fortune and the Red Bull, after 1625, were, unlike all other known public theatres, roofed over so that the yard became a covered pit.[1] This assertion, though vaguely referred to here and there, has really nothing at all to support it. The author of the idea thought that a roof would have made the two theatres more profitable and he collected a number of vague or irrelevant passages to satisfy himself that roofed they were. Leslie Hotson has cited convincing evidence that the Red Bull was not roofed in 1654 and 1655 (Hotson, p. 86), and there is no evidence that the Fortune ever was.

Finally, the sign used by the Fortune is referred to by a member of a rival company, Thomas Heywood. In his *English Traveller*, probably produced about 1627 (see above, iv. 565–7), Heywood has a scene near the end of Act IV in which the scheming servant Reignald has climbed up the front of the stage façade and waits there out of reach of his master. After he has been there some time the master bids him come down:

Old Lio. Sirra, come downe.
Reig. Not till my Pardon's sealed, I'le rather stand heere
    Like a Statue, in the Fore-front of your house
    For euer; Like the picture of Dame Fortune
    Before the Fortune Play-house.

                  (1633 edition, I_3^v–I_4.)

Reignald's comparison suggests that the Fortune sign was a statue of Dame Fortune rather than a picture, but either would satisfy the simile.

Though Edward Alleyn was certainly the moving spirit in the building of the second Fortune, he did not himself assume all the

performance, to support his statement, 'Like the round Globe, the square Fortune had but two entrance doors, set at opposite sides of the house: the one at the northeast, access by alley from Whitecross Street, the other at the southwest, access from Golden Lane. That the latter, the southwest, was the choice stage, stage-gallery, and lords' room side appears by the fact that the "carriage trade" rolled up not into Whitecross Street, but into Golden Lane at the southwest: "there were above six-score Coaches on the last Thursday in Golden Lane to heare the Players at the Fortune".' As usual the inferences go beyond the evidence: (1) The first Fortune was square; there is no evidence that the second was. Indeed, James Wright said in *Historia Histrionica*: '[Edward Alleyn] was Master of a Company of his own, for whom he Built the *Fortune* Play-house from the Ground, a large, round Brick Building.' (2) The evidence shows two doors, but not that they were set north-east and south-west. (3) The evidence shows *where* the Coaches were stationed, not *why*.

[1] W. J. Lawrence 'New Light on the Elizabethan Theatre', *Fortnightly Review*, xcix, New Series (1916), 820–9.

financial burden. The abstract of a lease dated 20 May 1622 and other papers preserved at Dulwich (see *Henslowe Papers*, pp. 28–30 and 112) show that he issued shares and half-shares in the new enterprise to comprise a total of twelve shares. The building was leased for a term of 51 years. Each share paid a ground rent of £10. 13s. 10d. per annum and an assessment of £83. 6s. 8d. for the construction of the theatre, and each sharer agreed that the building would not at any time be converted 'to any other vse or vses then as a playhouse for recreacōn of his Ma^ts: subiect[es].' Evidently most of the Palsgrave's players who had participated in the leases of the first Fortune in 1618 were no longer financially able, for only three of them—Richard Gunnell, Charles Massey, and Richard Price—bought shares in the new Fortune. The other share holders—John Fisher, William Gwalter, Adam Islipp, Edward Jackson, Anthony Jarman, Francis Juby, George Massey, Thomas Sparks, Thomas Wigpitt, and Alleyn himself—were investors. Later divisions or transfers of these shares are traced in the Dulwich papers. (*Henslowe Papers*, p. 112.)

When the first leases were signed on 20 May 1622 the building was unfinished, for the lease reads 'vpon part of which said ground there is intended to be erected and sett vpp a new playhouse'. (Ibid., p. 29.) It was still unfinished at the beginning of 1623. The pseudonymous author of *Vox Graculi, or Iacke Dawes Prognostication . . . For this yeere 1623* wrote: 'The Dugges of this delicate young bed fellow to the *Sunne* [i.e. the Spring] will so flow with the milke of *Profit* and *Plenty*; that (of all other) Some Players (if *Fortune*, turned *Phoenix*, faile not of her promise) will lie sucking at them with their fulsome forcastings, for pence and two-pences, like young Pigges at a Sow newly farrowed, for that they are in danger to meet with a hard *Winter*, and be forced to trauell softly on the hoofe.' (1623. Sig D₂.) But Jack Dawe evidently expected the theatre to be in operation by March, for in a later passage he includes in his prediction for the month of March the statement: 'As for thunder and lightning, you shall be sure to haue more store this Moneth, at the *Fortune* in *Golding-lane*, then in *Graues-end* Barge, or in *Westminster-hall*, in a long *Vacation*.' (Sig. H₄ᵛ.) The expectation of a spring opening was probably fulfilled. In the records of the Court of Request suit of Gervase Markham against a number of the backers of his journey from London to Berwick, Paul Tey, court messenger, reported that on or about 23 May 1623 he had warned 'Richard Clayton, Richard Grace, William Stratford and Abraham Pedle gent (all Actoʳs at the fortune neere Golding lane)'. (See above, ii. 682–3.)

Though the Palsgrave's company was no doubt delighted to be settled in its new theatre, their prospects were not rosy. They had lost repertory and costumes, and their struggle to get enough plays to keep going is revealed in the Office Book of the Master of the Revels. From 27 July 1623 to 3 November 1624 fourteen licences for new plays for them are known, by far the largest number known to have been licensed by the Master of the Revels for any company in a similar period. Such a struggle to build up a repertory is not productive of good plays: only one of the fourteen was ever published, Thomas Drue's *The Duchess of Suffolk.* (See above, iii. 284–6.)

In this period of struggle at the Fortune the dominant member of the organization was Richard Gunnell. (See above, ii. 454–8.) He had been a patented member of the Palsgrave's company at least since January 1612/13; he was a friend of the company's financial backer, Edward Alleyn, in whose diary he appears frequently; Gunnell and Charles Massey were the only members of the company to hold full shares in the new theatre; in their hour of need Gunnell wrote at least two of the Palsgrave's new plays for them, and he appears to have assumed the function of a manager. The document most indicative of his managerial function is one alluded to in a suit of 1654 found by Leslie Hotson (Hotson, pp. 52–54), an action deriving from the attempt of William and Margaret Wintershall (Gunnell's daughter) to collect a debt from Andrew Cane, the Fortune clown. The revealing document is a bond of 30 April 1624, in which Cane says

no money was ever lent or paid, or even intended to be secured thereon; but the said bond was only entered into by your orator and the said other obligors, being then the then Prince of Wales his Servants [error for Palsgrave's. See above, i. 148, n. 5] that played and acted at the Fortune Playhouse in Golding Lane . . . unto the said Richard Gunnell (another of the said Prince's then Servants and Players in the same house) only to oblige themselves to the said Mr. Gunnell to stay and play there. . . .

From a statement by William and Margaret Wintershall we learn that the other Palsgrave's men besides Cane who bound themselves to Richard Gunnell to continue together at the Fortune were Charles Massey, William Cartwright, William Stratford, Richard Price, and Richard Fowler.[1] These were the chief members of the Fortune troupe in 1624, and their bond to

---

[1] Hotson, pp. 52–53 from the bill and answer in a Chancery suit at the Public Record Office, C 10 32/31.

Gunnell probably indicates that he was in charge of the enterprise at that time.

That Gunnell managed the Fortune is again suggested by two of Sir Henry Herbert's Lenten entries eleven months later. During Lent the theatres were supposed to be closed, but for a fee the Master of the Revels often allowed them to remain open on certain days. (See below, vii. 3–4.) On these days the entertainment—at least in the public theatres—was often fencing, rope dancing, or vaulting, rather than play performances. In Lent of 1624/5 Sir Henry Herbert records his payments from the representative of the Fortune:

> From Mr. Gunnel, in the name of the dancers of the ropes for Lent, this 15 March, 1624. £1.0.0.
>
> From Mr. Gunnel, to allowe of a Masque for the dancers of the ropes, this 19 March, 1624. £2.0.0. (*Variorum*, iii. 66 n.)[1]

A fuller knowledge of the career of Richard Gunnell would illuminate Jacobean and early Caroline theatrical practice. He lived in the parish of the Fortune—St. Giles without Cripplegate—where his name appears frequently in the registers from 1614 to 1631, and one wonders if he may have lived in one of the houses connected with the theatre until he transferred his activities. In 1631 his house was in Redcross Street. (See above, ii. 456.)

In spite of Gunnell's efforts, the days of the Palsgrave's men at the Fortune were numbered. Before the end of Lent 1624/5, when the rope dancers were at the theatre, King James died (27 March), and all London theatres were certainly closed for a period of mourning. The mourning period was not yet completed when the

---

[1] This entry was missed by J. Q. Adams when he made his transcriptions for *Herbert*. Besides Malone's transcription, there is another, perhaps by Craven Ord, pasted into the Scrap-Books of J. O. Halliwell-Phillipps (*Noble Companies*, p. 2) now at the Folger Shakespeare Library. It shows interesting variants from Malone:

> For Lent—From Mrs Gunnill to allowe of a masque for the dancers of the ropes 19 March 1624. 10^s

'M^rs' could well be correct, since she could easily have served as a messenger for her husband, and it would be easy to misread 'M^r', much the more familiar abbreviation in these entries. Malone may have dropped the 'For Lent' deliberately, since all the entries he assembled at this point are Lenten ones. The variations in the fee are more puzzling, for they look nothing alike. At this time Herbert's regular fee for licensing a new play was £1. 0s. 0d.; it did not rise to £2. 0s. 0d. until much later (see above, iii. 265–6); surely £2. 0s. 0d. is too high for such a short script as a rope dancers' masque must have been.

terrible plague of 1625, the worst since the Black Death, seized London, and the theatres were probably not allowed to open from James's death until the end of November or the beginning of December. (See above, ii. 654–7.) This long period of inaction and disaster, when 35,417 plague deaths are recorded in London, broke every London company except the King's men. The Palsgrave's men did not reappear when the theatres opened again in the new reign. (See above, i. 151–3.)

Apparently they were succeeded at the Fortune by a new and only vaguely known troupe called the King and Queen of Bohemia's company. (See above, i. 260–9.) The new company was in existence before 10 September 1626, and since it included Richard Gunnell and two of the men who in 1624 signed the bond to continue to play together with him at the Fortune, it seems likely that the new troupe was made up of remnants of the Palsgrave's men, joined with others, perhaps a few of the old Lady Elizabeth's or Queen of Bohemia's men, to play with Gunnell at the Fortune. (See above, i. 260–4.) The evidence is very tenuous, but it makes the new troupe seem the most likely tenant of the Fortune for the next few years.

There is no indication that the Fortune under the tenancy of the King and Queen of Bohemia's players became any more respectable as a playhouse than it had been when the Palsgrave's men were there. In the middle of May 1626 the Fortune was the scene of a dangerous riot, involving, among others, a number of sailors who threatened to bring in the navy. The affair is known only through recognizances taken for the appearance of a number of the participants. Bonds were posted for James Carver, a sailor, 'touchinge a daungerous and great ryott committed in Whitecrosstreete at the Fortune Playhouse and especially for strikinge beatinge and assaulting Francis Foster the constable and Thomas Faulkner, an inhabitant at the Fortune Playhouse'; for Thomas Alderson, a sailor, 'touchinge a greate and daungerous ryott committed in Whitecrosstreete at the Fortune Playhouse, and for joyninge with the rest of the Riotters in beatinge and assaultinge of Thomas Faulkener an inhabitant at the Fortune Playehouse, and being charged in the Kinges name to yeelde and keepe the peace hee saide hee cared not for the Kinge, for the Kinge paide them noe wages and therefore hee cared not, And further sayinge hee would bringe the whole Navy thither, to pull downe the playehouse'; and for the appearance of Richard Margrave, a sailor, 'for publishinge certaine discoveries of an intended assemblie at the Beare Garden, for revenge of an injurye done to a saylor, and

that there would be a capten a drumme and cullors goe with them,
and afterwards for denyinge itt on examinacion'.

Bonds were posted by Robert Francke and William Collison,
both sailors of Blackwall, for the appearance of Patrick Gray of
Blackwall 'touching a dangerous ryott at the Fortune Playhouse,
and callinge to his fellow-saylors to knocke them all downe that
were present'; for Robert Franke, sailor of Blackwall, 'touchinge
a daungerous and greate ryott committed in Whitecrosse-
streete at the Fortune Playhouse, and for givinge out that if they
the saylers were not putt in a stronger then the New Prison,
they would all be fetched out before the next morowe'; and for
William Collison of Blackwall, sailor, 'concerninge a daungerous
and greate ryott committed in Whitecrostreete at the Fortune
Playhouse, and for assaultinge and strikinge of Edward Heather
the Headboroughe'. (*Middx. Co. Rec.* iii. 161–3.)

Rioting sailors were not unusual in London, but in this instance
there are suggestions that their actions were not only violent but
were directed toward the theatre. Alderson threatened that the
navy would come to pull down the Fortune, and the men are
charged not only with beating a constable and a headborough,
but two of them are said to have assaulted Thomas Faulkner,
'an inhabitant of the Fortune Playhouse'. Presumably Faulkner's
residence means that he was a functionary of the theatre, probably living in one of the houses attached, but nothing else is
known of his theatrical associations.

Two years later the Fortune was again the site of riotous actions
in the events leading up to the lynching of the notorious Doctor
Lambe, but this time the rioting was begun by apprentices, and
the sailors were trying to protect the victim. Of the death of
Lambe, a protégé of the hated Duke of Buckingham, there are
several accounts, most particularly the one printed in the anonymous pamphlet published in Amsterdam in 1628, entitled, *A
Briefe Description of the notorious Life of Iohn Lambe, otherwise
called Doctor Lambe. Together with his Ignominious Death.*

Vpon Friday being the 13. of Iune, in the yeare of our Lord 1628.
hee went to see a Play at the *Fortune*, where the boyes of the towne,
and other vnruly people hauing obserued him present, after the Play
was ended, flocked about him, and (after the manner of the common
people, who follow a Hubbubb, when it is once a foote) began in a
confused manner to assault him, and offer violence. He in affright
made toward the Citie as fast as he could out of the fields, and hired
a company of Sailors, who were there present to be his guard. But
so great was the furie of the people, who pelted him with stones, and

other things which came next to hand, that the Sailors (although they did their endeauour for him) had much adoe to bring him in safetie as farre as *Moore-gate*. ($C_3{}^v$–C_4.)

The boys who began the assault are called apprentices by Sir Francis Nethersole in the account of the affair which he wrote to the Queen of Bohemia: 'On Friday last Dr. Lambe, of whom her Majesty has heard so much, being at a play at the Fortune, was espied by certain prentices, who fell upon him at his going home ...'. (*C.S.P., Dom.*, 1628–9, p. 169.) Since even the popular ballad called 'The Tragedy of Doctor *Lambe*' (H. E. Rollins, *A Pepysian Garland*, p. 280) mentions the Fortune as the place where the rioting began, the association of the lynching of Lambe and the Fortune theatre was evidently fixed in the public mind.

How long after the Doctor Lambe riot the King and Queen of Bohemia's company remained at the Fortune is not clear. In July 1629 their manager, with William Blagrave, deputy to the Master of the Revels, leased a plot of ground from the Earl of Dorset on which they built the Salisbury Court theatre. (See above, vi. 87–88.) This new activity must have diverted most of Gunnell's energy from the Fortune, but there is no evidence that he abandoned it.

The Fortune, like all other London theatres, was closed because of the plague from 17 April to 12 November 1630. (See above, ii. 657–8.) After Sir Henry Herbert allowed the players to resume, the King and Queen of Bohemia's company continued under restraint by the neighbouring justices, but unfortunately their petition does not say what the neighbourhood or the theatre was. The Lord Chamberlain's Warrant Books carry a notice of the petition, though not the document itself, and there are no other known references to it. 'A petition of the King & Queene of Bohemia's Players for leaue to exercise their quality beeing restrayned by ye Iustices therabout[es]. Answered (vizt) His Matie: is graciously pleased that the pet^{rs} haue free liberty to exercise their quality of playing without restraint; any former Act of prohibition to ye contrary notwithstanding./ Dec. 13. 1630./' (*M.S.C.* ii. 403.) The parish of St. Giles without Cripplegate had been particularly hard hit by the plague of 1625 (see F. P. Wilson, *The Plague in Shakespeare's London*, pp. 187–8), and it may be that the justices there were somewhat panicky, but the petition affords no evidence that the justices of St. Giles are those concerned.

By the end of 1631 all the known members of the King and Queen of Bohemia's company were members of other troupes or

dead (see above, i. 268–9), and it seems likely that another company of actors, the King's Revels company, came into the Fortune
in that year. The prologue to Marmion's *Holland's Leaguer*, which
the new Prince Charles's (II) company acted at the Salisbury
Court for six consecutive days in early December 1631, begins:

> *Gentle spectators, that with gracefull eye*
> *Come to behold the Muses Colonie,*
> *New planted in this* soyle; *forsooke of late*
> *By the Inhabitants, since made fortunate*
> *By more propitious starres. . . .*
>
>   (1632 quarto A₄ᵛ.)

Since the prologue goes on to refer to the Globe, the Phoenix, and
by inference, the Blackfriars, and since 'this soyle' means the
Salisbury Court, it seems most likely that 'made fortunate' refers
to the Fortune theatre, and all but completes the roster of the
active London theatres in 1631—Globe, Blackfriars, Phoenix,
Salisbury Court, and Fortune—excepting only the Red Bull. The
predecessors of Prince Charles's (II) company at the Salisbury
Court were the King's Revels company, who therefore seem assigned to the Fortune theatre by this prologue. (See above, i.
304–7.)

The King's Revels company, though better known than the
King and Queen of Bohemia's men, did not succeed in raising
the level of Fortune performances much, for when Alexander
Gill sneered with delight at the failure of Jonson's *Magnetic Lady*
at Blackfriars in October 1632, it was the lowness of the Fortune
which he chose to contrast with the distinction of Blackfriars:

> Is this youʳ Loadestone *Ben* that must Attract
> Applause and Laughter all each Scæne and Acte?
> Is this the Childe of your Bedridden witt,
> An[d] none but the Black-friers to foster ytt?
> Iff to the Fortune you had sent youʳ Ladye
> Mongest Prentizes, and Apell-wyfes, ytt may bee
> Youʳ Rosie Foole might haue some sporte begott
> Wᵗh his strang habitt, and Indeffinett Nott.
>
>   (Herford and Simpson, *Ben Jonson*, xi. 346–7,
>   from Bodleian MSS. Ashmole 38, p. 15.)

Though Gill's opinion of Jonson can be discounted, his estimate
of the Fortune audience must conform to general opinion, else his
sneer loses its force.

The only play of about this time which can be assigned to the
theatre is one written by William Heminges, son of the veteran
actor of the King's company. Edmond Malone noted from the lost

manuscript of Sir Henry Herbert's Office Book that 'Soon after his father's death he [William Heminges] commenced a dramatick poet, having produced in March, 1632-3, a comedy entitled The Coursinge of a Hare, or the Madcapp, which was performed at the Fortune theatre, but is now lost.' (*Variorum*, iii. 189.) Presumably the play was produced by the King's Revels company.

How long that company continued to play at the Fortune is not known, but before the middle of July 1634 they had returned to the Salisbury Court. On 18 July Thomas Crosfield, a Fellow of The Queen's College, Oxford, recorded in his diary a visit from Richard Kendall, wardrobe keeper to the Salisbury Court company, then visiting Oxford and playing at the King's Arms. In the budget of London theatrical information which Kendall gave Crosfield is a list of the London companies, including 'The Fortune in Golden Lane, yᵉ cheife Mr Wᵐ Cartwright, Edward Armestead, John Buckle, John Kirke.' (See above, ii. 688-9.) This new troupe whose London theatre was the Fortune in 1634 is another shadowy group known as the 'Red Bull-King's players' because they had usually been playing at the Red Bull. (See above, i. 270-82.) In the provinces they are generally called the King's players, though no connexion with the King's men of Blackfriars and the Globe can be demonstrated. No other record of their tenancy of the Fortune is known for more than a year after Thomas Crosfield's note, but in March 1635/6 the Mayor of Canterbury wrote to the Privy Council to complain about the activities of a troupe of actors who had just left Canterbury after playing there for over a week. The dates show that they were playing in Lent, when performances at the Fortune would have been at least restricted. (See below, vii. 1-9.) The mayor says that '. . . their night plays continued until midnight, to the great disorder of the city, whereof daily complaints came to the writer. Finding that these plays proved a nursery for drunkenness and disorder, especially in that time of abstinence . . .'. In a later letter the mayor identifies the company: 'The players complained of are of the company of the Fortune play house, and the principal of them were Weekes and Perry.' (*C.S.P., Dom.*, 1635-6, pp. 321 and 355.) What went on at the Fortune at least part of the time the company was absent on the road is shown by an entry in Sir Henry Herbert's Office Book made five days after the beginning of Lent, and apparently a week or ten days before the company reached Canterbury: 'From Vincent—For dancing on the Ropes this Lent at yᵉ Fortune by Blagrove 7 March 1634—2ˡⁱ'.[1]

[1] Neither Malone nor Chalmers printed this entry, and it is therefore not

In early May the Red Bull-King's company was back at the Fortune, perhaps having returned at the end of Lent (17 April). Another entry in the Office Book of the Master of the Revels shows their presence and records a practice probably more common than the extant records show: 'Received of ould Cartwright for allowing the [Fortune] company to add scenes to an ould play, and to give it out for a new one, this 12th of May, 1636,—£1.0.0'. (*Variorum*, i. 424.) The bracketed addition is Edmond Malone's; presumably he identified the theatre from adjacent entries which he found no reason to copy. Since Thomas Crosfield had listed William Cartwright, Senior, among 'ye chiefe' at 'The Fortune in Golden Lane' in July 1634, and here Sir Henry Herbert records him as carrying out a licensing arrangement for the company in May 1636, it may be that Cartwright had succeeded Gunnell as manager of the theatre. He had held stock in the Fortune in 1618; he had signed the bond with Gunnell in 1624; he is frequently mentioned in the diary of the company's financial backer, Edward Alleyn, who owned his portrait, and he lived in the parish of the theatre. (See above, ii. 402–4.) Gunnell had been superseded at least by 7 October 1634, when his burial is recorded in the registers of the parish of St. Bride, Fleet Street. (See above vi. 93–94.) Since Gunnell had acquired an important interest in the Salisbury Court theatre of that parish in 1629, Cartwright could have succeeded him at the Fortune several years before his death.

The revised play which William Cartwright persuaded the Master of the Revels to allow the Fortune players to present as a new one was destined to go unacted, at least for some time, for the very day he licensed it Sir Henry Herbert sent out orders closing all London theatres because of the plague. The theatres remained dark, except for one short interval, for nearly seventeen months. (See above, ii. 661–5.)

During and immediately after this protracted plague closing there must have been many adjustments among the hard-pressed companies, adjustments of which the reduction and transfer of Queen Henrietta's men, and the formation of the new company called Beeston's Boys or the King and Queen's young company are the best-known examples. (See above, i. 236–41 and 324–9.) What

to be found in Adams, *Herbert*. It comes from a manuscript transcript in what appears to be a nineteenth-century hand (possibly that of Craven Ord). The transcript has been cut up into separate items and pasted into various of Halliwell-Phillipps Scrap-Books. This one is pasted into the book labelled *Fortune*, p. 46. William Vincent was a fairly well-known leader of a troupe of jugglers and tight-rope dancers. He lived in the parish of the Fortune. (See above, ii. 612–13.)

the Red Bull-King's company did in this time of distress, no records show. Their theatre, however, is referred to after the opening in much the same contexts as before. In the highly allusive *Praeludium* performed about this time at the Salisbury Court as an opener for Thomas Goffe's *Careless Shepherdess* (see above, iv. 501–5), Thrift, a citizen, having heard much discussion of private theatre plays, decides to leave the Salisbury Court and get his money back:

> And I will hasten to the money Box,
> And take my shilling out again, for now
> I have considered that it is too much;
> I'le go to th' Bull, or Fortune, and there see
> A Play for two pense, with a Jig to boot.
>
> (1656 quarto, B$_4$^{v}.)

About the same time Jasper Mayne, whose *City Match* was being acted at Blackfriars shortly after the reopening following the plague (see above, iv. 847–50), wrote in his verses on the death of Ben Jonson (d. 6 August 1637):

> Scorne then their censures, who gav't out, *thy Witt*
> As long upon a *Comœdie* did sit
> As *Elephants* bring forth; and that *thy blotts*
> And *mendings* tooke more time then *Fortune plotts*.
>
> (*Jonsonus Virbius*, 1638, E$_3$^{v}.)

Jigs and slapdash plots may have been customary fare at the Fortune, but the players there could also meddle in politics as well as their betters. In these years, immediately before the out-break of hostilities, passions were running high in London, and the temptation for the players to exploit them was very great; various records show that they succumbed more often than before. Davenant's *Britannia Triumphans* (7 January 1637/8, see above, iii. 199–200) was unusually explicit in its anti-Puritan and anti-democratic implications; Massinger's lost *The King and the Subject* was censored by both King Charles and the Master of the Revels (late May 1638, see above, iv. 794–6) for its veiled attack on Royal financial measures; the Red Bull players and the author were ordered to appear before the Attorney-General in late September 1639 for scandalous attacks on aldermen, proctors, and the government in a lost anonymous play, *The Whore New Vamped* (see above, v. 1441–2) which they had acted 'many days together'; in early May 1640 the King and Queen's young company was suppressed and their manager jailed for acting without licence an unnamed play concerned with 'passages of the K.s journey into the Northe' (see above, i. 332–3); on 26 February 1641 the Puritan inhabitants of the district of Blackfriars petitioned Parliament to suppress the Blackfriars theatre (see above, i. 64); and on 6 May 1641 William Davenant, himself both an active dramatist and the manager of the King and Queen's young company in succession to the jailed William Beeston, fled the country in terror because of his involvement in the Army Plot. (See above, iii. 195.) In such an environment it is not surprising that the company at the Fortune also presented dangerous political material to its audience.

The affair is first reported—along with a great deal about the King's troubles with the Covenanters—in a letter of 8 May 1639, written by Edmund Rossingham to Viscount Conway:

> Thursday last [2 May] the players of the Fortune were fined 1,000 *l.* for setting up an altar, a bason, and two candlesticks, and bowing down before it upon the stage, and although they allege it was an old play revived, and an altar to the heathen gods, yet it was apparent that this play was revived on purpose in contempt of the ceremonies of the Church; if my paper were not at an end I would enlarge myself upon this subject, to show what was said of altars. (*C.S.P.*, *Dom.*, 1639, 140–1.)

More details of the players' clash with the authorities were set forth in the anonymous anti-episcopal pamphlet, *Vox Borealis, or The Northern Discoverie, By way of Dialogue between Jamie and Willie* ('the yeare coming on, 1641'), but I am suspicious of this account because it retails in late 1640 events of May 1639 as if they had just happened, and its titles seem too pat as anti-episcopal propaganda. The account in *Vox Borealis* reads:

> In the meane time let me tell ye a lamentable Tragedie, acted by the Prelacie, against the poore Players of the *Fortune* Playhouse, which made them sing
>
> *Fortune my foe, why dost thou frown on me? &c*
>
> [for] they having gotten a new old Play, called *The Cardinalls conspira[c]ie*, whom they brought upon the *stage* in as great *state* as they could, with *Altars*, *Images*, *Crosses*, *Crucifixes*, and the like, to set forth his pomp and pride. But wofull was the sight to see how in the middest of all their *mirth*, the Pursevants came and seazed upon the poore Cardinall, and all his Consorts, and carryed them away. And when they were questioned for it, in the High Commission Court, they pleaded *Ignorance*, and told the Archbishop, *that they tooke those examples of their Altars, Images*, and the like, *from Heathen Authors*. This did somewhat asswage his anger, that they did not bring him on

the Stage: But yet they were fined for it, and after a *little Imprison-*
ment gat their *liberty*. And having nothing left them but a few old
Swords and Bucklers, they fell to Act the *Valiant Scot*, which they
Played five dayes with great applause, which vext the Bishops worse
then the other, insomuch, as they were forbidden Playing it any
more; and some of them prohibited ever Playing againe. (B₂–B₂ᵛ.)

It would be pleasant to accept these additional details as part of
the history of the Fortune theatre and its company, but *Vox
Borealis*, though he gives his readers no inkling of the fact, is a
year and a half late with his details, and the title, *The Cardinal's
Conspiracy*, nowhere else recorded (see above, v. 1300–1), fits
too neatly into the campaign of vilification of Archbishop Laud
for easy acceptance. *The Valiant Scot* is extant, but there is no
other indication of the company which owned it or the theatre
in which it was performed (see above, v. 1233–6); and again the
title seems too pat for chance at the time of the Bishops' War and
the London glorification of the Covenanters, especially in the
light of the lines which immediately follow those already quoted:

Well (quoth *Willie*) let the Bishops be as angry as they will, we
have acted the *Valiant Scot* bravely at *Berwicke*: and if ever I live
to come to *London*, Ile make one my selfe to make up the number,
that it may be Acted there too and that with a new addition; for
I can tell thee, here's matter enough, and ye ken that I can Fence
bravely, and flish flash, with the best of them.

These suspicions that the new details set out in 'the yeare coming
on, 1641' are propaganda rather than facts are increased by the
verbatim repetition of the *Vox Borealis* account in the following
year, 1642, in another Puritan pamphlet, *A Second Discovery by
the Northern Scout*.

Six months after the troubles at the Fortune about their ridicu-
ling of the ceremonies of the Church, a functionary of the theatre
was summoned for infringement of the rights of the all-powerful
King's company at Blackfriars. The Lord Chamberlain's warrant
books carry the entry:

Appʳhension　Another [*warrant*] for Iohn Rodes of
　　　　　　　yᵉ fortune Playhouse vpon yᵉ complaint
of the black fryers Company for selling their Playes.
eod [i.e. 28 October 1639] Ios: Butler messengʳ.

(*M.S.C.* ii. 391.)

Probably there were two men named John Rhodes who were involved in Caroline theatrical activities. (See above, ii. 544–6.) One

of them is said by John Downes and Charles Gildon to have been a wardrobe keeper at Blackfriars. He may or may not have been the same John Rhodes who owned shares in the Fortune in 1637. The man who was summoned to answer the complaint about selling plays in 1639 was presumably the Fortune shareholder, since the warrant identifies him with that theatre. If he had sold the plays for performance at the Fortune, he was foolhardy, but so were other members of the company, as the affair of the candlesticks and the bowing at the altar shows, but the whole matter is very obscure.

In any event the days of the Red Bull-King's company at the Fortune were numbered. They were forced out of that theatre and went to the Red Bull, to be replaced by Prince Charles's (II) company. There are two records of the exchange. Edmond Malone copied an extract from the Office Book of the Master of the Revels: 'At Easter [5 April] 1640, the Princes company went to the Fortune, and the Fortune company to the Red Bull.' (*Variorum*, iii. 241.) The same exchange is recorded with more details by John Tatham. For some unknown play he wrote a prologue, and almost immediately published it in his *Fancies Theater*, 1640 (Stationers' Register, 15 October). The prologue complains to the new audience at the Red Bull that the company has played to small houses at the Fortune and has been forced out, allegedly by the machinations of Prince Charles's company.

> *A Prologue spoken upon removing of the late Fortune*
> *Players to the Bull.*
>
> Who would rely on Fortune, when *shee's* knowne
> An *enemie* to Merit, and hath shewne
> Such an example here? Wee that have pay'd
> Her tribute to our losse, each night defray'd
> The charge of her attendance, now growne poore,
> (Through her expences) thrusts us out of doore.
> For some peculiar profit; shee has t' ane
> A course to banish Modesty, and retaine
> More dinn, and *incivility* than hath been
> Knowne in the *Bearwards Court*, the *Beargarden*.
> Those that now sojourne with *her*, bring a noyse
> Of *Rables*, *Apple-wives* and Chimney-boyes,
> Whose shrill confused Ecchoes loud doe cry,
> Enlarge your *Commons*, Wee hate *Privacie*.
> Those that have plots to *undermine*, and strive
> To blow their Neighbours up, so *they* may thrive,
> What censure they deserve, *wee* leave to you,
> To whom the judgement on 't belongs as due.

Here Gentlemen, our Anchor's fixt; And wee
(Disdaining Fortunes mutability)
Expect your kinde acceptance; then wee'l sing
(Protected by your smiles our ever-spring;)
As pleasant as if wee had still possest
Our lawfull Portion out of Fortunes brest:

. . . . .

($H_2{}^v$–H_3.)

The company which now took over the Fortune had been formed in 1631, and first acted at the private theatre, Salisbury Court, and later at the Red Bull. (See above, i. 302–15.) Its composition is much better known than that of the Red Bull-King's troupe which it succeeded. The principal players were Mathew Smith, Richard Fowler, Ellis Worth, and the clown, Andrew Cane, formerly a goldsmith. (See above, ii. 576–7, 439–40, 625–7, and 398–401.) It appears that Cane had already made a popular reputation at the Red Bull before he came to the Fortune, for references to him during the interregnum and later sometimes call him Cane of the Fortune and sometimes Cane of the Red Bull. *The Stage-Players Complaint,* written in the autumn of 1641 (see above, i. 317, n. 1) is sub-titled 'A pleasant Dialogue betweene Cane of the *Fortune,* and Reed of the *Friars'.* The two comedians (after the first two speeches Cane is called Quick, and Reade, Light) have a few quips at each other, but mostly they lament the times and the plague closing (5 August to late November [see above, ii. 666–7]) which keeps them poor. The two woodcuts on the title-page are evidently intended to represent Cane and Reade, but they may well be old blocks. The lines of the dialogue are theatrically un-illuminating, except for the implication that Reade was best known for his nimble dancing and Cane for his rapid speech, but the sub-title and the use of the names suggest that in these last years of the theatre Cane was the great attraction at the Fortune, and Timothy Reade (see above, ii. 540–1) at the Salisbury Court (Whitefriars).

Still later testimony confirms Andrew Cane's popular reputation as the chief attraction at the Fortune, though items sometimes refer to his earlier years at the Red Bull. *Mercurius Pragmaticus* (*for King Charls II*) for the week of 22–29 January 1649/50 sneers at the Parliamentarians: 'But your own Play-houses at *Westminster, Whitehall, Darby-house, Somerset-house, &c.* are the only Stages where Players must come, and who those players must be, I'le tell you; all in Parliament Robes K——s F——s and Rebels; those are the men now in request: *Andr. Cane* is out of date & all other his complices. . . .' (As quoted by Hotson, *Commonwealth and Restoration Stage*, p. 46.) Edmund Gayton (1608–66) is evidently referring to Prince Charles's (II) company at the Fortune, two of whose principal players he mentions—though it is possible that he had in mind their earlier days at the Red Bull—when he writes in his *Pleasant Notes upon Don Quixot*, 1654:

> I have known upon one of these *Festivals*, but especially at *Shrove-tide*, where the Players have been appointed, notwithstanding their bils to the contrary, to act what the major part of the company had a mind to; sometimes *Tamerlane*, sometimes *Jugurth*, sometimes the Jew of *Malta*, and sometimes parts of all these, and at last, none of the three taking, they were forc'd to undresse and put off their Tragick habits, and conclude the day with the merry milk-maides. And unlesse this were done, and the popular humour satisfied, as sometimes it so fortun'd, that the Players were refractory; the Benches, the tiles, the laths, the stones, Oranges, Apples, Nuts, flew about most liberally, and as there were Mechanicks of all professions, who fell every one to his owne trade, and dissolved a house in an instant, and made a ruine of a stately Fabrick. It was not then the most mimicall nor fighting man, *Fowler*, nor *Andrew Cane* could pacifie; Prologues nor Epilogues would prevaile; the Devill and the fool were quite out of favour. Nothing but noise and tumult fils the house, untill a cogg take 'um, and then to the Bawdy houses, and reforme them. . . . (p. 271.)

Late into the Restoration Cane's drawing-power at the Fortune was still remembered. In his *Thermae redivivae: the City of Bath Described*, 1673, Henry Chapman introduced his appendix with the statement: 'THE APPENDIX, Without which a Pamphlet now a dayes finds as as [*sic*] small acceptance as a Comedy did formerly, at the *Fortune* Play-house, without a Jig of *Andrew Kein's* into the bargain.' And even later Cane seems to be cryptically alluded to in *Remarks upon E. Settle's Narrative*, 1683: 'His *Post-script* is like the Fools Part in a *Fortune-Playhouse-Comedy*, to make the sixpenny Gallery Sport; you there finding him a perfect *Jack Pudding*,[1] and like another *Merry Andrew*, telling the Jesuites,

---

[1] Was Jack Pudding a stage name? There is a coincidence of name and theatre in the verses which Sir Aston Cokayne wrote for the 1653 edition of Richard Brome's *Five New Plays*. Cokayne looks forward to better days when the London theatres can open again. After mentioning the three private theatres and the Globe, he continues:

> Our *Theaters* of lower note in those
> More happy daies, shall scorne the rustick Prose

[*continued on* p. 172]

what He, the *Worshipful Protestant Poet* would have done, had he been of their *Consult.*' (E₂ᵛ, p. 16.)

But Andrew Cane was not the only memorable actor in Prince Charles's company at the Fortune in the last two years of the Caroline theatre. In *Knavery in all Trades: Or, The Coffee-House*, published in 1664, and often ascribed to John Tatham, who wrote the 1640 prologue 'spoken upon removing of the late Fortune Players to the Bull', there is a passage in Act III in which a group of gentlemen in a coffee-house indulge their reminiscences of the London theatre before the wars, and incidentally confirm Gayton's memories of Mathew Fowler's roles. Two of the nameless gentlemen tell suggestive anecdotes of performances by Prince Charles's company at the Fortune. After some talk of the spectacular revival of Shakespeare and Fletcher's *Henry VIII* (Lincoln's Inn Fields, January 1663/4?), and the Third Gentleman's remark, 'sir, they say 'tis done rarely well', the Fourth Gentleman and the Fifth Gentleman flaunt their memories of the past:

> *fourth.* I cannot believe it, 'tis impossible they should do any thing so well as I have seen things done.
>
> *fifth.* When *Taylor Lowen*, and *Pollard* were alive.
>
> *fourth.* Did you not know *Benfield*, and *Swautted*? [all five King's men at the Blackfriars and Globe]
>
> *fifth.* Did I not know 'em? yes, and hum'd them off a hundred times.
>
> *fourth.* But did you know *Mat Smith, Elis Worth,* and *Fowler* at the Fortune?
>
> *fifth.* Yes, and I will tell you by a good token; *Fowler* you know was appointed for the Conquering parts, and it being given out he was to play the Part of a great Captain and mighty Warriour, drew much Company; the Play began, and ended with his Valour; but at the end of the Fourth Act he laid so heavily about him, that some Mutes who stood for Souldiers, fell down as they were dead e're he had toucht their trembling Targets; so he brandisht his Sword & made his *Exit*; ne're minding to bring off his dead men; which they perceiving, crauld into the Tyreing house, at which, *Fowler* grew angry, and told 'em,

> Of a *Jack-pudding*, and will please the Rout,
> With wit enough to beare their Credit out.
> The Fortune will be lucky, see no more
> Her Benches bare, as they have stood before.

$(A_2-A_2ᵛ.)$

Similarly, the account in the *Kingdom's Weekly Intelligencer* for 2–9 January 1648/9, of raids on the Phoenix and the Salisbury Court, notes that the soldiers 'went also to the Fortune in Golden-lane, but they found none there but John Pudding dancing on the Ropes'.

Dogs you should have laine there till you had been fetcht off;
and so they crauld out again, which gave the People such an
occasion of Laughter, they cry'd that again that again, that
again.

fourth. I but what d'ye call him was the man; he plaid the devil
in Doctor *Faustus*, and a fellow in the Gallery throwing a
Tobacco-Pipe at him; I hope to see thee (quoth He) e're long as
bad as I am, what's that quoth the fellow? the Son of a Whore
quoth He. (D$_4$^{v}–E$_1$.)

Perhaps something like the ludicrous incident of the fierce Fowler
and the terrified Mutes is what the anonymous author of the
satirical broadside, *The Last Will and Testament of the Doctors
Commons*, printed in June 1641, had in mind when he listed among
his legacies: 'Item, I will and bequeath all my large Bookes of
Acts, to them of the Fortune Play-House . . . in regard they want
good action. All my great Books of Acts to be divided between the
Fortune and the Bull; for they spoyle many a good Play for want
of Action.' (Quoted by H. E. Rollins, *Studies in Philology*, xviii
[1921], 270.)

Most of the plays performed by Prince Charles's men at the
Fortune in these late years must have been revivals, as the anecdotes of Gayton and Tatham indicate, but there is a record of at
least one of their new plays, though the piece is now lost. In June
1641 Sir Henry Herbert licensed a play for the company according
to an entry which neither Malone nor Chalmers printed in their
extracts from his Office Book; it is found only in a cutting from
a transcript, perhaps by Craven Ord, and now pasted into one of
Halliwell-Phillipps' Scrap-Books at the Folger Library: '23^d Iune
1641 Rec͞ed for the licensinge a booke for the Fortune comp.
called the Doge and the Dragon. 2^{li}' (See above, v. 1321–2.) This
is the last precisely datable record of activities at the Fortune
before Parliament issued its order closing all playhouses on
2 September 1642. (See above, ii. 690.)

But the Fortune did not cease to function as a playing-place
after the publication of the Parliamentary order. For a number of
years it has been known that there were a good many more or less
surreptitious performances in London between the official closing
of the theatres and Davenant's cautious performances a decade
and a half later.[1] For these performances the Red Bull, the Fortune,
and the Salisbury Court are the houses most frequently mentioned.

[1] See Hyder E. Rollins, 'A Contribution to the History of the English
Commonwealth Drama', *Studies in Philology*, xviii (1921), 267–333 and
xx (1923), 52–69, and Hotson, pp. 3–81, 133–66.

What companies performed is unknown, and generally play titles are not mentioned, but it is probable that at least a few and possible that a majority of Prince Charles's men were involved in the illegal performances at the Fortune. As a rule notices have been preserved for only those performances which were raided; it can be assumed that there must have been a good deal more activity at the theatres than the extant notices record.[1]

The *Weekly Account* for 27 September to 4 October 1643 notes:

> The Players at the Fortune in Golding Lane, who had oftentimes been complained of, and prohibited the acting of wanton and licentious Playes, yet persevering in their forbidden Art, this day [Monday, October 2] there was set a strong guard of Pikes and muskets on both gates of the Playhouse, and in the middle of their play they unexpectedly did presse into the Stage upon them, who (amazed at these new Actors) it turned their Comedy into a Tragedy, and being plundered of all the richest of their cloathes, they left them nothing but their necessities now to act, and to learne a better life.[2]

The effectiveness of this suppression may be doubted, though it is true that there are no more specific records of plays at the Fortune for the next four years. A letter of Thomas Forde, though it could well be dated later (see Hotson, p. 73, n. 60), has been assigned to about 1643 by Hyder Rollins. The letter was first published in Forde's *Faenestra in Pectore. Or, Familiar Letters*, 1660, p. 56:

> The Souldiers have routed the Players. They have *beaten* them out of their *Cock-pit*, *baited* them at the *Bull*, and *overthrown their Fortune*. For these exploits, the Alderman (the Anagram of whose name makes *A Stink*) [Thomas Atkins] moved in the House, that the Souldiers might have the Players cloaths given them. *H.M.* stood up and told the Speaker, that he liked the Gentlemans motion very well, but that he feared they would fall out for the *Fools Coat*. But you know who has Acted that part, and may very well merit that, among the rest of his gifts. (*Studies in Phil.* xx [1923], 53.)

Forde could be referring to the raid of 2 October 1643, but there were later raids, and one could even suspect that Forde, like later writers, had improved his letters for publication in 1660.

Exhibitions of some kind certainly did continue at the Fortune, for a year and a half after the plundering by the soldiers there is a

---

[1] For instance, Sir Humphrey Mildmay saw unnamed plays or rope dancing at unnamed theatres on 18 July, 21 August, and 16 November 1643. (See above, ii. 680.)

[2] Rollins, *Studies in Phil.* xviii (1921), 277–8. It is the news summary of this item from the first page of the pamphlet which is quoted in *C.S.P., Dom.*, 1641–3, p. 564.

record that the fencers were using the house in Golding Lane as they had long used other public theatres. *Mercurius Veridicus* for 19–26 April 1645 reports that 'The same day a Waterman and a Shoomaker met at the Fortune Playhouse to play at severall Weapons, at which (though they had but private summons) many were present, and in the middest of their pastime, divers of the Trained Bands beset the house and some Constables being present, had choise of fit men to serve the King and Parliament.' (Hotson, p. 17.)

In 1647 there was evidently a good deal of playing in the London theatres, and several accounts name the Fortune as one of the houses in use. The satirical pamphlet, *The Parliament of Ladies*, issued on 26 March 1647, asserts that 'A motion was then made for putting down of playes . . .'. (Rollins, *Studies in Phil.* xviii [1921], 279.) A sequel entitled *The Ladies, A Second Time, Assembled in Parliament*[1] is much more specific:

> The House then adjourned for that day, and on the morrow assem-
> bled againe, where the first thing they fell upon, was, a Complaint
> that was made against Players, who contrary to an Ordinance, had
> set up shop againe, and acted divers Playes, at the two houses, the
> Fortune, and Salisbury Court. Whereupon it was demanded what
> Plaies they were, and answer being given, that one of them was the
> scornefull Lady, the house tooke it in high disdaine, and as an abso-
> lute contempt of their power; and therefore ordered that Alderman
> *Atkins* should make a journey on purpose to suppresse them; and also
> ordered that an Act should be passed to prohibit that Play to be
> herafter acted. . . . (Rollins, op. cit., p. 279.)

The account is, of course, satiric, but it was based on fact, as the Parliamentary records show. Rollins points out that two or three weeks earlier, on 16 July 1647, the Commons had ordered the Lord Mayor and the Justices of Peace 'to take effectual Care speedily to suppress all publick Plays and Playhouses, and all Dancings on the Ropes'. (*Journals of the House of Commons*, v. 246, as quoted in Rollins, op. cit., p. 280.) Though the order is said to have been put into effect it did not stop the playing, witness a later account, on 11 August, which reads:

> A complaint was made of players acting plays publicly at the
> Fortune in Golding-lane and in Salisbury-court. The House wondered
> at the neglect of the justices of the peace therein to permit them,
> especially at this time. It was moved that the Commander-in-Chief
> of the Guard of the Houses might take care to suppress them, but

[1] The Rollins date of 13 August is in error; the date should be 2 August.

considering the dangerous season of the plague, the House, hoping that the justices of peace will observe their orders, passed a vote that order be given to the justices to take care speedily to suppress them. (*C.S.P., Dom.*, 1645–7, p. 599.)

The enforcement of this order is perhaps what *Mercurius Melancholicus* refers to on 4 September 1647, when he reminds Luke Harruney (Henry Walker) 'of the unfortunate accident which happened at the Fortune Playhouse, the Actors instead of *Actus primus, Scaena prima*, being taken away by some industrious Officers, to prevent such dangerous Assemblies, and so the Play was spoyled'. (Hotson, pp. 25 and 75, n. 97.)

But in spite of orders for the suppression of theatres and the arrest of players, performances at the Fortune and other London playhouses were not permanently stopped. Parliament was informed that playing still went on, and the *Kingdom's Weekly Intelligencer* for 18–25 January 1647/8 pointed out 'it is very observable, that on Sunday *January* 23. there were ten Coaches to heare Doctor *Ushur* at *Lincolns* Inne, but there were above sixscore Coaches on the last Thursday in Golden lane to heare the Players at the *Fortune*'. (Rollins, op. cit., p. 286.)

On 9 February 1647/8 Parliament issued 'An Ordinance for Suppression of all Stage-Playes and Interludes' which was more severe than earlier ones. The Lord Mayor, Justices of the Peace, and Sheriffs of London, Westminster, Middlesex, and Surrey were ordered

to pull downe and demolish, or cause or procure to be pulled downe and demolished all Stage-Galleries, Seates, and Boxes, erected or used . . . for the acting, or playing, or seeing acted or plaid, such Stage-Playes, Interludes, and Playes aforesaid . . . and all such common Players, and Actors of such Playes and Interludes . . . to cause to be apprehended, and openly and publikely whipt in some Market Towne. . . . And it is hereby further Ordered and Ordained, That all and every summe and summes of Money gathered, Collected, and taken by any person or persons, of such persons as shall come to see, and be Spectators of the said Stage-Playes, and Interludes, shall be forfeited and paid unto the Church-wardens of the Church or Parish where the said summes shall be so collected and taken, to be disposed of to the use of the poore of the said Parish. . . . And it is hereby further Ordered and Ordained, That every person or persons which shall be present, and a Spectator at any such Stageplay, or Interlude, hereby prohibited, shall for every time he shall be so present, forfeit and pay the summe of five shillings to the use of the Poore of the Parish. . . . (W. C. Hazlitt, *The English Drama and Stage* . . . [1869], pp. 67–69.)

Even these harsh measures were not soon, or at any rate not effectively, carried out, for the *Kingdom's Weekly Intelligencer* reported in the week of 12–19 September 1648 that 'Stage-playes were daily acted either at the *Bull* or *Fortune,* or the private House at *Salisbury-Court'*. (Hotson, op. cit., pp. 38 and 77, n. 150.) Raids on performances were still taking place four months later. The same periodical reports in its issue of 2–9 January 1648/9 that 'The Souldiers seized on the Players on their Stages at Drury-lane, and at Salisbury Court. They went also to the Fortune in Golden-lane, but they found none there, but John Pudding dancing on the Ropes, whom they took along with them. . . .' (Hotson, op. cit., pp. 40 and 77, n. 159.)

This is the last notice of any entertainment at the Fortune theatre. The severe Parliamentary order of February 1647/8 was finally carried out. A series of manuscript notes about the destruction of several of the theatres found in a copy of the 1631 edition of Stow's *Annales* at Thirlestane House, Cheltenham, includes this one: 'The Fortune Playhouse betweene White Crosse streete and Golding lane was burnd downe to the ground In the yeare 1618. And built againe with brick worke on the outside in ye yeare 1622. And now pulled downe on the inside by these Souldiers this 1649.' (Folger Shakespeare Library, Phillipps MS. 11613.)

How thorough the soldiers were in their demolition at this time we have no precise evidence to tell us, but by July 1656 the building had been neglected so long that it was in ruinous condition. The report of the surveyors of the property for the Court of Assistants of Dulwich College noted above states: 'And ffurther though ye sd building did in our opinions cost building: about Two thouzand pound yet in as much as greate pt of ye tymber is Rotten: ye Tyles much broaken and decayed and ye brick walls much shaken: and ye Charge for demollishing ye same will bee Chargable and dangerous, vppon these consideracōns our opinion is that: ye sayd Materialls may not bee more worth then eightty pound.' (*Henslowe Papers,* p. 96.) In spite of this great decay, Dr. Thomas Smith of Cockermouth had heard a rumour two years later that the Fortune was to be restored to its old use as a play-house. On 15 October 1658 he wrote to his friend, Sir Daniel Fleming: 'Sir William Davenant, the poet laureate, has obtained permission for stage plays, and the Fortune playhouse is being trimmed up.' (*Hist. MSS. Com.* 12, Appendix, Part vii, Fleming MSS, p. 23.) Other records of Davenant's plans and activities prove that Doctor Smith was misinformed about the theatre and about the exact type of performance he planned.

The fate of the building can be traced in the Dulwich College records. On 5 March 1659/60 the Court of Assistants of the College signed an order for the lease of the ruinous building, and an advertisement was inserted in *Mercurius Publicus* for 14–21 February 1660/1:

An Advertisement

The *Fortune* Play-house, scituate between *Whitecross-street* and *Goulding-lane*, in the Parish of St. *Giles Cripple-gate*, with the Ground thereto belonging, is to be Let to build upon, where 23 Tenements may be erected, with Gardens; and a Street may be cut through, for the better accomodation of the Building. Inquire of Mr. *Jenkins*, a scrivener in *Black-Friers*.

No tenant was immediately found, and the Court of Assistants sold the material to William Beaver for £75. (*Henslowe Papers*, p. 95 n.) Beaver, however, did not remove every trace of the building, for William Maitland notes in 1739: 'The first Playhouse (for ought I can learn) that was erected in the Neighbourhood of the City of *London*, was situate between *Whitecross-street* and *Golden-lane*, in a Place still denominated *Playhouse-yard*; where, on the North Side, are still to be seen the Ruins of that Theatre.' (*History of London* [1739], ii, p. 1370.)

THE SECOND GLOBE[1]

Adams, John Cranford, *The Globe Playhouse: Its Design and Equipment* (1942; 1961, rev. ed.).

[1] The name of the theatre, perhaps the most familiar of all theatre names, is of unknown origin. Edmond Malone said: 'I formerly conjectured that The Globe, though hexagonal on the outside, was perhaps a rotunda within, and that it might have derived its name from its circular form. But, though the part appropriated to the audience was probably circular, I now believe that the house was denominated only from its sign; which was a figure of Hercules supporting the Globe, under which was written, *Totus mundus agit histrionem.*' (*Variorum*, iii. 66–67.) He does not, as has sometimes been said, assert that he got his information from the notes of William Oldys, or indicate where he did get it. The quotation, Professor Ernst Robert Curtius points out in his *Europäische Literatur und Lateinisches Mittelalter* (1948; English translation 1953, pp. 140–1), comes from the *Policraticus* of John of Salisbury, with 'agit' substituted for 'exerceat'. The sign gives the only known point to the exchange in *Hamlet*, ii. ii. of the Folio text: 'Do the Boyes carry it away?/I that they do my Lord, *Hercules* & his load too.'

Harrison's suggestion (Penguin ed.) that the motto prompted the Seven Ages of Man speech in *As You Like It*, a play which seems to date from about the time of the opening of the first Globe, is attractive, but less compelling. Contemporary allusions to the Globe sign are curiously rare.

Adams, pp. 234–66.

Baldwin, Thomas Whitfield, *The Organization and Personnel of the Shakespearean Company* (1927), pp. 90–117 and 332–62.

[Braines, W. W.], *The Site of the Globe Playhouse Southwark* (second edition, 1924), published for the London County Council.

Chambers, *E.S.* ii. 414–34.

Hayward, Wayne Clinton, 'The Globe Theatre, 1599–1608', MS. Thesis, The Shakespeare Institute, Stratford-upon-Avon (1951).

Hodges, C. Walter, *The Globe Restored: A Study of the Elizabethan Theatre* (1953).

Hotson, Leslie, *Shakespeare's Wooden O* (1959).

Nagler, A. M., *Shakespeare's Stage* (1958).

Reynolds, George F., 'Was there a "Tarras" in Shakespeare's Globe?', *Shakespeare Survey*, iv (1951), 97–100.

Shapiro, I. A., 'The Bankside Theatres: Early Engravings', *Shakespeare Survey*, i (1948), 25–37; and ii (1949), 21–23.

[Sharers' Papers], *M.S C.* ii (1931), 362–73.

The Globe theatre in regular use as a second theatre by the King's company from 1614 to 1642 was not the structure popularly referred to as 'Shakespeare's Globe'. That building had been burned to the ground during a spectacular performance of *Henry VIII* (*or All is True*) on the afternoon of 29 June 1613.[1] A new Globe theatre, generally called 'the second Globe' by modern writers, but not by the subjects of James I and Charles I, was built on the old foundations[2] by the six actors of the King's company and their lay associate, who had held shares in the first

[1] This sensational event is one of the most fully attested occurrences in the early seventeenth-century theatre. The day after the fire two alert printers had ballads ready at Stationers' Hall: Simon Stafford entered 'the sodayne Burninge of the "Globe" on the Bankside in the Play tyme on Saint Peters day last 1613', and on the same day Edward White presented for registration 'A doleful ballad of the generall overthrowe of the famous theater on the Bankesyde, called the "Globe" &c by William Parrat'. (Arber, iii. 528.) Though none of the copies Stafford and White presumably printed is known to have survived, it may be that Parrat's ballad is the one preserved in a seventeenth-century manuscript which has been frequently reprinted. (Adams, 254–5; Chambers, *E.S.* ii. 420–2).

Letter writers, poets, and chroniclers recorded the fire: *Chamberlain*, i. 467; Sir Henry Wotton, *Reliquiae Wottonianae* (ed. 1672), p. 425; Thomas Lorkin (Birch, *Court and Times of James the First*, i. 253); Ben Jonson, 'An Execration upon Vulcan' (Herford and Simpson, *Ben Jonson*, viii. 208–9); Edmund Howes (John Stow, *Annales* . . . *Continued* (both 1615 and 1631), Iiii); and John Taylor, *The Nipping or Snipping of Abuses* (1614), K3v.

[2] See below, p. 183.

Globe at the time of the fire—the actors Richard Burbage, William Shakespeare, John Heminges, Henry Condell, William Ostler, John Underwood, and Richard Burbage's brother, Cuthbert Burbage.[1] This was the original group which had leased the site of the first Globe on 21 February 1598/9, save that the actors Condell, Ostler, and Underwood had, by 1614, succeeded to the places of the deceased Kempe, Phillips, and Pope.

The plot of ground which the original group had leased for thirty-one years from Sir Nicholas Brend is described in some detail in the lease.[2] This property consisted of two irregular plots, both on the south side of Maid Lane (not the north side as has been frequently argued and as the lease specifies), and divided, one plot from the other, by an unnamed lane. The northernmost plot, adjacent to Maid Lane, was 156 feet long on the Maid Lane side, and extended 88 feet back on one side and 100 feet back on the other. The second plot, even more irregular, lay still further south, on the other side of the unnamed lane; it was 220 feet long adjacent to the lane, and varied in depth.[3] At the time of the original lease in 1598/9 the property had consisted of seven gardens, and it was large enough to contain, eventually, not only the theatre but the taphouse, tenement, and garden which the Sharers' Papers of 1635 seem to show were also held by the 'housekeepers'.

These housekeepers were paid rent for the use of their theatre by the rest of the company, a rent which in 1635—and presumably for many years before—consisted of half the takings from the galleries and boxes and all the receipts at the tiring-house door.[4] Such an

---

[1] It is not clear just when Underwood acquired his share, perhaps after the fire but before the rebuilding. (See Baldwin, *Organization and Personnel*, pp. 100–2.)

[2] The lease is found in the documents of a suit of Thomasina Ostler, widow of William, against her father, John Heminges, in 1615. The suit was first reported and the copy of the lease transcribed by C. W. Wallace in *The Times* (London) 2 and 4 October 1909. A convenient transcription is printed by Sir Edmund Chambers in *William Shakespeare: A Study of Facts and Problems*, ii. 58–62. The problem of the exact dimensions and precise location of the plot is authoritatively discussed in a volume prepared for the London County Council by W. W. Braines, *The Site of the Globe Playhouse Southwark*, Second edition, 1924. See also I. A. Shapiro, *Shakespeare Survey*, i (1948), 25–37.

[3] See the charts and plans, *The Site of the Globe Playhouse Southwark*, frontispiece, and pp. 39 and 44.

[4] *M.S.C.* ii. 365. The Sharers' Papers from which the statement is taken are summarized above, i. 43–47. The estimates made by both the actors and the housekeepers in these papers give a fair idea of the receipts at the Globe and Blackfriars in the year 1634-5. The most detailed analysis of

organization, by which the housekeepers, except for Richard Burbage's brother, Cuthbert, were made up of a group of the actors themselves, is unique to the King's company so far as is known.[1] It was used also for Blackfriars. Unfortunately the actors found it impossible to control the disposal of housekeepers' shares when members of the company died. From 1619, when Richard Burbage died, until 1635, when Benfield, Pollard, and Swanston, leading members of the Caroline company, petitioned for the right to buy housekeeping shares, half or more of these shares were in the hands of heirs of deceased King's men, and only a minority were enjoyed by actors of the current company. A decree of the Lord Chamberlain in 1635 ordered three shares to be sold to Benfield, Pollard, and Swanston, and the sale presumably put the majority of the shares in the hands of the actors again. They may have continued so until the Globe was demolished, but the matter is uncertain: it is not known what happened to the shares of John Shank after his death in January 1635/6. He left three shares in the Globe to his wife, and, if she succeeded in holding them, the majority of the housekeeping shares were again in the hands of outsiders during the last five years of the history of the company.[2]

The new Globe theatre, which was built for the company at the expense of these seven housekeepers, was probably opened in the late spring of 1614. The date is indicated by the accounts of Edmund Howes and John Chamberlain. The opening phrase of Howes's account of the burning of the first Globe shows that he must have written before the next St. Peter's Day (29 June 1614):

Also vpon S. *Peters* day last, the play-house or Theater called the *Globe*, vpon the Banck-side neere London, by negligent discharging of a peale of ordinance, close to the south side thereof, the Thatch tooke fier, & the wind sodainly disperst yᵉ flame round about, & in a very short space yᵉ whole building was quite consumed, & no man hurt: the house being filled with people, to behold the play, viz. of

these figures is that made by T. W. Baldwin, *The Organization and Personnel of the Shakespearean Company*, pp. 344–5. He concludes that in this year the total receipts at the Globe were about £1,195, at the Blackfriars £2,170.

[1] There was an exception for a short period, from October 1618 to May 1621, when a group of the Palsgrave's players appear to have held the first Fortune in a similar joint tenancy. (See above, i. 137-44.)

[2] For the fullest discussion of the history of the housekeepers' shares in both the first and second Globe, see Baldwin, *The Organization and Personnel of the Shakespearean Company*, pp. 90–111. For the will of John Shank see above, ii. 646–8.

Henry the 8. And the next spring it was new builded in far fairer manner then before.[1]

But though Howes indicates that the new theatre had been completed by 29 June 1614 it cannot have been completed very long before, for Chamberlain wrote of it as new on 30 June 1614, in a letter to Lady Alice Carleton: 'I have not seen your sister Williams since I came to towne though I have ben there twise . . . the next she was gon to the new Globe to a play. Indeed I heare much speach of this new play-house, which is saide to be the fayrest that ever was in England . . .'. (*Chamberlain*, i. 544.) Chamberlain's comment on the superiority of the rebuilt theatre is echoed by John Taylor, the Water Poet, who adds what seems to be a smug commendation of the housekeepers who courageously rebuilt immediately after their heavy loss:

> *Epigram* 22
>
> As Gold is better that's in fire tride,
> So is the bankeside Globe that late was burn'd:
> For where before it had a thatched hide,
> Now to a stately Theator is turn'd.
> Which is an Emblem, that great things are won,
> By those that dare through greatest dangers run.[2]

The second Globe was built at a cost to the housekeepers of around £1,400,[3] and it appeared to its patrons as much more

---

[1] John Stow, *Annales . . . of England . . . Continued . . . by Edmond Howes* (1615), Iiii.

[2] *Taylors Water-work or The Sculler Travels from Tiber to Thames* (Second edition, 1614), G₄. Not in the first edition of 1612. Another epigram of Taylor's seems to say that he was present at the fire.

> *Epigram* 33
> *V pon the burning of the Globe.*
> Aspiring *Phaeton* with pride inspirde,
> Misguiding *Phoebus* Carre; the world he firde:
> But *Ouid* did with fiction serue his turne,
> And I in action sawe the Globe to burne.
> (*The Nipping or Snipping of Abuses* [1614], K₃ᵛ.)

[3] This is the figure given in 1635 by John Shank, the principal comedian and a leading sharer in the King's company. (See above, i. 45, from *M.S.C.* ii. 368.) In the Court of Requests suit of 1619–20, *Witter v. Heminges and Condell* (*Nebraska University Studies*, x [1910], 305–36). John Heminges, business manager of the company, says that the assessment on one share was about the sum of £120. There were 14 shares at the time, though Heminges,

splendid than the theatre which had burned: John Chamberlain heard it spoken of as 'the fayrest that ever was in England'; John Taylor says that it is improved to a 'stately Theator'; Edmund Howes says 'it was new builded in a farre fairer maner than before'. There is no evidence, however, that the new splendour of the second Globe involved any fundamental change in structure or any notable increase in size from 'Shakespeare's Globe'. A rent return made in 1634 describes the theatre as 'built w[ith] timber, aboute 20 yeares past, upon an old foundation . . .', and a corrected rent return repeats: 'The Globe playhouse nere Maidelane, built by the Company of Players with timber about 20 yeares past uppon an old foundacion . . .'.[1] These old foundations consisted of piles, for the area was marshy: in John Norden's map of the South Bank, revised and published in 1600 under the title *Civitas Londini*, the Globe is shown between two ditches (see I. A. Shapiro, *Shakespeare Survey*, i [1948], 28–29 and Plate VII), and Ben Jonson, in his comments on the burning of the first Globe in 'An Execration upon Vulcan', speaks of Vulcan's cruel stratagem

> Against the *Globe*, the Glory of the *Banke*.
> Which, though it were the Fort of the whole Parish,
> Flanck'd with a Ditch, and forc'd out of a Marish,
> I saw with two poore Chambers taken in,
> And raz'd, e're thought could urge, This might have bin
> See the worlds Ruines! nothing but the piles
> Left! and wit since to cover it with Tiles.
> (Herford and Simpson, *Ben Jonson*, viii. 208–9.)

Since the piles upon which the first Globe was erected remained after the fire and were used as a foundation for the second, no significant increase in size seems possible. About the capacity of the new theatre there is one specific estimate, made twice by a contemporary observer. When Thomas Middleton's violently anti-Spanish play, *A Game at Chess*, was enjoying its spectacular success at the Globe in August 1624 (see above, i. 9–14 and iv.

---

apparently by a slip, seems to indicate 12, implying a total assessment of £1,680 or possibly £1,440. Professor Wallace, who discovered and first published the papers of the *Witter* v. *Heminges and Condell* suit, said that he had 'other contemporary documents showing the cost was far less than £1,400' (*The Times* [London], 2 October 1909), but he never published them, and I know of no clue what or how reliable these other contemporary documents are. It is noteworthy that the statement of Heminges in 1619–20 and of Shank in 1635 are in rough agreement.

[1] W. Rendle in *Walford's Antiquarian*, viii (July–December 1885), 214.

870–9) the Spanish Ambassador wrote to Madrid long and detailed accounts of the affair. He says: 'The actors whom they call here 'the King's men' have recently acted, and are still acting, in London a play that so many people come to see, that there were more than 3000 persons there on the day that the audience was smallest. . . .' Later he repeats the same estimate: 'It cannot be pleaded that those who repeat and hear these insults are merely four rogues because during these last four days more than 12,000 persons have all heard the play of *A Game at Chesse*, for so they call it, including all the nobility still in London.'[1] Since the Ambassador's other statements about this affair are generally verifiable and accurate, his estimate of the capacity crowds at the Globe is persuasive. In any case no other specific contemporary statement about the size of this theatre is known; indeed, the Ambassador's two statements constitute all but one of the known contemporary estimates of the capacity of *any* Elizabethan theatre.[2]

The external appearance of the second Globe as it looked some time between 1637 and 1644 is recorded by Wenceslaus Hollar in a preliminary drawing and in his *Long View of London*, published in Amsterdam in 1647. In the etching the labels 'The Globe' and the 'Beere bayting h' have been accidentally exchanged, but in

[1] Edward M. Wilson and Olga Turner, 'The Spanish Protest against *A Game at Chesse*', *Mod. Lang. Rev.* xliv [1949], 476–82.

[2] The other contemporary estimate is that which Johannes de Witt made of the Swan theatre in 1596. He said the Swan would accommodate 3,000 persons in its seats. (See below, vi. 250.) Most of the numerous modern discussions of the capacity of the Globe are concerned with 'Shakespeare's Globe', not with the theatre built in 1614. These estimates are commonly based on analyses of figures which are extant for *other* Elizabethan public theatres—the receipts at Henslowe's playhouses and the cubic capacity derived from his specifications in the Fortune building contract. Such estimates differ widely, since they are subject to uncertainties about the meaning of some of Henslowe's figures. For what it is worth, we may take the fact that several of these estimates of Elizabethan theatre capacities had approximated the Spanish Ambassador's number of 3,000 many years before this version of his report was discovered and published in 1949. Alfred Harbage estimated the capacity of the Rose in the 1590's as 2,500 (*Shakespeare's Audience*, p. 34); Sir Walter Greg thought that the capacity of the first Fortune, built in 1600 and largely modelled on the first Globe, might have approximated 3,000 (*Henslowe's Diary*, ii. 134–5). In deriving spectator capacity from cubic capacity modern estimates based on modern experience have probably been too low in most instances because of their failure to take into consideration the smaller physique of the average Elizabethan or their greater toleration of excessive crowding. This point is effectively—if emotionally—made by Leslie Hotson (*Shakespeare's Wooden O*, pp. 285–303).

the preliminary drawing the buildings are not labelled.[1] The structure shown in both the drawing and the etching is round. The twin huts which show above the gallery roof in both pictures are large and conspicuous, extending far into the yard; between them is an odd onion-shaped tower unique in pictures of early London theatres, and of unknown function.

Part of the Globe establishment, though presumably not a part of the theatre building and therefore not identifiable in the engravings, was a taphouse. The existence of this common feature of entertainment enterprises[2] is established for the second Globe by the Sharers' Papers of 1635. In the petition of Benfield, Pollard, and Swanston to be allowed housekeepers' shares of the Globe and Blackfriars they say: 'Wheras the sayd Houskeepers out of all their gaines haue not till o^r Lady day Last payd aboue 65^{li} p ann' rent for both Houses, toward[es] which they rayse

---

[1] See I. A. Shapiro, *Shakespeare Survey*, i (1948), 34–37 and Plate XIII; and *Shakespeare Survey*, ii (1949), 21–23 and Plates XI and XII. Other pictures said to show the second Globe are erroneous. The picture of this theatre in J. Q. Adams, p. 260, is really the 'Beere bayting h' of the Hollar *Long View*, but Professor Adams, like others, including John Cranford Adams, *The Globe Playhouse*, pp. 333–4 (but corrected in the 1961 edition), failed to see that the labels had been confused. Another plate captioned 'The Bear Garden and the Second Globe' (*The Globe Playhouse*, p. 82) comes from J. C. Visscher's *View of London*, dated 1616. This engraving has been shown to be inaccurate, derivative, and based on drawings made before the second Globe was built. (Shapiro, *Shakespeare Survey*, i. 27–28 and 30–31.)

[2] The taphouse at the first Globe is noted in the anonymous ballad on the burning of that theatre:

> No shower his raine did there downe force
> In all that Sunn-shine weather,
> To save that great renowned howse;
> Nor thou, O ale-howse, neither.
> (Chambers, *E.S.* ii. 421.)

The taphouse at the first Fortune is noted in the lease of the playhouse to members of the Palsgrave's company on 31 October 1618 of 'All that his great building now vsed for a playhowse and comonly called by the name of the ffortune . . . togither wth one messuage or Teñte therevnto adioyning called the Taphowse nowe in the occupacõn of one Marke Brigham . . .'. (*Henslowe Papers*, pp. 27–28.) The taphouse at the second Fortune is noted in the lease of a share in the theatre to Charles Massey, 20 May 1622: 'all that part or parcell of ground vpon part whereof lately stood a Playhouse or building called the ffortune with a Taphouse belonging to the same . . .'. (Ibid., p. 29.) It was still there in 1656, according to 'm^r. Jarman & m^r. Tanners view of the fortune play house ground & theire report thereupon'. They wrote on 18 July 1656 of 'ye sd late playhouse and Tapphouse: belonging to ye same . . .'. (Ibid., pp. 95–97.)

betweene 20 & 30^{li} p ann' from the Taphowses & a Tenemt & a
Garden belonging to the p^{r}misses . . .'. (*M.S.C.* ii. 366.) The actors
might have been more specific, but I take their plural to mean that
there was a taphouse for the Blackfriars and one for the Globe;
presumably 'a Tenemt & a Garden' were both part of the Globe
properties, but I know of no evidence that they were used by
audiences or actors. Presumably one of the houses they mention
is that which William Rendle saw referred to in a document
among the loose scraps in the parish papers of St. Saviour's,
Southwark, a copy of a return to the Earl Marshal in 1634:

PLAYHOUSE AND HOUSE, SR MATHEW BREND'S INHERITANCE.

The Globe playhouse, nere Maid lane, built by the company of
players, with the dwelling house thereto adjoyninge, built w^t timber,
aboute 20 yeares past, upon an old foundation, worth 14^{li} to 20^{li}
per ann., and one house there adjoyning, built about the same tyme
with timber in the possession of Wm Millet, gent, worth per ann, 4^{li}.
(*Walford's Antiquarian*, viii [July–December 1885], 214.)

The appearance of the interiors of the first and second Globe
theatres[1] have been frequently, but not always responsibly,
discussed. The documentary evidence about them is almost nil.
For years the standard discussions were those of Adams, pp.
244–9 and 257–60, and in more detail, though intermingled with
the features of other theatres, Chambers, *E.S.* iii. 103–54. Several
of their conclusions or assumptions have been modified by later
investigations, particularly by the implications about other
public theatres in Professor George Fullmer Reynolds's authoritative volume, *The Staging of Elizabethan Plays at the Red Bull*

---

[1] A picture of the interior of an early seventeenth-century theatre called
Theatrum Orbi has been published, but it has nothing to do with the Southwark playhouse. Richard Bernheimer published an article entitled 'Another
Globe Theatre' in the *Shakespeare Quarterly*, ix (1958), 19–29. He calls
attention to a plate showing the interior of a theatre labelled *Theatrum
Orbi* published in Robert Fludd's *De Naturali, Supernaturali, Praeter-
naturali, et Contranaturali Microcosmi Historia*, Oppenheim, 1619. The
illustration appears in a chapter on mnemotechnics called 'De Animae
Memorativae Scientia, qui Vulgo Ars Memoriae Vocatur'. The plate shows
a theatre not at all appropriate for Fludd's text, and Mr. Bernheimer
thinks that it is a picture of a real theatre. After analysing the features of
the architecture he suggests that the building belongs to some German
town—Kassel?—and that it was given certain English characteristics for
the use of English comedians. In any case, it was not intended to represent
the Globe in London, and it is not at all clear what the tennis-court-like
interior really depicts.

Theater, 1605–1625, published in 1940. The most notable modification suggested by Reynolds is his casting of serious doubt on the existence of a permanent structural inner stage at the Red Bull theatre during these years, and, by implication, at other theatres of the time. Other noteworthy accounts are C. Walter Hodges's *The Globe Restored*, 1953, an admittedly imaginative study, but composed with a good knowledge of the documentary evidence and, most significantly, written by a stage designer with theatrical experience; and Alois Nagler's small volume, *Shakespeare's Stage*, 1958, written with close fidelity to the documents and informed by an unusually wide knowledge of all contemporary European theatres and their antecedents. These later studies, both concerned with the first rather than the second Globe, do not differ radically from Adams and Chambers, except to cast further doubts on the existence of permanent inner and upper stages, to suggest a much greater use of 'free-standing' scenic elements, and to emphasize much more fully the practicability and use of the various features of the stage.

The most widely disseminated and discussed accounts of the Globe interior are those of John Cranford Adams in *The Globe Playhouse*, 1942, popular because of its explicit detail, and of Leslie Hotson in *Shakespeare's Wooden O*, 1959, popular because of its fervent statement and its radical position. Unfortunately, neither of these popular books is reliable.

The Adams study is sadly confused, partly because it is based on evidence derived indiscriminately from plays irrelevant for his purpose—plays written before the first Globe was built or after it was burned, plays written for companies other than the Lord Chamberlain–King's men, plays written for other public theatres, such as the Fortune and Red Bull, and even from plays written for private theatres, St. Paul's, Blackfriars, the Phoenix, and the Salisbury Court.[1] Another pervasive source of Adams's confusion was pointed out by Professor George Fullmer Reynolds, at that time the chief authority on the staging of Elizabethan plays. Reynolds commented:

Professor Adams, in short, treats the Elizabethan plays most of the time as if they were written by some very realistic modern dramatists, and this is a third and most important reason for doubting him. . . . But as a statement of the uses of the various parts of the stage, this book is almost as completely modern in its assumptions,

[1] For the enumeration of about fifty of these irrelevant plays from which Adams draws evidence for the Globe see *Modern Philology*, xl (1943), 359–61.

and therefore as misleading, as those imaginative treatises put out by German writers about 1900.[1]

The most explicit and extensive refutation of many of the contentions of Adams about the first Globe is to be found in Wayne Clinton Hayward's unpublished thesis, 'The Globe Theatre, 1599–1608', Shakespeare Institute, Stratford-upon-Avon, pp. 115–214.

The other most widely read book on the interior of the Globe, *Shakespeare's Wooden O*, is largely a piece of special pleading for Leslie Hotson's surprising contention that Elizabethan plays were presented at court and in the public theatres in the round, or on an arena stage, an idea which he had previously set out in *The Sewanee Review* in 'Shakespeare's Arena' (lxi [1953], 347–61) and in the entertaining book, *The First Night of Twelfth Night*, 1954.

In *Shakespeare's Wooden O* Hotson follows the method of the late nineteenth and early twentieth-century theatre studies: i.e. tacitly assuming that all seventeenth-century theatres were more or less identical over the period from 1576 to 1642, he collects statements indiscriminately from English, Spanish, French, Italian, and German sources of any date within the period, or even as early as 1520 or as late as 1762, and from stage directions and speeches in plays written for the little-known private theatre in St. Paul's or for the large and vulgar Red Bull, or even for the

---

[1] Review in *Journal Eng. and Ger. Phil.*, xlii (1943), 124–6. The same exposure of the basic method used in *The Globe Playhouse* is more fully stated by Reynolds in his destruction of Adams' 'evidence' for a tarras as a basic structural feature of the Globe:

'More significant, however, is the underlying principle which causes Adams to look for a tarras at all, and which motivates his whole book; the idea that the more realistically and literally every hint of stage directions and textual allusions as to stage settings and equipment is carried out the better. Applying similar interpretations to the Elizabethans that one would to Ibsen or Pinero or any other realistic modern dramatist, Adams arrives at a detailed inventory of stage equipment and construction and tries for a naturalistic consistency easy for a modern reader to accept, but quite foreign not only to the Elizabethan stage but to that of the eighteenth century and early nineteenth as well. Lawrence and Granville-Barker, in the correspondence already referred to, emphasized the inapplicability of this theory to the Elizabethans, and I have submitted evidence that shows how far their actual practice was from carrying it out. [*The Staging of Elizabethan Plays at the Red Bull*, pp. 39–48.] Not only does Adams's theory show a fundamental misunderstanding of Elizabethan stage-craft; it seems to indicate a misconception of dramatic illusion in general. This is a late date to have to insist that dramatic illusion has little to do with an illusion of reality. Yet that is the basis on which Adams seems to be arguing all through his book.' (*Shakespeare Survey*, iv [1951], 98–99.)

Oxford and Cambridge colleges. This is the method employed by Kilian, Brodmeier, Brandl, Genee, and Tolman: to offer as proof what is really an uncontrolled series of illustrations for predetermined conclusions, a method which was exposed and superseded in 1940 by Professor Reynolds's *The Staging of Elizabethan Plays at the Red Bull.*

Actually *Shakespeare's Wooden O* is only partly concerned with the second Globe theatre, but that playhouse is most conspicuously drawn to the attention of its readers by the book's title and by the fascinating fictional account in the first chapter, 'Scandal Packs the Globe' (pp. 14–49). In this story Hotson describes in lively detail what the readers see when on Saturday, 14 August 1624 'mine host Richard Austen of the Boar's Head' secures for them the services of the knowledgeable old actor, William Strange, who 'boasts the magic initials 'W. S.', and is but two years the late dramatist's junior'. This 'active old stager' takes the readers from their 'substantial dinner' at the Boar's Head Tavern to attend a performance of Middleton's *A Game at Chess* at the second Globe.

There was indeed a performance of that play at that theatre on that date, and there are more extant contemporary comments on the performances of this play than for those of any other in the period 1576–1642. (See above, iv. 870–9.) Unfortunately none of these accounts provides any evidence for the curtained houses or mansions on the stage or for the basement tiring-house which are the essentials of Professor Hotson's reconstruction of the staging as witnessed by the readers of *Shakespeare's Wooden O.* After having predisposed his readers to his own fanciful picture of the Globe on the afternoon of 14 August 1624 Hotson devotes his next nine chapters to his collection of quotations, assembled, as indicated above, from relevant as well as from fantastically remote sources, and to entertaining indictments of what he calls 'modern academic prejudice'. The reliance throughout on the initial fictional chapter, which soon becomes reality for the author and is used as evidence (e.g. p. 248), is succinctly illustrated by the statement about this imagined Shakespearean theatre on page 152: 'The reality which rises before us shows not one feature of resemblance to the fancied "Globe" of the stage-historians or of the "restorers".' This fascinating transformation of fancy into reality and vice versa characterizes most of the book, and painfully obscures and distorts the interesting new evidence which is scattered throughout.

Actually Hotson has retreated (but without specific admission) from his extreme position in the earlier article and book, namely, that all playing-places in sixteenth- and early seventeenth-century England, whether at court, at the universities, or in public theatres, were 'arena' stages, completely surrounded on all sides by a standing as well as a seated audience—a position only dubiously supported by the slight evidence he originally offered, and flatly contradicted by all three extant contemporary pictures of Elizabethan stages, particularly the only very clear one, that of the Swan in 1596, and by Peter Streete's contract for building the Fortune in 1600, all of which show a stage set against one wall. Though the Fortune contract specifies a square building, several of the known theatres were indeed round, as many references imply, and the galleries of several of them—perhaps all—did run round the house as the Swan drawing shows, but this is quite different from Hotson's originally argued arena stage, cut off from all walls and to be entered only from below by means of trapdoors. The audience in the pit of the second Globe and of other Elizabethan public theatres has long been conceived of as standing on only three sides of the stage. There is nothing in *Shakespeare's Wooden O* to necessitate the alteration of this conception.

So long as Hotson argued, as in the original article and book, that the standing audience completely surrounded the stage, he was forced to the hypothesis that the tiring-house was underneath the stage and that the actors' only access was through trapdoors. Now that he has tacitly abandoned his standing audience on the fourth side and allowed the stage to stand against one wall, as shown in the Swan drawing and specified in the Fortune contract, his hypothesis of the basement tiring-house is no longer necessary, but he clings fervently to it, with many citations of French, Italian, and medieval illustrations. He cites no convincing evidence at all from Elizabethan plays or from contemporary English documents, except a number of the frequently noted trapdoor entrances from graves or pits or hell. There is nothing in *Shakespeare's Wooden O* to demonstrate that the tiring-house, so frequently mentioned in the literature of the time, was a basement under the stage at the second Globe.

The structural houses, or mansions, which Hotson insists were always on all stages of the time are a different matter. They are a vital necessity for him if he is to cling to his basement tiring-house and still account for the hundreds of examples in Elizabethan plays of entrances which are clearly not from below. If there was always a house or two on stage over one or another of the trapdoors, then the entrance from below could be concealed, and visible entrance could be made through an ordinary door, as the great majority of entrances in seventeenth-century plays obviously require. For theatre historians the only new feature of this hypothesis about temporary stage houses, or mansions, is Hotson's fervent insistence that they were invariably present in the performances of all plays in all theatres, as an arena stage with a basement tiring-house would require. Many scholars have written about the use of temporary houses in Elizabethan staging, ever since Peter Cunningham published his *Extracts from the Accounts of the Revels at Court* . . . in 1842, and especially since Professor Feuillerat organized and indexed this material in 1908, 1910, and 1914. The Revels accounts show clearly that such houses were commonly used in the presentation of plays at court in the reign of Elizabeth and before. A number of items in Henslowe's lost inventories (first published by Edmond Malone in 1790) were probably stage houses, though their character is not so clear in Henslowe's inventories as in the Revels references. The occasional use of temporary houses in the public theatres was suggested in 1905 by Professor Reynolds (*Modern Philology*, iii [1905–6], 73) and developed in 1940 in *The Staging of Elizabethan Plays at the Red Bull* (pp. 131–63) and by Alois Nagler in *Shakespeare's Stage* (pp. 34–65, *passim*). Sir Edmund Chambers recognized the probable use of practicable tents—a form of house or mansion—in the public-theatre staging of *Richard III* and of *Henry V* (*E.S.* iii. 106). The question really raised by Hotson does not concern the existence of houses in the sixteenth- and seventeenth-century English theatre; they have long been known. His real question is: Were stage houses an essential of every production of the time, public or private, at court, in the universities, in the London theatres? And his answer is an endlessly reiterated Yes. The evidence he produces to support his answer indicates the use of houses in medieval performances, in French performances, in Italian performances, in university performances, in court performances of the time of Elizabeth, but with all his reiteration he has not made a case for the invariable use of stage houses in the commercial theatres of London in the seventeenth century. In certain scenes, such as that of the opposed tents in the last act of *Richard III*, they may well have been used at the second Globe, as Reynolds suggested they were at the Red Bull, but that they were essential to the production of all plays at the Globe or at the other theatres of the time has certainly not been demonstrated; and, in view of the paucity of allusions in the thousands of available stage directions of the period, it seems unlikely.

Hotson's further insistence that the Lords' Room, or highest

priced box, was located directly behind and above the stage at
the second Globe and at all other sixteenth- and seventeenth-
century English theatres is another unproved and unlikely contention. The Swan drawing shows 'orchestra' at the left of the
stage and only slightly above it. In his *Dictionary* of 1611 Cot-
grave defined *orchestra* as 'the Senators, or Noblemens Place in a
Theatre, betweene the Stage, and common Seats; also, the Stage
it selfe'. In the *Procemium* to his *Guls Hornbook* (1609) Dekker
has the words 'but when at a new play you take vp the twelue-
penny roome next the stage'. W. J. Lawrence, in *The Elizabethan
Playhouse and other Studies* (pp. 29–40), makes a good case for
this position and for the supposition that in at least some theatres
the Lords' Room had *formerly* been located over the stage. Here
again Hotson has tried to derive a universal practice from selected
and inadequate evidence.

The large and diverse collection of comments, speeches, and stage
directions in *Shakespeare's Wooden O* adds more doubts to those
of Reynolds, Hosley (*Shakespeare Survey*, 1957, 1959, and 1960,
and *Shakespeare Quarterly*, 1954, 1957), Hodges (1953), and Nagler
(1958), that a permanent inner stage and a permanent upper
stage were standard structural features of Elizabethan public
theatres, including the second Globe. Places for discoveries and
for speeches and actions 'aloft' were certainly required now and
then, but they were not required so often or so long as was formerly supposed.[1] It now seems likely that the stage directions
'discovers' or 'aloft' or 'above' may well have been carried out
by the use of temporary structures or of parts of the theatre
ordinarily used for other purposes.

As we turn from the physical characteristics of the second
Globe to its use by the King's men in the Jacobean and Caroline
period, it is well to remember that by 1616 it was no longer
the only theatre—or even the principal theatre—of the company,
but a secondary and socially inferior playhouse. By the time the
second Globe was finished the King's company was already well
established in its custom of alternating between two of its own
theatres, the Globe for summer performances and the Blackfriars
for winter.

No doubt one of the original reasons for the acquisition of
Blackfriars was the company's resolve to exploit more effectively
the socially superior audiences in London. At any rate this is the

---

[1] Reynolds, *The Staging of Elizabethan Plays at the Red Bull*, and Hosley,
Shakespeare Survey, x. 77–89, xii. 35–46, and *Shakespeare Quarterly*, viii.
15–31.

audience they did come to exploit, and gradually the Globe became a secondary theatre for the company, and Blackfriars the
principal house of the King's men. (See above, vi.12–15.) By 1620 at
the latest most of the company's extant new plays were prepared
for Blackfriars, and when there was a slip in the arrangements,
prologues or epilogues are sometimes very frank in their statement of the inferiority of the Globe and its customary audience.
A very good example is furnished by one of the late Blackfriars
dramatists, James Shirley, who wrote nearly all his plays for
private theatres—the Phoenix or Cockpit in Drury Lane, the
Salisbury Court, the Werburgh Street theatre in Dublin, and
Blackfriars. (See above, v. 1064–170.) He wrote *The Doubtful Heir*
for the Dublin theatre, where it was first produced (see above, v.
1105–7), but when he returned to write for the King's company in
1640 he brought *The Doubtful Heir* with him, expecting that it
would be acted at Blackfriars. It was acted at the Globe instead,
and Shirley expressed his disappointment and his opinion of the
Globe and its customary audience in the Prologue for the play,
which he included in his collection of his own poems four years
after the closing of the theatres.

> *A Prologue at the* Globe *to his Comedy call'd*
> The doubtfull Heire, *which should have*
> *been presented at the* Black-Friers.

> *Gentlemen,* I am onely sent to say,
> Our Author did not calculate this Play,
> For this Meridian; the Bank-side he knowes,
> Is far more skilful at the ebbes and flowes
> Of Water then of Wit: He did not mean
> For the elevation of your Poles this Scene.
> No shews, no frisk, and what you most delight in,
> (Grave understanders) here's no Target fighting
> Upon the Stage, all work for Cutlers barrd,
> No Bawd'ry, nor no Ballads; this goes hard.
> The wit is clean, and (what affects you not)
> Without impossibilities the plot;
> No Clown, no squibs, no Divell's in't; oh now
> You Squirrels that want nuts, what will ye do?
> Pray do not crack the benches, and we may
> Hereafter fit your palats with a Play.
> But you that can contract your selves, and sit
> As you were now in the *Black-Friers* pit,
> And will not deaf us with lewd noise, or tongues,
> Because we have no heart to break our lungs,

Will pardon our vast Scene, and not disgrace
This Play, meant for your persons, not the place.
(*Poems &c.* [1646], *Narcissus* D$_4$ᵛ–D$_5$.)

Such a frank declaration of the inferiority of the Globe audience to the Blackfriars audience seems rather dangerous in the light of the reputation for violence of Caroline public-theatre audiences.[1] Perhaps the actor really delivered a milder version of the Prologue and Shirley sharpened his barbs to ease his spleen before he published it.

The usual dates of the company's summer season at the Globe are nowhere set down, but it seems to me likely that they usually played at Blackfriars through the three winter terms of the law courts, from about the first week in October to some time in May.[2]

But though the Globe was normally only a summer theatre after 1609, there is evidence that at least once, and probably much oftener, it had occasional use in the spring. During Lent, in the Jacobean and Caroline period, the use of London theatres was restricted, though not totally forbidden as had been the case in earlier years. (See below, vii. 1–9.) Usually the managers seem to have bought a Lenten dispensation allowing them to use their theatres on all except 'sermon days' (Wednesdays and Fridays) and Holy Week. But the entertainment at the playhouses during Lent did not always consist of plays, for several allowances for rope dancers, vaulters, or fencers to use theatres during this period are extant. One of Sir Henry Herbert's records not copied by Malone or Chalmers reads: 'From the Dutchman——at ye Globe by Blagrove 16 March 1634.—2ˡⁱ'[3] What the Dutchman did and what he was paying for is suggested by a record of a similar payment, four years before, and also dated during the season of Lent: 'Reced of Mͬ Lowins for allowinge of a Dutche vaulter att their house 18 ffeb: 1630.'[4] I should assume that the

---

[1] See G. E. Bentley, *Shakespeare and his Theatre*, pp. 110–27.

[2] For a discussion of the evidence for the dates see above, vi. 15–17.

[3] From an independent transcript of Sir Henry Herbert's manuscript, probably made by Craven Ord, and now pasted into various volumes of Halliwell-Phillipps's Scrap-Books at the Folger Shakespeare Library. This extract is in the volume labelled *Globe*, p. 133.

[4] From the same transcript in the same Scrap-Book s, (Lowin, p. 19). Chalmers notes this entry in his *Supplemental Apology* . . . (1799), p. 209 n., whence it is copied into *Herbert*, p. 47. The Chalmers transcript, however, is in indirect discourse, in a long series of items, some of which are in quotation marks, but not this one. He reads 'Houses' and explains '[the Globe, and Blackfriars]'. He also says Lowin was licensed, which is not quite accurate. After the retirement of John Heminges, the financial transactions of the King's company were generally handled by John Lowin and Joseph Taylor. (See above, ii. 499–506.)

same Dutchman is involved in both records and that each notes a Lenten dispensation to allow the vaulter to entertain in a King's men's theatre. Though the first record definitely specifies the Globe, the second could mean either Globe or Blackfriars. I think, however, that both refer to the Globe, since vaulters, fencers, and rope dancers are elsewhere recorded at public theatres, but not, so far as I know, in private theatres during the reign of Charles I.

Such off-season entertainment at the Globe was not, I should surmise, unusual during the last twenty-five years of its existence. The company cannot have found it advantageous to maintain an empty theatre for seven months of the year if any revenue from it were obtainable. Vaulters, fencers, and rope dancers, though often named in vague general references of the time, were not important enough to literate people to have their precise activities commonly recorded, and very few of their specific performances are known. I must admit, however, that I have found only one—or possibly two—records which indicate non-dramatic use of the Globe in the months when the company was playing at Blackfriars. Such a suggestion for its utilization is mostly speculation.

During the summer season the Globe, however inferior in esteem and profit to the company's winter theatre, saw not only the performance of plays which had originally been put on at Blackfriars, but of a number which were written to be performed in the summer on the Bankside. Not many of them can be certainly identified now, but if Edmond Malone's assessment of the entries in Sir Henry Herbert's Office Book can be trusted, there must have been more than forty of them. Malone said:

> In the summer season the stage exhibitions were continued, but during the long vacation they were less frequently repeated. However, it appears from Sir Henry Herbert's Manuscript, that the king's company usually brought out two or three new plays at the Globe every summer.
>
> *   *   *   *   *
>
> It appears from Sir Henry Herbert's Office-book that the king's company between the years 1622 and 1641 produced either at Blackfriars or the Globe at least four new plays every year. (*Variorum*, iii. 153 and 166.)

Malone's total of eighty or more new plays licensed for the company by Herbert cannot be substantiated now, but we should not expect it to be, for Malone and Chalmers did not pretend to copy all the entries, but only those which, for one reason or another, interested them. Even so, as many as forty-nine of these new plays licensed for the King's men between 1622 and 1641 can be

identified. (See above, i. 101–8.) Most of the entries we still have
do not name the theatre for which the play was planned, but I
think it justifiable to assume that plays which were licensed in
June, July, or August were ordinarily intended for the Globe;
plays licensed in October, November, December, January,
February, March, and April were ordinarily for Blackfriars.
Plays licensed in May or September might have been intended for
either theatre, the May licences in particular depending for their
assignment on the lateness of Easter and the consequent date of
the closing of the Easter term of the law courts. There are extant
eleven records of licences to the King's men for the performances
of new plays in June, July, and August (Globe) and thirty licences
for new plays in the months presuming a Blackfriars opening.
The discrepancy between these figures and the 50–50 division
implied by Malone I should take as an indication that a higher
proportion of the June, July, and August licences was for lost or
inferior plays which did not interest Malone or Chalmers and
whose licences, therefore, were not copied.

It could be argued that a certain number of the plays licensed
in the summer were intended only to be tried out on the Globe
audience but really planned for normal production at the more
profitable Blackfriars. James Shirley's *The Doubtful Heir* may be
an example. In any case, the plays licensed in months implying
a Globe production are these:

1622, 22 June. Fletcher (and Massinger?), *The Sea Voyage.*
  Herbert says 'This piece was acted at the Globe'. (See above,
  iii. 411–14.)
1623, 29 August. Fletcher and Rowley, *The Maid in the Mill.* (See
  above, iii. 376–80.)
1624, 12 June. Middleton, *A Game at Chess.* Various independent
  records of Globe performances. (See above, iv. 870–9.)
1627, 6 June. Massinger, *The Judge.* Lost. (See above, iv. 793–4.)
1629, 8 June. Massinger, *The Picture.* The 1630 title-page names
  both Globe and Blackfriars. (See above, iv. 808–10.)
1629, 29 July. Brome, *The Northern Lass.* Herbert's comment is
  not, strictly speaking, a licence, but for our present purposes
  it is even better. Malone says '*The Northern Lass . . .* was acted
  by the King's Company on the 29th of July, 1629'. The title-
  page of the first edition says it was acted 'at the Globe, and
  Black-Fryers'. (See above, iii. 81–84.)
1633, 13 June. Massinger, *The Unfortunate Piety.* Lost. (See
  above, iv. 820–1.)

1634, 6 June. Massinger, *A Very Woman, or The Prince of Tarent.*
The first edition of 1655 only says 'acted at the Private-House
in *Black-Friars*'. (See above, iv. 824–8.)

1635, 1 August. Davenant, *News from Plymouth.* The epilogue for
the play was printed in *Madagascar*, 1638, with the title 'Epilogue, To a Vacation Play at the Globe'. (See above, iii. 209–11.)

1638, 2 and 5 June. Massinger, *The King and the Subject.* Lost.
(See above, iv. 794–6.)

1640, 1 June. Shirley, *The Doubtful Heir, or Rosania, or Love's
Victory.* The title-page of the first edition, 1652, mentions only
Blackfriars, but the prologue had been printed by Shirley in his
Poems &c. 1646, with the title '*A Prologue at the* Globe *to his
Comedy call'd* The doubtfull Heire, *which should have been pre-
sented at the* Black-Friers'. (See above, vi. 193–4 and v. 1105–7.)

I must leave it to others to try to analyse the features of these
plays which differentiate them from the plays planned for
Blackfriars, but the distinctive materials and methods of *A Game
at Chess, The Northern Lass,* and *News from Plymouth* would
seem to me to be fairly obvious.

There are a number of other plays belonging to the King's
company for which the licensing date is unknown or unrevealing,
but which are known from other records to have been acted at
the Globe in the period 1616–42, though not necessarily to have
opened there. Four or five of them were clearly prepared for an
original Globe production, but for most the evidence is ambiguous.
The plays are the following:

Beaumont and Fletcher, *A King and No King.* Title-page of the
first edition, 1619, says 'Acted at the Globe'. (See Chambers,
E.S. iii. 225.)

Beaumont and Fletcher, *Philaster.* Title-page of the first edition,
1620, says 'Acted at the Globe'; second edition, 1622, 'Acted,
at the Globe, and Blacke-friers'. (See ibid. iii. 222–3.)

Fletcher (and Jonson and Massinger?), *Rollo, Duke of Normandy, or
The Bloody Brother.* Seen by Mildmay at the Globe, 23 May 1633.
(See above, iii. 401–7.)

Fletcher (and Massinger?), *The Prophetess.* Herbert received the
benefit of a Globe performance of 21 July 1629. (See above,
iii. 394–7.)

Fletcher (and Massinger?), *Sir John van Olden Barnavelt.* The
prompt manuscript carries names of King's men; correspondence shows it was acted between 14 and 27 August 1619. (See
above, iii. 415–17.)

Glapthorne, *Albertus Wallenstein*. Title-page of the first edition, 1639, says 'Acted with good Allowance at the Globe'. (See above, iv. 477–9.)

Heywood, *A Challenge for Beauty*. Title-page of the first edition, 1636, says it was acted '*At the* Blacke-friers, *and at the* Globe'. (See above, iv. 562–3.)

Heywood and Brome, *The Late Lancashire Witches*. Title-page of the first edition, 1634, says 'lately Acted at the *Globe*' ; a petition of the King's players shows that it was almost ready to be acted on 20 July 1634. (See above, iii. 73–76.)

Massinger, *The Emperor of the East*. Title-page of the first edition, 1632, says 'diuers times acted, at the *Blackfriers*, and *Globe* Play-houses', though it was licensed 11 March 1630/1. It was published with a Blackfriars prologue, a court prologue, and an unspecified epilogue. (See above, iv. 777–81.)

Massinger, *The Unnatural Combat*. Title-page of the first edition, 1639, says 'As it was presented by the Kings Majesties Servants at the Globe'. (See above, iv. 821–4.)

Shakespeare and Fletcher, *Henry VIII*. No early quartos. A newsletter of August 1628 says twice that the Duke of Buckingham saw *Henry VIII* at the Globe on Tuesday (5 August?). (See above, i. 22–23.)

Shakespeare, *Othello*. The title-page of the first quarto, 1622, says '*diuerse times acted at the* Globe, and at the Black-Friers'. (See Greg, *Bibliography*, ii. 523.)

Shakespeare, *Pericles*. Sir Henry Herbert says of a gratuity from Benfield received 10 June 1631 in the name of the King's company, 'This was taken upon Pericles at the Globe'. (*Variorum*, iii. 177 n.)

Shakespeare, *Richard II*. On 12 June 1631 Herbert recorded that he received of John Shank in the name of the King's company £5. 6s. 6d. 'for the benefitt of their summer day, upon yᵉ second daye of Richard yᵉ Seconde, at the Globe'. (*Variorum*, iii. 177 n.)

Shakespeare, *The Taming of the Shrew*. The title-page of the 1631 quarto says 'acted by his Majesties *Seruants at the* Blacke Friers *and the* Globe'. (Greg, *Bibliography*, i. 204.)

Webster, *The Duchess of Malfi*. The title-page of the first edition, 1623, says '*Presented priuatly, at the Black-Friers* ; *and publiquely at the Globe*'. (Ibid. ii. 535.)

Anonymous, *The Merry Devil of Edmonton*. The title-page of the first edition, 1608, says '*Acted, by his Maiesties Seruants, at the Globe*', and the statement is repeated on the title-pages of the editions of 1612, 1617, 1626, and 1631. Continued production as well as printing is indicated by Jonson's statement in the prologue to *The Devil is an Ass* (1616) calling the play 'your dear delight', and by its performance at court by the King's company in 1618, 1630/1, and 1638. (See above, i. 133.)

The evidence cited seems to me sufficient to allow some confidence that each of these plays did indeed have Globe performances during the years 1616–42, for the inferior reputation of the Bankside theatre would surely not tempt any publisher to claim Globe performances for a play which had been acted at Blackfriars only. Most of these twenty-eight plays, I should surmise, enjoyed performances at both theatres, as did a number of others in the company's repertory (see above, i. 108–34) for which evidence so far discovered points either to Blackfriars performance only or to production at neither theatre. The plays in the list most surely written with the Globe in mind are *Sir John van Olden Barnavelt*, because of the date of performance and the date of the historical material on which the play is based; *The Late Lancashire Witches*, for the same reasons; *The Unnatural Combat*, because the title-page mentions only the Globe, though Waterson, the publisher, had issued or sold a number of plays before, including Massinger's own *Picture* and *Emperor of the East*, both of which were said on his title-pages to have been performed at both the Globe and Blackfriars. With less confidence I should suggest *Albertus Wallenstein* and *A Challenge for Beauty*, because of the character of the plays.

Summer performances at the Globe may have continued until all playing was prohibited by order of Parliament on 2 September 1642. (See above, ii. 690.) During the troubled summer of 1642, however, playing surely cannot have been very profitable, for in the preceding April James Shirley was already complaining of small audiences (see above, i. 67–68), and it would not be surprising to learn that the summer of 1642 saw few performances at the Globe.

During the years in which the theatres were officially closed, performances of plays in London are recorded with somewhat unexpected frequency.[1] Often the theatre used is not mentioned, but though there are records of performances of one sort or another at the Red Bull, the Fortune, the Phoenix, the Salisbury Court, and the Hope, there is no mention of surreptitious acting

---

[1] See Hyder Rollins, 'A Contribution to the History of the English Commonwealth Drama', *Studies in Philology*, xviii (1921), 267–333; and Hotson, pp. 3–81.

at the Globe. It may be that the omission is only chance, but one notes that only the Hope among the named theatres is south of the Thames, and that none of the entertainment mentioned there consisted of a play. Perhaps the actors during the Common-wealth feared to venture across the river.

The Globe continued to stand for nearly two years after the beginning of the wars. Its final destruction is recorded in a series of manuscript notes on six of the London theatres found in a copy of Stow's *Annales*, 1631, once lodged at Thirlestane House, Cheltenham, and now Folger Shakespeare MS. Phillipps 11613: 'PLAY HOUSES. The Globe play house on the Banks side in Southwarke. . . . And now pulled downe to the ground, by Sʳ Mathew Brand, On Munday the 15 of April 1644, to make tennements in the roome of it.' (F. J. Furnivall, *The Academy*, xxii [No. 547, 28 October 1882], 314–15.) The destruction of the Globe, though not the date, is confirmed by a document dated 6 July 1653, found by Halliwell-Phillipps, and now preserved in the Folger Library: 'The Jurie of the Sewers for the Easte parte of Surrey vpon their Oathes Saie That vpon a viewe made of the Sewer in Maide Lane nere the place Where the Globe Playhouse lately stood. . . .'

THE HOPE

Adams, pp. 324–41.

Briley, John, 'Of Stake and Stage', *Shakespeare Survey*, viii (1955), 106–8.

Chambers, *E.S.* ii. 448–71.

Greg, W. W. (ed.), *Henslowe Papers* (1907), 19–22 *et passim*.

Hotson, pp. 59–70.

Kingsford, C. L., 'Paris Garden and the Bear-baiting', *Archaeologia*, Second Series, xx (1920), 155–78.

Shapiro, I. A., 'The Bankside Theatres: Early Engravings', *Shakespeare Survey*, i (1948), 25–37.

—— 'An Original Drawing of the Globe Theatre', *Shakespeare Survey*, ii (1949), 21–23.

The Hope was a dual-purpose house, carefully planned to facili-tate the entertainment of its patrons either with the performance of plays on its stage or with the baiting of bears and bulls in its arena. It was built to replace the old bear-garden,[1] and its double

---

[1] For the early history of the bear-garden and of the site see Chambers, *E.S.* ii. 448–65, supplemented by C. L. Kingsford, *Archaeologia*, Second Series, xx (1920), 155–78.

function is clearly set out in the contract which Philip Henslowe and Jacob Meade made with the carpenter, Gilbert Katherens, on 29 August 1613, just two months after the burning of the near-by Globe. (W. W. Greg, *Henslowe Papers*, pp. 19–22.) The builder agrees to tear down the old bear-garden, and on or near the same site to

newly erect, builde and sett vpp one other Same place or Plaiehouse fitt & convenient in all thinges, bothe for players to playe Jn, And for the game of Beares and Bulls to be bayted in the same, And also A fitt and convenient Tyre house and a stage to be carryed or taken awaie, and to stande vppon tressells good substanciall and sufficient for the carryinge and bearinge of suche a stage. . . . And to builde the same of suche large compasse, fforme, widenes, and height as the Plaie house Called the Swan. . . . And shall also builde the Heavens all over the saide stage to be borne or carryed w^{th}out any postes or supporters to be fixed or sett vppon the saide stage. . . . (Ibid., p. 20.)

At several other points in the contract Henslowe and Meade, instead of giving specifications, only reiterate that their new combination theatre and bear-garden is to be like the Swan. They do indicate three galleries, the first of which is to have posts 'Twelve footes in height and Tenn ynches square'. The height of the second and third galleries is not given, but presumably they diminished in height like those specified in Henslowe's contract for the Fortune (see above, vi. 142), since the posts for the second gallery are required to be eight inches square and those for the third, seven inches square. There are to be 'Two Boxes in the lowermost storie fitt and decent for gentlemen to sitt in'. The foundation is to be of brick at least thirteen inches above the ground. The bull house and stable are to provide accommodations for six bulls and three horses. The roofs of both theatre and stable are to be tiled (because of the recent fate of the Globe?); Katherens is required to 'builde two stearecasses w^{th}out and adioyninge to the saide Playe house in suche convenient places as shalbe moste fitt and convenient for the same to stande vppon, and of such largnes and height as the stearecasses of the saide playehouse called the Swan, nowe are or bee.' (Loc. cit.)

The Hope, frequently called the Bear Garden, especially in its later years after it had been deserted by the major London dramatic companies, was evidently a round building, as the demolished bear-garden on the same site had been.[1] The round

[1] After his visit to the bear-garden on 23 August 1584 Lupold von Wedel described the place as 'a round building three stories high'. (Trans.

shape of Henslowe and Meade's new combination theatre and bear-garden is shown in the best contemporary pictures: the drawing by Wenceslaus Hollar and his engraving of the same in his *Long View of London*, published at Amsterdam in 1647.[1] The circular shape of the building is also indicated in a deposition made at the sign of the Dancing Bears, on the Bankside in Southwark, by John Baxter, aged 57, before Sir Thomas Fowler, Francis Mitchell, Thomas Foster, and Francis Poulton, a commission appointed by the Court of Exchequer, who took depositions on 26 September and 10 October 1620. Baxter deposed that he knew the buildings erected by Henslowe: 'ffirst one house was thereon built, nowe called the house for the young beares; there is another house there called the house for the white beares and the playhouse called the hope, wch were erected and built by Phillip Hensloe and now held in possession of Jacob Mead or his ass^s . . .'. In answer to another question John Baxter deposed: 'To the tenth he saith that hee verely believeth that those buildings aforesaid were sett vppon the kings land for that at the first driving of the pyles for the foundacon of the hope Playhouse the workmen had incroached vppon the Bishopp of Winchesters land whereof Mr Allen being advertised that it would breed discord thereafter [and] coming thither advised Mr Hensloe to alter his Circle of the Playhouse and sett it altogether vppon [the] kings lands wch was accordingly done . . .'.[2]

The new dual-purpose Hope must have been round, inside as well as outside. The internal shape is repeatedly indicated in two

Gottfried von Bülow, *Transactions of the Royal Historical Society*, New Series, ix [1895], 230.) Thomas Platter, who visited the bear-garden in 1599, said: 'The play house is built in circular form; above are a number of seated galleries; the ground space under the open sky is unoccupied. In the midst of this a great bear is fastened to a stake by a long rope.' (Chambers' translation, *E.S.* ii. 456, from Gustav Blinz, 'Londoner Theater und Schauspiele im Jahre 1599', *Anglia*, xxii [1899], 460.)

[1] The importance of these two pictures has been shown by I. A. Shapiro in two articles in the *Shakespeare Survey*, i (1948), 25–37 and ii (1949), 21–23. In the engraving the labels for the Globe and the Bear Garden, or Hope, have been accidentally exchanged. The Hope is the structure marked 'The Globe'.

[2] P.R.O. Exchequer Bills, Answers, &c., James I, Surrey (E. 134.18 Jas. I, M.10). The depositions in this suit all concern the location of the present and former bear-baiting buildings and whether they were on the King's land or on the Bishop of Winchester's land. A number of modernized extracts from these depositions were printed by C. L. Kingsford, *Archaeologia*, Second Series, xx (1920), 175–7. Long extracts—none too accurate—were copied out and inserted into J. O. Halliwell-Phillipps's Scrap-Book labelled *Hope*, now in the Folger Shakespeare Library.

passages written by John Taylor, the Water Poet, in his *Bull, Beare, and Horse, Cut, Curtaile, and Longtaile*, 1638.

> Being growne into Maturity and strength,
> And having hither past the seas, at length,
> At *Beare-Garden*, (a sweet Rotuntious Colledge)
> Hee's taught the Rudiments of Art and knowledge.
>
> (D₅.)

. . . . .

> But leaving stately horses, it is found
> The Beare-garden is circular, or rovnd,
> Where *Iack-an-Apes* his horse doth swiftly run
> Hir circuit, like the horses of the Snn [*sic*]
>
> And quicke as lightning, his will trace and track,
> Making that endlesse round his Zodiacke.
>
> (E₃ᵛ.)

The Hope was evidently one of a group of buildings devoted to the maintenance of the sport of bear- and bull-baiting. Besides the theatre, Gilbert Katherens agreed

> to new builde, erect, and sett vpp the saide Bull house and stable wᵗʰ good and sufficient scantlinge tymber plankes and bordes and p[ar]ticōns of that largnes and fittnes as shalbe sufficient to kepe and holde six bulls and Three horsses or geldinges, wᵗʰ Rackes and mangers to the same, And also a lofte or storie over the saide house as nowe it is . . . [and to] fynde and paie for . . . all other thinges needfull and necessarie for the full finishinge of the saide Plaie house Bull house and stable. . . . (*Henslowe Papers*, p. 21.)

By 1620 there were other necessary buildings as well. In his depositions before the Exchequer commission in 1620, quoted above, John Baxter testified that he knew the buildings erected on the old dog-yard: 'ffirst one house was thereon built, nowe called the house for the young beares; there is another house there called the house for the white beares, and playhouse called hope. wᶜʰ were erected and built by Phillip Hensloe and now held in the possession of Jacob Mead or his assˢ. . . .' John Taylor also speaks in his deposition of the house 'for white bears another house for young beares built by Phillip Hensloe'; and, in his answer to the interrogatories of the Bishop of Winchester, Taylor testified that 'the ground lying on the West side of the play house where the bull house and hay house now stands was anciently A doggyard belonging to the beare garden'.

The contract and the testimony would seem to indicate a group of seven buildings: the Hope, the bull-house, the stable for horses,

the hay-house, the house for white bears, the house for young
bears, and (one would assume) a house for bears neither white nor
young. But it may be that the stable is the same as the hay-house,
and it seems that one of the bear-houses was converted at some
time before 1620 to a dwelling, for the Bishop of Winchester's
fifteenth interrogatory was: 'Item whether you doe knowe or
haue heard that the house of one Michael ffrancis together with his
garden one the west side of the Playe house were once p[ar]cell
of the Bearegarden And his nowe [dwellinge?] house was a beare
house.' To which Peter Tompson answered: '. . . that Michaell
ffrauncis his house together wth his gardens on the west side of
the playhouse were reputed parcell of the beare garden and his
now dwelling house was A beare house for to keepe young beares
in'. And Luce Bachelor agreed with him, testifying: 'she doth
knowe of hir owne knowledge that the house and garden wherein
Michaell frauncis in the Interr named now dwelleth was parcell of
the beare garden and was a beare house to keep young bears in'.
Neither the Bishop's interrogatory nor the deposition of Peter
Tompson nor of Luce Bachelor gives the date of the conversion of
the house for young bears into a house for Michael Francis, but one
infers that the conversion took place after the Hope was completed.
Yet John Baxter's deposition indicates that in 1620 there was
still 'one house . . . nowe called the house for young beares'. I can
only conclude that in 1620 there still clustered about the Hope a
bull house, a stable-hay-house, a young-bear-house, a white-bear-
house, and a principal bear-house.

　　One final implication about the Hope is to be found in the depositions at the Dancing Bears before the commission of the Court
of Exchequer. Three deponents testify to the enlarging of the
Hope before September 1620. The thirteenth of the Bishop's
interrogatories was: 'Item do you knowe the newe buildinges
called the Hope Playhouse and was it not erected vppon p^te of
the Landes and Tenementes known by the name of the Bear-
garden belonging to the Bishopp of Winchester.' Peter Tompson
deposed: 'To the thirteenth Interr he saith that at the erecting of
the new playhouse called the hope about seaven yeares since by
Mr Phillip Hensloe he the said Mr Hensloe did ptly by threats and
partly by intreats get and had from William Glover who dwelt
vppon part of the Bishops lands A piece of his backside to erect
and sett vpp part of the said playhouse called the hope and that
he did three seuerall tymes enlarge his playhouse vppon the said
Glovers lands but to what quantity this deponent remembereth
not.' Tompson's testimony was confirmed by Luce Bachelor, who

deposed: '. . . and she believeth it to be true for that there hath
been land taken three severall tymes out of hir fathers yard for
the erecting of the new playhouse wch land hir father held vnder
Mr Paine his lease made by the Bishopp of Winchester'. The
testimony of Katherin Glover, wife of Jeremy Glover, age 39, is
similar: 'To the thirteenth Interr this deponent saith that she
knoweth the newe buildinge called the hope playhouse and that
part thereof was built vppon Willm Glovers yard being this de-
ponentes husbands father wch he held vnder A lease from the
Bishopp of Winchester.'

These depositions seem to indicate that on three occasions between the beginning of construction in 1613 and the interrogation
of witnesses in September and October 1620 the Hope had been
enlarged. If so, no other evidence of the alteration in the structure
of the playhouse is known. I am led, however, by the use of the
plural in the Bishop's interrogatory—'the newe buildinges called
the Hope Playhouse'—to suspect that the three deponents are
also using the word 'playhouse' to refer to the whole group of
buildings devoted to bull- and bear-baiting. It is noteworthy that
Gilbert Katherens's contract calls for the erection of only three
buildings, the theatre, the bull-house, and the stable. The various
deponents, however, refer to at least two other buildings: the
house for young bears and the house for white bears, and to three
if the hay-house is not the stable of the contract. It may be that
the testimony that Henslowe 'did three seuerall tymes enlarge his
playhouse vppon the said Glovers lands' refers to the erection of
new housing for bears and not to alterations in the structure of
the theatre. Or it could be that the alteration of the young bear-
house into a dwelling for Michael Francis involved the encroach-
ments on Glover's land, though this seems less likely.

Whatever the later additions, the new playhouse itself was
supposed to be ready for players before the end of 1613;
Katherens's contract called for the Hope to be finished by
30 November 1613, but the opening may have been delayed.
(Chambers, *E.S.* ii. 468 and 370–1.) In any case, the first event
which can be associated with the new theatre took place in the
following autumn. It is described by the irrepressible Water Poet
in a series of doggerel pamphlets, the first of which begins with
the announcement:

> . . . *I*, Iohn Taylor Waterman, *did agree with* William Fennor, *(who
> arrogantly and falsely entitles himselfe the Kings Majesties* Riming
> Poet) *to answer me at a triall of Wit, on the* seuenth of October last
> 1614 *on the* Hope *stage on the* Bank-side, *and the said Fennor receiued*

*of mee ten shillings in earnest of his coming to meet me, whereupon I
caused* 1000 *bills to be Printed, and diuulg'd my name* 1000 *wayes and
more, giuing my Friends and diuers of my acquaintance notice of this*
Bear-garden *banquet of dainty Conceits.* . . . (*Taylors Revenge* [1615];
All the Workes of Iohn Taylor, the Water Poet [1630], Nn₁ᵛ–Nn₂.)

The dastardly Fennor failed to show up, and the heroic chal-
lenger was left alone on the Hope stage to quell the defrauded
audience. After several lines of description of their rage and
violence, Taylor continues:

> But I (to giue the Audience some content)
> Began to act what I before had ment:
>
>   .   .   .   .   .
>
> Then came the players, and they play'd an act,
> Which greatly from my action did detract.
> For 'tis not possible for any one
> To play against a company alone,
> And such a company (I'll boldy say)
> That better (nor the like) e'r play'd a Play.
> In briefe, the Play my action did eclips,
> And in a manner seal'd vp both my lipps.
>
> (Ibid., Nn₃.)

The repeated use of bear-baiting figures and allusions in the
series of pamphlets on the affair[1] is apparently thought by the
author-combatants to be appropriate to the house, not to the two
opponents.

The dramatic company which Henslowe and Meade intended as
co-tenants with the bears and bulls at the Hope was the Lady
Elizabeth's men—presumably 'such a company (I'll boldly say)
That better (nor the like) e'r play'd a Play'. In this troupe the
leading actor was Ben Jonson's protégé, Nathan Field. (See above,
ii. 434–6 and iii. 299–303.) It may well have been as a favour to
Field—whom he specifically links with Richard Burbage as a
great actor in the dialogue (v. 3. 85–88) of the play—that Jonson
broke his custom of preparing plays for the King's men (see above,
iv. 608) and wrote *Bartholomew Fair* for presentation by Field's
company at the Hope. Jonson's *Induction* records its performance
at the Hope on 31 October 1614 and furnishes more specific information about theatre customs and production than one finds
in any other play of the time.

---

[1] There are three pamphlets: *Taylors Revenge*, 1615; *Fennors Defence*,
1615; and *A Cast over the Water . . . given gratis to W. Fennor, the Rimer from
London to the King's Bench*, 1615. They are reprinted together in *All the
Workes of Iohn Taylor*, . . . (1630), Nn₁ᵛ–Oo₆.

The production of such a play as *Bartholomew Fair* by a dramatist of Jonson's standing, if not their rescue of the hard-pressed
Water Poet, might have been expected to establish the Lady
Elizabeth's men at the Hope, but the company did not get on well
with Philip Henslowe, and some time in 1615 they drew up a list
of complaints against him. (*Henslowe Papers*, pp. 86–90.) Most
of these complaints pertain to financial matters involving costumes
and personnel, but one of them refers to the company's promised
compensation for 'lying still one daie in forteene for his baytinge'.
(Ibid., p. 88.) This matter of the days for baiting and the days for
playing at the Hope was an inevitable source of irritation for any
group of actors at the house. The customary apportioning of days is
now very difficult to determine, for the extant records of baiting
days are contradictory and may indicate changes in the programme as well as errors in the records. The players' complaint
against Henslowe mentions baiting once a fortnight, but
Henslowe's agreement (ibid., pp. 123–5), made a few months
before, on 7 April 1614, with Robert Dawes, an actor in the Lady
Elizabeth's company, stipulated (if the interlineations are properly placed) that Henslowe and Meade were to have '[one day of]
every fower daies, the said daie to be chosen by the said Phillip
and [Jacob] . . . monday in any week on which day it shalbe lawful
for the said Philip [and Jacob their administrators] and assignes
to bait their bears and bulls ther, and to use their accustomed
sport and [games] . . .'. (Ibid., p. 125.)

Perhaps the 'one daie in forteene', mentioned in the players'
complaint, for which Henslowe had agreed to pay compensation,
was an extra day over and beyond the stipulated 'one day of every
fower daies' of the original agreement. Or it may be that in these
records 'forteene' is an error for 'fower' or vice versa. Baiting
about every four days is the implication of a statement in the
theatrically knowledgeable pamphlet, *Vox Graculi, or Iacke Dawes
Prognostication*, 1623: 'The Dogge-dayes will all this yeere rage
twice a weeke, and that very furiously; but their forest out-rage
will be about the *Beare-garden*.' (G₁ᵛ.) Fifteen years after the
prognostication of Jack Dawe, John Taylor, the Water Poet,
rejoiced that after the plague closing of 1636–7 the bear-baiting
days were three a week:

> Our *Beares*, and *Bulls*, and *Dogs*, in former state,
> The streets of *London* do perambulate,
> And honest sport, and lawfull merriment,
> Shall thrice a weeke be shew'd, to give content.
> (*Bull, Beare, and Horse* . . . [1638], D₇ᵛ.)

A statement in a manuscript note of about 1656 or 1657 on the destruction of the theatre buildings in London gives the same two-a-week programme as the one implied by Jack Dawe: 'The Hope on the Banks side in Southwarke, commonly called the Beare Garden. A Play house for Stage Playes. On Mundayes, Wedensdayes [*sic*], Fridayes and Saterdayes. And for the Baiting of the Beares On Tuesdayes and Thursdayes. the Stage being made to take vp and downe when they please.'[1] Perhaps the fervour of London aficionados fluctuated. Since the bear-masters seem always to have had a controlling interest in the Hope, they could probably demand as many baiting days as they thought the traffic would bear.

Whatever the apportioning of playing-days and baiting-days, actors are not constituted to accommodate graciously to the competition of bears. It should not be surprising that the conflict of the Lady Elizabeth's men with the powerful and astute Philip Henslowe brought about the breaking of the company as a regular metropolitan troupe. It appears only in the provinces in the next few years, and sometime in 1615 it was replaced at the Hope by Prince Charles's (I) company, an organization which absorbed four of the actors who had formerly been Lady Elizabeth's men. (See above, i. 176–9.)

On 20 March 1615/16 the ten leading members of the reconstituted Prince Charles's (I) company signed an agreement with Jacob Meade and Edward Alleyn, the former actor and heir of the recently deceased Philip Henslowe.[2] In discharge of an old debt owed to Philip Henslowe for loans and costumes, the actors of Prince Charles's company agreed to pay to Alleyn one fourth of their takings 'out of & for the whole galleryes of the playehowse comonly called the hope'; and they further agreed that they 'shall and will playe at the said howse called the hope, or elsewheare wth the likinge of the said Edward & Jacob accordinge to the former Articles of Agreem^t had & made wth the said Phillipp & Jacob'. (See above, i. 198–9 and n. 2.)

But the new tenants did not stay long. They address their creditor and former collegue, Edward Alleyn, in a letter undated

---

[1] Manuscript note in a copy of Stow's *Annales* (1631), at Thirlestane House, Cheltenham, reported by F. J. Furnivall, *The Academy*, xxii, no. 547 (28 October 1882), 315, now Folger Phillipps MS. 11613.

[2] Alleyn had been joint Keeper of the Bears and Mastiffs with Henslowe from 1604–5 to 1614–15. After Henslowe's death he continued as keeper until his own death in 1626. (*M.S.C.* vi [1961], p. 125.) The position should have been lucrative, but fees were often in arrears. (See John Briley, 'Of Stake and Stage', *Shakespeare Survey*, viii [1955], 106–8.)

but probably written in the winter of 1616–17 (see above, i. 200–1
and n. 3), confessing that they too have left the Hope in part because of their own troubles about bear-baiting: 'S^r J hope you
mistake not o^r remoouall from the bankes side: we stood the
intemperate weather, 'till more Jntemperate Mr Meade thrust vs
over, taking the day from vs wch by course was ours. . . .' Though
bear-baiting is not specifically named, the fact that Jacob Meade,
partner with Alleyn in the Hope, had never had any connexion
with plays but was Keeper of the Bears makes his purpose in
taking over a day from the actors clear enough.

From this time on there is no known record of the regular
association of any standard London company with the Hope.
The usual context of allusions to the theatre appears in 1621 in
Henry Farley's *St. Pavles-Chvrch her Bill for the Parliament*, when
Zeale laments the frivolous interests of Londoners:

> To see a strange out-landish Fowle,
> A quaint Baboon, an Ape, an Owle,
> A dancing Beare, a Gyants bone,
> A foolish Ingin moue alone,
> A Morris-dance, a Puppit play,
> Mad *Tom* to sing a Roundelay,
> A Woman dancing on a Rope;
> Bull-baiting also at the *Hope*;
> A Rimers Iests, a Iuglers cheats,
> A Tumbler shewing cunning feats,
> Or Players acting on the Stage,
> There goes the bounty of our Age:
> But vnto any pious motion,
> There's little coine, and lesse deuotion.

$$(E_4-E_4{}^v.)$$

In his scorn for people who will allow the cathedral to decay
while popular amusements flourish, Zeale has obviously cited all
the vulgar catch-pennies he can recall. It is noteworthy that
he mentions only one theatre and that a good proportion of his
popular amusements are associated at one time or another with
that house—apes, bears, rope dancers, bull-baiting, rimers' jests,
tumblers, players acting on a stage.[1]

---

[1] Probably the variety of the entertainment at the Hope seemed nothing
new to Londoners. All London public playhouses appear to have accommodated more miscellaneous spectacle than we are accustomed to associate
with theatres, and the bear-garden tradition had long been one of variety.
Lupold von Wedel, after his visit to Southwark on 23 August 1584, described the programme at the Bear Garden:

These dogs were made to fight singly with three bears, the second bear

Clearly the Hope was not wholly abandoned by the players, though the great companies of London seem to have shunned it, probably because less tainted theatres became available: first the Phoenix or Cockpit (1617), then the new Fortune (1622–3), and finally the Salisbury Court (1629–30). But in 1620 the building was still locally known as a theatre, for in the depositions taken on 26 September and 10 October 1620 in the Exchequer suit the commissioners repeatedly speak of it as a theatre, and it is called 'the Playhouse', 'the hope playhouse', 'the new playhouse', 'the new playe house called the Hope', and 'the newe buildinge called the hope playhouse' more than twenty times in the depositions of at least six different Southwark witnesses, old and young, male and female.

Moreover, in Hilary Term 1621 Edward Alleyn said that: '. . . the said Phillipp Henslowe . . . did erect and build the house Called the Hope now imployed and used for a game place for baitinge his Ma^ts Beares and Bulls and for a playhouse to wch use it is imploied and used att this daye . . .'.[1] Actors as well as bears at the Hope are also mentioned in *A North Country Song*; though the date cannot be fixed, it must be after 1614, since the substitution of stage for stake can refer only to the Hope:

> When I'se come there, I was in a rage
> I rayl'd on him that kept the Beares,
> Instead of a Stake was suffered a Stage,
> And in Hunkes his house a crue of Players.[2]

being larger than the first, and the third larger than the second. After this a horse was brought in and chased by the dogs, and at last a bull, who defended himself bravely. The next was, that a number of men and women came forward from a separate compartment, dancing, conversing and fighting with each other [a jig?]: also a man who threw some white bread among the crowd, that scrambled for it. Right over the middle of the place a rose was fixed, this rose being set on fire by a rocket: suddenly lots of apples and pears fell out of it down upon the people standing below. Whilst the people were scrambling for the apples, some rockets were made to fall down upon them out of the rose, which caused a great fright but amused the spectators. After this, rockets and other fireworks came flying out of all corners, and that was the end of the play. (*Transactions of the Royal Historical Society*, Second Series, ix [1895], 230.)

[1] Exchequer Bills and Answers, temp. Jac. I, Surrey No. 165, quoted in the Halliwell-Phillipps Scrap-Book, *Hope*, p. 14, Folger Shakespeare Library. Though Halliwell-Phillipps does not make his source clear, it must be part of Alleyn's answer in the suit of *William Henslowe* v. *Edward Alleyn* in the Court of Exchequer.

[2] *Wit and Drollery* (1661), F_6^v. Unfortunately this name of Hunks does not fix the date, for there were at least two, and probably more, bears called Hunks. The Schedule of Bulls and Bears annexed to a lease of the Bear

The most frequently mentioned activity at the Hope continued to be bear-baiting, and its appeal was by no means confined to the vulgar, as Henry Farley would like to imply. There was regular bear- and bull-baiting for the King and the Prince (see below, *Annals*, vii. 27, 28, 35, 36 *et passim*), and though royalty is not known to have attended the public performances at the Hope, ambassadors did. John Chamberlain wrote to Sir Dudley Carleton on 12 July 1623: 'The Spanish ambassador is much delighted in bare-baiting. He was the last weeke at Paris-garden where they shewed him all the pleasure they could both with bull, beare, and horse, besides Jackanapes, and then turned a white beare into the Thames where the dogs baited him swimming, which was the best sport of all.' (*Chamberlain*, ii. 507.)

Bear-baiting at the Hope was not always such unalloyed pleasure as it appears to have been on the afternoon of the visit of the Spanish Ambassador. Two years later there is a grim item in the accounts at St. Saviour's, in which parish the Hope was located: 'Sept. 7. Item, paide for a shrowde to put in the boy that was kilde in the Beargarden, 00–01–06.'[1]

Baiting and occasional plays seem not infrequently to have been supplemented by other forms of entertainment at the Hope, and the miscellaneous activities recorded by John Taylor in 1614

Garden dated 15 December 1590 includes 'Item, one greate beare called Tom Hunkes, x. li.' (*Archaeologia*, Second Series, xx [1920], p. 175) ; several years later Sir John Davies refers to 'old Harry Hunkes, and Sakersone' (Epigram xliii in *Epigrammes and Elegies* [n.d.], D₂ᵛ) ; Thomas Dekker refers (in his timely *Worke for Armorours* (1609), (B₂) to 'monsieur *Hunkes* . . . his old shoulders' ; and Henry Peacham speaks of 'Hunks of the Beare-garden' (in his verses for *Coryats Crudities* [1611], k₄ᵛ). Twenty-one years is surely too long for any bear to stand up to the dogs in this bloody sport. Probably there was a still later Hunks—as Taylor's *Bull, Beare, and Horse* . . . (1638) shows that there was a later Nan and George and a later bull called Jugler. Alternatively, the line in the song in *A North Country Song* could mean 'in what we have been accustomed to think of as the house of Hunks'.

[1] The Halliwell-Phillipps Scrap-Book, *Hope*, p. 149, Folger Shakespeare Library. The only citation Halliwell-Phillipps gives is 'Acc. 1625–1626 St. Saviours MSS.'. Presumably his source was 'the Sexton's MS. note[s]' referred to by Halliwell-Phillipps's *Outlines*, Sixth edition (1886), ii. 343. The registers themselves do not give accounts like this. Unfortunately, it is not clear when the boy was killed. If the accounts quoted ran from Lady Day to Lady Day, then September of the year 1625–6 would have been September 1625, when plague deaths were 2,550 (see above, ii. 668) in the first week and there were certainly no public performances in the Bear Garden. If the accounts ran from Michaelmas to Michaelmas, then the date was September 1626 and the boy may have been killed in connexion with a public exhibition. If so, one would expect allusions elsewhere to such an event.

and suggested by Henry Farley in 1621 are several times recorded during the reign of Charles I. Prize-fights were occasional features at all the public theatres especially during Lent. (See below, vii. 1–9.) But special association of such exhibitions with the Hope is suggested by two passages published in 1631 and 1632. For John Stow's *The Annales of England . . . from the First Inhabitation . . .*, Edmund Howes wrote the continuation to 1631 published in that year. In it Howes boasts of the large number of London theatres, names half a dozen, and continues: 'besides the new built Beare garden, which was built as well for playes, and Fencers prizes, as Bull bayting . . .'. (Iiiiᵛ.) The same customary usage is indicated by Nicholas Goodman in the following year. Goodman was describing the view of the three Bankside theatres—the Globe, the Hope, and the Swan—which could be seen from the bawdy-house called Holland's Leaguer. It is noteworthy that in his allusion to the Hope, though he names only prize-fights and animal-baiting as the activities there, he says that they did *most* possess it: '. . . the other was a building of excellent *Hope*, and though *wild beasts* and *Gladiators*, did most possesse it, yet the Gallants that came to behold those combats, though they were of a mixt Society, yet were many Noble worthies amongst them . . .'. (*Holland's Leaguer* [1632], F₂ᵛ.) Similar exhibitions are recorded by Sir Henry Herbert, who extended his function as Master of the Revels to the licensing of odd variety shows as well as of plays. Generally his licences for itinerant entertainers did not mention theatres, but in 1632 two of them did:

[For a prise from] Blagrove playd at ye Hope ye 13. Iune 1632.
[1632. For a warrant to] Grimes for shewing ye Camell for a yeare from 20 Iune [The Hope Theatre. Herbert's Diary.][1]

Whether these supplements to baiting continued at the Hope until the closing of the theatres, I cannot tell, though I should assume that they did. The late references, however, are all to baiting. In 1638 John Taylor, the Water Poet, published *Bull, Beare, and Horse, Cut, Curtaile and Longtaile*, one of his crude and entertaining verse effusions devoted mostly—allowing for his customary free association—to bear- and bull-baiting and dedicated to 'Mʳ *Thomas Godfrey*, Keeper of the Game for Beares, Bulls, and Dogges'. He says that the Bear Garden maintained three

---

[1] From a MS. copy of the Office Book which Halliwell-Phillipps cut up and pasted into his Scrap-Book labelled *Hope*, p. 46, now in the Folger Shakespeare Library. The words in brackets were written in by him to replace words destroyed in cutting up the manuscript.

bulls, twenty bears, and seventy mastiffs, and in an appended
list he gives the names of four bulls and nineteen bears. The
account is a current one, for though he several times laments the
long plague closing, once saying that the bull had been idle 'this
18 Moneths at least', the lines

> And that we have obtain'd againe the Game
> Our *Paris-Garden* Flag proclaimes the same.
>
> (D₇ᵛ.)

were evidently written after the plague restriction was lifted on
2 October 1637 and before the piece was entered in the Stationers'
Register on 25 October 1637. In such a current and detailed
pamphlet it is notable that the home of the bears and the bulls is
never called the Hope, and no use of the house by actors is ever
suggested. Indeed the name Hope appears so seldom in the late
years that one is sometimes tempted to think that the repeated
allusions to bear-garden activities may refer to some other
structure, but it is only the name which has fallen into disuse.
That the bear-garden remained the same as the Hope is shown by a
mock advertisement in *The Man in the Moon* for 13–20 February
1649/50:

A Match, a match; Gentlemen, pray stand off: *Be it known unto all
men by this presents, that I the* Man in the Moon, *in behalfe of my Dog*
Towzer, *doe challenge all the Dogs, Bitches, Puppies, and all in the
Citie of* Westminster; *to play with them all one after another, severally
three Courses at the* Winsor-Bull, *at the* Hope *on the Bank-side, on*
Thursday Feb. 28. *for three* Crownes *a Dog . . . hee desireth* Godfrey *to
see that his* Bull *be ready. . . .* (Quoted by Hotson, p. 64.)

And the identification is confirmed by the manuscript note (see
below) of the destruction of the theatre in 1656 which calls it 'The
Hope on the Banks side in Southwarke, commonly called the
Beare Garden'.

In the order of Parliament suppressing all 'publike Stage-
Playes', 2 September 1642, there is no mention of bear-baiting or
bull-baiting. (See above, ii. 690.) There was, however, a later order,
issued December 1642, requiring that 'the Masters of the Bear-
Garden, and all other persons who have interest there, be enjoined
and required by this House, that for the future they do not permit to be used the game of bear-baiting in these times of great
distraction until this House do give further orders herein'. (J. P.
Collier, *History of English Dramatic . . .* [1879], iii. 102.) It has
often been assumed that this order effectively stopped bull- and

bear-baiting until the Restoration, but Professor Hotson has collected ample evidence to show that it did nothing of the kind. (Hotson, pp. 59–70.) Until 1656 baiting continued with some regularity on the Bankside, but in that year came the end of the Hope. A series of contemporary manuscript notes in a copy of the 1631 edition of Stow's *Annales* records the pulling down of six London theatres between 1644 and 1656. The account of the Hope reads:

The Hope on the Banks side in Southwarke, commonly called the Beare Garden. A Play house for Stage Playes On Mundayes, Wedensdayes Fridayes and Saterdayes. And for the Baiting of the Beares on Tuesdayes and Thursdayes, the Stage being made to take vp and downe when they please. It was built In the yeare 1610. And now pulled downe to make tennementes, by Thomas Walker a Peticoate Maker in Cannon Streete, on Tuesday the 25 day of March 1656. Seuen of Mr Godfries Beares, by the command of Thomas Pride then hie Shriefe of Surry were then shot to death, On Saterday the 9 day of February 1655 [i.e. 1655/6], by a Company of Souldiers.[1]

Though we have no other record of the petticoat maker's destruction of the building, there are at least two other allusions to Colonel Pride's destruction of the bears (Hotson, p. 69), an action which must have made further operation of the bear-garden impossible, and thus, perhaps, enabled Thomas Walker the petticoat maker to get the property as a bargain.

NEWINGTON BUTTS

Adams, pp. 134–41.
Chambers, *E.S.* ii. 404–5.

The extremely obscure Newington Butts theatre, a mile south of London Bridge, was in operation by 1580; it is last known as a playing-place in 1594.

THE RED BULL

Adams, pp. 294–309.
Chambers, *E.S.* ii. 445–8.
Fleay, Frederick Gard, *A Chronicle History of the London Stage, 1559–1642* (1890), pp. 270–97.

[1] From a copy at Thirlestane House, Cheltenham, when reported by F. J. Furnivall; now Folger Phillipps MS. 11613.

Hotson, pp. 82–87.

Jeaffreson, John Cordy, *Middlesex County Records*, iii (1888).

Lawrence, W. J., 'New Light on the Elizabethan Theatre', *Fortnightly Review*, xcix, New Series (1916), 820–9.

Reynolds, George F., *The Staging of Elizabethan Plays at the Red Bull Theater, 1605–1625* (1940).

Rollins, Hyder E., 'A Contribution to the History of the English Commonwealth Drama', *Stud. Phil.*, xviii (1921), 267–333.

Sisson, Charles J., 'The Red Bull Company and the Importunate Widow', *Shakespeare Survey*, vii (1954), 57–68.

Van Lennep, William, 'The Death of the Red Bull', *Theatre Notebook*, xvi (1961–2), 126–34.

Wallace, C. W., *Three London Theatres of Shakespeare's Time*, University of Nebraska Studies, ix (1909), pp. 5–51.

In spite of various pieces of litigation about it, less is known of the building of the Red Bull theatre at the upper end of St. John's Street, Clerkenwell, than of the Fortune or the Globe or the Hope. The earliest and clearest statement of its origin is found in a petition of the provincial player Martin Slater (see above, ii. 574–5), a petition probably to be dated not long before June 1605 when the Duke of Holstein left England after a visit to court beginning in the previous November.

Martyn Slatiar to [the King?]

Is one of his Majesty's servants and has been chosen by the Duke of Holstein to select a company of comedians to attend his Grace here or elsewhere, and having made choice of them is unprovided of a house to play in, as others of their profession have. The petitioner willing to show himself in the best manner he could for his Grace's service together with one Aaron Holland, servant to the Earl of Devonshire, having jointly the lease of the house betwixt them for 30 years, has altered some stables and other rooms, being before a square court in an inn, to turn them into galleries, with the consent of the parish who have subscribed their name to a petition, with due consideration for divers causes, and especially towards the poor of the parish, who have allowed them 20s. a month towards their maintenance; and likewise for the amending and maintaining of the pavements and highways have bestowed upon the same 500l. Since which time the Privy Council have stayed the finishing of the same. They pray to have such privilege as others of their quality have, and to finish the work. (*Hist. MSS. Com.*, Cecil Papers, xvii [1938], 234.)

Though Slater's connexion with the Red Bull is not confirmed in the various later suits about the theatre, that of Aaron Holland very frequently is. Holland had leased from Anne Beddingfield the Red Bull property. Thomas Woodford in a Court of Requests suit of 1619 says that Holland being

lawfullie possessed of and in one messuage or tenemente with thappurtenaunces [Com]onlie called and knowne by the name of the Redd Bull scituate in the parish of S^t [James] Clerkenwell aforesaid . . . did afterwardes erecte builde and sett vpp in and vpon some parte of the same messuage or tenement diuers and sundry buildinges and galler[ies wch he afterwardes] leased for a playhouse . . . After w^ch . . . Aron Holland . . . did by his Indenture of lease [bearinge date the . . . day of . . .] in the third yeare of [the] reigne of yor Matie . . . made betwene the said Aron Holland of the one partie and Thomas Swynnerton of the other partie demise and graunt a seaventh parte of the said playhowse and gallaries with a gatherers place there[to] belonginge or apperteyninge vnto the said Thomas Swynnerton. . . .[1]

A few details about the theatre property are added three years later, on 25 October 1625, by Woodford in a Chancery Bill. There he describes the property as

one Messuage or Tenement now commonly called or knowne by the name or signe of the Red Bull at the vpper end of St John street with the Gardens Courts Cellars Wayes & liberties therevnto belonging or apperteyning sometymes in the tenure of one John Waintworth or his assignes . . . in the parish of St James at Clerkenwell aforesaid did lately erect & set vp in & vpon part of the premisses diuers & sundry buildings & galleries to serue & to be vsed for a Playhouse or a place to play & present Comedies Tragedies & other matters of that qualitie. . . . (Hotson, p. 327.)

These two documents indicate that the original Red Bull was an inn whose 'square court'[2] and stables Holland remodelled

---

[1] Wallace, *Three London Theatres*, pp. 17–18, from an uncalendared Court of Requests Bill. Later documents in the suit and its conclusion are transcribed and discussed in Hotson, pp. 82–86 and 327–47.

[2] Presumably a theatre 'before a square court' was square, and thus resembled the most recently built London theatre, the nearby Fortune, and not the Fortune's immediate predecessor, the Bankside Globe, which was circular or polygonal, as was the later Hope. There has been some confusion about the shape of the Red Bull, since the epilogue of the 1607 edition of Day, Rowley, and Wilkins' *Travailes of the Three English Brothers* refers to 'Some that fill vp this round circumference'. The title-page says that the play was acted by the Queen's men, who appear to have been at the Red Bull in 1607. But the Queen's men had previously been at the Curtain, as the draft patent shows, and the Stationers' Register entry for the play says 'as yt Was played at the Curten'. Evidently the *Travailes of the Three English*

into a theatre, and that he was leasing shares in his new playhouse in 1605. Later documents show that the lease to Thomas Swinnerton was for a one-eighteenth, not a one-seventh share, that money was paid to Phillip Stone at the 'Great Gate leading to the sayd Play house', and that one of the part owners of the theatre in 1618 was a man named John Attree who died before 1623. (Hotson, pp. 327–47, and Sisson, op. cit.)

There is no evidence that Martin Slater's company for the service of the Duke of Holstein ever performed in London. The earliest occupants known for the Red Bull were the members of Queen Anne's company, which was there until 1617. Swinnerton was a member of this troupe, and Slater seems to have been, though he generally appears in provincial records rather than London ones.[1] Indeed, no known records assign any company to the Red Bull before 1609, or probably 1607 (see Chambers, *E.S.* ii. 231 and iii. 220–1).

Since Swinnerton and Slater, both Queen Anne's men, had interests in the Red Bull very early, if not from the beginning, and since their company had been having trouble with the landlords of the Boar's Head, which their draft patent of 1603 or 1604 calls, together with the Curtain, 'their now vsuall Howsen' (Chambers, *E.S.* ii. 229–30), it has been inferred that Holland prepared his new Red Bull with the Queen's company in mind. The possibility is somewhat increased by the further statement in the draft patent that Queen Anne's men may play not only in the Boar's Head and the Curtain theatres but 'Aswell . . . *as in* any other play howse not vsed by others, by the said *Thomas Greene, elected, or by him hereafter to be builte*'. (Ibid.) These clear implications that the company intended to move and possibly to build led Professor Charles Sisson to conclude that Aaron Holland designed the Red Bull for the use of Queen Anne's men under a bargain with them, and that this conjectured agreement

---

Brothers was written for performance at the Curtain before the Queen's men moved to the Red Bull, and the epilogue refers to the shape of the Curtain, not that of the Red Bull.

[1] See above, i. 158–60 and ii. 574–5. Slater's association with the Queen's men is probably the grounds for the Duke of Holstein's selection of him, for the Duke was the Queen's brother, who had been visiting court since November 1604. The Duke of Holstein's company is somewhat puzzling; no other mention of it is known. Since Slater is several times associated with touring Queen Anne's companies, one wonders if it could have been a touring branch of the Queen's men for which he had got the Duke's patronage, expecting to play with them in London when he could, and then to go back to the Continent with the Duke at the end of his visit.

is the reason for the odd provision in the draft patent for a play-house 'hereafter to be builte' by Greene, the most prominent member of Queen Anne's company. The hypothesis is very persuasive, if not yet demonstrable.

The Red Bull was apparently a large theatre, though no estimates of its capacity are recorded. In the Preface to the 1673 edition of his collection of drolls, *The Wits; or, Sport upon Sport*, Francis Kirkman says of the later Red Bull: '*these small things were as profitable, and as great get-pennies to the Actors as any of our late famed Plays. I have seen the* Red Bull *Play-House, which was a large one, so full, that as many went back for want of room as had entred*'. (A₂ᵛ.) One would assume a size not notably inferior to that of the Fortune and the Globe, since these two theatres had been built in the preceding five or six years for the principal competitors of Queen Anne's men, and the Red Bull would surely have been planned to compete with the existing new theatres.

Kirkman's allusion to the theatre as a familiar playing-place for drolls is probably the grounds for the erroneous statement, still sometimes repeated, that the picture of a stage with half a dozen characters from different drolls upon it, printed as the frontispiece to the 1662 edition of *The Wits, or Sport upon Sport*, is a representation of the stage of the Red Bull. Kirkman, however, never refers to his uncaptioned frontispiece, and since the picture shows an indoor stage with two candelabra and footlights, it clearly does not represent the Red Bull.[1]

At the beginning of our period in 1616 the Red Bull had been occupied, probably for ten or eleven years, by Queen Anne's company. Here they had brought out or revived such plays as Webster's *White Devil* and *The Devil's Law Case*, Heywood's Four Ages plays, *The Four Prentices of London, The Rape of Lucrece*, and *A Woman Killed with Kindness*, Dekker's *If it be not Good the Devil is in it*, Cooke's popular *Greene's Tu Quoque*, Marlowe's *Edward II*, Rowley's *A Shoemaker a Gentleman*, and the anonymous *The Honest Lawyer*. Of course there were many others not so easily identifiable now. For years the principal playwright of the troupe had been Thomas Heywood, a patented member of the company from before the time of the transfer to the Red Bull. For this theatre it is likely that Heywood wrote a good proportion of the output he mentioned in his epistle to *The*

---

[1] Apparently the frontispiece of *The Wits* was never alleged to be a picture of the Red Bull stage until 1809. For a discussion of the frontispiece see *The Wits: or, Sport upon Sport*, edited by John James Elson, 1932, Appendix ii.

English Traveller: 'two hundred and twenty [plays] in which I haue had either an entire hand, or at the least a maine finger'.

The principal actor and apparently the manager of the troupe at the Red Bull had been, until his death in 1612, Thomas Greene of *Greene's Tu Quoque*. After him Heywood's friend, Christopher Beeston (see above, ii. 363–70) had taken over a large part of the management of the affairs of the company. Thomas Heywood said in his deposition in the *Worth* v. *Baskervile* suit of 1623:

... the complainants and the rest of their then Company [i.e. Queen Anne's men], both before and synce the decesse of Thomas Greene did repose their mayne Trust and Confidence in Hutchinson alias Beeston, for and concerning the Managing of their Affayres, he having a kynde of powerfull Comaunde over the complainants and their then fellow Actors in that behalfe [insomuch as at one tyme they trusted him three yeares together or thereabouts with their moneys gotten by their labours and paynes in Acting or Playing, without any accompt thereof made vnto the complainants or Company to my knowledge.] (Sisson, op. cit., p. 64.)

In spite of the fact that Heywood also testified in this suit that under the leadership of Beeston 'there hath bin eight or nyne pounds in a day received at the dores and Galeries' of the Red Bull (loc. cit.) the company seems to have been in straits during the years 1612 to 1617. (See above, i. 158 ff.) Beeston was sued for debts incurred for company costume materials, and other members said that he had kept their accounts fraudulently. (Wallace, *Three London Theatres*, pp. 32–51.) Nevertheless (perhaps one should say consequently) Beeston managed to construct in 1617 the new Phoenix or Cockpit theatre in Drury Lane, the second operating private theatre in town. To this new playhouse he moved Queen Anne's company from the Red Bull about the end of February 1616/17. They left the Red Bull deserted for only a few days, however, for on 4 March 1616/17 the new Cockpit was sacked by a Shrove Tuesday mob and the company returned to the Red Bull. It is not unlikely that their losses in costumes and probably in play books were great.

Three months were enough for repairs to the Cockpit, for on 3 June 1617 the company was said to be 'now comme, or shortlie to comme from the said Playhowse called the Redd Bull to the Playhowse in Drurie Lane called the Cockpitt'. (*Baskervile* suit, Fleay, *Stage*, pp. 285–6.)

At the Red Bull the Queen's men were succeeded by Prince Charles's (I) company which had come from the Hope on the Bankside, where they were financed by Edward Alleyn. (See above, i. 198–203.) They may have transferred as early as April 1617, for under that date is a receipt in the accounts of the Prince of Wales for the delivery of 'one other messuage from St Iameses to the Red Bull with a message to the players'. (*M.S.C.* vi. 146–7.) Their playing at the Red Bull is indicated by an entry made by Edward Alleyn in his diary under the date of 3 October 1617: 'I went to ye red bull & R̸ for ye younger brother, but 3. 6. 4.' (William Young, *The History of Dulwich College*, ii. 51.) The play is lost (see above, v. 1448–9) and the meaning of the diary is not so clear as it might be, but I take it that Alleyn received from the players as part payment of their debt to him the sum of £3. 6s. 4d. which had been taken at performances of *The Younger Brother* at the Red Bull.

A threat to pull down the Red Bull and the Cockpit was made by London apprentices about a year after their depredations at the Cockpit. On 12 February 1617/18 the Privy Council wrote the Lieutenants of Middlesex to warn them of the threat. (See above, i. 163.) Apparently adequate protective measures were taken, for nothing further is heard of the malicious plans of the apprentices.

After the death of Queen Anne on 2 March 1618/19 her company of players was without a patron, and Christopher Beeston sought a new service and new tenants for his theatre. He entered the service of the Prince of Wales and moved the Prince's company from the Red Bull to his new Phoenix. Though the evidence is not clear, it appears that the evicted and patronless Queen Anne's company came back to the Red Bull, where they were reorganized under the name of the Company of the Revels. At the Red Bull this company performed in the next three years Markham and Sampson's *Herod and Antipater*, Massinger and Dekker's *The Virgin Martyr*, Thomas May's *The Heir*, I. C.'s *The Two Merry Milkmaids*, and the anonymous play *The Two Noble Ladies and the Converted Conjurer*. (See above, iv. 734–5; iii. 263–6; iv. 835–7; iii. 101–4; and v. 1426–7.)

During this company's tenancy of the Red Bull in March 1621/2 a felt-maker's apprentice named John Gill was injured by a sword in the hands of one of the actors, Richard Baxter. He threatened to bring down the apprentices on the Red Bull unless Baxter gave him satisfaction and recompense for his surgeon's bill of ten shillings. The threatening letter was turned over to Middlesex authorities, and no violence is known. (See above, i. 166–7.)

One could assume that Gill had been seated on the stage during the performance of a play at the Red Bull when he was hurt by Baxter's sword, but prizes played by fencers were not unknown at the Red Bull[1] and he may have been injured during such a contest.

Some time in late 1622 or early 1623 the struggling Queen Anne–Revels company was succeeded at the Red Bull by Prince Charles's (I) company, who had previously moved from the Phoenix to the Curtain. (See abov,e i. 205–8.) Around the time of the company's transfer, Sir Henry Herbert recorded two plays which were acted at the Red Bull:

The Princes Players—A french Tragedy of the Belman of [Paris contayning 40] sheetes written by Thomas Drickers & Iohn [Day, for the company] of the Readbull this 30 Iuly 1623 1^{li} o.

For the lady Eliz: Players. September A new Comedy called the Cra Marchant [or come to my Cuntry] house contayninge 9 sheetes may bee acted [this 12th Septr 1623] Written by William Bonen 3. o. o.
It was acted at the Red Bull & licensed without [my hande to itt because] they were none of the foure companys. (Halliwell-Phillipps Scrap-Books, *Theatres of Shakespeare's Time*, pp. 51 and 53.)

The records make it clear enough that both plays were performed at the Red Bull, but they do not reveal so clearly by whom or just when. The first entry might be simply redundant in its naming of the company, or it might suggest that Dekker and Day wrote the piece for a previous company at the Red Bull but the Prince's men took it over. The second licence is more confused. Clearly the play had already been acted at the Red Bull when it was licensed to Lady Elizabeth's men, and something irregular is indicated by the phrasing and by the abnormally large licensing fee. The identity of the actors who are 'none of the foure companys' is not clear.

A more notorious play also acted at the Red Bull, and probably by Prince Charles's company, was the topical *Late Murder of the Son upon the Mother, or Keep the Widow Waking* performed in September 1624. (See above, iii. 252–6.) In the suit about the play as performed at the Red Bull, Thomas Dekker deposed that instructions for the writing of the play were given to him and to

---

[1] Sir Henry Herbert's Office Book records at least two such matches: '1622. 21 Martii. For a prise at the Red-Bull, for the howse; the fencers would give nothing. 10s.' (*Herbert*, p. 48) and an undated entry, 'For a prise playd at the Redd bull by M^r [Allen & Mr Lewkner] gentlemen—10^s. for the house 10^s' (Halliwell-Phillipps Scrap-Books, Folger Library, *Theatres of Shakespeare's Time*, p. 53.)

John Webster, John Ford, and William Rowley by Ralph Savage, a man who is otherwise unknown, but who must have been concerned with the management of the company at the Red Bull. One of the ballads composed on the events of the play is alleged to have been sung on the streets and even, at the direction of Aaron Holland, under the windows of the widow who was the victim of the sub-plot. The company at the Red Bull seems to have been enterprising, if not very subtle.

On 27 March 1625 King James died, and all London theatres were closed. Before his funeral the plague had increased danger- ously, and it is likely that no theatres were allowed to reopen before the end of November. (See above, ii. 654–7.) Such a disaster in the theatre wrecked most of the London companies, but Prince Charles's men were additionally hurt in that they not only lost their patron, who took over his father's company, the King's men, but several of their principal actors who were joined to it. The troupe disappears in 1625.

There are suggestions but no clear proof that the Red Bull theatre was altered in this plague period. The most datable reference comes from a plague pamphlet written by '*W. C.* Pastor at *White Chappell*' and dedicated to the Lord Mayor, Sheriffs, and Aldermen 'and the rest of the Godly Citizens *and Officers, who haue eyther stayed in* their Places and Duties during this Visitation: or sent their large and Comfortable Benuolence for the Poore'. The pamphlet is dated 1625, and references in the Dedicatory Epistle suggest that W. C. was writing in late September or early October of the plague year:

. . . I walking hourely through the valley of the shadow of Death, (burying forty, fifty, sometimes sixty a day, and in the Totall, more than two thousand alreadie) . . . if any . . . thinke I deale too farre and too freely in this Confession. I aske no more but to forbeare his judgment, til they be vnder the hand of God, as we haue bin now three moneths and more . . . who sees more than forty thousand Chris- tians . . . laid in the dust, in little more then twice forty dayes. (A$_3$^{v}, A$_5$ and A$_5$^{v}.)

The figures suggest that he wrote with the plague bills before him, and they fit the reports of deaths for the 84 days from 1 July to 22 September. (See above, ii. 668.) His comment on the theatres, therefore, was apparently made in late September or early October of 1625. He says in his prayer:

And when other Churches were fasting and praying, we alas, were masking, feasting and playing: And when as thy Gospell had glutted vs, so as holy Lectures, begun to bee now held, like meate out of season, and preaching in some places to bee put downe, yet euen then O Lord, were the Theatres magnified, and enlarged, where Satan is serued and sinne secretly instilled, if not openly professed. (B_2^v.)

The only theatre definitely known to have been altered about this time is the Fortune, which was rebuilt in 1622; it is William Prynne's much more specific but less datable record which makes it appear that W. C. was referring to the Red Bull as well as to the Fortune. Prynne says in the Epistle to *Histriomastix*:

*The Fortune   *two olde Play-houses* being also lately reedified,
and Red bull.   enlarged, and one **new Theatre* erected, the
*White Friers   multitude of our London Play-haunters being
Playhouse.   so augmented now, that all the ancient Divels
                     Chappels (for so the Fathers stile all Play-
                     houses) being five in number, are not sufficient
                     to contaric their troopes, whence wee see a
                     sixth now added to them. . . . (*Histriomastix*
                     [1633], First Epistle Dedicatory, $*_3^v$.)

Prynne's date is not so clear as W. C.'s. Though *Histriomastix* was not published until 1633, it had been entered in the Stationers' Register on 16 October 1630, and parts of the treatise are said to have been written well before that. Ordinarily the rebuilding date of early 1625 or before, set by *London's Lamentation*, might be thought too early to have been referred to by Prynne in a publication of 1633 as 'lately'; but since Prynne refers in the same passage to the Fortune construction of 1622 as 'lately', he offers no contradiction to the sermon date.

Though the Epistle of *Histriomastix* is specific enough in its reference to particular theatres, the pamphlet is extremely vague. The evidence for the enlargement of the Red Bull in or shortly before 1625 is thus embarrassingly slight, but it cannot be ignored. One can only conclude that some enlargement took place in the 1620's—perhaps in 1625—but that nothing at all is known about it.

W. J. Lawrence wanted to be much more specific about the alterations in this theatre. He argued (loc. cit.) in his usual entertaining fashion that the reconstruction involved the roofing of the yard, and that thereafter the Red Bull offered in its cheapest accommodations the same shelter from the elements as did the private theatres. The argument consists mostly of 'it stands to reason', 'naturally', and 'one cannot doubt'; very little solid factual evidence is ever offered. Since Lawrence's essay appeared

(1916) Hotson has cited (pp. 86–87) fairly conclusive evidence that the Red Bull yard was open to the sky in 1654 and 1655, and consequently that the enlargement of 1625 is most unlikely to have included a roof for the yard. Hotson also pointed out that the addition of a large roof to walls not built to support it would have been both difficult and expensive. This objection of his is reinforced by later evidence that the original walls of the Red Bull theatre were probably just the walls of the old Red Bull Inn, and would thus already have been subjected in 1605 to greater stress than the inn builders had calculated. Whatever the vaguely known enlargement of about 1625, then, it is most unlikely to have included a roof for the pit.[1]

After 1625 the Red Bull is more obscure than it had been in the days of Queen Anne's men and Prince Charles's (I) company. Its plays must have attracted only the slightest literary attention,

[1] It was Lawrence's notion of a roof, making the Red Bull a completely enclosed and artificially lighted house like the private theatres, which led him to revive the discredited identification of the frontispiece of *The Wits* as a representation of the Red Bull stage, and to scatter the assumption through the pages of his widely used *Physical Conditions of the Elizabethan Public Playhouse*, 1927 (pp. 4, 8–9, 14, 87, 129).

There is sad confusion about the pre-war theatre in William Van Lennep's article 'The Death of the Red Bull'. He says:

A picture of its exterior as it stood in Clerkenwell is to be found in the large map of London and Westminster, published by Richard Newcourt in 1658 (Pl. 4). Notice the theatre was completely circular. The structure on the right of it must have been the main entrance on St. John Street, close to the Fleet River. The stage that extended well into the yard is not shown; it had been removed when Parliament had closed the theatres in 1642. The theatre looks much like the Globe Playhouse, but larger and without the superstructure or huts that adorn Shakespeare's theatre. It was a huge theatre, originally built in 1600 and enlarged in 1632. (Op. cit., p. 126.)

The date of the original construction is wrong, and, unless we completely discard the testimony of W. C., the date for the enlargement must be wrong. The plate for the article, which is entitled 'Red Bull Theatre from R. Newcourt's map of London and Westminster, 1658' and shows the features described, is taken from Faithorne's 1658 engraving of Newcourt's drawing, entitled 'An Exact Engraving of the Cities of London and Westminster and the Suburbs thereof . . .'. In this map there is no theatre in the area of the Red Bull. The buildings, orchards, and gardens shown in the plate come from the Bankside area of the map; indeed the plate shows part of the shore of the Thames and the bows of two boats at the top. In Faithorne's engraving the building is labelled 'Beare garden'. The plate made for Van Lennep's article cuts off the part of the engraving with the label, and consequently must have been misplaced in Van Lennep's notes. As depicting the Bear Garden, the features of the engraving, so contradictory of our knowledge of the Red Bull, are readily accounted for.

for the publishers mostly ignored them. Nearly 500 editions and issues of plays and masques were published in the reign of Charles I (1625–49) and about 150 of those editions name a theatre on the title-page.[1] But the name of the lowly Red Bull is added to their title-page statements by the printers only six times in the reign of Charles I, and four of the six examples occur on the title-pages of old plays and refer to productions in the time of Queen Anne's company at the theatre.[2] Obviously the publishers of Caroline London thought that most Red Bull plays were not worth printing, or if they did print one they thought that a title-page association with the Red Bull would sell no copies.

For a decade after 1625 the occupancy of the Red Bull is uncertain. As we have seen, the last Jacobean tenants, Prince Charles's (I) company, had ceased to exist at the death of King James. Their successors, after an interval at least as long as the plague-closing, appear to have been a vaguely known troupe usually called the King's players when on tour and the Red Bull company when in London. (See above, i. 270–82.) The first clear notice of this organization is found in an entry by the Master of the Revels in his Office Book: 'from Mr. Hemming [the usual financial agent of the King's men], in their company's name, to forbid the playing of Shakespeare's plays, to the Red Bull Company, this 11 of April, 1627,—5*l.* 0. 0.'. (*Variorum,* iii. 229.)

The unusual size of the fee—one of the largest recorded in the Office Book—suggests an unusual favour granted by Sir Henry, as indeed it was, plays in print being ordinarily beyond the control of the company. Apparently the troupe at the Red Bull had made use of the cheap repertory to be acquired by the purchase of a First Folio; perhaps they went too far in bringing to London plays which they had performed without hindrance in the country.

Two and a half years later—in November and December 1629—a French troupe visited London and presented at least one play at the Red Bull. On 8 November 1629, Thomas Brande wrote:

. . . certain vagrant French players, who had beene expelled from their owne countrey, *and those women,* did attempt, thereby giving just offence to all vertuous and well-disposed persons in this town, to

[1] Fifty-nine title-pages name the Cockpit or Phoenix in Drury Lane; forty-eight Blackfriars; and eleven the Salisbury Court, which was not built until 1629.

[2] The four old plays are Heywood's *Four Prentices of London* and his *Rape of Lucrece*; Rowley's *A Shoemaker a Gentleman*; and Dekker's *Match Me in London*.

act a certain lascivious and unchaste comedye in the French tonge at
the Blackfryers. Glad I am to saye they were hissed, hooted, and
pippin-pelted from the stage, so as I do not thinke they will soone
be ready to trie the same againe. . . . (Collier, *History of English
Dramatic Poetry* [1879], i. 452–3.)

The same performance is twice noted from another point of
view by William Prynne:

	. . . as they have now their female-Players in Italy, and other forraigne parts, and as they had such *French-women Actors*, in a Play[t] not long
[t]In Michael.	since personated in *Blacke-friers Play-house*, to
Terme, 1629.	which there was great resort.

*　*　*　*　*

They had in those dayes some few women Actors: which in his
10. Homily upon *Mathew*, he stiles *Fœminae Theatrales*: Theatricall
women: In imitation of these some French-women, or Monsters
rather on Michaelmas Terme 1629. attempted to act a French Play,
at the Play-house in Black-friers: an impudent, shamefull, unwomanish, gracelesse, if not more then whorish attempt. (*Histriomastix*,
Ee₃ᵛ–Ee₄ and Ggg₃ᵛ.)

In his Office Book Sir Henry Herbert records three separate
performances by the French visitors, with a comment on their
reception somewhat different, at least on one occasion, from those
of Brande and Prynne:

For the allowing of a French company to playe a farse at Black-
fryers, this 4 of November, 16[2]9,—2*l*. 0*s*. 0*d*.

For allowinge of the Frenche [company] at the Red Bull for a daye,
22 Novemb.,—[2*l*. 0*s*. 0*d*.]

For allowinge of a Frenche companie att the Fortune to play one
afternoone, this 14 Day of Decemb. 1629,—1*l*. 0*s*. 0*d*.

I should have had another peece, but in respect of their ill fortune,
I was content to bestow a peece back. (*Variorum*, iii. 120.)

These records are puzzling. If the French were hooted from the
Blackfriars stage, how did they dare risk the Red Bull and the
Fortune? The audiences and the houses in Blackfriars and Drury
Lane would surely be more understanding than those in St. John's
Street and Golding Lane; the hooting and pippen-pelting are more
familiar at the Red Bull than at Blackfriars. Herbert's accounts
note the visitors' bad luck at the Fortune but not at the Blackfriars, and Prynne says there was great resort to them at Blackfriars. I suspect some confusion in Brande's letter, but the date

seems to verify his association of the uproar with the Blackfriars performance and not with the others. It would be interesting to find other news letters about the visitors of 1629.

In the next five years there are no records of a company at the Red Bull, though several for the Red Bull–King's company in the provinces. Presumably their London theatre was used by them much of the time in these years, but metropolitan performances can only be conjectured.

Not until 1634 do we have any clear evidence of a troupe performing in St. John's Street. In the summer of that year the King's Revels company played in Oxford on a provincial tour, and Richard Kendall, wardrobe-keeper for the company, visited his friend Thomas Crosfield, a Fellow of The Queen's College. Kendall told Crosfield a good deal about the five London companies and their theatres, information which Crosfield set down in his diary. (See above, ii. 688–9.) The entry for the third company reads: '3. The Princes Servants at ye Red-bull in St Johns street, ye cheife Mr Cane a goldsmith, Mr Worth Mr Smith 2000^li.' There is no mention of the Red Bull–King's company and no indication of how long Prince Charles's (II) men had been at the theatre at the time of Kendall's visit, 18 July 1634.

This company of the child Prince Charles (see above, i. 303–23) is first found playing at the Salisbury Court theatre, but several members had once been actors at the Red Bull, and the transfer of the company to that house is not surprising. The date of the transfer is unknown, but it was some time between January 1631/2 and July 1634. At the Red Bull the company appears to have remained until 1640, except for frequent summer tours. About the time of Kendall's account to Crosfield they left their theatre to accompany the King and Queen on a summer progress, and several other records of the company show them touring rather than playing in their London theatre. (See above, i. 310–13.) Prince Charles's company, unlike its immediate predecessor at the Red Bull, was sufficiently distinguished to perform several times before the King at court, and several times before the young Prince Charles after the setting up of his separate establishment. (See *M.S.C.* vi. 152–4.)

Like all other London theatres the Red Bull was closed because of plague from May 1636 until October 1637, except for one week. (See above, ii. 661–5.) How the players supported themselves in such a time no one knows.

In the year following the reopening there are records of two disturbances at the theatre. Recognizances were taken in January

1637/8 for the appearance of Thomas Pinnocke, a silk-weaver, to answer 'for menacing and threatening to pull downe the Redbull playhouse and strikinge divers people with a great cudgell as he went alonge the streets'. Only seven months later Thomas Jacob was similarly charged 'for committing a greate disorder in the Red Bull playhouse and for assaulting and beating divers persons there'. (*Middlesex County Records*, iii. 168.)

In the following year there was a more serious difficulty at the theatre, when Prince Charles's company succumbed to the perennial temptation of the actors and staged a play which was much too specific in its presentation of contemporary controversial figures. The play was an anonymous lost piece called *The Whore New Vamped* (see above, v. 1441–2), known only from the scandalized remarks of the Privy Council on its production:

> Complaint was this day made that the stage-players of the Red Bull [have for] many days together acted a scandalous and libellous [play in which] they have audaciously reproached and in a libel [represented] and personated not only some of the aldermen of the [city of London] and some other persons of quality, but also scandalized and libelled the whole profession of proctors belonging to the Court of [Probate], and reflected upon the present Government.

> .   .   .   .   .

> In the play called 'The Whore New Vamped', where there was mention of the new duty on wines, one personating a justice of the peace, says to Cain. 'Sirrah, I'll have you before the alderman;' whereto Cain replies, 'The alderman, the alderman is a base, drunken, sottish knave, I care not for the alderman, I say the alderman is a base, drunken, sottish knave.' Another says, 'How now Sirrah, what alderman do you speak of?' Then Cain says, 'I mean alderman [William Abell], the blacksmith in Holborn;' says the other, 'Was he not a Vintner?' Cain answers, 'I know no other.' In another part of the play one speaking of projects and patents that he had got, mentions among others 'a patent for 12*d*. a piece upon every proctor and proctor's man who was not a knave.' Said another, 'Was there ever known any proctor but he was an arrant knave?' (*C.S.P., Dom.*, Charles I, 1639, pp. 529–30.)

Such attacks on the unpopular proctors are likely enough to have given the play a run of 'many days together'; one wonders that the Master of the Revels had not acted earlier, as he had done with previous plays whose political allusions were too specific. (See *Herbert*, pp. 18–23.) The mention of Andrew Cane, or Keyne, as an actor in the scandalous play testifies to the popularity of this comedian of Prince Charles's company at the Red Bull. In the last years of the Caroline theatre his name appears frequently. (See above, ii. 398–401.)

There is no record of the punishment of the players for their popular attack on aldermen and proctors, but the Council was sweeping enough in its demand for an investigation. The order of 29 September directs that:

the Attorney-General be hereby prayed forthwith to call before him, not only the poet who made the play and the actors that played the same, but also the person that licensed it, and having diligently examined the truth of the said complaint, to proceed roundly against such of them as he shall find have been faulty, and to use such effectual ex[pedition] to bring them to sentence, as that their exemplary punishment may [check] such insolencies betimes. (Loc. cit.)

Whatever happened to the dramatist or the Master of the Revels, the players at the Red Bull cannot have been long suppressed or disgraced, for within six weeks they were presenting plays before the court at Richmond, and the offending Andrew Cane later received payment for them. (*M.S.C.* ii. 394.)

In the following spring Prince Charles's men left the Red Bull again and were succeeded by the Red Bull–King's company [confusing nomenclature] which had been at the theatre before. Sir Henry Herbert noted in his Office Book the exchange of playhouses: 'At Easter 1640, the Princes company went to the Fortune, and the Fortune company to the Red Bull.' (*Variorum*, iii. 241.) The exchange of theatres is also recorded in the prologue for an unknown play which John Tatham published in his *Fancies Theater*, 1640, entitled '*A Prologue spoken upon the removing of the late Fortune Players to the Bull*'. It implies that Prince Charles's company was a noisy troupe which had intrigued to get the Fortune, and it appeals to the Red Bull audience:

> Onely wee would request you to forbeare
> Your wonted custome, banding *Tyle*, or Peare,
> Against our *curtaines*, to allure *us* forth.
>
> (See above, i. 315–16.)

Such implications of the conduct of audiences at the Red Bull are common enough, but they are not usually so politely phrased.

This is the last record of playing at the Red Bull before all theatres were closed at the beginning of the war. One can only assume that the Red Bull–King's troupe continued in St. John's Street for the next two and a half years until the closing order was issued.

After the Parliamentary closing order of 2 September 1642 playing was no longer authorized at any London theatre, but since Professor Rollins's examination of the Commonwealth newsbooks it has been known that there were a good many performances in the old playhouses between the time of the closing order and the Restoration.[1] A number of different playhouses were used in these lean years, but the most popular appear to have been the Red Bull, the Fortune, and the Salisbury Court. Usually the newsbook allusions to activities in the theatres give very little specific information about performances; the allusions generally occur in accounts of raids or in satiric remarks about the new government. Between the closing order of September 1642 and the dismantling of several theatres in March 1648/9 there are a number of references to Red Bull performances, though the most active theatre in these years appears to have been the Fortune. (See above, vi. 173 ff.)

Early in the year 1648 the Red Bull actors appear to have felt free enough to advertise, for the issue of *Perfect Occurrences* for 28 January to 4 February 1647/8, under the date *Thursday Feb. 3*, carries the note: '*Tickets were thrown into Gentlemens Coaches, thus.* At the Bull this day you may have Wit without Money, *meaning a Play.*' (p. 402.)

Such defiance did not, however, go unnoticed, for in its issue of 7–14 February 1647/8 *A Perfect Diurnal* records much more drastic Parliamentary action. Under the date of 9 February the journal prints an ordinance which passed its third reading and was sent to the Lords.

Whereas the Acts of Stage Playes, Interludes, and common Playes . . . hath been prohibited by Ordinance of this present Parliament, and yet is presumed to be practised by divers in contempt thereof. Therefore for the better suppression of the said Stage-players, Interludes and common Players, It is Ordained by the Lords and Commons in Parliament That all Stage playes, and the players of Interludes and common players, shall be taken to be Rogues, and punishable within the Statutes of the 39 year of the Reigne of Queen *Elizabeth* and the seventh year of the Reign of King *James*, and lyable to the paines and penalties therein contained. . . .

And it is further Ordained, That the Lord Mayor, Justices of the peace, and Sheriffs of the City of London and Westminster, and the Counties of Middlesex and Surrey, or any two or more of them, shall and are authorized to pull downe and demolish, to cause or procure to be pulled down and demolished all Stages, galleries, Seates, and

---

[1] See Rollins, Hotson, and Van Lennep, op. cit. The following account is mostly a selection, reorganization, and slight expansion of their material.

Boxes . . . within the said City of London and Liberties thereof, and
other places within their respective jurisdiction, and all such common players and interludes to be proceeded against as Rogues (if they
still persist.)

And that every person which shall be present, and a Spectator at
any such Stage play, or Interlude hereby prohibited, shall for every
time he shall be so present, forfeit and pay the sum of five shillings
to the use of the Poor of the Parish, where the said person shall at
that time dwell or sojourn, being convicted thereof by his own confession, or proof of any one witnesse upon Oath, before any one
Justice of Peace. (pp. 1909-10.)

It might be thought that such specific provisions, together with
the fines which would be alluring to local authorities, would put
an end to all London playing at the Red Bull and elsewhere, but
such was not the case. Seven months later, according to *The
Kingdom's Weekly Intelligencer* for 12-19 September 1648, the
House of Commons was informed that 'Stage-playes were daily
acted either at the *Bull* or *Fortune*, or the private House at
Salisbury-Court, and that many scandalous Books and Ballads
are daily published'. (pp. 1082-3.) And in the following January
wholesale raids were carried out in an apparently flourishing
theatre district. *The Kingdom's Weekly Intelligencer* for the week of
2-9 January 1648/9 carries the account under the date of 2 January:

The Souldiers seized on the Players on their Stages at Drury-lane
and Salisbury Court. They went also to the Fortune in Golden-lane,
but they found none there, but John Pudding dancing on the Ropes,
whom they took along with them. In the meane time the Players
at the Red Bull, who had notice of it, made haste away, and were all
gone before they came, and tooke away all their acting cloathes with
them. . . . (p. 1210.)

The good fortune of the Red Bull players in comparison with
that of those at the other three theatres is suggestive. Had they
arranged for warnings? Did they have friends in influential positions? Something of the sort seems likely, for it is notable that in
the account of the dismantling of the theatres two months later
the wrecking of the Salisbury Court, the Phoenix, and the Fortune
is mentioned, but not that of the Red Bull, which continued to be
used. (See F. J. Furnivall in *The Academy*, xxii, no. 547 [28 October
1882], 315) from a manuscript now in the Folger Shakespeare
Library.

There may have been an intermission in playing at the Red
Bull, but nine months later a raided performance is noted in
A Perfect Diurnal for 17-24 December 1649, under date of

20 December: 'There being some Actors privatly playing neer St. *Iohns* street, whereof one giving information to some Souldiers, some Troopers went from the Mewes seized upon the Players, and took away their Sword and Cloths.' (p. 18.)

Perhaps 'privatly' means in some private house and not in the Red Bull theatre, but St. John's Street was not a district of great houses. Certainly it was at the theatre in St. John's Street that the raid of 22 January 1649/50 took place. The royalist newsbooks are more detailed in their accounts of this one. *Mercurius Pragmaticus (for King Charles II)* for the week of 22–29 January even names the most popular of the Red Bull actors taken in the raid. He jeeringly addresses Parliament:

> If you be destitute of something to do, you may go hang yourselves for a pastime to the people; I believe you would have more spectators then the *Players* in *St. John's street*; yes and Lords and Ladies too would laugh more to see the *Juncto* and State hang, then any Play in the world Acted.
>
> But your own Play-houses at *Westminster, Whitehall, Darby-house, Somerset-house &c* are the only Stages where Players must come, and who those Players must be, I'le tell you; all in Parliament Robes K——s F——s and Rebels; those are the men now in request *Andr. Cane* is out of date & all other his complices: alas poor players they are acting their parts in prison, for their presumption to break a Parliament Crack. On Tuesday *Janu* 21 [22] 1649. bee it known unto all men, the State *Janizaries* rob'd the Play-house in *St. Johns streete*, imprisoned the Players, and listed all the Lords Ladies and Gentlewomen, who are either to serve the States or pay money, if their mightynesse please to command it for so great a contempt as breaking an Act made upon the Stage at *Westminster.* . . .

Another account of the raid, with more sneers at Parliament, is printed in *The Man in the Moon* for the week 23–31 January 1649/50:

> Sure the *Play* at *Westminster* is almost at an end, for the *Foole* hath done his *part*, and is fetch'd off the *Stage* with a *vengeance*; Exit *Philip* the *Foole*, but a knavish one Ile promise you; which made the *Tragedians* at *Westminster*-Hall presently so mad for him; that they thought, the hideous *Storm* that fetch'd him away, had carried him to those other *Comedians* in Saint *Johns* street: which drove them presently thither, with two or three *Companies* of the *Rebells*; seized on the poor *Players*, uncased them of their *Cloaths*, disarmed the Lords and Gentlemen of their Swords and Cloakes; but finding him not to be there, they hung the poore *Players* Cloathes upon their Pikes, and very manfully marched away with them as *Trophies* of so wonderfull a *victory*; there was taken at this Fight

about seven or eight of the chiefe Actors, some wounded, all their Cloaths and Properties, without the loss of one man on our side. . . . (pp. 313–14.)

Perhaps this raid, with its heavy casualties for the players, finished performances at the Red Bull for a time, but customary playing there is implied two years later in a mock announcement published in *The Laughing Mercury* for 22 September 1652:

The Jackanapeses are to be all in Pease-porridge and red *Liveries*, with a Linnen Silk-Ribbon cross their shoulders made all of wooden parchment, and the twelve Celestiall Signes and Planets in Plate-gold embroidered round thereon in *Highgate-sund*; when they return back the *Players* are to meet them as they come from *Sturbridge-Faire* in a *Galley-Foyst*, and to sayle with them to the *Red-Bull*, where they are to Act a *bloody-Sea-fight*, before them in a Land *Water-worke*, written by the Ghost of Fryar *Bacon*, at the very instant that the Brazen-head spake to him, and said, *Times past.* (p.192.)

It was probably during this and the immediately following years that the brief farces called drolls came to be popularly acted, especially at the Red Bull. The form, best known from Francis Kirkman's collections of 1662 and 1673, was suited for itinerant players and threatened theatres. The only name connected with these pieces is that of Robert Cox (see above, ii. 414–15), who was both their principal actor and, according to Kirkman, their author, though most of them are merely excerpts and adaptations from well-known plays. The Red Bull is the only theatre definitely associated with Cox and the drolls. The second edition of *Acteon and Diana*, 1656, says that the pieces in the collection were 'By Rob. Cox Acted at the *Red Bull* with great applause', and Kirkman says in the Preface to his larger collection of 1673 that at performances of the drolls he had '*seen the* Red Bull *Play-House, which was a large one, so full, that as many went back for want of room as had entred*'. (Preface, A₂ᵛ.) And Gerard Langbaine describes Cox as an excellent comedian who, when the stage was suppressed, 'betook himself to making Drolls or Farces . . . which under the Colour of Rope-dancing, were allow'd to be acted at the *Red-Bull* Play-house by stealth, and the connivance of those straight lac'd Governors'. (*Account of the English Dramatick Poets*, p. 89.)

'Under Colour of Rope-dancing' seems to mean 'as part of a rope-dancing performance'; at least that was clearly the programme on two occasions at the Red Bull in 1653. The first is advertised by the facetious *Mercurius Democritus* in his issue celebrating the great victory over the Dutch fleet. Toward the end of the issue of 1–8 June 1653 *Mercurius* prints an advertisement under the heading

A Challenge to the dancer on the Ropes.

At the *Red-Bull* in St *Johns street* on Thursday next, being the Ninth of *June* 1633 [i.e. 1653]. There is a Prettie conceited fellow that hath challenged the *Dromedary* lately come out of *Barbary*, to dance with him *Cap a Pee*, on the Low Rope . . . As also running up a board with *Rapiers*, and a new countrey Dance called the *Horn-Dance*, never before presented; performed by the ablest Persons of that *Civill quality* in *England*. There will also appear a merry conceited Fellow which hath formerly given content.

And you may come and return with safety. (p. 463.)

Professor Rollins was convinced that the merry conceited fellow who had formerly given content was Robert Cox, and the sequel seems to prove him right. It is noteworthy here that the advertising is very assured, implying, as does the 'formerly given content', that performances were customary at the Red Bull at this time. Three weeks later performances were still going on, but not with safety. The same journal reports in its issue of 22–29 June 1653:

There were in the Suburbs of the City of *Nodnollshire*, two heavy Routs this last week, the one was of the *Sodom Py-woman*, the other of the Dancers of the Ropes, both betrayed by some of their own Quality . . . The Rope dancers having imployed one Mr *Cox* an *Actor* . . . to present a modest ha[r]mlesse jigge, calle[d] *Swobber*, yet two of his own quallity, envying their poor brother should get a little bread for his Children, basely and unworthily betrayed him to the Souldie[r]s, and so abused many of the Gentry that formerly had been their Benefactors, who were forced to pay to the Souldiers 5*s.* a piece for their comming out, as well as for going in,

An action, so superlatively base,
Would bush the Devil in an Anticks face.

(p. 487.)

This raid, like several of the others previously recorded, was evidently just an annoyance, and not an attempt at permanent closing, for general allusions in the journals suggest that the town took for granted public entertainment at the Red Bull later in the year. It is asserted in *Mercurius Fumigosus* for 15–22 November 1654 that 'Two *cross-legg'd Creatures* called *Sutorians*, having a great minde to learn the right Art of Preaching, would the other day needs go to the *Red-Bull* to learn *speech* and *Action* of the *Players* before they come to *Exercize* or hold *forth*.'

However continuous acting at the Red Bull may have been at this time, it was still illegal, and one of the accounts of a raid at the end of the year asserts that the players had become over-confident of their immunity. *The Weekly Intelligencer* for 26 December–2 January 1654/5 notes under date of Monday 1 January that 'The players at the *Red-bull* were on the last Saturday [29 December 1654] despoiled of their acting cl[o]aths by some of the soldiery, they having not so ful a liberty as they pretended.' *A Perfect Account of the Daily Intelligence* for 27 December–3 January 1654/5 asserts that the actors were already dressed at the time of the raid, and adds the unusual comment 'but the Souldiery carryed themselves very civilly towards the Audience' (p. 1663). *Mercurius Fumigosus* for 27 December–3 January gives the name of the play as *Wit without Money.* (p. 247.) It may be coincidence that this is the only play twice cited in interregnum performances, but one suspects a journalistic satisfaction in an appropriate title, especially since *Mercurius Fumigosus* breaks into verse about the soldiers,

> *Who Acting better then the Players yet,*
> *Left them* sans *money, Cloaths or Witt.*

The betrayal of Robert Cox at the Red Bull by two jealous players in June 1653 was not unique in the troubled affairs of hard-pressed Cromwellian actors. The facetious *Mercurius Fumigosus* in his issue for 9–16 May 1655 implies that jealousies were endemic.

A Dumb *Comedy* is next Week to be Acted at the *Red Bull*, if the *Players* can but agree and be honest among themselves; which will be the best, though hardest Scaene they can Act.

> *Pitty that those that Act in various shapes,*
> *Should 'mongst themselves prove worse then Mymick Apes.*
> *True* Roscians *learn by Action, and Civill be*
> *To all; but those Act ill, 'can't with themselves agree.*
> *For whilst they quarrell which the most should share,*
> *They are tane napping, as* Moss *did take his Mare.* (pp. 394–5.)

Possibly jealousies among the actors led to the sterner raid of 14 September 1655, but it is likely that a more determined policy of the Cromwellian government was the real cause. Both the Hope and Blackfriars were eliminated as places of entertainment in this year, and the Red Bull could scarcely expect continued toleration. J. Banks wrote in a letter to Joseph Williamson that this raid was a rout which involved many broken crowns (*C.S.P., Dom.*, 1655, p. 336), and *Mercurius Fumigosus* (12–19 September

1655, p. 546) says that at the Red Bull 'a great Rowt was given, some Prisoners taken'. A fuller account is in *The Weekly Intelligencer* for 11–18 September 1655, under date *Friday Sep. 14.*

This Day proved Tragicall to the *Players* at the *Red Bull*, their Acting being against an Act of Parlament, the Soldiers secured the persons of some of them who were upon the Stage, and in the Tyrinhouse, they seized also upon their cloaths in which they acted, a great part whereof was very rich, it never fared worse with the spectators then at this present, for those who had monies paid their five shillings apeece, those who had none to satisfie their forfeits, did leave their Cloaks behind them, the Tragedy of the Actors, and the Spectators, was the Comedy of the soldiers. There was abundance of the Female sex, who not able to pay 5*s.* did leave some gage or other behind them, insomuch, that although the next day after the Fair, was expected to be a new *Faire* of Hoods, of Aprons, and of Scarfs, all which their poverty being made known, and after some check for their Trespasse, were civilly restored to the Owners. (pp. 38–39.)

There was sufficient talk of this very thorough raid to make the occasion the subject of a ballad, which was reprinted in a collection in the following year.

A Song

1.

The fourteenth of September
I very well remember,
   When people had eaten and fed full,
Many men, they say,
Would needs go see a Play,
   But they saw a great rout at the red Bull.

2.

The Souldiers they came,
(The blind and the lame)
   To visit and undo the Players;
And [from] women without Gowns,
They said they would have Crowns;
   But they were no good Sooth-sayers.

3.

Then *Jo: Wright* they met,
Yet nothing could get,
   And *Tom Jay* i' th' same condition:
And the fire [tire?] men they
Wou'd ha' made 'em a prey,
   But they scorn'd to make a petition.

4.

The Minstrills they
Had the hap that day,
  (Well fare a very good token)
To keep (from the chase)
The fiddle and the case,
  For the instruments scap'd unbroken.

5.

The poor and the rich,
The whore and the bitch,
  Were every one at a losse,
But the Players were all
Turn'd (as weakest) to the wall,
  And 't is thought had the greatest losse.
          ([John Phillips], *Sportive Wit*, 1656, Ff_4^v–Ff_5.)

The ballad writer seems to assume that Red Bull performances
were a normal attraction in 1655, and his allusions to actors, tire
men, musicians, and a varied audience suggest a fully organized
theatrical enterprise of the pre-war type. But the raid must have
been more business-like than most of the others, for allusions to
specific performances at the Red Bull disappear for a few years.
It may be these years which James Wright had in mind when he
referred in *Historia Histrionica*, 1699, to seasonal activities at the
Red Bull 'in Olivers time'. After telling of the playing of a troupe
of old Caroline players, including John Lowin, Joseph Taylor,
Thomas Pollard, Nicholas Burt, and Charles Hart, at the Cockpit
in 1648, and the raid on their performance of Fletcher's *Bloody
Brother*, Truman continues:

Afterwards in *Oliver's* time, they used to Act privately, three or
four Miles, or more, out of Town, now here, now there, sometimes in
Noblemens Houses, in particular *Holland-house* at *Kensington*, where
the Nobility and Gentry who met (but in no great Numbers) used to
make a Sum for them, each giving a broad Peice, or the like. And
Alexander Goffe, the Woman Actor at *Blackfriers*, (who had made
himself known to Persons of Quality) used to be the Jackal and give
notice of Time and Place. At Christmass, and Bartlemew-fair, they
used to Bribe the Officer who Commanded the Guard at *Whitehall*,
and were thereupon connived at to Act for a few Days, at the *Red
Bull*; but were sometimes notwithstanding Disturb'd by Soldiers.
(See above, ii. 695.)

This raid by no means marked the end of the Red Bull, but the
performances there after Davenant had begun his experimental

musical and scenical performances in 1656 belong more properly to the beginnings of the Restoration theatre than to the end of the Caroline. (See Van Lennep, op. cit.) Sometimes distinguished actors were there, and Pepys went to the theatre, or intended to, in August 1660, March 1660/1, May 1662, and April 1664. But on the last occasion he saw not a play but 'a rude prize fought, but with good pleasure enough'. Such entertainment seems to have been the usual fare during the last years of the Red Bull. The Player in the first scene of Davenant's *The Play-House to be Let* (summer 1663) tells the House-keeper to respond to the request of the indigent fencers:

> Tell 'em the *Red Bull* stands empty for Fencers,
> There are no Tenents in it but old Spiders.

And the final notice of the theatre is of this sort, a handbill for a prize fight at eight weapons to be held at the Red Bull on the afternoon of 30 May 1664. (Van Lennep, pp. 133–4.) After the great fire in September 1666, nothing more is heard of the theatre.

The Reputation of the Red Bull Theatre

Though Londoners of the seventeenth century were scarcely inclined to treat any theatre with undue respect, the Red Bull was the subject of more sneers than any other playhouse of the time. Of course the Puritans tended to sneer at, or to castigate, all theatres, but they generally made no distinctions, and they were not often specific at all. More tolerant writers often sneered at the Fortune or the Curtain, sometimes at the Globe, and now and then at the Phoenix. The Fortune appears commonly to have been associated with the Red Bull, in part, no doubt, because during most of the period they were the only theatres in the district north of the City. But there are more admiring or non-committal references to the Fortune than to the Red Bull, and fewer condescending ones. As the Curtain falls into disuse, the Red Bull reigns supreme in ignominy. Such a reputation might have been expected in the twenties or thirties when the private theatres attracted all the prestige, but even in the earlier days before the Phoenix and the Salisbury Court had been built, violence and vulgarity seem to be the usual associations with the Red Bull.

The miscellaneous references to this theatre are strikingly consistent in their implications about the characteristics of the usual audience. On 29 and 30 May and 1 June 1610 recognizances were taken for the appearance of five men—four of them felt-makers—

to appear at the next Sessions of the Peace for the County of Middlesex to answer 'for that he and others made a notable outrage att the playhouse called the Red Bull'. (*Middlesex County Records*, ii. 64–65.) Three years later, on 3 March 1612/13, similar recognizances were taken for the appearance at the next jail-delivery of Alexander Fulsis 'suspected to have pict a purse and iii li. in money in the same purse out of the pocket of one Robert Sweete at the Red Bull in St. John's Street'. (Ibid., p. 86.) Nine years later felt-makers were again a source of trouble at the Red Bull when one of their apprentices, while sitting on the stage there, was injured by an actor's sword. The apprentice wrote a letter threatening 'Mr. Baxter and the other Redbull players to ruyn theire house and persons' by the might of the apprentices unless he was recompensed. One hundred persons assembled riotously in Clerkenwell, but there is no record that they damaged the theatre or the actors. (Ibid. ii. 165–6 and 175–6.)

Similar extra-theatrical entertainment at the Red Bull is reflected in the record of recognizances taken before a Justice of the Peace on 16 January 1637/8 for the appearance of a silk-weaver named Thomas Pinnocke to appear to answer 'for menacing and threatening to pull downe the Redbull playhouse and striking diverse people with a great cudgell as he went alonge the streets'. (Ibid., ii. 168.) Seven months later Thomas Jacob was conducting himself in much the same way at the theatre and on 23 August 1638, friends gave recognizances for him to appear to answer 'for committing a greate disorder in the Red Bull playhouse and for assaulting and beating divers persons there'. (Ibid.)

The well-known description of holiday theatre violence in Edmund Gayton's *Pleasant Notes on Don Quixote*, 1654, 'the Benches, the tiles, the laths, the stones, Oranges, Apples, Nuts, flew about most liberally, and as there were Mechanicks of all professions, who fell every one to his owne trade, and dissolved a house in an instant, and made a ruine of a stately Fabrick' (see above, ii. 690–1), probably refers to events at the Fortune and Red Bull. There are three reasons which make such an identification likely: (*a*) similar actions are recorded for these two theatres elsewhere, but not for others in Gayton's time (b. 1608); (*b*) five of the nine plays named by Gayton, in the longer passage of which these lines are a part, can be identified as belonging to the Fortune and Red Bull repertories, and of the four others only one, *The Merry Devil of Edmonton* can be associated with any other Jacobean or Caroline repertory. *The Merry Devil* belonged to the King's men, and Gayton's mention of it may suggest that such holiday riots

were not unknown at the Globe; (c) the notable actors Andrew
Cane and Richard Fowler, named near the end of Gayton's description, spent the last ten years of the Caroline period at the Fortune
and Red Bull.

These repeated associations of violence and petty crime with
the Red Bull make that theatre the appropriate setting for popular fictional accounts involving such activities. The ballad in the
Pepys collection called *Dice, Wine, and Women, or the Unfortunate Gallant gull'd at London*, undated, but printed by Thomas
Langley, who published from 1615 to 1635, utilizes the popular
association when the young man up from Cornwall sings:

> 8. Then thinking for to see a play,
>   I met a Pander by the way:
>   Who thinking I had money store,
>   Brought me to Turnboll to a whore:
>   Ere from that house I rid could be
>   It cost ten pound my setting free.
>
>   .   .   .   .   .
>
> 9. Most of my money being spent,
>   To *S. Iohns* street to the *Bull* I went,
>   Where I the roaring Rimer saw,
>   And to my face was made a daw:
>   And pressing forth among the folke,
>   I lost my purse, my hat and cloke.
>
>   (Rollins, *The Pepys Ballads*, i. 237–41.)

The association of vulgarity with Red Bull performances seems
quite justified by the affair of *The Late Murder of the Son upon
the Mother, or Keep the Widow Waking* performed there in
September 1624. (See above, iii. 252–6.) This play was written
hurriedly by Dekker, Ford, Webster, and Rowley to capitalize on
a sensational matricide and the equally sensational drunken
debauch of a well-to-do widow of West Smithfield, not far from
the theatre. Though the play is lost, many details about it are
given in the Star Chamber proceedings, including the facts that
it was acted at the Red Bull and advertised by a leering ballad
with the sub-title of the play as a refrain, and this conclusion:

> And you whoe faine would heare the full
> discourse of this match makeing,
> The play will teach you at the Bull,
> to keepe the widdow wakeing.

This composition was sung on the streets, and there is an allega-
tion that the managers of the Red Bull sent singers to warble the

ballad under the window of the disgraced widow. The fact that
the son-in-law of the victimized widow named the actors at the
Red Bull, the managers of the theatre, and the authors of the
play in his complaint against the seducers of his mother-in-law no
doubt seemed quite congruent with the reputation of the theatre.

References to the dramatic fare on the stage of the Red Bull
commonly assume general recognition among the literate of the
inferior, if not ridiculous, character of the plays. George Wither's
first satire 'Of the Passion of Love' in his *Abuses Stript and Whipt*,
1613, describes one of the more contemptible lovers:

> Then he thats neither valorous nor wise,
> Comes ruffling in, with shamelesse brags and lies,
> Making a stately, prowd, vaine-glorious show;
> Of much good matter, when tis nothing so.
> In steed of lands, to which he ne're was heire,
> He tels her tales of castles in the ayre.
> For martiall matters he relates of fraies,
> Where many drew their swords and ran their waies.
> His *Poetry* is such as he can cull,
> From plaies he heard at *Curtaine* or at *Bul*,
> And yet is fine coy Mistres-*Marry muffe*,
> The soonest taken with such broken stuffe.
>
> (C_4^v.)

Thomas Tomkis assumes that his audience is familiar with the
same reputation for the Red Bull in his *Albumazar*, acted before
the King at Trinity College, Cambridge, on 9 March 1614/15. Here
the popular clown, Trincalo, after his introductory soliloquy,
hears the object of his ridiculous love calling him: 'O 'tis *Armellina*:
now if she have the wit to beginne, as I meane shee should, then
will I confound her with complements drawne from the Plaies
I see at the Fortune, and Red Bull, where I learne all the words I
speake and vnderstand not.' (1615 ed., II i. C_4^v–D_1.)

A few years later Peter Heylen made a similar implication about
the character of the plays at the Red Bull in his verses about the
performance of Barton Holyday's *Technogamia*, acted by Christ
Church men before the King at Woodstock, 26 August 1621.
(See above, iv. 589–96.)

> He hath a zelous sword if you he heares
> Be sure heele cut of your rebellious eares,
> fly to ye Globe or Curtaine with your trul,
> Or gather musty phrases from ye Bul,
> This was not for your dyet . . .

(Cavanaugh, ed., *Technogamia*, xxxv; from a Folger manuscript.)

The same assumptions are made in *Wit at Several Weapons*, where the audience must take for granted the simplicity and nonsense of Red Bull plays. In II. i the clown, Pompey Doodle, servant to Sir Gregory Fop, and 'a piece of puff-paste, like his Master', aids Sir Gregory's wooing by presenting the lady with a ruff and asking that she starch it herself. When the puzzled lady inquires the reason for Sir Gregory's silly request, Pompey Doodle replies:

> There lyes his main conceit, Lady, for sayes he, In so doing she cannot chuse but in the starching to clap it often between her hands, and so she gives a great liking and applause to my present, whereas if I should send a Puppy, she ever calls it to her with a hist, hisse, hisse, which is a fearefull disgrace, he drew the device from a Play, at the Bull tother day. (Beaumont and Fletcher Folio, 1647. Kkkkkk₂.)

Thomas Carew's opinion of Red Bull plays and players was not unlike Holyday's and Fletcher's, though it may be that his judgement should be discounted somewhat, since he was writing in anger at the failure of his friend Davenant's play at Blackfriars:

> . . . . . *they'l still slight*
> *All that exceeds Red Bull and Cockepit flight.*
> *These are the men in crowded heapes that throng*
> *To that adulterate stage, where not a tong*
> *Of th' untun'd Kennell, can a line repeat*
> *Of serious sense: but like lips, meet like meat.*[1]

Even the resident players themselves sometimes regretted the traditional noise and vulgarity at the Red Bull, and the Company of the Revels, newly arrived at that theatre in 1619 (see above, iii. 101–4) seem to have attempted to reform it, according to the prologue of their comedy, *Two Merry Milkmaids, or the Best Words Wear the Garlands*.

> This Day we entreat All that are hither come,
> To expect no noyse of Guns, Trumpets, nor Drum,
> Nor Sword and Targuet; but to heare Sence and Words,
> Fitting the Matter that the Scene affords.
> So that the Stage being reform'd, and free
> From the lowd Clamors it was wont to bee,

---

[1] Commendatory verses to William Davenant's *The Just Italian* (1630), A₃ᵛ–A₄. The naming here of the Cockpit or Phoenix where Queen Henrietta's men, a good troupe with good plays, were performing at this time is puzzling. Note that after naming two theatres Carew continues about 'that adulterate stage' as if he had a singular antecedent. Did he insert 'Cockepit' hastily because of some pique?

Turmoyl'd with Battailes; you I hope will cease
Your dayly Tumults, and with vs wish Peace.

(1620 ed.)

Similar to the noise and battles of the Red Bull plays are the
devils also associated with their performances. Samuel Pepys
noted in his diary on 30 October 1662:

> I would not forget two passages of Sir J. Minnes's at yesterday's
> dinner. . . . The other, Thos. Killigrew's way of getting to see plays
> when he was a boy. He would go to the Red Bull, and when the man
> cried to the boys, 'Who will go and be a devil, and he shall see the
> play for nothing?' then would he go in, and be a devil upon the stage,
> and so get to see plays.

Since Killigrew was born in London in 1612, and is said to have
attended Thomas Farnaby's school in the parish of St. Giles
Cripplegate, the environment is right for the boy. One would guess
the date of his devilish activities to have been about 1620 to 1625.
Even if Sir John's story is apocryphal, he could himself have been
well acquainted with the Red Bull at this time (he was born in
1598/9), and he and his auditors clearly assumed the common
appearance of devils in Red Bull plays during Killigrew's boy-
hood.

John Cleveland also implies that devils were common in Red
Bull plays when he writes in his *Character of a Country Committee-
man*:

> A Committeeman by his name should be one that is possessed,
> ther's number enough in the compellation to make it an Epithite for
> Legion; he is *persona in concreto* (to borrow the Solecisme of a moderne
> Statesman) you may translate it by the red bull phrase and speak as
> properly, enter seven devills *solus*. (1649 edition A₄.)

In Caroline times it was usual to associate outmoded dramatic
forms with the Red Bull. The outraged Puritan citizen in the
Praeludium, written around 1638 for Thomas Goffe's *Careless
Shepherdess* (see above, iv. 501–5) at the Salisbury Court theatre,
says:

> And I will hasten to the money Box,
> And take my shilling out again, for now
> I have considered that it is too much;
> I'le go to th' Bull, or Fortune, and there see
> A Play for two pense, with a Jig to boot.
>
> (1656 ed., B₄ᵛ.)

About the same time Jasper Mayne, himself a playwright, assumed the same popular estimation of Red Bull plays when he wrote in his poem to the memory of Ben Jonson:

> Thy *Scœne* was free from *Monsters*, no hard *Plot*
> Call'd downe a *God* t' untie th' unlikely *knot*.
> The *Stage* was still a *Stage*, two entrances
> Were not two *parts* oth' *World*, disjoyn'd by *Seas*.
> Thine were *land-Tragedies*, no Prince was found
> To swim a whole *Scœne* out, then oth' *Stage* drown'd;
> Pitch't fields, as *Red-Bull* wars, still felt thy doome,
> Thou laidst no sieges to the *Musique-Roome* . . .
> (*Jonsonus Virbius*, 1638, E₄.)

In the same year Ralph Bride-Oake, in his commendatory verses for the collection of Thomas Randolph's poems, makes a similar implication about the plays of the repertory of the Red Bull:

> The sneaking Tribe, that drinke and write by fits,
> As they can steale or borrow coine or wits,
> That Pandars fee for Plots, and then belie
> The paper with—*An excellent Comedie*,
> *Acted* (more was the pitty,) *by th' Red Bull*
> *With great applause*, of some vaine City Gull;
> That damne Philosophy, and prove the curse
> Of emptinesse, both in the Braine and Purse.
> (*Poems, with the Muses' Looking-Glass* [1638], sig**.)

A late allusion asserts that the performances of the company at the Red Bull were bad even when the play itself was not. Professor Hyder Rollins quotes satirical broadsides of June 1641 entitled *The Late* [and *The Last*] *Will and Testament of the Doctors Commons*:

> Item, I will and bequeath all my large Bookes of Acts, to them of the Fortune Play-House, for I hold it a deed of charity, in regard they want good action.
> All my great Books of Acts to be divided between the Fortune and the Bull; for they spoyle many a good Play for want of Action. (Op. cit., p. 270.)

The association of the Fortune with the Red Bull is here more than the usual conjunction of the two North London public theatres, for the companies of the Fortune and the Red Bull had exchanged theatres just fourteen months before. The Master of the Revels noted in his Office Book: 'At Easter 1640, the Princes company went to the Fortune, and the Fortune company to the Red Bull.' (*Variorum*, iii. 241.)

The same kind of allusion to the old and inferior plays of the
Red Bull is made by the young Abraham Cowley. In the third
act of his play, *The Guardian*, produced at Trinity College, Cambridge, on 12 March 1641/2 (see above, iii. 176–9), Captain Blade
asserts that the company was still acting a fifty-year-old play at
the Red Bull. He admonishes the shouting old man, Truman:

> First leave your raging, Sir: for though you should roar like
> *Tamerlin* at the Bull, 'twould do no good with me.
> *Tru.* I *Tamerlin*? I scorn him, as much as you do, for your ears.
> I'll have an action of slander against you, Captain.
>   (1650 ed., C₃^v.)

In the same year that Cowley's play was acted, another fifty-
year-old play, Thomas Heywood's naïve *Four Prentices of London*,
is assigned to the Red Bull repertory. A. C. Generosus (Peter
Hausted?) writes in his *Satyre against Separatists*:

> Go on brave *Heroes*, and performe the rest,
> Increase your fame each day ayard at least,
> 'Till your high names are growne as glorious full
> As the foure *London* Prentices at the *Redbull*:
>
> .   .   .   .   .
>
> So may you come to sleep in Fur at last,
> And some *Smectimnian* when your dayes are past
> Your funerall Sermon of six houres rehearse,
> And *Taylor* sing your praise in lofty verse.
>   (1642 ed., A₃^v–A₄.)

Acting of a character appropriate to such out-of-date plays is
attributed to the Red Bull by Richard Flecknoe in his character
'Of a Proud one': 'She looks high, and speaks in a *Majestick tone*,
like one playing the *Queens* part at the *Bull*, and is ready to say,
blesse ye my good people all, as often as she passes by any company.'[1]

The later seventeenth-century writers who speak reminiscently
about the Caroline theatre also agree in their condescension towards the Red Bull. Sir Aston Cockayne wrote in his Præludium
for Richard Brome's *Five New Plays*, 1653, an anticipation of
the revival of playing at the old theatres. He looked forward to
better times when:

> Our *Theaters* of lower note in those
> More happy daies, shall scorne the rustick Prose

---

[1] *Enigmaticall Characters* (1658), F₂. Though Flecknoe is writing late,
his familiarity with the Caroline stage is shown by his reference in the same
collection to the King's man, Joseph Taylor, playing Mosca in Jonson's
Volpone.

Of a *Jack-pudding*, and will please the Rout,
With wit enough to beare their Credit out.
The Fortune will be lucky, see no more
Her Benches bare, as they have stood before.
The Bull take Courage from Applauses given,
To Eccho to the *Taurus* in the Heaven.

(A₂–A₂ᵛ.)

Edmund Gayton, who shows great familiarity with the Caroline theatre in his *Pleasant Notes upon Don Quixote*, wrote: 'I have heard, that the Poets of the Fortune and red Bull, had alwayes a mouth-measure for their Actors (who were terrible teare-throats) and made their lines proportionable to their compasse, which were *sesquipedales*, a foot and a halfe.' (1654 edition, D₄ᵛ.) Familiarity with the Red Bull was also shown by Edward Howard when he wrote about the Restoration theatre in the year 1671:

. . . we find the most irregular, and illiterate, obscene and insipid Plays crowded with audiences, where they with better exercise to their bodies sweat for company, than improve their wit, learning, or manners, to do all which should be the use of Plays; whilest the most fortunate of our present Poets may perhaps conceive them-selves little less than sacred, in having this vogue, or stream of applause bestowed on their Plays, as if it were the only proper in-cense to be offer'd to *Parnassus* in their behalfs: but we may remember that the Red Bull writers, with their Drums, Trumpets, Battels, and Hero's, have had this success formerly, and perhaps have been able to number as many Audiences as our Theatres, (I will not presume to make the comparison otherwise) so likewise the Sock of that stage as well as the Buskin is not so Rank but that it may in some degree tread with our present writers, witness the Farce, *alias* the comedy *Tu quoque*, no less than a mate for most of the modern of either denomination, and yet of happy memory, in point of audiences, as I doubt not many of ours of the like Genius will be, when they have liv'd as long.[1]

---

[1] *The Six Days' Adventure, or The New Utopia* (1671), A₄ᵛ—a. It is in-teresting to note the familiarity with Red Bull affairs displayed in Howard's casual comparison with *Greene's Tu Quoque*, for that play was written for a Red Bull company, and Thomas Greene, the clown of the troupe, was famous in his role of Bubble. The text makes capital of his reputation:

Ger. Why then wee'le goe to the Red Bull; they say *Green's* a good Clowne.
Bub. Greene? *Greene's* an Asse.
Scatt. Wherefore doe you say so?
Bub. Indeed I ha no reason: for they say, hee is as like mee as euer he can looke.
Scatt. Well then, to the Bull.

(*Greene's Tu Quoque* [1614], G₂ᵛ.)

Finally, long after the closing of the theatres, a familiarity with the status of the Red Bull is still displayed by James Wright. In his *Historia Histrionica* of 1699 he writes that the Fortune and Red Bull 'were mostly frequented by Citizens, and the meaner sort of People'. (See above, ii. 693.)

Of all the Jacobean and Caroline theatres in London it is clear that the Red Bull was the least reputable, yet in the twenty-two years following Parliament's closing of all playhouses the extant records seem to indicate more playing at the Red Bull than in any of its former rivals. One is tempted to speculate on the relationship of these two conditions.

THE RED LION INN

The only known record of the Red Lion Inn in the parish of Stepney in East London as a playing-place comes from the year 1567. See Chambers, *E.S.* ii. 379–80.

THE ROSE

Adams, pp. 142–60.
Chambers, *E.S.* ii. 405–10.
Shapiro, I. A., 'The Bankside Theatres: Early Engravings', *Shakespeare Survey*, i (1948), 25–37.
Wallace, C. W., 'Shakespeare and the Globe', *The Times* (London, 30 April 1914), pp. 9–10.

Only one piece of evidence can be cited to show that the Rose theatre, built by Philip Henslowe in 1587 and operated by him for sixteen years, was ever in use as a place of entertainment after 1616. Edmond Malone annotated his mention of the Rose in a list of London theatres as follows: 'The Swan and the Rose are mentioned by Taylor the Water-poet, but in 1613 they were shut up .... After the year 1620, as appears from Sir Henry Herbert's office-book, they were used occasionally for the exhibition of prize-fighters.' (*Variorum*, iii. 56 n.)

J. Q. Adams (op. cit., p. 160 and n. 3) thought that the Rose had been either torn down or converted into tenements about 1606. Noting that some have said 'the Rose was standing so late as 1622' he comments: 'The chief source of this error is a footnote by Malone in *Variorum* III, 56; the source of Malone's error is probably to be seen in his footnote, *ibid.*, p. 66.' On the page referred to Malone quotes several extracts from Sir Henry Herbert's Office Book referring to prize-fighters, rope dancers, and Lenten allowances for the Red Bull and the Fortune, the Cockpit company and the King's men; Adams seems to imply that Malone added the Swan and the Rose in error when the Master of the Revels had mentioned only the Red Bull and the Fortune. But Malone's extracts from Herbert's manuscripts are only samples; Malone generalized on what he read, not on what he copied. As a matter of fact, another passage from Herbert's Office Book, not copied by Malone, does show the Swan being used for fencers in August 1623. (See below, vi. 250.) Under the circumstances one cannot say that Malone was in error, only that his evidence is uncomfortably contradictory, for other records seem to indicate that on 25 April 1606 the Rose playhouse was no more.

C. W. Wallace, in his article 'Shakespeare and the Globe', summarized several entries from the Records of the Sewer Commission for Kent and Surrey concerning the Rose. Several times Philip Henslowe was amerced for it, but on 4 October 1605 'return was made that it was then "out of his hands"'. On 14 February 1606 'Edward Box, of Bread-street, London, was amerced for the same. It was then still standing, but immediately afterwards disappeared. The last notice concerning it was on April 25, 1606, when Box owned the site. It was then referred to as "the late Playhouse in Maid-lane"'.

One could wish that both Malone and Wallace had been more complete in their transcriptions. 'The late Playhouse' could mean the building lately used as a playhouse, not the site of the building now demolished, as Wallace seems to imply from his 'still standing' in the preceding sentence.

All the present state of our information allows is the statement that we have no records of plays at the Rose after 1603; that it is called 'the late Playhouse' in 1606, and that Malone says that Herbert's Office Book shows it being used occasionally for prize-fights after 1620. There is no certain depiction of it in views or maps dating after 1606. (See I. A. Shapiro, 'The Bankside Theatres', *Shakespeare Survey*, i [1948], 25–37.) So far as I know there are no clear allusions to it in the Jacobean and Caroline period.

THE SWAN

Anon., 'A Note on the Swan Theatre Drawing', *Shakespeare Survey*, i (1948), 23–24.

Adams, pp. 161–81.

Chambers, *E.S.* ii. 411–14.

Hodges, C. Walter, 'De Witt Again', *Theatre Notebook* (1950–51), 32–34.

Holmes, Martin, 'A New Theory about the Swan Drawing', *Theatre Notebook*, x (1955–6), 80–83.

Hulshof, A. and Breuning, P. S., 'Brieven van Johannes de Wit aan Arend Van Buchel en anderen', *Bijdragen en mededeelingen*, Historisch Genootschap, Utrecht, lx (1939), 87–208.

Shapiro, I. A., 'The Bankside Theatres: Early Engravings', *Shakespeare Survey*, i (1948), 25–37.

Southern, Richard, 'Colour in the Elizabethan Theatre', *Theatre Notebook*, vi (1951–2), 57–58.

Wallace, C. W., 'The Swan Theatre and the Earl of Pembroke's Servants', *Englische Studien*, xliii (1910–11), 340–95.

The Swan theatre, the westernmost of the four Bankside public playhouses, was built by Francis Langley and opened in the year 1595 or 1596.[1] Of all the Elizabethan, Jacobean, and Caroline theatres, the Swan is the only one whose interior is known to us from a detailed contemporary picture, one drawn by Johannes de Witt during a visit to London, probably in the summer of 1596, but extant only in a copy of the drawing and the accompanying letter made by de Witt's correspondent, Arend Van Buchel.[2] Though this picture, perhaps originally drawn from memory and extant only in a copy, may be inaccurate in details, it is our best guide to the appearance of the interior of an Elizabethan public

---

[1] See Adams, pp. 161–2 and Chambers, *E.S.* ii. 411–12. On its circular shape see I. A. Shapiro, 'The Bankside Theatres'. An interesting suggestion that the exterior walls were timber with flint conglomerate filling and that the columns within were wooden, painted in a convincing imitation of marble, is set out by Richard Southern 'Colour in the Elizabethan Theatre'.

[2] The best of the many reproductions of this drawing, as well as of the accompanying letter, are to be found in *Shakespeare Survey*, i (1948), 23–24 and Plates II and III. See also the Hulshof and Breuning article. Martin Holmes (loc cit.) has made the interesting suggestion that the sketch represents the theatre during a rehearsal, not a regular performance. This suggestion would account for many of the features of the sketch, such as the absence of spectators in the galleries and the presence of the few watching figures in the gallery over the stage. These watchers, Mr. Holmes suggests, are actors, not members of a paying audience.

theatre. Contradiction of any of the features of this sketch—a common practice among many of our theatre reconstructors—should be received with scepticism unless accompanied by over-whelming evidence. In his accompanying text de Witt says:

Theatrorum autem omnium [Theatre, Curtain, Rose, Swan] prestantissimum est et amplissimum id cuius intersignium est cygnus (vulgo te theater off te cijn) quippe quod tres mille homines in sedilibus admittat, constructum ex coaceruato lapide pyrritide (quorum ingens in Brittannia copia est) ligneis suffultum columnis quæ ob illitum marmoreum colorem, nasutissimos quoque fallere posse[n]t.

By 1616 this theatre had been superseded by the newer public playhouses—the Globe, the Fortune, the Red Bull, and the Hope—and no Jacobean or Caroline company is certainly known to have made regular use of it, though it was still standing years later. Occasional references show that it was used now and then, apparently for shows and possibly in one year by a regular company. Edmond Malone said that 'After the year 1620, as appears from Sir Henry Herbert's office-book, they [the Rose and the Swan] were used occasionally for the exhibition of prize-fighters'. (*Variorum*, iii. 56, n. 5.) Though none of these entries about the Swan got into print from Sir Henry's records, one of them is found in a manuscript copy of the office-book, perhaps that made by Craven Ord, which Halliwell-Phillipps cut up and pasted into one of his scrap-books. The extract is undated, but it follows one dated 23 August 1623: 'For a Prise playd at the Princes armes or [the Swann by Tho⁵] Musgrave & Renton . . .   10ˢ·¹

The only evidence that the Swan was ever used for plays after 1616 is to be found in the manuscript *Account Book of the Overseers of the Poor of the Liberty of Paris Garden, 1608–1671*, from which Professor C. W. Wallace published extracts. I quote all from the year 1614 on:

Aprill the 25. 1614
Item frõ the players of the swann playhowsse   .   . iijˡⁱ xᵈ
Aprill the 20th 1615
Reč frõ the swann play howsse 0 19 2
Monday Aprill the 9th 1621
Receiued of the players 5 3 6
(Wallace, op. cit., p. 190)

¹ Halliwell-Phillipps Scrap-Books, Folger Shakespeare Library, volume labelled *Theatres in Shakespeare's Time*, p. 127. The bracketed words were written by Halliwell-Phillipps to replace those cut off in cutting up the manuscript. For a brief discussion of the manuscript Halliwell-Phillipps had, see J. Q. Adams, 'The Office-Book, 1622–1642, of Sir Henry Herbert, Master of the Revels', *To Dr. R.* (1946), 1–9.

The break in the sequence between 1615 and 1621 suggests
that there was not enough use of the theatre between April 1615
and April 1620 to enable the overseers to collect fees from the
occupants—if any. The surprisingly large sum collected in 1621—
larger than that in 1611, 1614, and 1615, and about the same as
that in 1612 and 1613—implies that in the year ending in April
1621 some company was enjoying reasonable success at the Swan.
Perhaps one of the many provincial troupes managed a London
season; if so, the Lady Elizabeth's men, whose licence of 20 March
1617/18 allowed them to perform in London and who played there
regularly before 1615/16 and after 1621,[1] are the most likely
candidates. Or it could be that the Lady Elizabeth's company had
succeeded Prince Charles's (I) company at the Phoenix a year
earlier than has been supposed, and that the Prince's men played
at the Swan several months before they settled at the Curtain,
which was before June 1622. (See above, i. 204–5.) Neither possibility has much to support it except the uncertainty of the date
of the change of tenants at the Phoenix before June 1622. The
record of the rather large sum collected by the Overseers of
the Poor from players at the Swan in April 1621 shows that
the theatre was presumably showing plays that year, but it points
up the inadequacy of our knowledge of theatre tenancy.

After 1621 we know only of prize-fighters as tenants of the Swan,
though one would think the place equally suitable for other
irregular entertainers. By 1632 the theatre is said to be unused
and in bad repair. Nicholas Goodman speaks of it in that year as
it appeared from the famous house of prostitution, Holland's
Leaguer:

. . . three famous *Amphytheators* [i.e. the Globe, the Hope, and the
Swan] which stood so neere scituated, that her eye might take view
of them from her lowest *Turret* . . . the last which stood, and as it
were shak'd handes with this Fortresse, beeing in times past, as
famous as any of the other, was now fallen to decay, and like a
dying *Swanne*, hanging downe her head, seemed to sing her owne
dierge. . . .[2]

---

[1] See above. i. 177–83. Perhaps it is relevant to note that the 1630
title-page of Middleton's *A Chaste Maid in Cheapside* says 'often acted at
the Swan on the Banke-side, by the Lady Elizabeth her *Seruants*'. The
statement has generally been taken to indicate occupancy of the Swan
by the Lady Elizabeth's men about 1611, when the play was presumably
first produced. (See Chambers, *E.S.* ii. 257 and iii. 441.) I suppose it is possible that a 1621 performance at the Swan could be referred to.

[2] *Holland's Leaguer* (1632), F₂ᵛ. For a short account of the pamphlet see
above, iv. 747.

Though her head may have been hanging, the Swan, or what appears to be the Swan, was still standing five years later. Two of the designs which Inigo Jones drew for the production on 7 January 1637/8 of the first scene of William Davenant's masque *Britannia Triumphans* (see above, iii. 199–200) are views of London from the south, showing the Bankside. One is drawn from a point of view more distant from the Bankside than the other, and therefore shows a wider area, but in more distant perspective. Both views show a round structure with a flag flying, on a site which can only be that of the Swan. (See Shapiro, loc. cit.) The display of the flag would proclaim the fact that a performance was taking place or impending at the theatre. One fears to push the literal accuracy of the Jones sketches too far, yet they were prepared for the delectation of a courtly audience which could be expected to recognize discrepancies.

It is unsatisfactory to have so little information about the use of the Swan theatre in the Jacobean and Caroline period. The available evidence makes it clear enough that during these years the playhouse was never the regular home of any major London company for an appreciable period. But what use *did* it have, and when was it torn down or converted to other uses? Surely there must be records or allusions somewhere which will provide fuller answers to these questions than I have been able to give.

THE THEATRE

Adams, pp. 27–74.
Chambers, *E.S.* ii. 383–400.

This first public theatre in England was built in 1576 and pulled down in December 1598 in preparation for the building of the first Globe.

THEATRES AT COURT

THE FIRST JACOBEAN BANQUETING HOUSE

[Braines, W. W.], 'The Parish of St. Margaret, Westminster', London County Council *Survey of London*, xiii, Pt. 2 (1930), 116–20.

Chambers, *E.S.* i. *passim*.

Cook, David, and Wilson, F. P., *Dramatic Records in the Declared Accounts of the Treasurer of the Chamber, 1558–1642*, Malone Society Collections, vi (1961), *passim*.

Palme, Per, *Triumph of Peace: A Study of the Whitehall Banqueting House* (1956), pp. 1–3, 115–18.

Neither the first nor the second Royal Banqueting House erected at the command of James I in the precincts of Whitehall Palace was primarily a theatre, but both were used so frequently for the gala court performances of masques and plays that a few facts about them are useful for the student of Jacobean and Caroline theatrical activities.

There had been a number of preceding buildings—in the reigns of Henry VIII, Edward VI, and Elizabeth several temporary banqueting houses had been built, and in 1581 there was constructed a more elaborate permanent structure that lasted until James's reign. This building, erected on the site used for the two later banqueting houses, was 'made in maner and forme of a long square, three hundred thirtie and two foot in measure about', and about forty feet in height. It had 'two hundred ninetie and two lights of glasse'. (Holinshed, *Chronicles*, 1587, iii. 1315, sig. Lllll$_{ii}$^{v}; Chambers, *E.S.* i. 16.) It was used for twenty-five years, and then in 1606 'the King puld downe the old rotten, sleight builded banquetting house at Whitehall, and new builded the same this yeare [1607] very strong and stately, beeing euery way larger than the first . . .'. (Stow, *Annales* [1631], sig. Ffff$_2$.) It is this banqueting house we are concerned with here.

The location, ground plan, and dimensions of the new building can be seen in a sketch plan made by John Smythson in 1618. (See the reproduction in Per Palme, *Triumph of Peace*, p. 116.) It lay between Whitehall 'Square' on the west and Sermon Court or Chapel Court on the east; larger maps and plans show that it lay between the Holbein Gate and the Palace Gate. Across the 'square' to the west and in full view of the Banqueting House windows, from which privileged spectators often watched, was the Tiltyard. Other royal playing-places frequently used for command performances were close by; about fifty yards to the north-east was the Great Hall, and about one hundred yards to the south-west was the Cockpit.

Smythson's sketch plan shows that King James's Banqueting House of 1606 was a large rectangular room, 120 feet long and 53 feet wide. Pillars along three sides—east, north, and west—supported galleries on three sides of the hall, and under these galleries, apparently between the pillars and the wall, were erected temporary degrees (scaffolds, bleachers) and boxes on those occasions when the Banqueting House was used for plays or masques. (For the most illuminating description of the interior see below, pp. 256–8.)

The beginning of the dramatic use of the new structure appears to have been the dancing of Ben Jonson's *Masque of Beauty* on 10 January 1607/8. (See Herford and Simpson, x. 455–9). It pretty surely marked the opening, for on 5 January, five days before the performance, John Chamberlain had written Sir Dudley Carleton: 'The maske goes forward at court for Twelfth day, though I doubt the new roome wilbe scant redy', and three days later, on the 8th, he wrote again: 'Sir, We had great hope of having you here this day, and then I wold not have geven my part of the maske for many of theyre places that shalbe present . . . for the shew is put of till Sonday by reason all thinges are not redy.' (*Chamberlain*, i. 252.)

For the next ten years there was a masque or barriers (a form of tourney in which the combatants fought on foot with pike and sword across a wooden barrier) in the new house every year, often more than one. (See the Chamber Accounts, *M.S.C.* vi [1961], 102–17.) In the first three years of its existence no plays are known to have been performed there, though a number are recorded as performed in the Hall, the Great Chamber, and the Cockpit; but beginning in 1610 the Banqueting House was used for plays several times each year. Plays continued to be produced, however, in the other Whitehall playing-places, especially the Cockpit, for which almost as many royal performances are recorded as for the Banqueting House. (Ibid.)

One of the last masques in the series at the first Banqueting House was Jonson's *Pleasure Reconciled to Virtue* on 6 January 1617/18. (See above, iv. 669–72, and Herford and Simpson, x. 573–86.) The occasion was described in unusual detail by Orazio Busino, Almoner to the Venetian Embassy, and scattered passages in his account give details about the interior of the Banqueting House. Busino says in one part:

Of the masques, the most famous of all is performed on the morrow of the feast of the three Wise Men according to an ancient custom of the palace here. A large hall is fitted up like a theatre, with well secured boxes all round. The stage is at one end and his Majesty's chair in front under an ample canopy. Near him are stools for the foreign ambassadors. On the 16th of the current month of January [i.e. in the Venetian calendar; 6 January, English calendar], his Excellency was invited to see a representation and masque, which had been prepared with extraordinary pains, the chief performer being the king's own son and heir, the prince of Wales, now seventeen years old, an agile youth, handsome and very graceful. At the fourth hour of the night we went privately to the Court, through the park. On reaching the royal apartments his Excellency [i.e. the Venetian Ambassador] was entertained awhile by one of the leading cavaliers until all was ready, whilst we, his attendants, all perfumed and escorted by the master of the ceremonies, entered the usual box of the Venetian embassy. . . . Whilst waiting for the king we amused ourselves by admiring the decorations and beauty of the house with its two orders of columns, one above the other, their distance from the wall equalling the breadth of the passage, that of the second row being upheld by Doric pillars, while above these rise Ionic columns supporting the roof. The whole is of wood, including even the shafts, which are carved and gilt with much skill. From the roof of these hang festoons and angels in relief with two rows of lights. Then such a concourse as there was, for although they profess only to admit the favoured ones who are invited, yet every box was filled notably with most noble and richly arrayed ladies, in number some 600 and more according to the general estimate. . . .

At about the 6th hour of the night the king appeared with his court, having passed through the apartments where the ambassadors were in waiting, whence he graciously conducted them, that is to say, the Spaniard and the Venetian, it not being the Frenchman's turn, ho and the Spaniard only attending the court ceremonies alternately by reason of their disputes about precedence.

On entering the house, the cornets and trumpets to the number of fifteen or twenty began to play very well a sort of recitative, and then after his Majesty had seated himself under the canopy alone, the queen not being present on account of a slight indisposition, he caused the ambassadors to sit below him on two stools, while the great officers of the crown and courts of law sat upon benches. The Lord Chamberlain then had the way cleared and in the middle of the theatre there appeared a fine and spacious area carpeted all over with green cloth. In an instant a large curtain dropped, painted to represent a tent of gold cloth with a broad fringe; the background was of canvas painted blue, powdered all over with golden stars. This became the front arch of the stage, forming a drop scene, and on its being removed there appeared first of all Mount Atlas, whose enormous head was alone visible up aloft under the very roof of the theatre . . . [After the final dance] the prince went in triumph to kiss his father's hands. The king embraced and kissed him tenderly and then honoured the marquis [of Buckingham] with marks of extraordinary affection, patting his face. The king now rose from his chair, took the ambassadors along with him, and after passing through a number of chambers and galleries he reached a hall where the usual collation was spread for the performers, a light being carried before him. After he had glanced all round the table he departed, and forthwith the parties concerned pounced upon the prey like so many harpies. . . . The story ended at half past two in the morning and half disgusted and weary we returned home. (*C.S.P., Ven.*, 1617–19, pp. 111–14.)

The last recorded performance at King James's first Banqueting House is that of an unknown masque on 6 January 1618/19.[1] The Chamber Accounts show charges for the preparation of 'the banquettinghouse and the Lorde Chauncello^{rs} Chamber . . . for a masque', but the work is said to have been done in November and December. (*M.S.C.* vi [1961], 117.) We know that Prince Charles danced in a masque on Twelfth Night 1618/19 (*Chamberlain*, ii. 200), and this is presumably the one for which the Banqueting House was being prepared, for Lady Anne Clifford wrote in her Diary, '. . . the Prince had the Masque at night in the Banqueting House. The King was there but the Queen was so ill she could not remove from *Hampton Court* all this Xmas. . . .' (*Diary of Lady Anne Clifford*, p. 84.)

Six days later the Banqueting House burned to the ground. Various chroniclers and letter-writers recorded the event. John Chamberlain wrote to Sir Dudley Carleton on the 16th:

Since my last we have had here a great mischance by fire at White-hall, which beginning in the banketting house hath quite consumed yt, and put the rest in great daunger, but that there was so much helpe at hand . . . and the fire though yt was exceding furious kept from spreading further then the limits of that building, saving only that the vehemencie of the heat burnt downe one of the rotten tarasses or galleries adjoyning and tooke hold of the pulpit-place which was soone quenched. . . . Divers reports run how yt came, but the most current is that a mean fellow searching in the masking or tiring house with a candle for certain things he had hid there, fired some oyled painted clothes and pasteboords, with such other

[1] There was no Jonson masque this year, for Jonson left London for Edinburgh in the summer of 1618 and was not back before February 1618/19. (Herford and Simpson, *Ben Jonson*, i. 75–83.) Middleton's *Inner Temple Masque, or Masque of Heroes* was performed about this time, but evidently not before royalty. (See above, iv. 881–2.)

stuffe, and seeing he could not quench yt alone, went out and lockt the doore after him, thincking so to conceale himself.[1] (*Chamberlain*, ii. 201–2.)

Two entries in the Chamber accounts, the first for November 1613 to January 1613/14, and the second for January to March 1616/17, appear ironic as antecedents to the fate of the Banqueting House:

being Comaunded by the Lord Chamb[er]leine to watch continewally night by night in the banquettinghouse as well for preserving his Ma^t[^{es}] Stuffe therein as for feare of daunger or hurte by fire in the said house during the tyme the workemen wrought there . . . 42 nights.

and

for watchinge in the Bankettinge house for daunger of fyre. (*M.S.C.* vi [1961], 110 and 115.)

THE SECOND JACOBEAN BANQUETING HOUSE

[Braines, W. W.,] 'The Parish of St. Margaret, Westminster', London County Council *Survey of London*, xiii, Pt. 2 (1930), 116–39 and Plates 13–45.

Hotson, Leslie, 'Shakespeare's Arena', *Sewanee Review*, lxi (1953), 349–61.

Nicoll, Allardyce, *Stuart Masques and the Renaissance Stage* (1938), 28–53 *et passim*.

Palme, Per, *Triumph of Peace: A Study of the Whitehall Banqueting House* (1956).

Wilson, F. P., 'The Elizabethan Theatre', *Neophilologus*, xxxix (1955), 40–58.

Wittkower, Rudolph, 'Inigo Jones, Architect and Man of Letters', *Journal of the Royal Institute of British Architects*, Third Series, lx (1952–3), 83–88.

King James must have resolved to build a new Banqueting House when the ashes of the old one were scarce cold. Less than a fortnight after the fire John Chamberlain was writing to Sir Dudley Carleton, the King's ambassador at The Hague: '. . .

---

[1] Apparently there was looting, or what Chamberlain in this letter called 'much embeaseling, and much spoyle'. In a subsequent letter, of 23 January, he says 'There was a broker likewise hangd at his owne doore in Houndsdich, for receving goods stoln at the fire at White-hall'. (*Chamberlain*, ii. 205.)

there is speach of setting up the banketting house again very
speedilie and some will undertake for seven or nine thousand
pound (I know not whether) to make yt more faire and bewtifull
then before'. (*Chamberlain*, ii. 204.) The rumour Chamberlain
heard was evidently well founded, for three months later a model
and part of the specifications for the great building of Inigo Jones
were ready. On 19 April 1619 the Officers of the Works presented
to the Privy Council the following estimate:

> The whole Charge of the Banquetting house to be newe builte
> according to a modell therof made, beinge in Lengthe 110 foote,
> and in breadth 55 foote, the under story beinge arched 16 foote in
> haight, the upper story 55 foote highe, the masons worck, Carpenters
> worck, Bricklayers worck, plombers, plasterers, Joyners, Smithes
> worck, glasinge and Labourers' worck, with digginge, Ramminge
> and making the foundacions with scaffouldinge to all the saide
> worcks, will amount unto the some of 9850li.[1] (P.R.O., S.P. 14/108,
> no. 55, as quoted by Per Palme, op. cit., pp. 2–3.)

The estimated cost of the new building is eloquent of the importance which the King must have attached to it. Equally
indicative is the status of the men appointed to the Commission
for the Banqueting House: the Duke of Lennox, Steward of the
Household; the Earl of Pembroke, Lord Chamberlain; the Lord
Digby, Vice-Chamberlain; Sir Fulke Greville, Under Treasurer
of the Exchequer; and the Earl of Arundell. (P.R.O., A.O. 1/2489/
370, as quoted by Per Palme, op. cit., p. 53.)

The model referred to in the statement of the Officers of the
Works must have been a fairly substantial one, to judge from the
sum later paid Jones for constructing it: 'To Inigo Jones upon
the Councells Warr[t] dated 27 June 1619 for making two several
models the one for the Star Chamber, the other for the Banquetting House   xxxvij[li].'[2] Clearly the King and his Surveyor of
the Works, Inigo Jones, were resolved to erect a monument to
the splendour of Stuart triumphs. And they succeeded.

The historical and architectural importance of the new building
has frequently been pointed out by the art historians: Per Palme
says that 'The Banqueting House was undoubtedly the most

---

[1] This estimate, like most, was grossly exceeded. A bill of 1633 specifying
a good deal of the construction, comes to £14,940 4s. 1d. See L. C. C. *Survey,
The Parish of St. Margaret, Westminster*, p. 121.

[2] Peter Cunningham, *Extracts from the Accounts of the Revels at Court . . .,*
Shakespeare Society, vii (1842), xlv. Cunningham said vaguely that his
record came from 'the same accounts (*Treas: of the Chamber*)'. (Ibid.,
p. xxxiv.)

important, and the most expensive, single building project under-taken by the early Stuarts' (op. cit., p. 3); moreover, its signifi-cance went beyond its importance in its own period. It was the principal work of the greatest English architect of his time, and, says Rudolph Wittkower, '. . . everyone agrees that Inigo brought about a revolution, at once so thorough and irrevocable that, whether we like it or not, it determined the course of English architecture for almost three centuries'. (Rudolph Wittkower, 'Inigo Jones, Architect and Man of Letters', *Journal of the Royal Institute of British Architects*, Third Series, lx [1952–3], 83.)

The architectural importance of the Banqueting House, however interesting, is not the basis of its dramatic significance. But the environment, the royal expression of magnificence which this ceremonial hall was designed and decorated to set forth, and which regularly provided the setting for national expressions of honour and glory, like the royal reception of ambassadors, the final ceremony of the Order of the Garter on St. George's Day, and even the court masques whose almost invariable theme was honour and glory—this environment provided by the Banqueting House most certainly affected the status of the plays presented there and of the actors who performed them.

The interest of King James in this new structure, which promised so much as a setting for his magnificence and for the prestige of his reign, was evidently unflagging. On 28 October 1620 John Chamberlain wrote from London to Sir Dudley Carleton, at The Hague: 'The King is expected here on Monday or Tewsday though yt were somwhile in question whether he wold come any further then Tiballs, but the incommoditie of calling the judges and officers thether about pricking of sheriffes and such matters, as likewise the pleasure of seeing the forwardnes of his new building have as yt were perforce drawne him hither.' (*Chamberlain*, ii. 323.)

But it was another six months, two years after the Officers of the Works had presented their estimate to the Privy Council, before the new building was far enough along to accommodate part of the ceremonies of the Knights of the Garter on 23 April 1621. Again Chamberlain wrote to Sir Dudley Carleton, this time some-what tartly: 'This day the King kept St. Georges feast in the new built banketting roome, which is too faire and nothing sutable to the rest of the house [i.e. Whitehall Palace].' (Ibid., p. 367.) Almost another year was to elapse, however, before the major building work was completed and the account made. It is described under the date of 31 March 1622:

a Banquetting house at Whitehall with a vaulte under the same, in length CX foote, and in width LV foote within: . . . The first story to the height of XVI foote wrought of Oxfordshire stone cutt into Rustique on the outside, and Brick on the inside, the walles VIII foote thick wth a vaulte turned over on greate square pillers of Brick and paved in the Bottome wth purbeckstone, the walles and vaulting layde with finishing morter. The vpper story being the Banquetting house LV foote in height to the laying on of the roofe, the walles fyve foote di. thick, and wrought of Northamptonshire stone cutt in rustique . . . wth XIIII windowes of eache side and one greate windowe at the upper end, and fyve doores of stone wth Frontespeeces and Cartoozes, the inside brought vp wth brick finished over wth twoe orders of Collomnes and pillasters, part of stone and part of brick, wth their Architrave Freize and Cornish, wth a gallery vpon the twooe sides and the lower end, borne vpon greate Cartoozes of Tymber carved wth Railes and ballasters of Tymber, and the floore layde wth spruce deales, a strong Tymber roofe covered wth lead, and vnder it a ceeling devided unto a Frett made of greate Cornishes inrichd wth carvings, wth painting, glazing etc. (P.R.O., A.O. 1/2489/370, as quoted by Palme, p. 64.)

This account of the major structural work completed by the early spring of 1622 by no means marked the completion of the Banqueting House. It was ready for use, but carving, plastering, gilding, tapestry hanging, and painting went on for years; indeed, the most famous feature of the Banqueting House, the series of Rubens paintings in the ceiling, was not in place before late 1635. (See Per Palme, op. cit., pp. 77–81, and plates *passim*.) By that time the increasingly decorated hall had been in use for masques and plays for thirteen or fourteen years.

Gorgeous though the new building was, it was only a shell for masque and play performances even after all the decorating had been completed. Its use as a theatre was only occasional, and there were therefore no permanent seats or boxes or even a stage with the necessary back-stage space, so that for each performance fairly extensive temporary construction was required to provide accommodations for both actors and audience. One phase of such regularly recurring construction is illustrated by the record of payment to a boss carpenter in the year 1621–2. Though the precise days on which the carpenters did this part of their work are not recorded in the extant accounts, it is highly probable that they were preparing for the first masque to be given in the new hall, Ben Jonson's *Masque of Augurs*, which was danced there on the night of 6 January 1621/2. (See above, iv. 655–8, and Herford and Simpson, *Ben Jonson*, x. 635–40.) The account reads:

To Ralphe Brice Carpenter for frameinge and setting vpp xi[en] baies of degrees on both sides of the banquettinge house every bay conteyninge xvi[en] foote longe, beinge twoe panes in every of them; the degrees belowe beinge seven rowes in heighte; and two boordes nayled vpon every brackett the degrees in the midle gallery beinge fower rowes in heigthe and twoe boordes nailed vpon brackettes also with a raile belowe and another raile in the midle gallery being crosse laticed vnder the same; working framinge and settinge vpp of vpright postes wroughte with eighte cantes to beare the same woorke; the kinge findinge all maner of materialls and the woorkmanshipp onely at xxx[s] the baye the some of xvi[li]. x[s]. (P.R.O. E 351/3255, as quoted by F. P. Wilson, op. cit., p. 52.)

The work Ralph Brice did provided seats for the general spectators only. Presumably they were disposed like those in the ground plan that Inigo Jones drew for the production of *Florimene* in the Great Hall at Whitehall in 1635. It is notable that in his sketch there seem to be seven tiers of seats or degrees on the two sides of the hall, and four in the gallery at the back, just as Brice says he had constructed them in the Banqueting House in 1621–2. (See Nicoll, op. cit., p. 33.)

In addition to the temporary construction required to provide for the general audience, further construction was needed to provide a stage and a State for the King, though it seems unlikely that the State would have been constructed anew for each performance, since it was the most commonly used feature of the House. Antonio Busino reported, when he saw Jonson's *Pleasure Reconciled to Virtue* on 6 January 1617/18:

The stage is at one end and his Majesty's chair in front under an ample canopy. Near him are stools for the foreign ambassadors.

.   .   .   .   .

On entering the house, the cornets and trumpets . . . began to play . . . and then after his Majesty had seated himself under the canopy alone, the queen not being present on account of a slight indisposition, he caused the ambassadors [Spanish and Venetian] to sit below him on two stools . . . . (*C.S.P., Ven.*, xv [1617–19], pp. 111–12. See also above, iv. 669–72.)

The same position for the State is shown in Inigo Jones's sketched plan for the Hall at the performance of *Florimene*. In that plan the base of the State is 11 feet wide, with railings on the back and two sides and two broad steps leading up to it from the floor. The whole is set 43 feet from the back wall of the stage, 23 feet from the front. In designing scenery the sight lines were always, of course, drawn from the State. Though what Busino saw was in the old Banqueting House, and *Florimene* was performed in the Great Hall, there is no reason to think that arrangements were different in Inigo Jones's Banqueting House. Its dimensions were practically the same as those of the hall Busino describes; the Great Hall was about 20 feet shorter and about 15 feet narrower, and the measurements given for *Florimene* may well have been increased somewhat in the Banqueting House, but probably there was no change in the relative positions or general character.

The largest piece of temporary construction required for each performance was the stage. Again the sketch for *Florimene* shows the general character. In it the stage was placed at the lower (north) end of the hall (as in all Jacobean and Caroline instances where position is mentioned), and was built across the entire width of the hall (39 feet); it was 23 feet deep. For a few masques stage dimensions are recorded: for Jonson's *Masque of Blackness*, 40 feet square; for Shirley's *Triumph of Peace*, 40 feet by 27 feet; for Davenant's *Salmacida Spolia*, 42 feet by 28 feet. Since these recorded measurements are roughly similar, though they range in date from 1605 to 1640, and though the stages they describe were built for four different buildings, it would appear that they represent the usual court stage dimension. The common denominator for the four is Inigo Jones, who planned all of them, and who designed all the identifiable masques in the new Banqueting House. His usual stage appears to be about forty feet wide and about two-thirds as deep.

The stage was raised above the level of the hall floor, and though the recorded heights vary, six or seven feet seems to have been usual: seven feet for *The Triumph of Peace*, 1633/4; six feet for *Coelum Britannicum*, 1633/4; six feet for *The Temple of Love*, 1634/5; six feet for *The Triumphs of the Prince D'Amour*, 1635/6; seven feet at the front and eight feet at the back for *Salmacida Spolia* in 1639/40.

Between the front of this raised stage and the State was the dancing area used for the masques when the masquers 'came down'. Busino noted that, when he saw *Pleasure Reconciled to Virtue* in January 1617/18, after the King was seated on the State

The Lord Chamberlain then had the way cleared and in the middle of the theatre there appeared a fine and spacious area carpeted all over with green cloth. . . . [After the major spectacle] Finally twelve cavaliers, masked, made their appearance. . . . These twelve descended together from above the scene in the figure of a pyramid, of which the prince formed the apex. When they reached the ground the violins to the number of twenty-five or thirty began to play their airs. After they had made an obeisance to his Majesty, they began to dance in very good time. . . . When this was over, each took his lady, the prince pairing with the principal one among those who were ranged in a row ready to dance, and the others doing the like in succession, all making obeisance to his Majesty first and then to each other. (*C.S.P., Ven.*, xv [1617–19], 112–13.)

This was a normal feature of the masque; even the green floor covering which Busino noted was usual, as we know from several extant records of the payments to workmen for nailing down the green cloth.

Such arrangements as these for the preparation of the Banqueting House for the performance of plays or masques were made presumably with some regularity from 1621/2 to 1635. Unfortunately most of the specific records are lost. The leading companies were paid for performing many plays at court in these years, but few of the extant records say *where* at court, and usually the dates are only inclusive ones, as in the Lord Chamberlain's warrant for payment to John Heminges of £160 'for 16 Playes Acted before his Ma^ty betweene Christmas & Candlemas. 1628'. (*M.S.C.* ii. 349.) Even the records of the masques are very scrappy. Occasional records do, however, deviate into the specific and note that the work was done for the preparation of the Banqueting House. Clement Kinnersley, Yeoman of the Removing Wardrobe of Beds, presented a bill in November 1627 for 'himselfe, his man & Tenne Labourers Ten dayes for makeing read ye banquetting house twice for 2 playes & twice for healing[es]'. (*M.S.C.* ii. 348.) Many other records which do not specify where the play was acted or which hall was prepared for the masque very likely indicate performances in the Banqueting House.

During the last few years before the theatres were closed, the Banqueting House was not used for masques and apparently not for plays. The decision was the King's, and several correspondents mention the decision and the reason for it. Sir John Finett wrote to Viscount Scudamore on 1 November 1637:

Wee haue a stately buylding toward in Whytehall (but more stately for forme and use then for matter or substance being all of wood) to be imployd only for maskes and dancing, whyle the bancketting is to be reserved only or cheefly for Audiences, with apprehension of his Majesty that torches, wyth theyr smoake may disluster the pictures and guyldings there, which are sayd to haue cost above ten thousand poundes. (P.R.O., C 115/N8/8810, as quoted by J. P. Feil, *Shakespeare Survey*, xi [1958], 111.)

The same reason for building the new Masquing House and removing the performances from the Banqueting House is given
by the Reverend Mr. Garrard in a letter to Viscount Wentworth
in Ireland, dated 16 December 1637: '. . . a new House being
erected in the first Court at *Whitehall*, which cost the King 2500*l.*
only of Deal Boards, because the King will not have his Pictures
in the Banqueting-house hurt with Lights'. (William Knowler,
ed., *The Earl of Strafforde's Letters and Dispatches*, ii. 140.) Though
no one mentions the precise date of the last masque in the Banqueting House, it seems likely that it was in 1635, and the last
recorded masque performances of that year are the repeated
presentations of Davenant's *The Temple of Love* in February
1634/5. (See above, iii. 216–18.) Before the next masque season
of 1635/6 the Rubens paintings—certainly the most precious ob-
jects in the House subject to smoke damage—may have been in
place, for they were shipped to England in October 1635. (See
Per Palme, op. cit., pp. 79–80.) There are no recorded masque
performances in Whitehall between February 1634/5 and January
1637/8. During much of that time London suffered plague severe
enough to close the theatres from 12 May 1636 until 2 October
1637 (see above, ii. 661–5), and much of that time the court was
at Hampton Court, where between May 1636 and the end of
January 1636/7 the King's company presented fourteen plays.
But plague alone was not the whole reason for the disuse of the
Banqueting House, for the four plays given by the King's company just before this period and the four immediately after were
performed at the Cockpit, Blackfriars, or St. James's—none in
the Banqueting House. (See above, i. 51–52.) The bill of the King's
men for twenty-four plays at court in the year 1638–9 has been
preserved; each entry mentions the place of performance: the
Cockpit, Blackfriars, Somerset House, Hampton Court, and
Richmond; the Banqueting House is not named. (See *Herbert*,
pp. 76–77.)

Finally, the first masque presented in the new Masquing House,
Davenant's *Britannia Triumphans*, which was danced there on
7 January 1637/8, has a Preface which fairly clearly sums up the
history:

Princes of sweet and humane Natures have ever both amongst the
Ancients and Modernes in the best times, presented spectacles, and
personall representations, to recreate their Spirits wasted in grave
affaires of State, and for the entertainment of their Nobilitie, Ladies,
and Courts.

There being now past three yeers of Intermission, that the King and Queenes Majesties have not made Masques with shewes and Intermedij, by reason the roome where formerly they were presented, having the seeling since richly adorn'd with peeces of painting of great value, figuring the acts of King *Iames* of happy memory, and other inrichments: lest this might suffer by the smoake of many lights, his Majestie commanded the Surveyor of his workes, that a new temporary [*sic*] roome of Timber, both for strength and capacitie of spectators, should bee suddenly built for that use; which being performed in two moneths, the Scenes for this Masque were prepared.

(1637 ed., A₂.)

These various records show that the King's decision to keep dramatic performances out of the Banqueting House held, that after the Rubens paintings were in place Whitehall masques were not given until 1637/8 and then were transferred to the Masquing House, and that Whitehall plays were performed in the Cockpit or in the Great Hall.

For the rest of the reign the great Banqueting House was limited to nondramatic functions. The building itself, of course, is still standing, though 'as seen today the Banqueting House is, in the main, an early 19th Century reconstruction of Jones's achievement'. (Per Palme, op. cit., p. 91.) The interior is even more altered than the exterior and affords little suggestion now of the magnificent spectacles it housed in the reign of King Charles. The last and greatest of them all cast the King in the leading role, for it was through one of the centre windows in the western front that on the afternoon of 30 January 1648/9 King Charles stepped out on to the platform for his execution.

THE COCKPIT-IN-COURT

Adams, pp. 391–409.

Bell, Hamilton, 'Contributions to the History of the English Playhouse', *The Architectural Record*, xxxiii (1913), 262–7.

Boswell, Eleanore, *The Restoration Court Stage (1660–1702)*, (1932), pp. 10–21; 239–41; 346–9.

[Braines, W. W.,] 'The Parish of St. Margaret, Westminster', London County Council *Survey of London*, xiv (1931), Pt. iii. 23–29.

Chambers, *E.S.* i. 216–17, n. 2, and 234.

Cook, David, and Wilson, F. P., 'Dramatic Records in the Declared Accounts of the Treasurer of the Chamber, 1558–1642', *M.S.C.* vi (1961), *passim.*

Keith, William Grant, 'John Webb and the Court Theatre of Charles II', *Architectural Review*, lvii (February 1925), 49–55.

Nicoll, Allardyce, *Stuart Masques and the Renaissance Stage* (1938), pp. 146–8.

Spiers, W. L., 'An Autograph Plan by Wren', *London Topographical Record*, ii (1903), 23–26.

—— 'An Explanation of the Plan of Whitehall', Ibid. vii (1912), 56–66 with plan.

There had long been a cockpit in the precincts of the Palace at Whitehall. John Stow makes note of it in his *Survey of London*, 1598. Proceeding south from Charing Cross he mentions the galleries beside the tilt-yard, and goes on: 'Beyond this Gallerie on the left hand is the garden or orchyard belonging to the saide White hall. On the right hand bee diuers fayre Tennis courtes, bowling Allies, and a Cockepit, all built by king *Henry* the eight, and then one other arched gate with a way ouer it thwarting the streete from the kinges gardens to the saide Parke.' (Bb₃ᵛ–Bb₄.)

The building is shown in the Agas map of about 1570 and in Wyngaerde's sketch of perhaps a few years earlier. Both are reproduced in the London County Council *Survey of London* (xiv, Pt. iii, p. 23 and plate 9).

In spite of the fact that the octagonal building shown by Agas and Wyngaerde and mentioned by Stow was designed for cockfights, plays for the court had been presented there on numerous occasions before 1616. The Declared Accounts of the Treasurer of the Chamber show repeated charges for 'making ready the Cockepitt' in the early Jacobean period (*M.S.C.* vi. 98–123). Though these accounts often fail to record the character of the entertainment for which the house was prepared, several of them are specific enough to show that the occasions were sometimes cockfights and sometimes play performances. In December 1607 Sir Richard Coningsby and nine assistants worked six days in making ready the Cockpit in Whitehall 'three severall times . . . for the plaies' (fol. 189a). In January 1607/8 they prepared the Cockpit 'two severall times . . . for the plaies' (ibid.); and again in January 1608/9 they made ready the Cockpit 'two severall times . . . for the Playes' (fol. 211a). One of these plays must have been that 'presented by the Children of the blackfriers before his highnes in the Cockpitt at Whitehall iiij° Ianuarij 1608', for which Robert Keyser was paid £10 (*M.S.C.* vi. 47).

Another dramatic occasion is indicated by a payment made by Lord Harington for Princess Elizabeth between Michaelmas 1612 and Lady Day 1613: 'To her grac*es* plaiers for acting a Comedie in the Cocke pitt wᶜʰ her highnes lost to Mʳ Edward Sackvile on a

Wager v^{li}.' (*M.S.C.* vi. 150.) Perhaps this was the play given by the Lady Elizabeth's company and reported by John Chamberlain in a letter of 22 October 1612 containing an account of the reception of Elizabeth's prospective bridegroom: 'On Tewsday she sent to invite him [the Palsgrave] as he sat at supper to a play of her owne servants in the Cockepit'. (*Chamberlain*, i. 381.)

Other preparations for plays to be given at the Cockpit before 1616 are recorded in February 1608/9, November 1609, January 1609/10, December 1610, January, February, and March 1610/11, December 1611, and February–March 1615/16. (*M.S.C.* vi. 103–13 and 145.)

It seems likely that the majority of the preparations recorded in the Declared Accounts were preparations for plays, but certainly not all of them were. A series of payments to James Maxwell and nine assistants between March 1617/18 and May 1618 record two days' work in making ready 'the Cockpitt . . . for a play'; two days' work in making ready 'the Cockpitt . . . for Cocking'; four days' work 'there . . . for twoe severall plaies'; and four days' work in preparing the Cockpit for a purpose unspecified (p. 116). This sequence implies that the amount of labour required in changing the Cockpit from one function to another was appreciable, but little different from that required for the Great Hall.

Though the Cockpit seems to have been in fairly regular demand for dramatic performances at court, it was not the sole or even the primary theatre for royal performances; other Whitehall playing-places were in use at the same time. The variety is best shown in the payment to James Maxwell and assistants for six days of work in December 1617 and January 1617/18 in making ready 'the Banquettinghouse the Cockpitt and the Hall' in Whitehall 'for three severall plaies' (fol. 91a). Before the extensive remodelling of the Cockpit in the years 1629–32, the Hall seems to have been used for plays in Whitehall rather more than the Cockpit, unless the unspecified preparations at the Cockpit nearly always represent preparations for plays and very seldom for cockfights.

After 1616 the Cockpit was used for the presentation of occasional plays, as before, until 1622. There are records of the payment for preparation of the Cockpit, usually but not always specifying plays, in December 1616–January 1616/17 (nine times); October 1617; December 1617–January 1617/18; March–May 1618; September–November 1618; February–March 1618/19; April–May 1621; April–June 1622. (*M.S.C.* vi. 114–21.) From 1622 to 1630 no records of the use of the Cockpit have been found, but for most of these years the accounts are missing or scanty. (Ibid., pp. 121–3.) It may be that Cockpit performances are concealed by the incomplete records, but one suspects that the Cockpit had been superseded. The new Banqueting Hall came into use in 1622, and together with the Hall and the Great Chamber it may well have accommodated all play productions which would formerly have been assigned to the Cockpit.

But in the season of 1629–30 there came a change: a completely remodelled Cockpit was built in Whitehall, and this one was planned for plays. Apparently the new structure was on the same foundation as the old one, and it probably used the same walls, since the old Cockpit had been octagonal externally and the new one was octagonal internally but square externally. The site was the same. The name Cockpit is not helpful in determining the relationship of the two buildings, for the term was also used loosely for an area.[1]

That there was a new theatre in Whitehall about this time has long been known from a speech written by Thomas Heywood. This prologue was not printed with any play but was published by Heywood in his *Pleasant Dialogues and Dramas* . . ., 1637. In the section of this book called 'Sundry Fancies writ upon severall occasions' and consisting of court prologues and epilogues, there appear the verses entitled *A speech spoken to their two excellent Majesties, at the first Play play'd by the Queenes Servants, in the new Theater at White Hall*. After sixteen lines on Greek and Roman theatres and their destruction, Heywood concludes:

> 'But may this structure last, and you be seene
> Here a spectator, with your Princely Queene,
> In your old age, as in your flourishing prime,
> To out-strip *Augustus* both in fame and time.' (Q₄ᵛ.)

But though the existence of the new court theatre has long been known from Heywood's verses, its character was not known, and its date of opening was generally thought to have been 1632, 1633, or 1634. Now it can be shown that the date of opening was

---

[1] See Braines, p. 23. Miss Boswell found grants making clear the size and boundaries of the area called the Cockpit in the reign of Charles II. 'In view of the confusion which formerly reigned in regard to the name Cockpit and the extent of the buildings so called, a somewhat irrelevant note on this matter may perhaps be pardonable. In 1676, Charles made a grant of the Cockpit to Danby, and on the patent roll the property is described as abutting on Hampden House and garden to the south, the Tennis Court to the east, and St. James' Park to the north and west; and containing 210 feet in length, and in breadth, 140 feet at the south end and 80 feet at the north. This definition of the property is repeated in a grant to Princess Anne in 1684. . . .' (*Restoration Court Stage*, p. 21.)

5 November 1630. In 1631 the King's company presented a bill (now at the Folger Shakespeare Library) for plays acted by the premier troupe before the King from 30 September 1630 to 21 February 1630/1. The first four productions listed in the bill are bracketed 'At [H]ampton Court', but the next seventeen are bracketed 'At the [Co]ck-pit'. The new concentration on the Cockpit is suggestive, but more explicit is the title listed for the first production there on 5 November, 'An Induction for the Howse'. (See above, i. 27–28 and note.) This title, unique in the annals of the Jacobean and Caroline theatre, evidently represents a house-warming piece for the new court playhouse. The sixteen other performances by the King's company at the new theatre in the following three and a half months reflect the interest of the court in the new house. Moreover, Queen Henrietta's company presented sixteen plays at court in about the same period (see above, i. 249), and though the place of performance is not indicated, the fact that the number of court performances is the largest for any recorded year in that company's annals probably further reflects the attractions of the new house.

An opening date in 1630 is also indicated in the accounts of the Office of the Works, for these payments show that the interior work for the new court playhouse was being done in the accounting period which ran from 1 October 1629 to 30 September 1630. Since these accounts are most unusual, giving more detailed information than we have for any other Jacobean or Caroline theatre, they are worth extensive quotation.[1]

For the year 1 October 1629 to 30 September 1630 we find under the paymastership of Henry Wickes:

WHITEHALL

workeing and setting vp three wyndowes of Stone for ye newe staires leadeing to the Cockepitt . . . cutting & carveing divers Statues to be sett vp in the Cockpit playhouse . . .

Zachary Tyler Carver . . . ffor Cutting and Carvinge x^{en} Corynthian Capitalls for Collomes at xiij^s iiij^d the peece vj^{li} xiij^s iiij^d for Cutting and carving x^{en} other smaller Composita Capitall[es] for Collomes at xij^s the peece vj^{li}, ffor Cuttinge and Carvinge ij^{oe} Corinth pillauster Capitall[es] at xiij^s iiij^d the peece xxvj^s viij^d for

---

[1] The original transcriptions of these records were made by the late Professor F. P. Wilson, who most generously lent me his manuscript, with permission to use it as I saw fit. The extracts have been checked against the originals at the Public Record Office (E 351/3263–7). Any errors in the transcriptions are mine, not his. Part of the series is now printed in volume VI of the Collections of the Malone Society.

Cuttinge and Carvinge ij^{oe} Composita pillauster Capitall[es] at xxiiij^s. . .

Iohn Hooke Turno^r . . . for turninge x^{en} greate Pilla^{rs}: for the Cockepitt at viij^s the peece & iiij^{li} for turninge x^{es} smaller Pilla^{rs}: for the same place at vj^s the peece lx^s . . .

Mathew Goodricke Paynt^r vizt for pryminge stoppinge and payntinge stone Cullor in oyle divers Cornishes pendaunt[es] and mouldings in the viij^t Cant[es] of the Cockepitt wth the postes both belowe and in the gallery aboue in the insyde all Cont: in measure ccclvi ya:^{ds} did at xvi^d the yarde xxiij^{li} xv^s iiij^d, for new Couleringe over wth fayre blewe the viij^t vpper squares on the wall three of them beinge wholy shaddowed and the rest mended xl^s, for pryminge and payntinge like glasse xx^{ty} panes wch had bin Lightes xxx^s and for Clenzinge and washinge the gold of the pendaunt[es] and Cornishes and mendinge the same in divers places wth gold Cullor in oyle and mendinge the blew of the same in sondry places I^s.

Iohn Synsburye Richard Byndinge Iohn Barton and other Carpenters . . . for framinge and settinge vpp twoe stories of Collomns in the Cockepitt playhouse beinge x^{en} Collomns vppon eu^{r}y Story Corinthia and Composita finishinge the head[es] wth Architrave, freeze and Cornishe vppon each Story and finishinge a backe wrought wth crooked tymber behinde them wth five doores in the first Story and in the second story one open dore & iiij^{er} neeches in the same vpper Storye his Matie fyndinge all materiall[es] and they the woorkemanship only by agreem^{te}: xxxj^{li} x^s . . . for framinge and setting vp the Deegres in the galleryes over the Cockpitt Cuttinge fyttinge and naylinge Brackett[es] vppon the same woorkinge and settinge of vpright postes to the Ceelinge for the better strenthninge therof and bourding the same degrees three bourd[es] in highte wth a bourde to stay theire feete his Ma^{ty} fyndinge all the Materiall[es] and they woorkemanship by agreem^{te}: iiij^{li} xv^s x^d . . .

. . . to divers Artificers and labourers for expedicon in theire woorke vppon extraordinary hast and for bread and drinke amongst them woorkinge very late in the nighte vij^s.

In the accounts for the year 1 October 1630–30 September 1631, Henry Wickes, Paymaster:

WHITEHALL

Iohn Decreet Sergeaunte painter and other paintr^s for . . . sondry Extraordenary workes aboute the Cockpitt and Playhouse there and for attendaunce and directing the Carvers and Carpenters to followe the Designes and Draughtes given by the Surveyor . . .

Carpenters for sondry woorkes by them donne and performed aboute the Cockpitt and playhouse there . . .

Carvers for moulding and clensinge of twoe great Statuaes of Plaster of Parris for the Cockpitt mouldinge and castinge three

Ballastleavo[rs] and cuttinge and flutinge the Bodies of twoe Corinthian Columnes ciiij[s] . . .

Rewardes vizt to Iohn Damford Carpenter for his extraordenary paines the laste sõmer 1630 aboute whitehall and the Cockpitt xl[s]

In the accounts for the year 1 October 1631–30 September 1632, Henry Wickes, Paymaster:

WHITEHALL

Candlestickes of Iron beautified wth branches Leaues and garnished wth other ornament[es] to beare Lights in the Cockpitt x[en] at xxx[s] the peece xv[li] . . .

Iohn walker Property maker viz:[t] for hanging the Throne and Chaire in the Cockpit wth cloth bound about wth whalebone packthred and wyer for the better foulding of the same to come downe from the Cloud[es] to the Stage cutting fitting and soweing of Callicoe to couer all the roome ouer head wth in the Cockpitt cutting a great number of Starres of Assidue and setting them one the Blew Callicoe to garnish the Cloath there setting one a great number of Coppring[es] to drawe the cloth to and fro the king finding all manner of stuff and he the woorkmanshipp only allowed by agreem[t] the some of C[s]

Iohn Decreit[es] his Ma[ts] Serg[t] Paynter and other Painters . . . ffor new painting the freez in the Cockpitt ouer the Stage and for painting and guilding the braunches round about and before the Stage vj[li] xiiij[s]. iiij[d] . . . ffor repayring & mending twoe great peec[es] of paynted woorke that were done by Palma, thone being the Story of Dauid and Goliah, thother of Saules Conuersion w[ch] were much defaced C[s] ffor repayring mending and new varnishing vij[en] of the greate Emperoure Heades that were done by Titian being likewise much defaced lxx[s] . . . for diuers times Cullouring in Gould cullo[r] the Braunches of xv[e] Candlesticks in the Cockpitt wherof tenn smallor and twoe greater then thother about and before the Stage and for Hatching and Guilding them wth fine gould cullouring the great Braunches in the front of the stage and Hatching and Guilding all the ptes to be seene forwards allowed by agrem[t] x[li] in all

In the accounts for the year 1 October 1632–30 September 1633, Henry Wickes, Paymaster:

WHITEHALL

Empcõns and Provicõns . . . Candlestickes ij with diverse branches for the Cockpitt at Whitehall - - - xiij[li]. vj[s]. viij[d] . . . .

In the accounts for the year 1 October 1633—30 September 1634, Henry Wickes, Paymaster:

Iohn de Creet[es] Serg[t] Painter Mathew Gooodericke Paynter viz: . . . for mending the Statues in the Cockpitt altering the inscriptions and clenzing other woorke there xx[s] . . .

Not only do these records give details of the new court theatre called the Cockpit, but they serve to identify sketches now in the Worcester College Library[1] as the plans for the new theatre. A comparison of the items in the payment records with features of the drawings can leave no doubt that the Whitehall workmen were building the theatre shown in the sketches, some stages of which are presumably referred to in the accounts for 1630–1 as 'the Designes and Draughtes given by the Surveyor', i.e. Inigo Jones.

The ten 'Corynthian Capitalls' and the ten 'greate Pilla^{rs}' are shown in the first order of the proscenium of the stage elevation in the drawings. The ten 'other smaller Composita Capitall[es]' for the 'smaller Pilla^{rs}' are shown in the second order of the proscenium. The 'Cornishes pendaunt[es] and moulding' in the 'viij^t Cant[es] of the Cockepitt' correspond to the eight corners of the octagonal interior shown in the drawings. The sketch also shows the work of Synsburye, Byndinge, and Barton in 'settinge vpp twoe stories of Collomnes in the Cockepitt playhouse beinge x^{en} Collomnes vpon eu^{r}y Story Corinthia and Composita finishinge the head[es] wth Architrave, freeze and Cornishe vppon each Story'. It also shows the 'five doores in the first Story and in the second story one open dore & iiij^{er} neeches in the same vpper Storye'. Since only the ground-floor plan is preserved, the work in the galleries (pre-

---

[1] Hamilton Bell, who fully described and discussed the sketches (*Architectural Record*, 1913) thought they were the work of Inigo Jones, but William Grant Keith made what appeared to be a good case (*Architectural Review*, February 1925) that they were the work of Jones's assistant, John Webb. Various writers have accepted his attribution to Webb, but the argument will not stand. Keith argued first from the distinctive drawing habits of Jones and Webb, but such stylistic evidence is very slippery. Keith's most telling points were based on his assumed dates for the Cockpit pictures in the maps of Faithorne and of Vertue. He contended that the new Cockpit was not yet built in 1658, mistakenly accepting Faithorne's publication date as the date of all details of the original drawing; Faithorne shows a still octagonal Cockpit. Keith pointed out that the Worcester octagon-within-a-square sketches are for the Cockpit shown in Vertue's map made from Fisher's drawings of the 1660's, during Webb's active London career, and after the death of Inigo Jones. Keith concluded that the theatre of the Worcester plans was built in the early years of the Restoration. But now the identification of the payments of 1629 or 1630 with the plan for the new theatre rules out Webb as the originator of the Worcester drawings. Plans for a theatre opened in 1630 must have been made not later than 1628 or 1629. In 1628 John Webb was seventeen years old and apparently still at the Merchant Taylors' School (*D.N.B.*). If the manner of drawing really is Webb's, the Worcester College drawings must be Webb's copies of lost originals, presumably by Inigo Jones. The close resemblance of the proscenium to that of the Theatro Olympico at Vicenza, which Jones visited in 1613 and 1614, is striking.

sumably above what Mr. Bell calls the balcony) cannot be seen. Payment in 1630–1 'for moulding and clensinge of twoe great Statuaes of Plaster of Parris for the Cockpitt' is presumably for the statues to go on either side of the central door in the proscenium. And the payment for further cleaning and repairing in the year 1633–4 'for mending the Statues in the Cockpitt altering the inscriptions and clensing the other woorke there' refers to the stage statues and to the inscriptions partly deciphered by Bell from the Worcester drawing.

Since the Office of the Works payments make it evident that the Cockpit which was opened on 5 November 1630 with 'An Induction for the Howse' was the building shown in the Worcester College plans, close attention to those drawings is desirable; they are the only detailed plans extant for any Jacobean or Caroline theatre. Though the plans are fairly clear, an architect's explication of them and his elucidation of the dimensions and of a few details not visible in the reproductions, is illuminating. Mr. Hamilton Bell gave a professional elucidation in his description of the originals in *The Architectural Record* in 1913. He wrote:

It represents within a square building, windowed on three sides and on one seemingly attached to another building, an auditorium occupying five sides of an octagon, on the floor of which are shown the benches of a pit, or the steps, five in number, on which they could be set. These are curiously arranged at an angle of 45 degrees on either side of a central aisle, so that the spectators occupying them could never have directly faced the stage [but did not have their backs to the State]. Surrounding this pit on five sides is a balcony [evidently not the 'galleryes' of the payment to Synsburye, Byndinge, and Barton] ten feet deep, with, it would seem, two rows of benches on four of its sides; the fifth side in the centre, directly opposite the stage being partitioned off into a room or box, in the middle of which is indicated a platform about five feet by seven, presumably for the Royal State. Three steps descend from this box to the central aisle of the pit. To the left of and behind this royal box appears another enclosure or box, partitioned off from the rest of the balcony. . . .

The staircases of access to this auditorium are clearly indicated; one small door at the rear of the *salle* with its own private stairway, communicating with the adjoining building, opens directly into the royal box; as in the Royal Opera House in Berlin today.

There is another door, with a triangular lobby, into the rear of the left-hand balcony. Two windows are shown on each side of the house, opening directly into the theatre from the outer air.

The stage runs clear across the width of the pit, about thirty-five feet, projecting in an 'apron' or *avant scène* five feet beyond the proscenium wall and is surrounded on the three outward sides by a low railing of classic design about eighteen inches in height, just as in many Elizabethan Playhouses.

If one may trust an elevation of the stage, drawn on the same sheet to twice the scale of the general plan, the stage was four feet six inches above the floor of the pit. This elevation exhibits the surprising feature of a classic façade, Palladian in treatment, on the stage of what so far we have regarded as a late modification of a playhouse of Shakespeare's day. Evidently Inigo Jones contemplated the erection of a permanent architectural *proscenium*, as the ancients called it, of the type, though far more modest, both in scale and ornamentation, of Palladio's Theatro Olimpico at Vicenza, which we know he visited in about 1600, some twenty years after its erection.[1] This *proscenium*, given in plan and elevation, shows a semi-circular structure with a radius of fifteen feet, two stories in height, of the Corinthian or Composite order. In the lower story are five doorways, the centre of which is a large archway flanked by pedestals, on which are inscribed in Greek characters, Melpomene—Thalia; over these and over the smaller doors are tablets.

The second story [of the proscenium] contains between its lighter engaged columns, over the four side doors, niches with corbels below, destined to carry statues as their inscribed bases indicate. So far as these inscriptions are legible,—the clearest reading 'phocles', probably Sophocles, these were to represent Greek dramatists, most likely Æschylus, Euripides, Sophocles, and Aristophanes.[2]

The curved pediment of the central archway runs up into this story and is broken in the middle by a tablet bearing the inscription 'Prodesse et [&] Delectare,' which is flanked by two reclining genii holding garlands.

Above these are two busts on brackets, Thespis and Epicurus, or possibly Epichoarnus [I read Epicar—]. The space directly above this pediment is occupied by a window-like opening five by four feet . . . The pyramidal pediment above this opening projects above the upper cornice into a coved ceiling, which would appear from the rendering of the drawing to form an apse above the semi-circular stage. Behind the *proscenium* is a large space with staircases of approach,[3] two

---

[1] Jones visited the theatre again in 1613 and 1614. He describes it in notes dated Sunday 23 September 1613. At Worcester College (Drawing 84a) are three of Jones's sketches and a plan of the Theatro Olympico with dimensions. The sheet on which they are drawn is said to have been 'taken out of Inigo Jones' copy of Palladio in which it had at some time been inserted'. Presumably Jones had these sketches and the plan by him when he worked on his designs for the new Cockpit.

[2] The lettering has been obscured by the cross hatching. I read the inscriptions from left to right 'Agath—, —ectan—, Sophocles, Antiph—'. Perhaps the first was Agathon and the last was Antiphanes.

[3] So far as I can see only the staircase on the left has a door of access to the stage; there is no door to the other on this floor. It must have led from the floor below to the gallery above.

Inigo Jones's Drawings for the Remodell

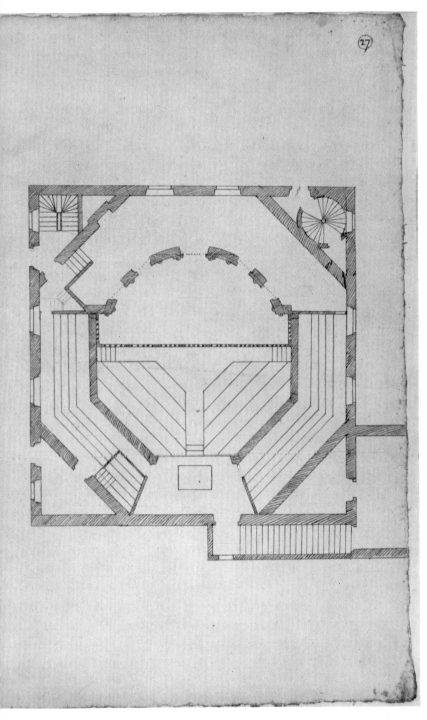

kpit-in-Court. Worcester College, Oxford

windows at the rear and apparently a fireplace for the comfort of the
waiting players. Communication with the front of the house is provided by a door in the proscenium wall opening into the stage door
lobby, whence the outside of the building may be reached.

There is no indication of galleries, unless some marks on the
angles of the front wall of the balcony may be interpreted without
too much license into the footings of piers or posts to carry one; the
total interior height shown in the elevation from what I have assumed
to be the floor of the pit to the ceiling being only twenty-eight feet
there would hardly have been room for more than one. The only staircases which could have served it are at the rear of the building in the
corners behind the stage wall . . .

The general dimensions would appear to be:

Total width of the auditorium	58 ft.
Total width of the pit	36 ft.
Total width of front stage or 'apron'	35 ft.
Total depth of the stage from the railing to the centre of the *proscenium*	16 ft.

The entire building is 58 feet square inside, cut to an
octagon of 28 feet each side.

Height from floor to ceiling	28 ft.
Height from stage to ceiling . .	about 23 ft. 6 in.
The lower order of the *proscenium* . . .	10 ft. 6 in.
The upper order of the *proscenium* . . .	9 ft. 6 in.

The scale on the drawing may not be absolutely correct, as measured
by it the side doors of the *proscenium* are only five feet high and two
feet nine inches wide; this, however, may be an error in the drawing,
since we have it on very good authority that Inigo Jones designed
without the use of a scale, proportioning his various members by his
exquisitely critical eye alone, subsequently adding the dimensions in
writing.

To these features of the Cockpit-in-Court as they are shown in
the plan and the elevation, one can now add a few others from the
Office of the Works accounts. The payments to the painter and
the carpenters show that there was a gallery, presumably above
what Mr. Bell calls the balcony. The painter Goodricke says 'the
gallery', but the carpenters say 'the galleryes'. I suspect that
there was only one, and that the carpenters used the plural to
refer to the different sides of the octagon, as is the case in various
carpenters' accounts for the preparation of galleries on the two
sides of the Great Hall.

The accounts of the painter Goodricke for 1629–30 show that
much of the interior of the theatre was painted to simulate stone,

but there was a good deal of colour too. The eight squares of the wall—presumably the eight sides of the octagon above a certain height—were painted a 'fayre blew'. Blue and gold were apparently the prevailing colours, since Goodricke was also paid for 'washinge the gold of the pendaunt[es] and Cornishes and mending the same in divers places wth gold Cullor in oyle and mendinge the blew of the same in sondry places'. And gold was the colour of the fifteen candlesticks 'about and before the stage' as well as of 'the great Braunch[es] in front of the stage'. The 'Blew Callicoe' which was cut and fitted by the property maker, John Walker, 'to couer all the roome ouer head' was garnished with stars which were probably gold. I assume that this blue cloth with stars covered the ceiling, but I am not sure why there were copper rings 'to drawe the cloth to and fro'. Perhaps this was a provision to pull the cloth aside so that the throne could descend.

The 'Throne and Chaire' which Walker bound with cloth, whalebone, and wire to facilitate folding was evidently the descending throne familiar in the public theatres. To the modern mind it seems a little incongruous for such a formal building as the Cockpit-in-Court.

The payment to Goodricke for 'pryminge and payntinge like glasse xx^{ty} panes wch had bin Lightes' suggests an effort to exclude daylight from the theatre. Most court performances were at night, however, and there may have been other reasons for painting out the twenty panes. Surely the four auditorium windows shown in the plan included more than twenty panes.

The position of the 'twoe great peec[es] of paynted woorke that were done by Palma', David and Goliath and Saul's Conversion, is obscure. In a public theatre they would have been painted cloths on the stage, but the character of the proscenium in this playhouse would not have allowed them there. Possibly they were hung on the diagonal walls at the back of the house.

The 'greate Emperours Heades that were done by Titian' are an interesting feature of the adornment of the theatre. It might have been guessed that they were placed in the niches in the upper level of the proscenium, but there are only four places and the inscription under one of them certainly reads 'Sophocles'. The phrasing used by De Critz (Decreits), 'vij^{en} of the greate Emperours Heades', implies that these heads were only those damaged among a larger number. Apparently all twelve of Titian's Twelve Caesars were housed at the Cockpit. Perhaps they were placed about the back of the house, as statues were in Jones's model at Vicenza.

The theatre made use of at least fifteen candelabra ('Candle-stickes of Iron'), most of which must have been elaborate, since ten of them cost thirty shillings apiece. The placing of this illumination is confusedly indicated by De Critz, who speaks of 'tenn smaller and twoe greater then thother about and before the Stage', and of 'the great Braunches [candelabra arms] in front of the stage'. Does he mean that the smaller candelabra were placed about the back of the stage and the two larger ones were suspended over the front of the stage? Perhaps these two were the 'Candlesticks ij with diuerse branches for the Cockpitt at White-hall' for which £13. 6s. 8d. was paid. The price suggests very elaborate work.

Finally, there are several items of payment for repairs or alterations in the Cockpit-in-Court after the Restoration, payments which sometimes shed light on the pre-war theatre. It is difficult to tell which of these items indicate restorations or minor alterations reflecting features of the 1630 theatre, and which provide for major alterations. The following seem to make implications about the court playhouse as it existed before its neglect began in 1642.

John Davenport, Master Carpenter, was paid for work done in November 1660 in

Makeing of v large boxes wth seuerall degrees in them at ye cockpitt and doores in them, taking vp the floore of ye stage and pitt and laying againe the floore of the stage & pitt pendant . . . making of two p[ar]titions in the gallery there for the Musick and players . . . making a paire of Stayres cont. [blank] stepps to goe into ye Gallery ouer the stage & incloseing the said stayres wth a doore in it Cont. about one square, making of two new doores goeing vnder the degrees and bourding vp one doore vppon the degrees, setting vp xj squares of p[ar]titioning vnder the degrees wth vj doores in them. (Boswell, p. 239, from P.R.O. Office of the Works Accounts.)

Mat-layers were paid for work done about the same time in: 'new matting some of the seats of ye degrees in ye Cockpit and the seats & floore where his Matie: sitts there, . . . new [matting] seuerall other seats and the flatt belowe the stage of the cockpit.' (Ibid.)

An order from the Lord Chamberlain on 24 November 1660 requires the Master of the Great Wardrobe to provide 'for the Cockpitt as much Greene Manchester Bayes lyned wth Canvas as will Cover the Stage and twenty faire gillt Branches wth three Socketts in each for Candles and Six Sconces for the Passages that are darke . . .'. (Ibid., p. 15, from the Lord Chamberlain's Warrant Books.)

An upholsterer's bill of about the same date lists 'For the Cockpitt att Whitehall . . . For hookes staples & buckrome employde about a Crimson velvett Canopie & for altring & mending the s^d Canopie 13.6.' (Boswell, p. 16.)

On 10 December 1662 the Lord Chamberlain issued a warrant

. . . for the upper tyring roome in the Cockpitt the walles being unfitt for the rich Cloathes, One hundred & tenn yards of greene bayes at three shill[ings] foure pence the yard One looking glasse of twenty seaven Inches for the Weomen Comedians dressing themselues. Twenty chaires & stooles three Tables two stands sixe Candlesticks two peeces of hangings and great curtaine rodds to make partitions betweene the Men & Weomen two paire of Andirons Two paire of Tonges two fire shovells & bellowes One Lanthorne & one Iron Pann, one proporty Bedd wth a redd Taffata Coverlet & taffata Curtaynes & quilt & one Couch. (Ibid., p. 18.)

In November 1662 there is a payment to bricklayers for '. . . Cuttinge way for 2 Chimneys & building them vp at the Cockpit playhouse & mending tileing there'. (Ibid., p. 240.)

How much of the old theatre is revealed in these accounts of repairs and alterations in 1660 and 1662 one cannot be sure, but I should hazard the following guesses: The five boxes built in 1660 were in the gallery, as shown by a later payment of 1670/1 for lodgings partly rebuilt in the 'vpper gallery & boxes lookeing downe into ye Cockpit playhowse'. (Boswell, p. 241.) These five boxes may well have been the restoration of old ones, for boxes were common in Caroline private playhouses, and confined spaces for ambassadors and court officials at Caroline command performances would have been convenient, as is amply shown by John Finett in his *Finetti Philoxenis*, 1656. The floor accounts I take to mean that the pit and the stage floors of the 1630 building were level, but in 1660 they were made pendant, i.e. raked. (See Boswell, p. 31.)

The partitions made 'in the gallery there for the Musicke and players' may have been new, but the entry reveals the fact that the old gallery ran behind the proscenium and presumably offered a floor behind the upper proscenium opening. Probably the music was there.

The fact that the matting payments call for 'new matting' and for only 'some of the seats' indicates that the old theatre had matting on the degrees and on the State; some of it now needed replacing.[1] I do not understand the need for matting under the

---

[1] There was matting on the floor of the Jacobean Cockpit. A Treasury payment was made in 1603–4 for 'Matt upon the Cockpitt being broken and torne withe Cockes fighting there'. (Quoted Braines, op. cit., p. 24 n.)

stage, but the entry shows that there was working-room there, presumably for the manipulation of the traps.

The green baize on the stage may well have been a replacement of decayed baize in the theatre of 1630. (See Boswell, p. 147.) The crimson velvet canopy for the State was mended in 1660, and therefore it can be taken as old and consequently a feature of the theatre before the war.

The entry of December 1662 indicates that there was both an upper and a lower tiring-room, the upper of which must have been used in part as a wardrobe. The room must have been large if it could hold twenty chairs and stools with three tables and two stands. The two fire-places provided are evidently in this upper tiring-room. The plan of 1630 shows a fire-place in the lower room, but the two in the upper tiring-room were probably new, as is suggested by the payments to the bricklayers.

Certainty about all the features of the Cockpit-in-Court is tantalizingly elusive. The Worcester plans do not show all parts of the house; the Office of the Works payments of 1629–34 do not reveal the beginning, only the later, stages of the construction; the Restoration accounts do not distinguish clearly between repairs necessary after eighteen years of neglect and Restoration alterations. Yet how much less are we forced back on conjecture about this theatre than about any other before the Restoration! The size, the proportions, the appearance of the stage, the disposition of the audience, and much of the ornamentation of the house are all clear enough.

One aspect of the new playhouse may be a little surprising. Since there is so much evidence of the use of scenic effect in the court theatre in masques and in a few plays like *The Queen of Aragon* and *The Royal Slave*, one might have expected that the greatest English scenic artist, Inigo Jones, would have made provision in his new court theatre for impressive display. But there is none.[1]

---

[1] One of several sources of confusion about scenic display at the Cockpit-in-Court is a sketch by Inigo Jones for a set behind a proscenium arch. The drawing is inscribed 'for ye cockpitt for my lo Châberlin 1639'. Simpson and Bell have associated the sketch with three others for the performance of Habington's *Queen of Aragon, or Cleodora*, which was produced at the Lord Chamberlain's expense on 9 April 1640. (See above, iv. 522–5 and *Designs by Inigo Jones*, pp. 131–2.) But *Cleodora* was produced in the Great Hall, not in the Cockpit-in-Court, and the other three sketches (two of which are labelled 'Cleodora') show the usual flat proscenium of Hall sketches, not the arched proscenium of the one made for the Lord Chamberlain. I can only guess that the sketch dated 1639 was prepared to back the central arch at the Cockpit-in-Court when the performance of 9 April 1640 was

Clearly spectacle was reserved for the Halls in Denmark House and Whitehall, the Banqueting House, and the Masquing Houses. Since the Cockpit-in-Court, unlike the others, was built for regular, not occasional, dramatic use, we have further evidence that even at the court of Charles I scenic effects were thought of as additional attractions, not essentials.

Though the Cockpit-in-Court was clearly not a theatre built for the exploitation of scenic spectacle, it could make use of scenic suggestion. The central door, and perhaps the two flanking doors, could be blocked by back scenes. Indeed, it is likely that we have three examples of sketches for such painted perspectives. Among the Inigo Jones drawings at Chatsworth are three labelled '1. A Pallas'; '2. An Army'; '3. A prison'. (Simpson and Bell, p. 135; reproduced in Nicoll, *Stuart Masques*, p. 147 and Keith, p. 55.) Mr. Keith has pointed out that the scale of these drawings shows that each of the planned paintings would fit nicely into the central opening of the Cockpit plan. Since these sketches, unlike most of the other scenic drawings Jones made, are designed for a narrow arched opening, it seems likely that they are intended for the Cockpit-in-Court.

The court enthusiasm for the new Whitehall theatre opened on 5 November 1630 is shown by the bill of the King's company, showing seventeen performances there in the course of fifteen weeks. (See above, i. 28–29.) And the new theatre was probably used at least ten more times in the same period, since Queen Henrietta's men gave sixteen unlocated performances in about nineteen weeks. The court records for 1631–2 are mostly not clear about the place of performance,[1] but 1632–3 shows no fall-

originally planned, and that this sketch was replaced by Simpson and Bell's number 362 when the place for performance was changed to the Hall. The proscenium opening in the sketch seems too tall and narrow for a full stage, but I must admit that the proportions of the opening are not so tall and narrow as the central door at the Cockpit-in-Court. (See also above, vi. 51–52.)

[1] There may have been one quite special performance at the theatre in this period, though the record does not make it clear whether the theatre or Cockpit lodgings are intended. On 5 May 1632 John Pory wrote to Viscount Scudamore: 'On Thursday night [3 May] my lo: Chamberlaine bestowed a feast and a playe upon the King and Queen at his lodging in the Cockpitt, which cost his lordship 1500ll. . . .' (J. P. Feil, *Shakespeare Survey*, xi [1958], 109, from Scudamore Papers at the P.R.O.) The coincidence of dates indicates that the rehearsal for this performance is the one which appears in a payment to the King's company for plays at court, 3 May 1632 to 3 March 1632/3: '20ll for the rehersall of one at the Cockpitt by which meanes they lost their afternoone at the House'. (*M.S.C.* ii. 360.) Though John Pory's letter seems to place the performance of the play in the Lord Chamberlain's

ing off in the use of the new playhouse; in the period from
November 1632 to April 1633 James Clegorne and his assistants
made ready the Cockpit for 'xxix^{en} playes'. (*M.S.C.* vi. 123.)
Again in 1638–9 the King's company performed seventeen times
at the Cockpit, five times in the spring, and twelve times in the
months of November and December.

But the Cockpit-in-Court did not become the theatre for all
command performances. Often the King was at Hampton Court
and sometimes at Richmond in the Christmas or the Carnival
season and had the plays there. Even in London the royal
performances were not always in the new theatre. The Hall
at Denmark (Somerset) Palace and the Great Hall in Whitehall
were still used for plays. All the pieces known to have been
produced with elaborate scenic effects were presented in these
two halls—*The Shepherds Paradise, The Faithful Shepherdess,
Florimene, The Passionate Lovers,* and *The Queen of Aragon.* For
four of the five set designs by Inigo Jones are still extant. But
the distinction between plays with scenery and plays without was
not so sharp as might be thought. Carlell's *The Passionate Lovers*
was produced with Jones's sets at Denmark House on 10 July
1638, but it was also performed at the Cockpit-in-Court and at
Blackfriars where the elaborate sets could not have been used.
(See above, iii. 122–3.) Again the concept of scenery as a special
display exhibition and not as an essential part of *any* play is
illustrated.

Performances at the Cockpit dwindled in the last year or so
before the war, as they must have done in the commercial theatres.
Sir Henry Herbert's entry for the last recorded performance at
the court playhouse before the war is eloquent: 'Un Twelfe
Night, 1641 [/42], the prince had a play called The Scornful Lady,
at the Cockpitt, but the kinge and queene were not there; and
it was the only play acted at courte in the whole Christmas.'
(*Variorum,* iii. 241.)

Before Parliament issued its closing order of 2 September 1642,
the King had deserted London, and the function of the Cockpit-
in-Court was gone. Its melancholy, deserted state is mourned in
a pamphlet which Thomason dated 4 October 1642. This piece,

Cockpit Lodgings, I incline to agree with Mr. Feil that probably only the
feast was there and the play was in the adjacent theatre. Indeed, the two
may have been connected, for when the Cockpit lodgings were partly
rebuilt, one of the payments of March 1670/1 notes that the 'vpper gallery
& boxes lookeing downe into ye Cockpit playhowse' were turned into
wardrobes. (Boswell, p. 241, from Office of the Works Accounts.)

called *A Deep Sigh Breath'd Through The Lodgings At White-Hall, Deploring the absence of the Court. And the Miseries of the Pallace,* probably reflects the feelings of many Londoners, though certainly not the majority.

In the Cockpit and Revelling Roomes, where at a Play or Masque the darkest night was converted to the brightest Day that ever shin'd, by the luster of Torches, the sparkling of rich Jewells. . . . Now you may goe in without a Ticket, or the danger of a broken-pate, you may enter at the Kings side, walke round about the Theaters, view the Pullies, the Engines, conveyances, or contrivances of every several Scaene, And not an Usher o' th' Revells, or Engineere to envy or finde fault with your discovery, although they receive no gratuitie for the sight of them. (A$_3$^{v}, quoted by G. Thorn-Drury, *R.E.S.*, i [1925], 462.)

There is no evidence that the Cockpit-in-Court was ever used for plays—as some of the commercial theatres were—during the prohibited period.[1] The court theatre was, however, as we have seen, reconditioned for use after the Restoration. Miss Boswell finds the repairs beginning in November 1660, and a printed prologue in the Thomason collection records the first performance: 'The Prologue to his Majesty At the first Play presented at the Cock-pit in Whitehall; Being part of that Noble Entertainment which their Majesties received Novemb. 19 from his Grace the Duke of Albemarle.'

Miss Boswell finds no evidence of performances at the theatre after 1664. The Cockpit was demolished or completely rebuilt in or about 1675, for a painting of about 1675 or 1676 shows a different and taller building on the site. (See Braines, op. cit., p. 28 and Plate 3.)

THE MASQUING HOUSE

[Boswell, Eleanore and Chambers, E. K.,] 'Dramatic Records: The Lord Chamberlain's Office', *M.S.C.* ii, Pt. 3 (1931), 321–416.
Feil, J. P., 'Dramatic References from the Scudamore Papers', *Shakespeare Survey*, xi [1958], 107–16.

[1] But there is a record of an official use of the court theatre during the Protectorate, an occasion which must have been very suggestive for William Davenant. The Lord Protector gave a banquet for members of the House of Commons at Whitehall on 20 February 1656/7. After dinner 'His Highness withdrew to the Cockpit; and there entertained them with rare music, both of voices and instruments, till the evening.' (Carlyle, Thomas, *The Letters and Speeches of Oliver Cromwell*, ed. S. C. Lomas [1904], iii. 15.)

Keith, William Grant, 'The Designs for the First Movable Scenery on the English Public Stage', *Burlington Magazine*, xxv (1914), 29–33, 85–98.

Wedgwood, C. V., 'The Last Masque', *Truth and Opinion: Historical Essays* (1960), 139–56.

The Masquing House in Whitehall, which some of the Puritans referred to contemptuously as 'The Queens Dancing-Barne', had a brief existence and only occasional dramatic use. It was built in 1637 to take over certain functions of the Banqueting House. Inigo Jones's magnificent building had only recently had its greatest adornments—the ceiling paintings by Rubens—finally installed (see above, vi. 265–6) and the King, fearful of damage to them and to the gildings, ordered the new building.

The new Masquing House was also built by Inigo Jones, and the first record of the project comes from an authorization to him:

A Warrant to Mr Suruayer to cause a great roome of Timber wth Degrees for Masques to bee presently built ouer the Tarras at Whitehall betwixt the banquetting house & the great Chamber According to such direccõns as hee had allready represented vnto his Ma^tye wth power to call together all the Officers & Mr Artizans of his Ma^t[es] sayd work[es] in their seuerall places respectiuely to bee imployed in the sayd worke & make a dispatch therof before Christmas. . . . Sept 29. 1637. (*M.S.C.* ii. 385.)

The work must have progressed rapidly, for a second Lord Chamberlain's warrant six weeks later seems to imply that the building is already well along: 'A warr^t to Mr Survayer to cause the Timber worke Iron worke & such other things as are usually found in the Office of ye work[es] to bee furnished in the new house built for Masques for two Masques to bee presented, the one for his Ma^tye and the other for the Queene Nou. 6. 1637.' (Ibid., p. 386.) The precise location as well as the dimensions of the new building are given in a letter written on 1 November 1637 by Sir John Finett to Viscount Scudamore:

Wee haue a stately buylding toward in Whytehall (but more stately for forme and use then for matter or substance being all of wood) to be imployd only for maskes and dancing, whyle the bancketting is to be reserved only or cheefly for Audiences, with apprehension of his Majesty that torches, wyth theyr smoake may disluster the pictures and guyldings there, which are sayd to haue cost above ten thousand poundes.

This fabrick is placed (that I may rightly fix your lordships imagination and fancy of it) wythin some ten foot of the bancetting

howse, extending in lenght toward the hall and gard chamber about
a hundred and ten foot, in bredth: ten or twelue foot into the fyrst
court; and about fyve and forty into that of the preaching place.
(P.R.O. C 115/N8/8810, as quoted by J. P. Feil, *Shakespeare Survey*,
xi [1958], 111.)

The dimensions of the new building given by Sir John, if I understand them correctly, indicate an area about the same size as
that covered by the two Banqueting Houses. The first hall built by
King James was 120 feet by 53 feet; Inigo Jones's hall was 110 feet
by 55 feet, and the new Masquing House, according to Finett, is
110 feet by about 55 or 57 feet. Apparently the Surveyor of the
Works wanted the new theatre for his masques to be the same
size as the old one. An elaborate set of working drawings prepared
by John Webb (see William Grant Keith, *Burlington Magazine*,
xxv [1914], 31) for Davenant's *Salmacida Spolia*, given in the
masquing house on 21 January 1639/40 (see above, iii. 213–15),
gives the dimensions of the hall on that occasion as 112 feet long,
57 feet wide, and 59 feet high, with a stage raised from 7 to 8 feet
above the floor. (B.M. Lansdowne MS. 1171, ff. 3b–4.) One or
two more details of the character of the new structure were noted
by George Garrard in two letters he wrote to Viscount Wentworth,
the first on 9 November 1637:

> Here are to be two Masks this Winter. . . . A great Room is now in
> building only for this Use betwixt the Guard-Chamber and Ban-
> queting-house, of Fir, only weather-boarded and slightly covered.
> At the Marriage of the Queen of *Bohemia* I saw one set up there, but
> not of that Vastness that this is, which will cost too much Money to
> be pulled down, and yet down it must when the Masks are over.
> (*Strafforde's Letters*, ii. 130.)

Garrard's second letter, written five weeks later on 16 December,
gives the figure he has heard of the cost of the new Masquing
House:

> Here are two Masks intended this Winter; the King is now in
> practising his, which shall be presented at *Twelfthtide*. . . . The other
> the Queen makes at *Shrovetide*, a new House being erected in the
> first Court at *Whitehall*, which cost the King 2500l. only of Deal
> Boards, because the King will not have his Pictures in the Banqueting-
> house hurt with Lights. (Ibid., p. 140.)

An authoritative statement of the short construction period
as well as a record of the first performance in the new house is
printed with the masque *Britannia Triumphans*, whose title-page

notes that it was 'By *Inigo Iones* Surveyor of his Majesties workes, and *William Davenant* her Majesties servant'. This masque was danced on 7 January 1637/8, and Sir Henry Herbert authorized its printing the next day. (See above, iii. 199–200.) The statement about the new Masquing House is found in the second paragraph:

There being now past three yeers of Intermission, that the King and Queenes Majesties have not made Masques with shewes and Intermedij, by reason the roome where formerly they were presented, having the seeling since richly adorn'd with peeces of painting of great value, figuring the acts of King *Iames* of happy memory, and other inrichments: lest this might suffer by the smoake of many lights, his Majestie commanded the Surveyor of his workes, that a new-temporary [*sic*] roome of Timber, both for strength and capacitie of spectators, should bee suddenly built for that use; which being performed in two moneths, the Scenes for this Masque were prepared. (A₂.)

An account of his troubles in handling the punctilious Spaniards at this first performance in the new building was written to Viscount Scudamore by Sir John Finett ten days after the performance. One or two of his details reflect some of the arrangements for spectators at the masque:

. . . I was twoo or three dayes after assaylled by his [the Spanish Ambassador's] steward who presenting me a list (wyth his lords particular recommendation) of one or twoo and twenty persons (all except three under title of Dons) they were introduced by a Tourndoore into the fyrst entry of the Maske-Roome (not the banckketing house but another buylt, next it, to save that and the pictures in it from harme by smoaking) where I bestowing them awhyle for theyr after ascent to a place appointed for them on the left hand of the kings chayre somwhat behynd and over it; certayne of the better sort of them, (ignorant of the way) tooke to the right hand, and entring there a doore (too readyly opened by Mr Controller), the rest following, they (altogether) passed up to a stand kept for the Frenche, where once seated I could not with civility remove them. . . . (P.R.O. C 115/N8/8814, quoted by J. P. Feil, loc. cit., p. 112.)

The second masque in the new structure, the one referred to by George Garrard as the Queen's masque at Shrovetide, in his letters to Viscount Wentworth about the season's plans, was Davenant's *Luminalia, or The Festival of Light* (see above, iii. 207–9), which the title-page says was 'Personated in a Masque at Court, By the Queenes Majestie, and her Ladies. On *Shrovetuesday* Night, 1637 [i.e. 6 February 1637/8]'. On 21 February Sir John Finett again wrote to Viscount Scudamore about his troubles in handling the Spaniards, who this time left in a huff, but he said nothing about the performance. (See J. P. Feil, loc. cit., p. 113.)

No other masque performances are known during the rest of 1638 or in 1638/9. James Birche heard that *Luminalia* was to be repeated at Easter for the entertainment of the Duchess of Chevreuse, and so wrote to Viscount Scudamore on 14 February 1637/8 (ibid., p. 113), but there is no record that the intention was ever carried out.

On 21 January 1639/40 Davenant's *Salmacida Spolia* was danced, both the King and the Queen appearing as masquers. (See above, iii. 213–15.) The performance was at Whitehall, in the Masquing House. Again it was intended to repeat the masque, this time at Shrovetide, 17–19 February 1638/9, and Secretary Vane wrote to Sir Thomas Roe of the plan. (*C.S.P., Dom.*, 1639–40, p. 459.) The intention may have been carried out, but no other record of it has been found.

Salmacida Spolia is the last of the Stuart masques; the occasion and its implications are brilliantly sketched by Miss C. V. Wedgwood in her essay, 'The Last Masque'. If any other masques besides Davenant's three were ever acted in the Masquing House, they are not now known. It is possible that there may have been some performances of plays in the Masquing House, but the new Cockpit-in-Court seems a more appropriate place for Whitehall performances, and no strictly dramatic use of the Masquing House is known.

The building did not long outlast the departure of the King from London, for on 16 July 1645 the House of Commons ordered that 'the boarded Masque House at *Whitehall*, the Masque House at *St. James*', and the Courts of Guard, be forthwith pulled down, and sold away; and that the Proceed thereof shall be employed towards the Payment of the King's poor Servants Wages'. (*Journals of the House of Commons*, iv. 210a.)

PROJECTED THEATRES

THE PROPOSED AMPHITHEATRE

A., G. E. P., 'Proposals for Building an Amphitheatre in London, 1620', *Notes & Queries*, Eleventh Series, x (1914), 481–2, 502–3.

Adams, pp. 412–17.

Hotson, Leslie, 'The Projected Amphitheatre', *Shakespeare Survey*, ii (1949), 24–35.

The scheme to build a large amphitheatre in London was a Jacobean projector's enterprise. Indeed, the only known literary reference assigns it to just this category. In Shakerley Marmion's *Holland's Leaguer* Agurtes says to Millicent:

> Nay more, if you can act it handsomely,
> You'll put a period to my undertakings,
> And saue me all my labour of proiecting,
>
> . . . . .
>
> My plots of Architecture, and erecting
> New Amphitheaters, to draw the custome
> From Play-houses once a weeke, and so pull
> A curse upon my head from the poore scoundrels.
>
> (1632 edition, ii. 3 [E₁ᵛ].)

But the allusion which Marmion put into the mouth of his character Agurtes in 1631 is to a revival of a scheme then more than ten years old. In 1620 three sergeants-at-arms in the King's service succeeded in obtaining a licence to erect in London a large amphitheatre to be used for a great variety of exhibitions, shows, and entertainments. The three licensees, John Cotton, John Williams, and Thomas Dixon, do not appear in other theatre records and were apparently showmen and entrepreneurs rather than actors.[1] A petition fourteen years later says that a

---

[1] Nothing certain is known about the men except that later documents call them 'Seriantes at Armes to his Maiestie'. Dr. Hotson suggests that John Dixon of the licence was the servant of the Lord Treasurer, who was alleged to be helping the notorious Sir Giles Mompeson in his exploitation of innkeepers and ale-sellers (op. cit., p. 26). A John Cotton was an officer of the Wardrobe from 1585 until 1630 (*M.S.C.* vi. 128–9) and he would have been conveniently placed for such a speculation. John Williams may have been the man of that name whom the Master of the Revels allowed to 'make *showe of an Elephant*' in 1623 (Chalmers, *Supplemental Apology*, p. 208), and the elephant man is probably the John Williams to whom the King allowed £270 'for the custody and keeping of an Elephant out of Spayne'. (Hotson, p. 26.) But the names are common, and these identifications must remain uncertain, though each cites an activity appropriate enough for an amphitheatre man.

Captain Robert Hassell was 'the first Inventor and profeser of the busines of the Amphitheater' (see below), but he is otherwise unknown, and his boast in 1634 is not necessarily a statement of fact. What the projectors proposed, and appeared at first to have succeeded in obtaining, is shown in their licence of 30 July 1620, discovered by Leslie Hotson:

... Whereas our welbeloved servants John Cotton, John Williams and Thomas Dixon three of the seriantes at armes in regard of their long se[r]vice done aswell vnto our deere Sistre Queene Elizabeth of famous memory as to our selfe ever since our coming to this our Crowne of England haue humbly peticioned vs that wee would be gratiously pleased to give license vnto them to build and prepare an Amphitheator vpon some convenient peece of ground neere our Citty of London for the exercise and practize of Heroique and maiestique recreacions aswell tending to the delight and enterteynment [of] forraigne Princes and Ambassadors and strangers and the Nobility and Gentry of this Realme as for the exercise of all manner of Armes and martiall discipline hereafter in these presentes mencioned and that they may receive and enioye the profittes and benefitts thereof for the Terme of thirtie and one yeeres, Wherefore wee . . . referred the consideracion of the true state thereof to some of the Lords of our Privy Councell calling vnto them the recorder of our Citty of London who haue certified vs of the good approvement of the Lord Maior and Councell of the said Citty therein, and did hold it fitt that the building might goe forwards so as it were done in such manner as might be proper and fitt for the performing of such exercises. And whereas the said John Cotton is willing to remit and release vnto the said John Williams and Thomas Dixon all such benefitts as shall or may be accrewing or due vnto him by the vertue of the said suite. Know yee that we . . . [allow them] at their costs and charges to buy and purchase in the name and to the vse of vs our heires and successors . . . such convenient peece or parcell of ground lying and being in or neere vnto our Citty of London as shalbe thought good by the said John Williams and Thomas Dixon . . . wee do covenant and grant to and with the said John Williams and Thomas Dixon . . . That wee our heirs or successors so soon as the said grounds shalbe so as aforesaid purchased and conveyed to vs our heires and successors shall and will by lettres Patents vnder our great Seale of England grant, deuise and to farme lett vnto the said John Williams and Thomas Dixon . . . the said parcell of ground for the terme of thirtie and one yeeres vnder the yeerely rent of forty shillinges and with such reasonable covenants as shalbe thought fitt. And therein also shall and will give free and full license and libertie power and authoritie vnto them their executors and administrators and assignes at their costs and charges to erect build and sett vpon the same parcell of ground one sufficient Messuage, house, or Amphitheator of free stone, brick, and strong tymber *with* all necessary outhouses stables, and oth*er* edifices . . . as may be most gracefull and fitt to accomodate all the exercise and pleasure hereafter menc*i*oned . . . that is to say the ryding and man*n*aging great horses, w*ith* exercise of Tilte, Turney, co*u*rse of field, Barriers, running at the ring and other martiall and manly exercises on horse backe the true vse of all manner of Armes for foot (vizt) the Pike, Partizan, Holberd, swords, muskett, pistoll or any other vsual or necessary armes whatsoever, the manner of Seafight*es* with Shippes and Gallies, embatelling of horses and foote, the rights to be *per*formed in Campe, seige or garrison w*ith* oth*er* docum*en*tes and instrucc*i*ons belonging to the honor and danger of a Martiall Co*u*rt w*ith* mathematicall & arithmeticall reading*es* necessary for martiall men. And likewise maskes or oth*er* shewes or invenc*i*ons, dancing, musique of all sorts, high and lowe winde instru*m*ents and oth*er*s, prospectives, exercises of the Olimpeyades, wrastling in oyled skins for prices or othe*r*wise, fightes w*ith* pike, partizan, and holbert heroique and maiestique playes in latin or in English and oth*er* pleasant delightfull and convenient shewes whatso-ever . . . fitt for the more stately and delectable publishing and sett-ing forth of the same, w*ith* a prohibicion to all Players wi*th*in the Citty of London and the Suburbes thereof to suspend and restraine them from their playes one day in every month throughout the yeere, giving them notice thereof fowerteene dayes before every such day of restraint Willing and com*m*anding all o*u*r Commissioners and all Maio*r*s, Sheriffes, Justices of peace Bayliff*es* Constables Headboroughes and all oth*er* officers and ministers for the tyme being that they nor any of them doe molest or trouble the said John Williams and Thomas Dixon . . . in the building setting vp or making of the said Amphi-theator in manner aforesaid . . . the thirtieth day of July in the eigh-teenth yeere of o*u*r Raigne. . . . (P.R.O., P.S.O. 2/44/14.)

With this licence should be considered another document found among the Tanner manuscripts at the Bodleian Library. This undated prospectus apparently belongs to the enterprise of 1620, since it accompanies the other documents about the attempt at that time.

The Exercise of many Heroick and Maiestick
*Recreations at his Ma*ties *Amphitheator.*

INPRIMIS *Tragedies, Comedies,* and *Histories, Acted* both in *Latine* and *English,* full of high State and Royall Representmen*tes* w*th* many variable and delightfull properties, w*th* Showes of great *Horse,* and riche *Caparisons,* gracefully prepared to Entertaine Foraigne *Princes,* and to giue content to the most *Noble* and *Worthyest* of his Ma*ties Admired* and happie *Kingdomes.*

THERE shall be Showne the manner of *Sea Fights* w*th* the resem-blance of Shipps and Gallies in very Exquisite and Singuler order, worthy the view of the most Noble and Generous beholders./

THERE shalbe showne the true vse of all manner of *Armes*, and Weapons for Foote, faire and richly Armed wth *Pike, Partizan, Holbert, Sword, Rapier, Muskett, Pistoll*, or any other vsuall or necessarie *Armes* whatsoeuer.

THERE shall allso be demonstrated many Excellent & Ingenious Experiences belonging to a *Campe, Seidge*, or *Garison* wth the *Manly* order, and Posture of a Souldier.

THERE will be allso, for delight and Recreation, *Musick* of all Sortes, *Winde Instrumentes*, high and Lowe, *String Instrumentes, Voices*, the best this Kingdome, or any other Nation can aford./

MASQUES of very Exquisite and Curious *Inuentions* wth the best *Dauncers* that can be, Mummeries allso, and *Moriskors*./

CURIOUS *Prospectiues* in this Kingdome vnnvsuall, of singuler rarietie, and high Invention, all possible Exercises of the *Olympiades*, as *Wrestling* in Oyled Skynnes for gold and siluer Collers, wth Other Inferiour prizes, *Wrestling* two or three against one, *Running, Jumping, Vauteing, Tumblinge, Danceing* on the Ropes, Gladiato^{rs} in equall and vnnequall Combate two or three against one, to approue the singularitie of Weapons wth the true and rightful vse of them./

STRANGE and vnvsuall *Padgeantes* wth very admirable and rare Inventions, neuer as yet brought forth to any Specula͠con in theise *Partes* of y^e *World*, wth all manner of *Pleasures* that may either delight the Eare, or content ye Eye in them./

THERE shall be seene the liuely *Figures* & pleasant demonstrations of y^e *Driades*, theire *Pastimes*, Natures, quallities and prime deriuations./

THE nymble *Niades* in their proper *Natures*, and delightfull pleasures, in and about y^e *Springes, Fountaines*, and *Waters*./

NOCTURNALLS of vnexpressable *Figures*; Visions, and *Apparitions Figureing deepe Melancholly* and vnusuall Representationes./

PASTIMES vsed in *Spayne* called *Joco del Tauro* and *Joco del Cano*./

ALL manner of *Fightings* of *Wilde Beasts* whatsoeuer can be procured for *Pastime*, Recreation and viewe. Besides an Infinite nomber of vnexpressed properties of Singuler Order & composure.

Meanes to accomadate all the expressed
properties are these./

AT ALL Tymes When *Wee* shall stand in neede of Fortie or Fiftie Great Horse to Ornifie with high State the *Sceane, Historie* or *Subiect*, A *Gentleman* his Maties Seruant and Commaunder in his *Highnes Stables* will be readie for vs./

WEE haue allso a *Captaine* of *Foote*, and his Offic^{ers} of Excellent Experience, and direction, readie at all Tymes./

CORNELIUS the *Dutchman* the *most admired man* of *Christendome* for singuler *Invention* and *Arte* wth diuers others of our *Nation*, that will vndertake for our *Sea Fightes, Prospectiues, Nocturnalls, Driades, Naides, Fire and Water-workes*./

FOR *Masques* and all other properties belonging to them, *Wee* are allreadie prepared wth Admirable Dauncers.

FOR our seuerall kindes of *Musick*, M^r. *Alphonso*. Mr *Innocent Laneire*, Mr *Bird*, Mr *Johnson*, and other great M.^rs in *Musick*./

GLADIATORS and *Sword* Men, good & sufficient store you all knowe.

FOR all Exercises of the *Olympiades* (being practized) no Nation is better to performe them, for high Courage *Actiuitie* and Strength./

FOR *Latine Playes*, the helpe of both the *Vniuersities*, when *Tyme* shall require for the Entertainment of *Princes*, or any *Embassadours* from foraigne *Nations*./

THE *English Actors* you knowe Sufficiently./

Consideraçons for the Vndertakers, and *all Patentees*./

1. What chardge may buyld the said *Amphytheator* and how soone.
2. How, and by what sufficient, and *Excellent* Men, all seuerall properties may be fitted, and made Gracefull according to the former Expressions, and to continew the concourse of *People* by wch money may be still comeing in.
3. As reasonable as may be coniectured what profitt may arise to the vndertakers to giue them satisfaction.

IT is concluded by diuerse and Judicious *Artizans* that haue conferred, and long consulted herein, that ten or Eleauen thousand poundes in *Bancke* may buyld ye said *Amphytheator* strong and faire, and that it is necessarie, to haue two thouzand poundes in *Bancke* when the *House* is buylt to furnish all properties *Gracefull* therevnto belonging.

WEE are alreadie prepared w^th *Men* of Excellencie for the vndertakeing of each seuerall propertie whatsoeuer.

WHILE the *House* is in buylding, all *Playes* and properties may be prepared that there may be no Tyme lost, for it is the most pretious thing that belongeth thereunto.

IT is desired that all those Gentlemen that resolue to be Vndertake^rs in this *Busienes* may aduise wth the best, and most Learned Councell they can, for the best Assureance of all theire proportions, Shares, and Rates./

WHEREAS it may be Imagined the chardge wilbe great, to accomodate, and furnish these Showes wth properties, and all other materialls, *It* will be so indeed, for some of the first and greatest Showes; But they will, or may be made continew many Yeares after for Exchange of *Sceanes*, and *Subiectes*, being well ordered, and preserued in the *Wardropp*, And thereby saue a great quantitie of money./

THERE is no *Laudable Way* or course that can deliuer vnto the *Vndertakers*, so easie, so great and so certaine a gaine as this doth offer, When you haue well aduised, and considered therevppon./ It is therefore requisite to hasten theire Accordance and Contractes the sooner. For halfe a yeare Tyme will proue to be the losse of asmuch money as will buyld the whole *House*, Which materiall *Pointe*, I

could Wishe that euery *Vndertaker* would well consider of./ (Bodleian
MSS. Tanner 89, ff. 51–54. First printed by G. E. P. A., loc. cit.)

The privileges granted by the licence and asserted in the prospectus are ludicrous in their pretensions; had they been proposed
five years earlier they would have fitted nicely into *The Devil is
an Ass*. It is difficult to imagine that they could ever have been
carried out at all in London without the resources of the court; it
is impossible that all the entertainments advertised could have
been made profitable. That the scheme was never carried out is
not surprising; the only surprise is that it got so far as it did and
was revived so often.

Perhaps a London riding-school could have furnished horses and
riders for the 'ryding and mannaging of great horses', but the
exhibitions of the tilt-yard were royal displays at Whitehall, and
it is curious that their commercial exhibition was ever allowed at
any stage of the licence. Masques and shows were also royal, but
not exclusively so, for masques were sometimes produced in city
halls or Inns of Court (see above, iii. 218–20 and v. 1154–9), and
the Lord Mayor's shows were famous. It was not social taboos
but expense which would have made them impossible for the
Amphitheatre, backed by the treasury of neither the King nor any
rich and proud City company.

The display of 'Pike, Partizan, Holberd, swords', &c., like the
fights, would have been easy enough to arrange with Masters of
Fence and the *habitués* of the Artillery Ground; wrestlers, tumblers,
vaulters, and rope dancers, too, were common in London, where
they sometimes exhibited in the theatres. But the profit from
displays of dancing and music in an amphitheatre for 12,000 seems
very dubious, in spite of the parade in the prospectus of the names
of leading composers and royal musicians. As for the proposed
performances of plays in Latin and English on days when all
London theatres were to be ordered to close, the audacity of the
suggestion is breath-taking. Latin plays were common enough at
the universities and were produced now and then at court, but for
12,000 London citizens in a public amphitheatre the proposal
cannot have been intended seriously. Even English plays for such
an audience envisaged the co-operation of the London actors,
and the carefully irrelevant statement of the prospectus, 'The
English Actors you knowe Sufficiently', suggests that the pro-
moters knew of the hostility they would surely evoke from all
leading actors with stock in their own companies.

Certain of the objections noted above, as well as others, were
brought to the attention of the King, and on 29 September 1620

he addressed to the Earls of Pembroke and Arundell, Lord John Digby, Sir Robert Naunton, Sir George Calvert, and Sir Fulke Greville, all members of the Privy Council, the following letter:

. . . Whereas at the humble Suite of our Servant*es* John Cotton, John Williams and Thomas Dixon, and in recompence of their services, Wee haue been pleased to Lycense them to buylde an *Amphitheator* which hath passed our Signet, and is stayed at our Priuie Seale, And findeing therein conteyned some such Wordes, and clauses as may in some Constructions, seeme to giue them greater Libertie both in pointe of Buylding, and vsing of Exercises then is any wayes to be *pe*rmitted, or was euer by vs intended Wee haue thought yt fitt to Commaund and giue Authority vnto you, or any foure of yo^u, to cause that allreadie passed to be Cancelled, and to giue order to our Solicitor Gennerall for the drawing vp of a New Warrant for our Signature to the same *pa*rties according to such directions, reservac͞ons as herewth Wee send you; Wherein Wee are mor *pa*rticuler both in the afmirmitiue [*sic*] and the Negatiue, To the End, y^t as, on the one side, Wee would haue nothing passe vs to remaine vpon Record (wch either for the Forme might not become vs, or for the substance might Crosse our many *Proclamations* pursued with so good success) for buyldings, or on the other side might giue them cause to Ymportune vs after they had ben at Charges. To which End, Wee wish that you call them before you, and let them knowe our Pleasure and Resoluc͞on therein. Giuen vnder our Signett at our Honour of Hampton Court the 29th of September in the 18th yeare of our Raigne of Great Britaine France & Ireland. (Tanner MSS. 89, f. 55–55^v.)

With this letter was enclosed a set of directions for the revisions of the licence, making the King's objections more explicit. A copy was discovered by G. E. P. A. in the Tanner manuscripts with the letter and the prospectus.

this is the Coppye of the Kings Direction Included in the kings letter

First That the Peticion^{ers} at theire owne chardg purchase a peece of Ground, in such a Convenient Place, as shall be alowed by our Commission^{ers} for Buyldin*ges* as perticularly that it fall not in such a Place as may hinder the intended Walkes in Lincolnes Inne Fields; or some such other publique Worke; and that [they] assure the Inheritance of the same vnto vs by firme Deed in Lawe./

Wee are then pleased to giue them License to set there on vpon a new Foundac͞on, such an *Amphitheator* as is by them desired, namely to hould Twelue thousand Spectato^{rs} at the least, *Prouided* it be buylt all of Bricke and Stone, the Walls to be of such thickness, as shalbe of necessitie for the continuance of such a Woorke, and for the safetie of so many People, wch shall be approued allso by our Commission^{ers} for buyldin*ges*, and that they shall not employ this, nor any parte thereof to dwelling houses, Stables, or otherwise whatsoeuer, but only to receiue the People in; at Tymes of Showes or Spectacles except one convenient Place of Dwelling in it for the *Man* wch shall keepe yt, wch shall be set out by our Com̄ission^ers for buylding. Neither that they erect any other house; Shedd, or Buylding whatsoeuer; there being enough to be hired of all vses and the motive to permitt this vpon a new foundac̄on being that none such can be found readie buylte./

Wee are likewise pleased, according to theire humble Suite to graunt them a Lease thereof for Thirtie yeares wth License (at all lawfull Tymes) to shew to theire best advantadge all kinde of Bayteing or Fighting of Beast*es*, Fenceing wth all Weapon*es*, Wrestling in any Sorte, Tumbling, danceing on Ropes, All kindes of Musick, all kinde of Playes, in what Languadge soeuer, the Prohibition wch they desire but one day in euery Month to be enlardged to one day in every Weeke, wth all kinde of Shewes whatsoeuer wch they can deuise, pleasant or delectable to the People Excepting Tilte, (wch no Subiect can set vpp w^thout our License) Torney, Course at the Field, Barriers and such like reserued for Solempnities and Trivmphs of Princes, and not to be vilified dayly in the Eyes of the Vulgar for money offered./

That they practise all these thinges only for Spectacle to the People, not pretending to make yt an *Academy* to instruct, or Teach the Nobilitie or Gentrie of this *Kingdome* a worke onely possible and fitt for Princes to Vndertake, and not to be mixed with *Mercenary* or *Mechanick* Endes; much less to haue a worke wch is so Noble, and hath been so long in our Princely resoluc̄on to be blasted, by being made the coulo[r] to delude wholy the good effects of our *Proclamations* and bringe in all kinde of Sordide houses vpon new Foundations wherew^th the Cittye allready aboundes. (Tanner MSS. 89, ff. 58–59.)

The Councillors, as directed, ordered the preparation of a new licence, and the order is also to be found in the Tanner manuscripts:

Februarie. 10th 1620 [/21]:   Geo: Caluert

His Ma^ts Attourney Gennerall is to prepare a Graunt readie for his Ma^ts Royall Signature, giueing License vnto John Cotton, John Williams and Thomas Dixon Seriant*es* at Armes to his Matie to buyld an *Amphitheator* according to the directions and reservac̄ons aboue written

            Pembroke   Arundell
            J. Degbye   Geo: Calue^rt
                             (Tanner MSS. 89, f. 58^v.)

The objections of the King are easy enough to appreciate. After his repeated proclamations against shoddy building and the increase of London housing (see N. G. Brett-James, *The Growth of*

Stuart London, pp. 79–104), his insistence on brick or stone and his restriction of living quarters to those for the keeper are proper precautions. The petitioners' definite proposal of a site in Lincoln's Inn Fields is here first revealed; the King had reason to be alarmed lest such a large building with its attendant crowds would impede public works, but his alarm must have been nothing compared with that of the company at the Cockpit in Drury Lane, whose house was only a hundred yards or so away, and who were themselves striving to attract 'the Nobility and Gentry of this Realme'. The stern denial of the proposal for tilts, tourneys, and barriers as 'not to be vilified dayly in the Eyes of the Vulgar for money offered' is just what was to be expected; here the wonder is that the projectors had the effrontery to make such proposals in the first place. The rebuke of the proposal 'to make yt an *Academy* to instruct, or Teach the Nobilitie or Gentrie' might also have been foreseen. One wonders if the projectors had heard vaguely and inaccurately of Edmund Bolton's plan for a Royal Academy; Kynaston's Musæum Minervæ of fifteen years later had something in common with what was proposed. (See above, iv. 716–17.)

It is odd that the King should have ordered the number of playing-days at the Amphitheatre to be quadrupled; could this be a concession to compensate for his restriction of the privileges originally granted? This new allotment must have sounded ominous to the London actors.

Why more than four months should have elapsed between the King's letter to the Council about a new licence and the Council's order for the preparation of the grant I cannot tell. Throughout the repeated attempts to get the Amphitheatre started one gets the impression that a struggle among court figures is going on in the background.

This licence of 1620–1 passed the Signet but not the Great Seal, and for five or six years the project was in abeyance. Then in the new reign, in 1626, it was revived with the support, perhaps at the instigation, of Endymion Porter. The new project seems to have been the same as the old one, with the restrictions ordered by King James. This attempt got as far as a warrant for a new licence. Under the date of 7 July 1626 the warrant is entered with the rubric 'License to build an Amphitheatre for martial sports & Interludes':

A License vnto John Williams and Thomas Dixon twoe of his Ma*jesties* Seriantes at Armes to purchase a convenient peece of grounde in Lincolnes Jnne fields or elsewhere neere London to build

an Amphiatheater which grounde is to bee conveyed to his Majestie
& his heires & successors with a Covenaunt that his Majesty wilbee
pleased to leause the same vnto them for: 31: yeeres with license to
build the said Ampheatheater & to exercise therin Marshall discipline
& other exercises for the recreacion & delightes of his Majesties subiects with a restraint to all playes & interludes & other sportes in
London & Suburbes one daie in euery weeke during the terme aforesaid when theis intended sportes shall begynne [.] his Majesties
pleasure signified by mr Alisbury Subscribed by mr. Attorney gennerall Procured by mr Endymion Porter.

Windebanck

[In another hand in the margin is 'stayed'.]

(P.R.O., S.P. 38/13/180ᵛ. Discovered by Leslie Hotson.)

The background of the staying of the licence of 7 July 1626 is
furnished by two letters concerning the project printed by John
Payne Collier in his *History of English Dramatic Poetry*. The Lord
Keeper wrote to Lord Conway:

My very good Lord,—I have perused this Bill, and do call to mynd
that about three or four yeres past, when I was Atturney Generall,
a patent for an Amphitheater was in hand to have passed; but upon
this sodain, without serch of my papers, I cannot give your lordship
any account of the true cause wherefore it did not passe, nor whether
that and this do varie in substans: neither am I apt upon a sodain to
take impertinent exceptions to any thing that is to passe, much less
to a thing that is recommended by so good a friend. But if upon
perusall of my papers, which I had while I was Atturney, or upon
more serious thoughts, I shall observe any thing worthy to be represented to His Majesty, or to the Councail, I shall then acquaint
your Lordship; and in the meanetyme I would be loth to be the
author of a motion to His Majesty to stay it: but if you fynd His
Majesty att fitting leasure to move him, that he will give leave to
thinke of it in this sort as I have written, it may do well, and I assure
your lordship, unless I fynd matter of more consequens then I observe on this sodain, it is not like to be stayed. And so I rest your
lordship's very assured to do you service.

Tho. Coventrye, Ch.

Canbury, 12 *August,* 1626.

(Collier, 1879 ed., i. 443–4.)

A second letter in the same correspondence shows why the
licence was stayed. Six weeks later the Lord Keeper wrote to
Lord Conway again.

My Lord,—According to His Majesty's good pleasure, which I
receaved from your lordship, I have considered of the graunt desired

by John Williams and Thomas Dixon, for building an Amphitheater
in Lincoln's Inne fields; and comparing it with that which was pro-
pounded in King James his tyme, doe finde much difference betweene
them: for that former was intended principally for martiall exercises,
and extraordinary shewes, and solemnyties for Ambassadors and
persons of honour and quality, with a cessation from other shews
and sports for one daie in a moneth onlie, upon 14 daies warning:
wheras by this new granut I see little probability of anything to be
used but common plaies, or ordinary sports, now used or shewed at
the Beare-garden or the common Playhouses about London, for all
sorts of beholders, with a restraint to all other plaies and shewes,
for one day in the weeke upon two daies warning: with liberty to
erect their buildings in Lincoln's Inne Fields, where there are too
many buildings already; and which place, in the late King's tyme,
upon a petition exhibited by the Princes comedians for setting up a
playhouse there, was certified, by eleven Justices of peace, under
their hands, to be very inconvenyent, And therefore, not holding
this new granut fitt to passe, as being no other in effect but to trans-
late the play-houses and Beare-Garden from the Bankside to a place
much more unfitt, I thought fitt to give your Lordship these reasons
for it; wherewithal you may please to acquaint his Majesty, if there
shalbe cause. And so remayn your lordship's very assured frende to
doe you service,

Tho. Coventrye.

Canbury, 28 *Sept.*, 1626.
Lo. Conway.

(Ibid., pp. 444–5.)

By 1626 the projectors had evidently settled on Lincoln's Inn
Fields as their site and secured Endymion Porter as their sponsor.
Possibly he had been concerned with the previous attempt,
though 1620 is a little early for his influence to have been very
great. But Porter's influence was not sufficiently great, even in
1626, after his patron Prince Charles had succeeded to the throne.
The patent was stayed, as the marginal note on the warrant shows.
Again one would like to think that protests from the London
dramatic companies carried some weight, but nothing in the correspondence suggests it.

Finally, Dr. Hotson has discovered that the amphitheatre project was revived yet again in 1634. There were some changes in
the fourteen years following the original proposal, and the new
group of projectors includes only John Williams of the original
trio; Williams is said to be 'very aged' and obviously was not
active in the new attempt to secure a patent. The new men are
of more courtly standing than the original projectors had been,
and they make the clever proposal that the amphitheatre be

named after Queen Henrietta-Maria. Nevertheless, there is no evidence that the renewal of the project got any further in 1634 than it had in 1620–1.

It hath formerly pleased yo*ur* most graceous father of blessed memory to grant licence vnto yo*ur* ma*jesties* seruants John Williams and Thomas Dixon Sergeants at armes for recompence, and reward of theire longe service to build an Amphitheat*or* on some Conuenient peice of ground nere to the Citty of London for presenting many noble, and worthy excercises menc*i*oned therin

And vppon yo*ur* pe*titioners* humble suite your ma*jestie* hath beene likewise pleased to signe another bill to Confirme the said graunt but with some few words of alterac*i*on which hath alsoe passed yo*ur* Ma*jesties* Royall signature.

In which bill there is nothinge desired (as wee can iudge) but may bee Conueniently permitted in this kingdome by reason of many such like propertyes are dayly practised by others albeit wantinge the grace, and excellency by vs intended.

> These three followinge reasons (as wee Conceaue) may be motives for the furtherance of his ma*jesties* graunts to the pe*titioners* li
>> The chardge of the purchase of the ground   1500
>> The house or Amphitheator   12000
>> The rent pe*r* An*num* duringe the tyme of the graunt   40ˢ

Profitt to ye Crowne

After the expirac*i*on of the terme to be lefft fully, and wholy to the Crowne for euer/

Hono*r* to ye Kingdome

In all Christendome is not now in vse any place soe prepared to accomodate soe many variable, and delightefull recreations and speculac*i*ons as this Amphitheat*or* may afford, for the entertainment of Princes Embassadors or Strangers of any forraine nation whatsoeu*r* which will be a graceous ornament to the Citty hono*r* to the kingdome and Content to honourable natives and others.

Benefitt to ye Commonwealth./

The exercises in that place may quickly enable the nobler sorte of gentry and others to many excellent and lawdable seruices of theire prince and Cuntrey: withdrawe many licentious, and vnlimited disposic*i*ons, from drunknes, lacivousnes, and such base or vnworthy inclinations. Besides it may bee an occasion to embusy diuers priuate consultac*i*ons, and Conventickles, with matters of pleasant levitye, and s[p]eculac*i*ons A pollecy oftentymes permitted in the beste, and most flowrishinge Commonwealthes

Latyne Scœnes also beinge presented for forraygne intertainm*entes* there wilbe demonstrated the delicacy of nature and educa-

*ci*on of gentlemen students in the universities whereby choise may be made of the most ingenious schollers, and pregnant disposic*i*ons for the service, and attendancy, peeres, or Cuntry

By meanes also of the exercises of the Olimpiads may bee pe*r*fected, and enabled many tryalls for hon*ourable* Cumbattes single, or otherwise so to renew the auncient, and honourable reputac*i*on of his m*ajesties* kingdome that were neuer formerly inferiour to any other kingdomes, or nations of the world for activity, Courage and strength./

This house beinge magnificen[t]ly built to accomodate a number of excellent p*r*opertyes, and inventions to entertaine Princes, Embassadors, Strangers, and hon*ourable* Natiues and Subiects.

It is therefore most humbly desired that the said Amphitheat*or* may be dedicated to the memorable honor of the Queens most excellent M*ajestie*, for it hath beene the auncient custome of greate Princes to be honored with the memory of sumptuous building*es* bridges Colledges and such like.

This house likewise will saue his m*ajestie* much money in entertaynment of princes, Embassadors or Strangers for this place may Content them with many Convenient and pleasant accomodac*i*ons

[The petition is endorsed '1634 Amphitheater'.]

(P.R.O., S.P. 16/281/44. First printed by Hotson, loc. cit.)

This petition, except for the newly proposed name and a few additional advantages set forth seems to differ little from the former proposals. There is no indication why the proposal was revived or who was really behind the renewal.

Finally, another petition has been discovered by Dr. Hotson, undated but later than that of 1634. New men of courtly standing have joined the enterprise.

To the Kinges most Excelent Majestie

The humble peticion of Sir Richard Young knight and baronet Sir Richard Darley knt Henry Murrey esq: attending his Majestie in his bedd Chamber John Willyams gent: And Capten Robert Hasell the first Inventor and profeser of the busines of the Amphitheater

Sheweth

That whereas your Roiall father of Blessed Memorie was plesed to grant leave unto John Willyams and Thomas Dixon, in recompence of their longe and faithfull service to build an Amphitheatre in or nere unto the City of London to present therin many Heroique & Maiestick recreations as in the sayd grant is mentioned. And that it hath bene likewise plesing to your gracious and princely goodnes to confirme the said grant admitting some fewe wordes of alteracion, as appereth by two grantes alredy passed the roiall Signature: And wheras Thomas Dixon one of the grantees is lately decessed, and the other very aged Your petiticioners moste humbly pray that this being a busines of so plesant, and famous a conscequence That it may not perish or fall for want of able and carefull prosecution: That your Majestie would be so graceously plesed as to grant that your *petitio*ners may be Joyned in your Majesties grant with the Surviving John Willyams for the building of the said Amphitheatre and for the better strengthning and expeditinge therof, who have allso with chardge, and humble patience longe expected the same, and prepared their good frendes with great summs of money for the building therof & fittinge many other necessarie accomodacions therunto belonginge. Humbly allso beseching (your roiall Majestie) would be so graceously plesed to give orderes to the right honorable the Lord Keeper, the Lord Chamberlaine of your Majesties house and the Secretarie Windebanke, that they three, or any twoe of them, To take their twoe grantes into their honorable Consideracions and to passe one of the twoe bookes immediately, which of them shall seme moste fittinge to their honorable Wisdomes

And your petitioners shall ever pray &c.

(Hotson, op. cit., p. 34; from Gibson Papers, MSS. Lambeth 930,
f. 131.)

These are the last of the documents to be discovered concerning the project for a London amphitheatre with a capacity of 12,000. The scheme seems much too grandiose ever to have been developed with commercial profit, but the repeated attempts to push it through show that a number of the subjects of Charles I thought differently.

DAVENANT'S PROJECTED THEATRE IN FLEET STREET

Adams, pp. 424–31.
Lawrence, W. J., *The Elizabethan Playhouse and Other Studies*, Second Series (1913), pp. 125–8.

Another theatre proposed but never built in Caroline times was a project of William Davenant, for which he got his patent past the Signet and the Privy Seal in 1639.

By 1639 William Davenant was an experienced man of the theatre. He had written for production at least ten plays and four court masques; and in the previous year he had attained the laureateship in succession to Ben Jonson, and triumphed over Thomas May and James Shirley. (See above, iii. 193–225.) His managerial ambitions, so conspicuously successful from 1656 to

1668, had evidently become virulent before he was 35, for within a year of the frustration of his new theatre plan he had succeeded in getting himself made Governor of the King and Queen's young company at the Phoenix in succession to the disgraced William Beeston.

Not much is known of the details of Davenant's plan of 1639, but that little suggests a very ambitious design. The first hint of what he intended is the licence which was printed in Rymer's *Foedera*.

De Licentiâ erigendi Theatrum concessâ Willielmo Davenant. *Charles* by the Grace of God, King of *England* . . . Know ye, that We . . . upon the humble Petition of our Servant *William Davenant* Gentleman, . . . do give and grant unto the said *William Davenant*, his Heirs, Executors, Administrators and Assigns, full Power, Licence and Authority, that he . . . and his and their Labourers, Servants and Workmen, shall and may lawfully, quietly and peacably frame, erect, new-build and set up, upon a parcel of Ground lying near unto, or behind the *Three Kings Ordinary* in *Fleet-street*, in the Parishes of *Saint Dunstan's in the West, London*, or in *Saint Bride's, London*, or in either of them, or in any other Ground in or about that place, or in the whole Street aforesaid, already allotted to him for that use, or in any other place, that is or hereafter shall be assigned and allotted out, to the said *William Davenant* . . . a Theatre or Playhouse, with necessary tireing and retiring Rooms and other places convenient, containing in the whole forty yards square at the most, wherein Plays, musical Entertainments, Scenes or other like Presentments, may be presented.

And We do hereby . . . grant to the said *William Davenant* . . . that it shall and may be lawful to and for him . . . from time to time to gather together, entertain, govern, privilege and keep, such and so many Players and Persons, to exercise Action, musical Presentments, Scenes, Dancing and the like, as he . . . shall think fit and approve for the said House, and such Persons to permit and continue, at and during the pleasure of the said *William Davenant* . . . from time to time, to act Plays in such House, so to be by him or them erected, and exercise Musick, musical Presentments, Scenes, Dancing or other the like, at the same, or other hours or times, or after Plays are ended . . . And that it shall and may be lawful to and for the said *William Davenant* . . . to take and receive of such our Subjects, as shall resort to see or hear any such Plays, Scenes, and Entertainments whatsoever, such Sum or Sums of Money, as is, are, or hereafter from time to time, shall be accustomed to be given or taken, in other Playhouses. . . .

And further . . . We do hereby give and grant to the said *William Davenant* . . . full Power, Licence and Authority, to continue, uphold and maintain the said Theatre or Playhouse, and tireing and retiring Rooms, and other places of convenience there, so to be erected and

built as aforesaid, and the same to repair and amend, when and as
often as need shall require . . . so as the Outwalls of the said Theatre
. . . be made or built of Brick or Stone, according to the tenor of our
Proclamations in that behalf, and so as under pretence or colour
hereof, the said *William Davenant* . . . do not erect or set up any
dwelling Houses or other Buildings, than as aforesaid . . . Witness
our self at *Westminster*, the six and twentieth day of *March*.

Per Breve de Privato Sigillo.
(Rymer, *Foedera*, xx. 377–8.)

The first notable fact in this licence is the location of the proposed large theatre in Fleet Street in the parish of St. Dunstan in
the West, or St. Bride's. This is the district of Blackfriars and the
Salisbury Court theatres; indeed, St. Bride's was the parish of the
Salisbury Court, and strong opposition from the troupes at those
two theatres and from their friends could be expected.

The next significant feature recorded in the licence is the size
of the building proposed, 'forty yards square', a very sizeable
area for a theatre, more than twice that specified in the Fortune
contract of 1600. It should be noted, however, that the document
says 'at the most' and that the area specified is apparently that of
the plot of ground, not necessarily that of the building. Nevertheless, such evidence as the licence presents implies a large house,
not a small private theatre like Blackfriars or the Salisbury Court.

The repeated permission for the presentation of 'Musick, musical Presentments, Scenes, Dancing or other the like' shows that
Davenant's ambitions in 1639 were surprisingly like those he
attained, under much greater difficulties, at Rutland House in
1656. The 'scenes' he proposed one would expect to be similar to
those attached to plays like *The Queen of Aragon* and *The Royal
Slave* recently given at court. Or perhaps he even hoped that some
of the devices from his own masques, *The Temple of Love, The
Triumphs of the Prince D'Amour, Luminalia*, and *Britannia
Triumphans*, could be transferred to his new theatre. W. J. Lawrence even went so far as to assert that the phrase of the licence,
'musical Presentments', was an adequate translation for *opera
musicale*. (Loc. cit.) None of these proposals sounds commercially
feasible in the theatrical situation of 1639, but then their
practical application was not a salient characteristic of the
grandiose schemes of either Davenant or his patron, Endymion
Porter.

The provision of the licence, that Davenant was to 'gather
together, entertaine, govern, privilege and keep, such and so many
Players and Persons . . . as he shall think fit and approve

for the said House', clearly provides for the assembling of a new company, and one is struck with the forecast of what Davenant actually did accomplish twenty years later. In 1639, before his theatre was fully allowed, he went so far as to begin recruiting his company. This we know from the notes of Richard Heton, manager of Queen Henrietta's company at Salisbury Court. In his scandalized indictment of the disloyalty of certain members of his own company Heton complains:

And some of them have treated upon Condicons for the Cockpit playhouse, some gone about to begge o^r house from the King, and one nowe of the cheife fellowes, an Agent for one that hath gott a grant from the King, for the building of a new playhouse wch was intended to be in Fleet Street, wch noe man can judge that a fellow of o^r Company, and a wellwisher to those that owe the house, would ev'r be an actor in. (See above, ii. 684.)

In the light of the fierce resentment that such raiding of other companies would rouse, to say nothing of the deadly threat of a large playhouse with courtly patronage and novel entertainment at the very doors of the Salisbury Court and Blackfriars, we may be sure that the attempt to block Davenant must have been frenzied. Courtiers, with more influence than any player could have, must have intervened, for three weeks after the date of the licence Davenant's patron, Endymion Porter, was writing to his agent at his house in the Strand:[1]

1639. April 16. Endymion Porter to Richard Harvey, at the writer's house in the Strand. I would have you solicit my Lord Duke, who is now in London, to know what he has done with my Lord Keeper concerning Mr. Davenant's patent; if he has procured the passing of it, follow it close and attend the sealing. It has already passed the signet and privy seal, and they are both paid for, there only remains the great seal to pay for. Disburse the money for it, and keep the patent until Davenant sends you the money, also by the next opportunity let me understand how much it comes to. (*C.S.P., Dom.*, 1639, p. 49. Vol. ccccxvii. 108.)

Mr. Davenant's patent had not passed the Great Seal, and someone with influence must have been preventing it. It would be pleasant to think that the opponent of Davenant and Porter was a friend of the players at Salisbury Court and Blackfriars,

---

[1] Porter's house was 'over against the New Exchange' (*C.S.P., Dom.*, 1639, p. 344) on the south side of the Strand. The proximity of this house to the proposed site of the new theatre makes one wonder if Porter had an interest in the land or buildings 'behind the *Three Kings Ordinary* in Fleet-street'.

one such as the Earl of Pembroke and Montgomery, but evidence
is lacking. That the project for the new theatre was effectively
stopped is shown by an indenture of the following September.

This Indenture made the second day of October . . . 1639. Between
the said King's most Excellent Ma^{ty} of the first part and William
D'Avenant of London Gent. of the other part. Whereas the said
King's most excellent Ma^{ty} by his highnes Letters patents under the
great Seal of England bearing date the six and twentieth day of
March last past . . . Did give and graunt unto the said William
D'Avenant . . . full power license and authority that they . . . shall
and may lawfully quietly and peacably frame erect new build and
sett up upon a parcell of ground lying neere unto or behinde the three
Kings ordinary in Fleet Streete in the pish of St. Dunstans in the
West London, or in St. Brides London, or in either of them, or in
any other ground in or about that place, or in the whole Streete
aforesaid already allotted to him for that use . . . [as in the licence of
26 March] . . . Now this Indenture witnesseth and the said William
D'Avenant doth by theis presents declare his Ma^{ts} intent meaning
at and upon the graunting of the said License was and is that he the
said William D'Avenant his heires Executors Administrators nor
Assignes should not frame build or sett up the said Theater or Playhouse in anie place inconvenient and that the said parcell of ground
lying neere unto or behinds the Three Kings Ordinary in Fleet
Street . . . or in any other ground in or about that place in the whole
Streete aforesaid, And is sithence found inconvenient and unfitt for
that purpose, therefore the said William D'Avenant doth for himselfe
his Heires Executors Administrato^{rs} and Assignes and every of them
covenante promise and agree to and wth o^r said Soveraigne Lord the
King his Heires and Successors That he . . . shall not nor will not by
vertue of the said License . . . frame erect new build or sett up upon
the said parcell of ground in Fleet Streete aforesaid or in any other
part of Fleet Streete a Theater or Playhouse, nor will not frame,
erect, new build or sett up upon any other parcell of ground lying
in or neere the Citties or Suburbs of the Cities of London or Westm^r
any Theater or Playhouse unles the said place shall be first approved
and allowed by warrant under His Mat^s signe manuell or by writing
under the hand and seale of the said Right Honble Thomas Earle of
Arundell and Surrey. In Witness whereof to the one p^t of this Indenture the said William D'Avenant hath sett his Hand & Seal the Day
and Yeare first above written.

William D'Avenant. L.S.

Signed Sealed and Delived
in the presence of
  Edw. Penruddoks
  Michael Baler.
      (Chalmers, *A Supplemental Apology* . . . [1799], pp. 188–90.)

This document shows that somehow Endymion Porter or his friends had got Davenant's patent past the great seal on 26 March 1639. Nevertheless, though the indenture revokes none of Davenant's essential privileges—witness the fact that in 1660 it was still considered a valid establishment of them (*C.S.P., Dom.,* Charles II, 1660–1, p. 114)—the restrictions on location were fatal. All good sites were eliminated, and the Earl of Arundel and Surrey was given full veto powers for any others. Probably Davenant and his friends did not pursue the matter much longer, for on 3 May 1640 William Beeston's company was suppressed, and by 27 June Davenant was confirmed as Beeston's successor in the managerial powers which he coveted. He cannot have enjoyed them long, for he was involved in the Bishops' Wars and later in the Army Plot, and he could have had little time for theatres.

Davenant's grandiose plan came to nothing in Caroline London, but it was not forgotten by its originator. It is the harbinger of his Commonwealth theatre and of his Restoration enterprises.

PRINTED IN GREAT BRITAIN
AT THE UNIVERSITY PRESS, OXFORD
BY VIVIAN RIDLER
PRINTER TO THE UNIVERSITY